SUPER TURBO

PROTECTS THE WORLD

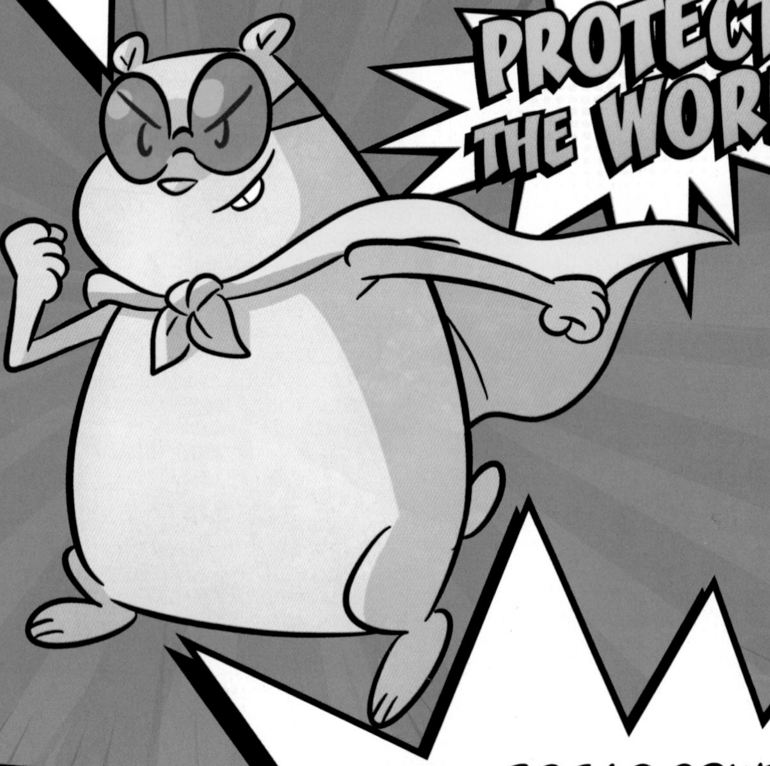

WRITTEN BY **EDGAR POWERS**

ILLUSTRATED BY **SALVATORE COSTANZA**

AT GLASS HOUSE GRAPHICS

LITTLE SIMON

NEW YORK LONDON TORONTO SYDNEY NEW DELHI

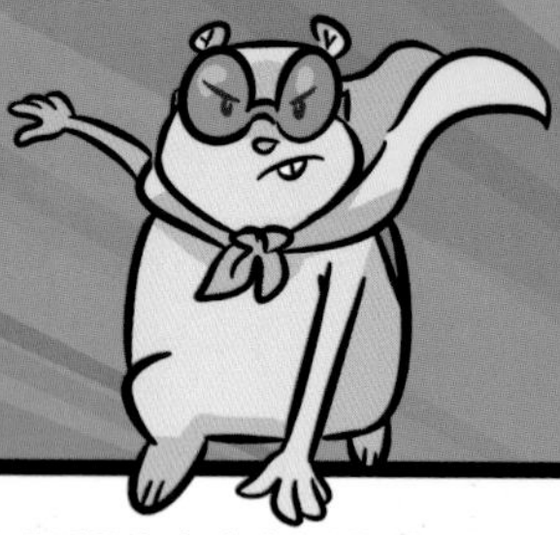

THIS BOOK IS A WORK OF FICTION. ANY REFERENCES TO HISTORICAL EVENTS, REAL PEOPLE, OR REAL PLACES ARE USED FICTITIOUSLY. OTHER NAMES, CHARACTERS, PLACES, AND EVENTS ARE PRODUCTS OF THE AUTHOR'S IMAGINATION, AND ANY RESEMBLANCE TO ACTUAL EVENTS OR PLACES OR PERSONS, LIVING OR DEAD, IS ENTIRELY COINCIDENTAL.

LITTLE SIMON
AN IMPRINT OF SIMON & SCHUSTER CHILDREN'S PUBLISHING DIVISION
1230 AVENUE OF THE AMERICAS, NEW YORK, NEW YORK 10020
FIRST LITTLE SIMON EDITION AUGUST 2021 * FOR INFORMATION ABOUT SPECIAL DISCOUNTS FOR BULK PURCHASES, PLEASE CONTACT SIMON & SCHUSTER SPECIAL SALES AT 1-866-506-1949 OR BUSINESS@SIMONANDSCHUSTER.COM. THE SIMON & SCHUSTER SPEAKERS BUREAU CAN BRING AUTHORS TO YOUR LIVE EVENT. FOR MORE INFORMATION OR TO BOOK AN EVENT CONTACT THE SIMON & SCHUSTER SPEAKERS BUREAU AT 1-866-248-3049 OR VISIT OUR WEBSITE AT WWW.SIMONSPEAKERS.COM. DESIGNED BY NICHOLAS SCIACCA * ART SERVICES BY GLASS HOUSE GRAPHICS * ART AND COLOR BY SALVATORE COSTANZA * LETTERING BY GIOVANNI SPATARO/GRAFIMATED CARTOON * SUPERVISION BY SALVATORE DI MARCO/GRAFIMATED CARTOON * MANUFACTURED IN CHINA 0521 SCP * 2 4 6 8 10 9 7 5 3 1 * LIBRARY OF CONGRESS CATALOGING-IN-PUBLICATION DATA NAMES: POWERS, EDGAR J., AUTHOR. | GLASS HOUSE GRAPHICS, ILLUSTRATOR. TITLE: SUPER TURBO PROTECTS THE WORLD / BY EDGAR J. POWERS ; ILLUSTRATED BY GLASS HOUSE GRAPHICS. DESCRIPTION: FIRST LITTLE SIMON EDITION. | NEW YORK : LITTLE SIMON, 2021. | SERIES: SUPER TURBO, THE GRAPHIC NOVEL ; BOOK 4 | AUDIENCE: AGES 5-9 | AUDIENCE: GRADES K-4 | SUMMARY: DURING CELEBRATE-THE-WORLD DAY AT SUNNYVIEW ELEMENTARY SUPER TURBO AND THE OTHER SUPERPETS PROTECT THE SCHOOL AND THE WORLD FROM WHISKERFACE. IDENTIFIERS: LCCN 2020027937 (PRINT) | LCCN 2020027938 (EBOOK) | ISBN 9781534478411 (PAPERBACK) | ISBN 9781534478428 (HARDCOVER) | ISBN 9781534478435 (EBOOK) SUBJECTS: LCSH: GRAPHIC NOVELS. | CYAC: GRAPHIC NOVELS. | SUPERHEROES—FICTION. | HAMSTERS—FICTION. | PETS—FICTION. | ELEMENTARY SCHOOLS—FICTION. | SCHOOLS—FICTION. CLASSIFICATION: LCC PZ7.7.P7 SN 2021 (PRINT) | LCC PZ7.7.P7 (EBOOK) | DDC 741.5/973—DC23 LC RECORD AVAILABLE AT HTTPS://LCCN.LOC.GOV/2020027937 LC EBOOK RECORD AVAILABLE AT HTTPS://LCCN.LOC.GOV/2020027938

CONTENTS

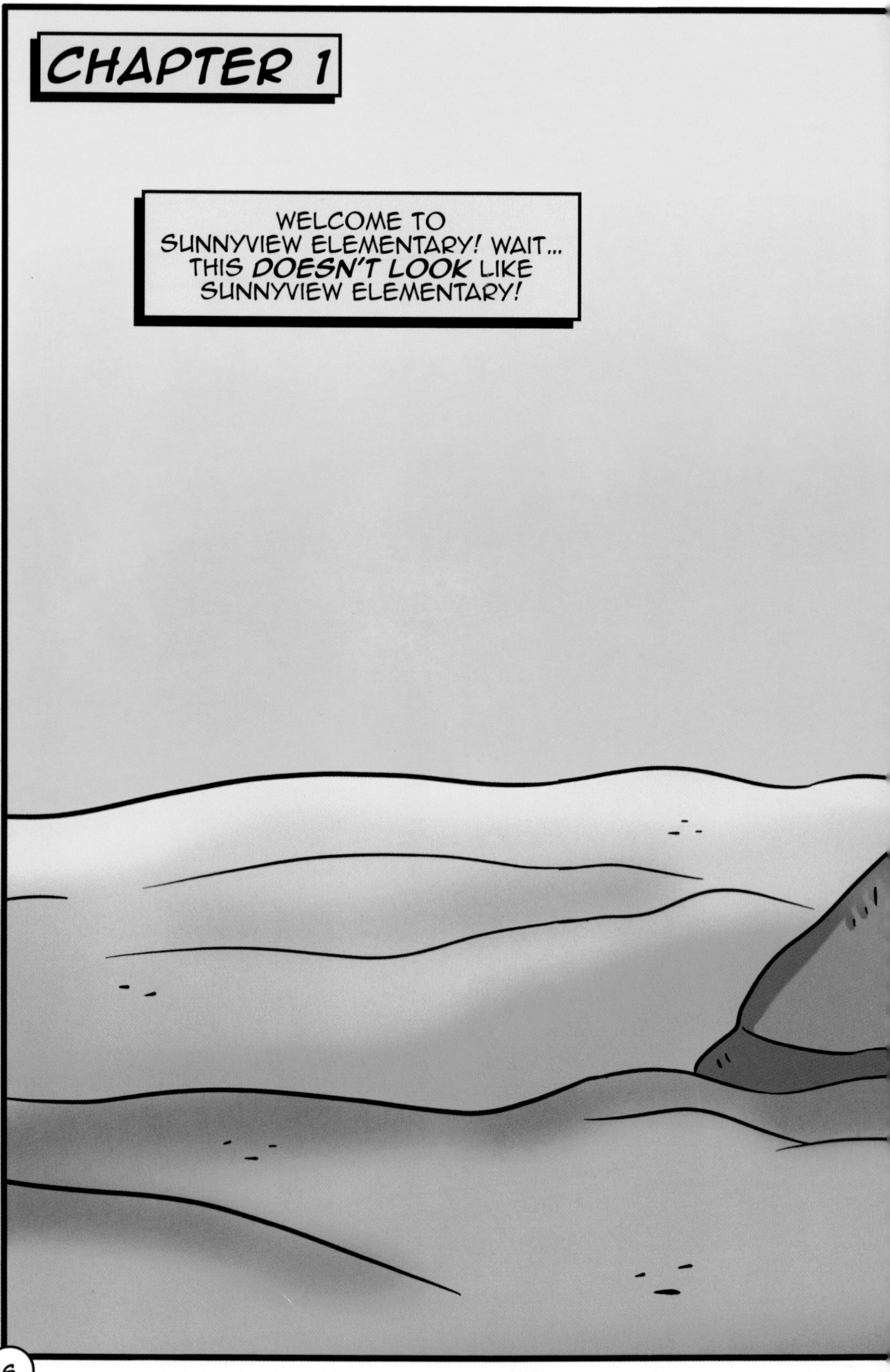
CHAPTER 1
WELCOME TO SUNNYVIEW ELEMENTARY! WAIT... THIS *DOESN'T LOOK* LIKE SUNNYVIEW ELEMENTARY!

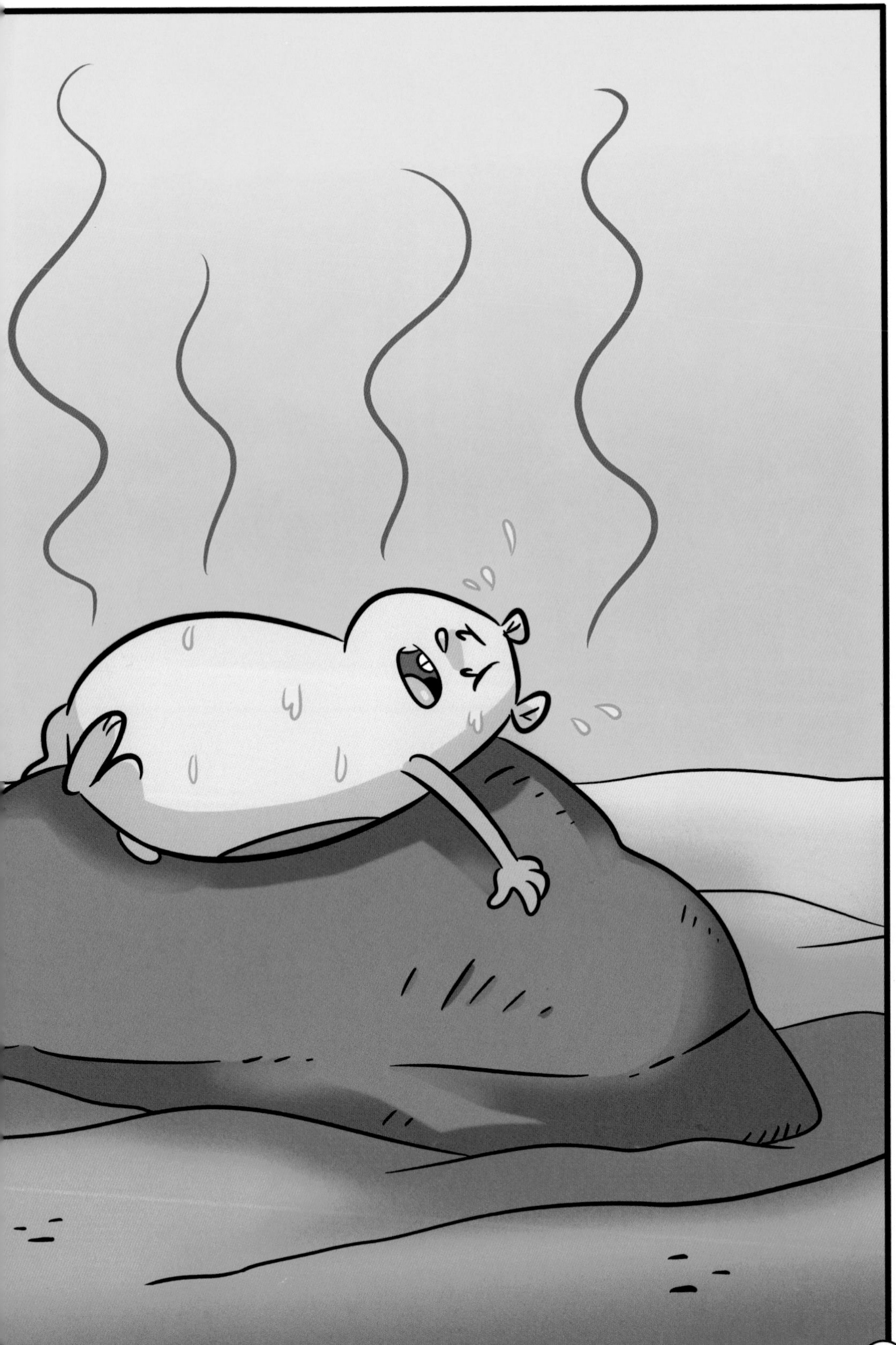

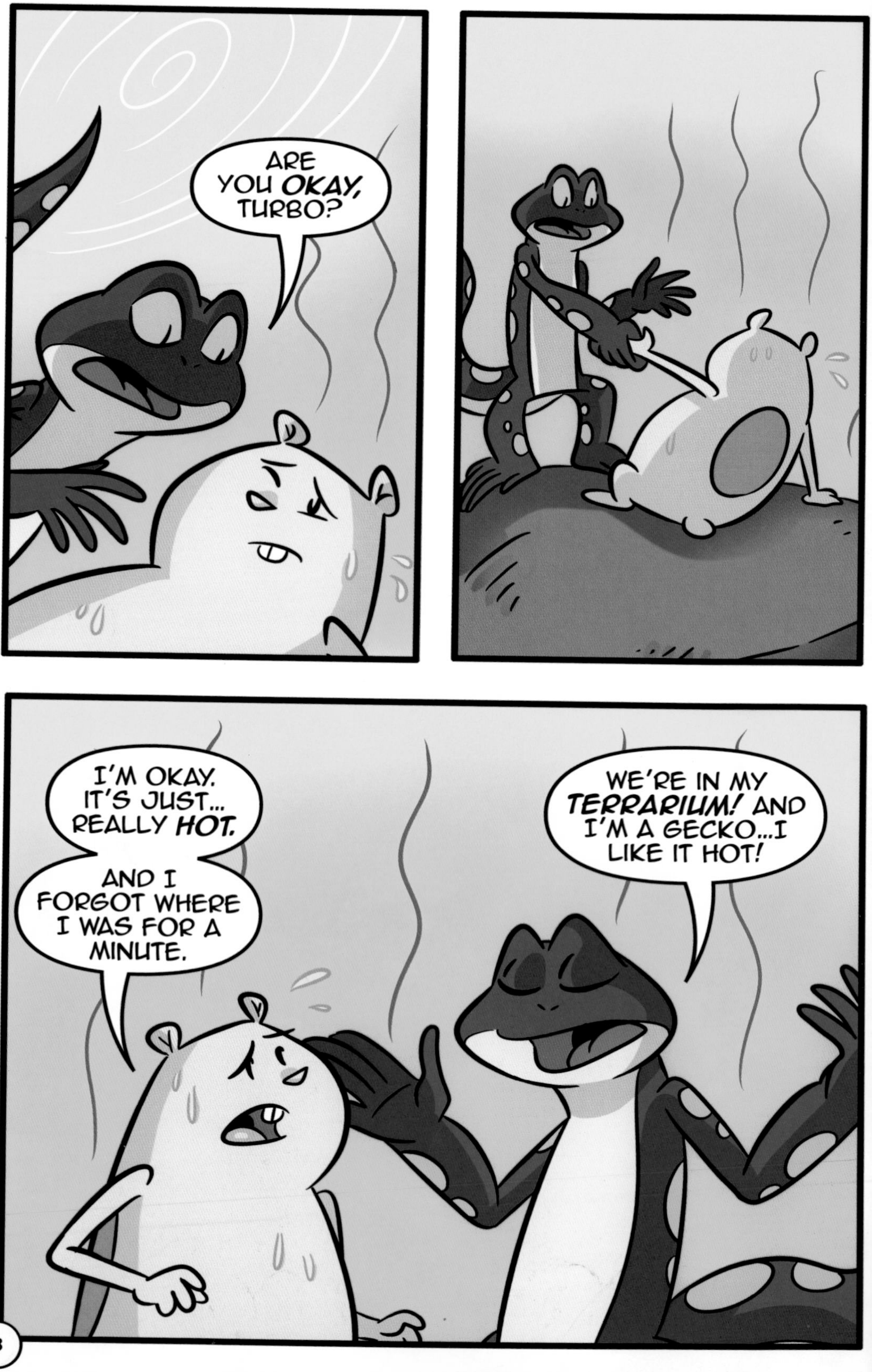
ARE YOU OKAY, TURBO?
I'M OKAY. IT'S JUST... REALLY HOT.
AND I FORGOT WHERE I WAS FOR A MINUTE.
WE'RE IN MY TERRARIUM! AND I'M A GECKO...I LIKE IT HOT!

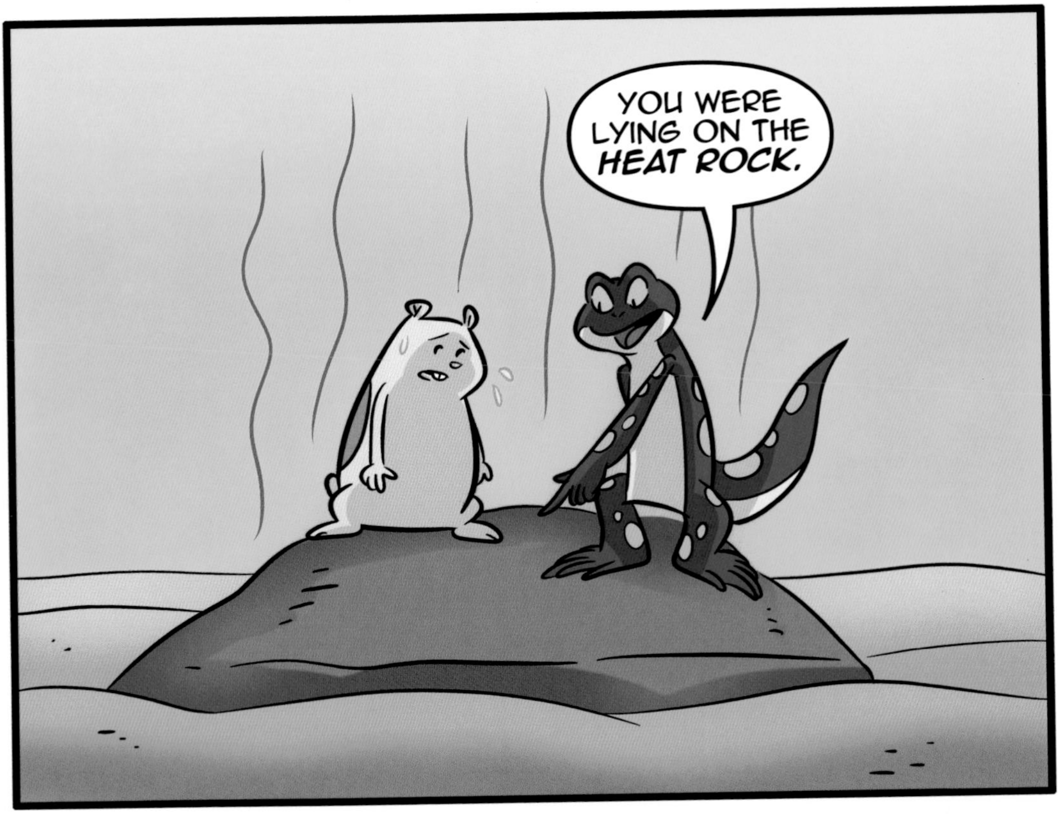
YOU WERE LYING ON THE *HEAT ROCK.*

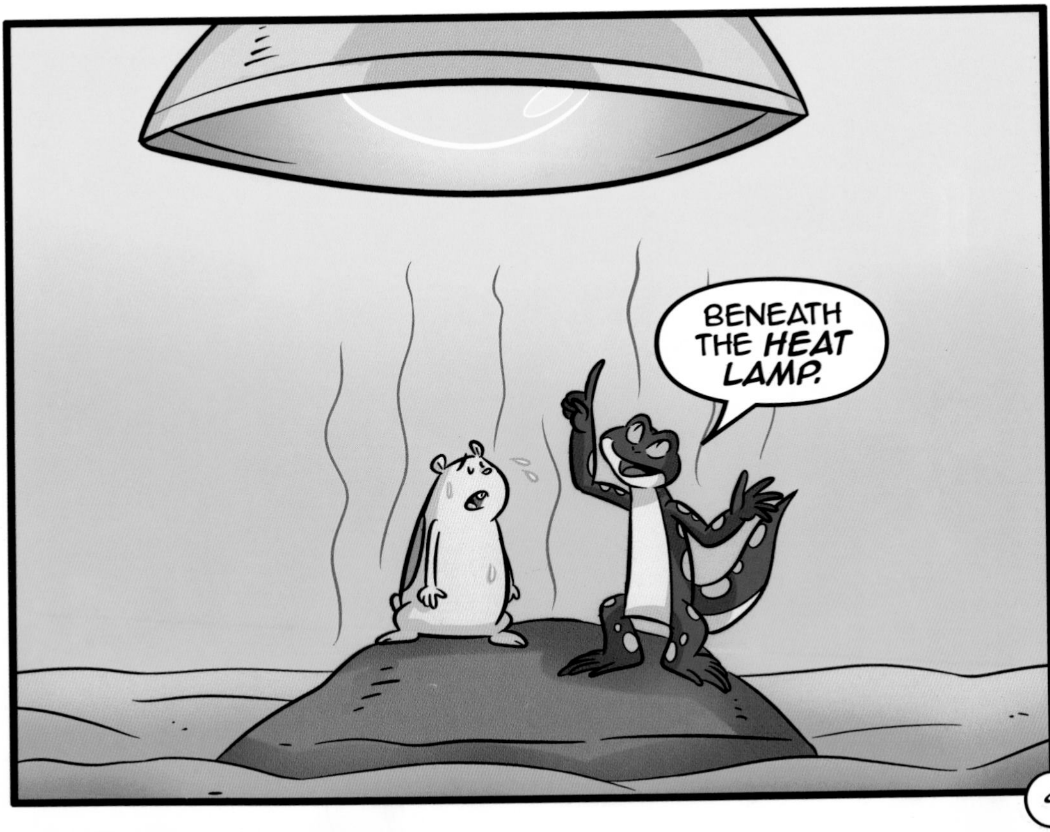
BENEATH THE *HEAT LAMP.*

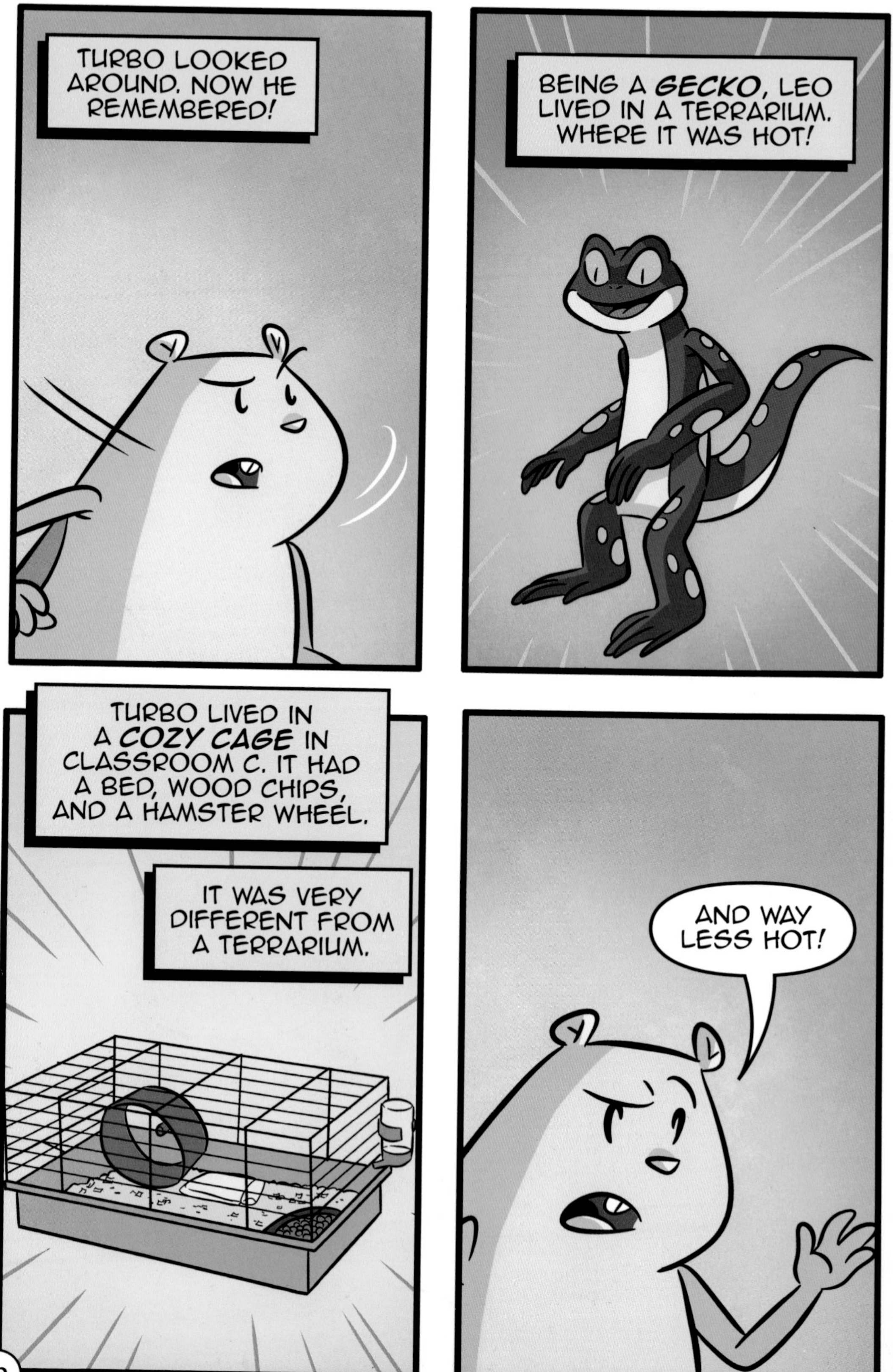
TURBO LOOKED AROUND. NOW HE REMEMBERED!
BEING A GECKO, LEO LIVED IN A TERRARIUM. WHERE IT WAS HOT!
TURBO LIVED IN A COZY CAGE IN CLASSROOM C. IT HAD A BED, WOOD CHIPS, AND A HAMSTER WHEEL.
IT WAS VERY DIFFERENT FROM A TERRARIUM.
AND WAY LESS HOT!

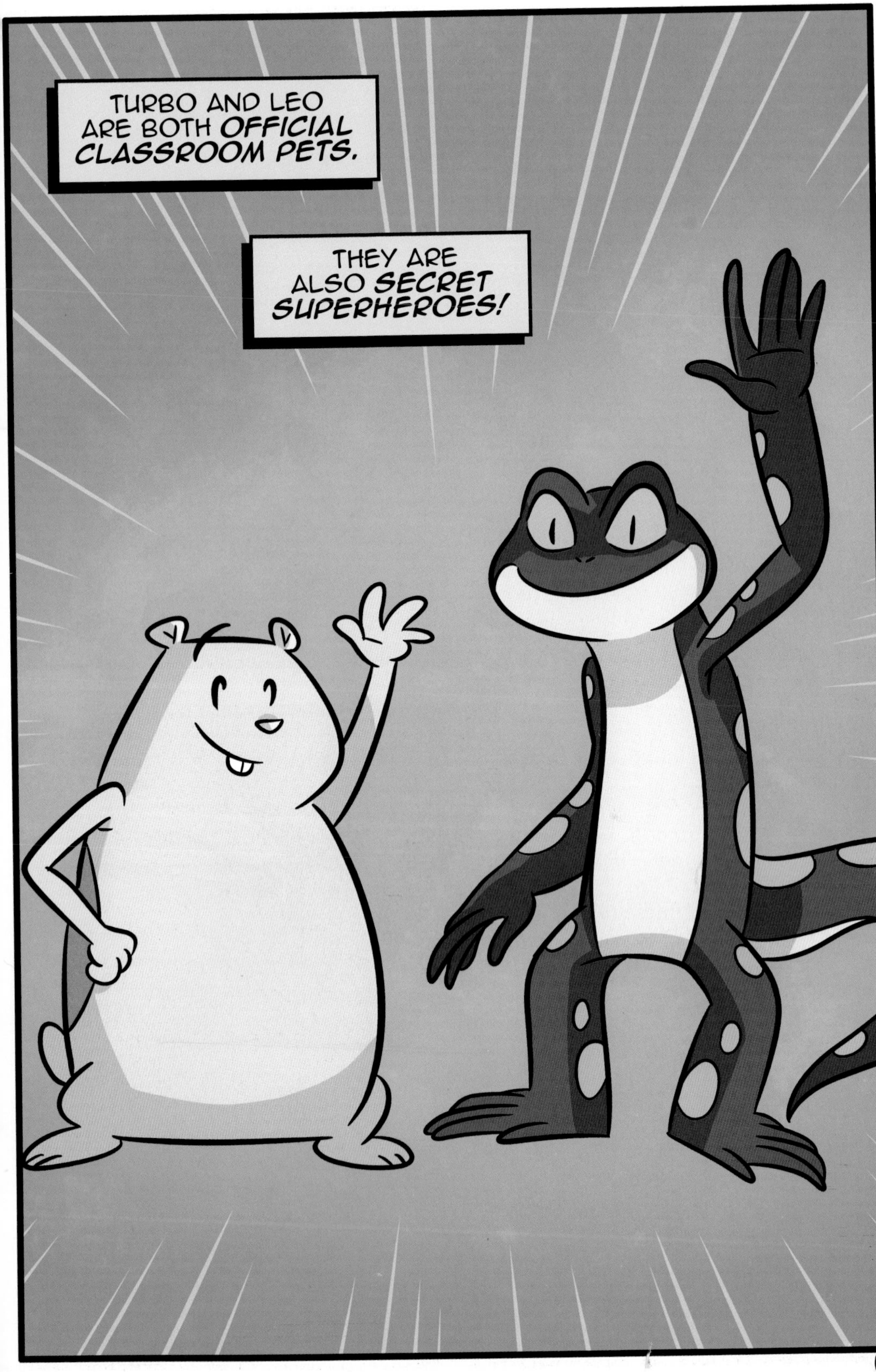
TURBO AND LEO ARE BOTH OFFICIAL CLASSROOM PETS.
THEY ARE ALSO SECRET SUPERHEROES!

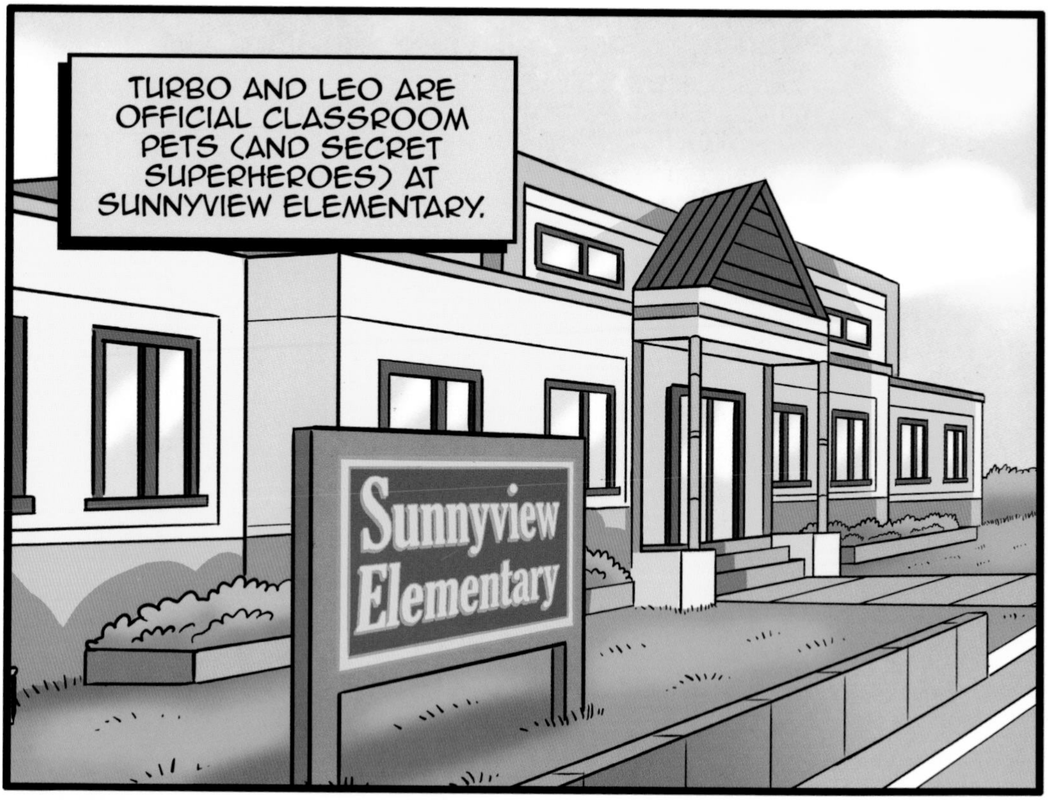
TURBO AND LEO ARE OFFICIAL CLASSROOM PETS (AND SECRET SUPERHEROES) AT SUNNYVIEW ELEMENTARY.
Sunnyview Elementary

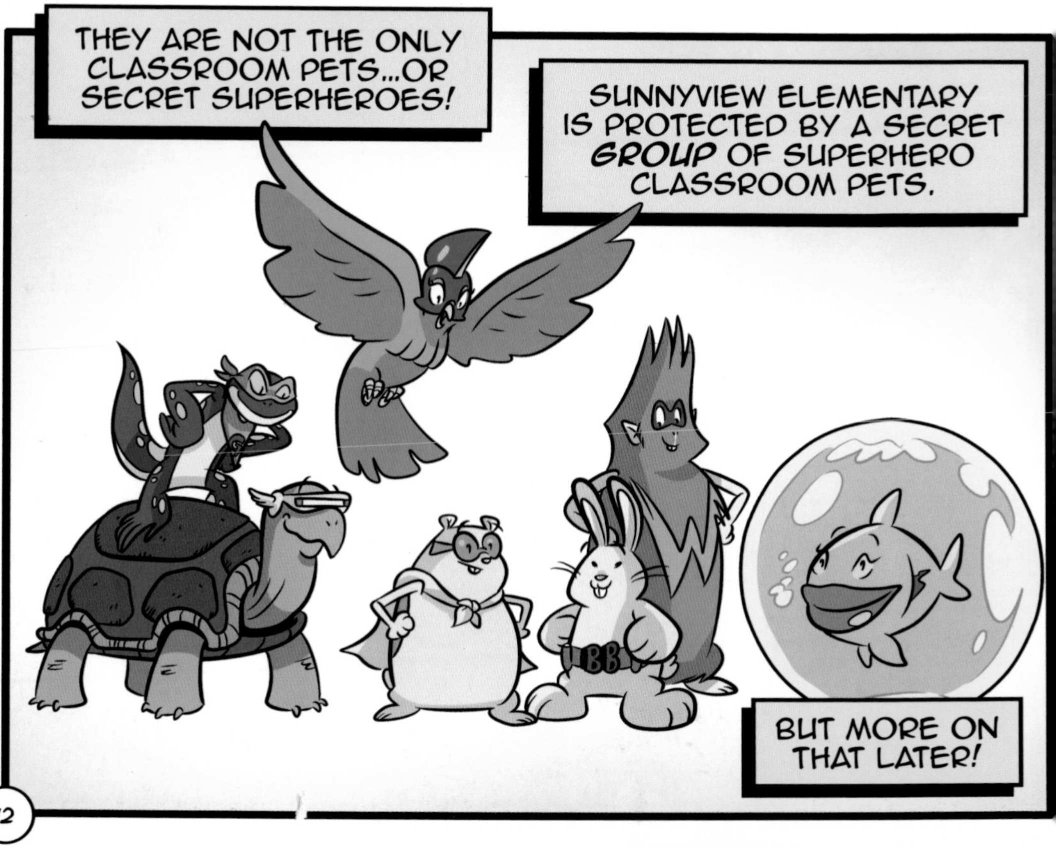
THEY ARE NOT THE ONLY CLASSROOM PETS...OR SECRET SUPERHEROES!
SUNNYVIEW ELEMENTARY IS PROTECTED BY A SECRET *GROUP* OF SUPERHERO CLASSROOM PETS.
BB
BUT MORE ON THAT LATER!

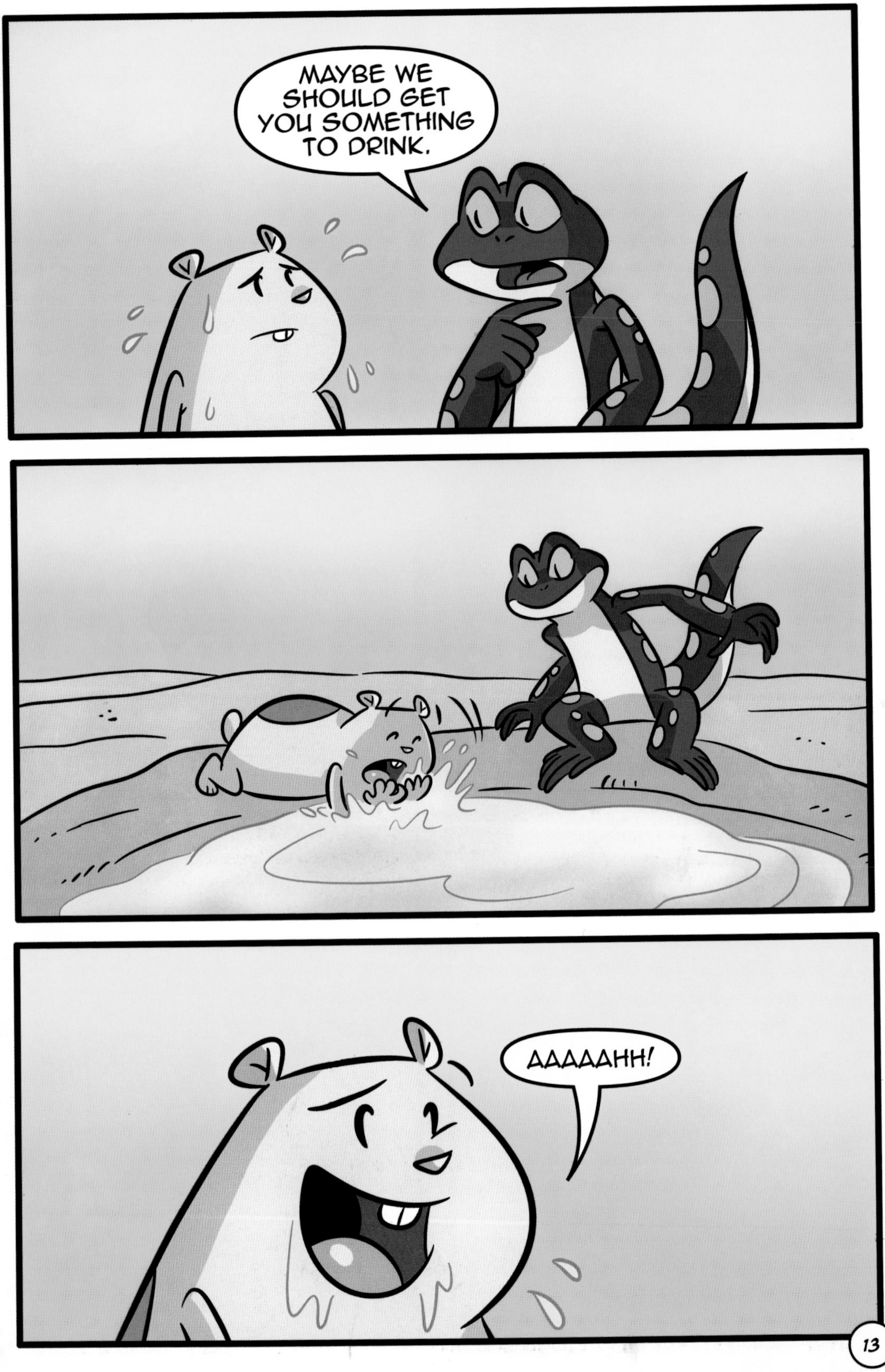

MAYBE WE SHOULD GET YOU SOMETHING TO DRINK.
AAAAAHH!

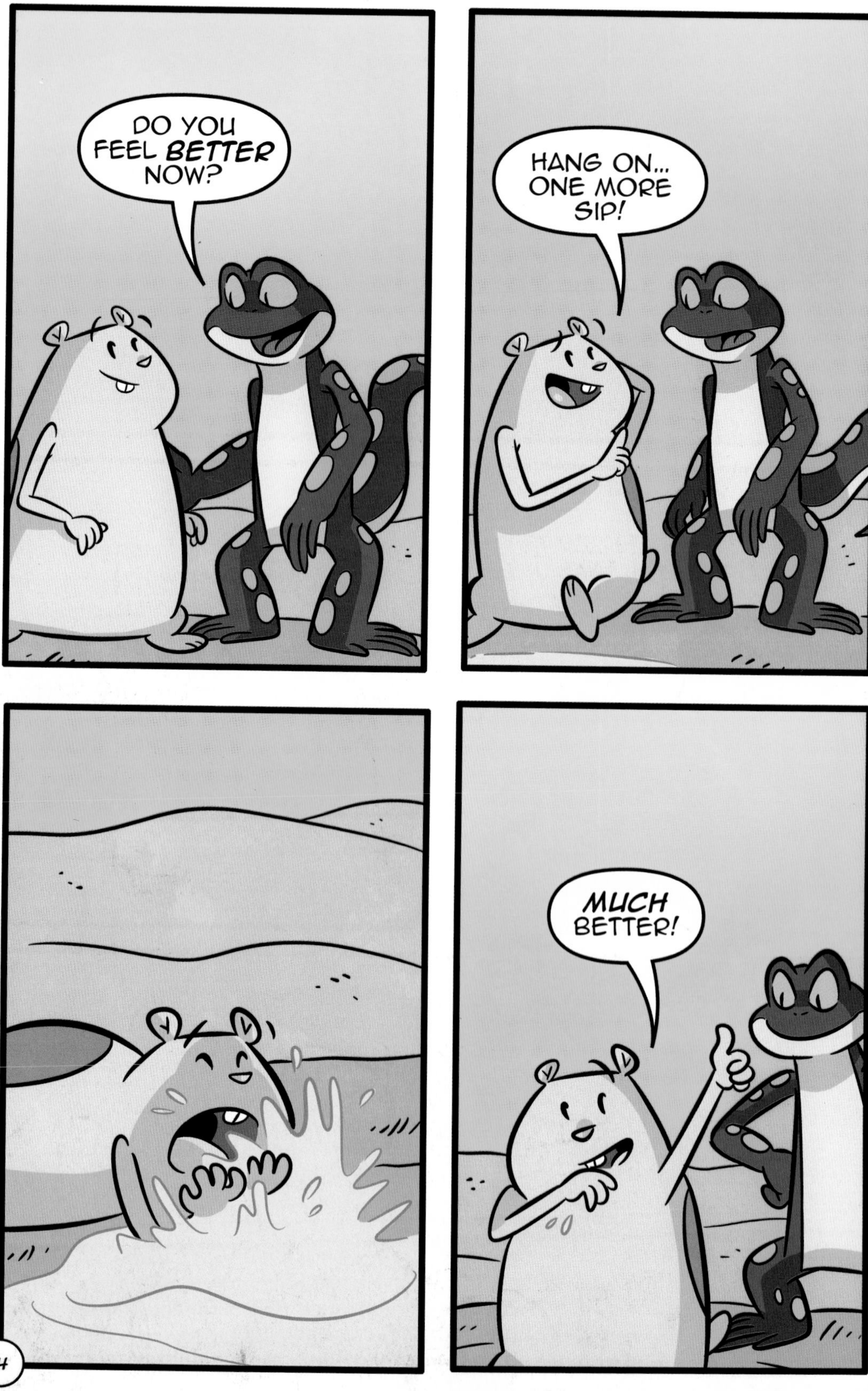
DO YOU FEEL BETTER NOW?
HANG ON... ONE MORE SIP!
MUCH BETTER!

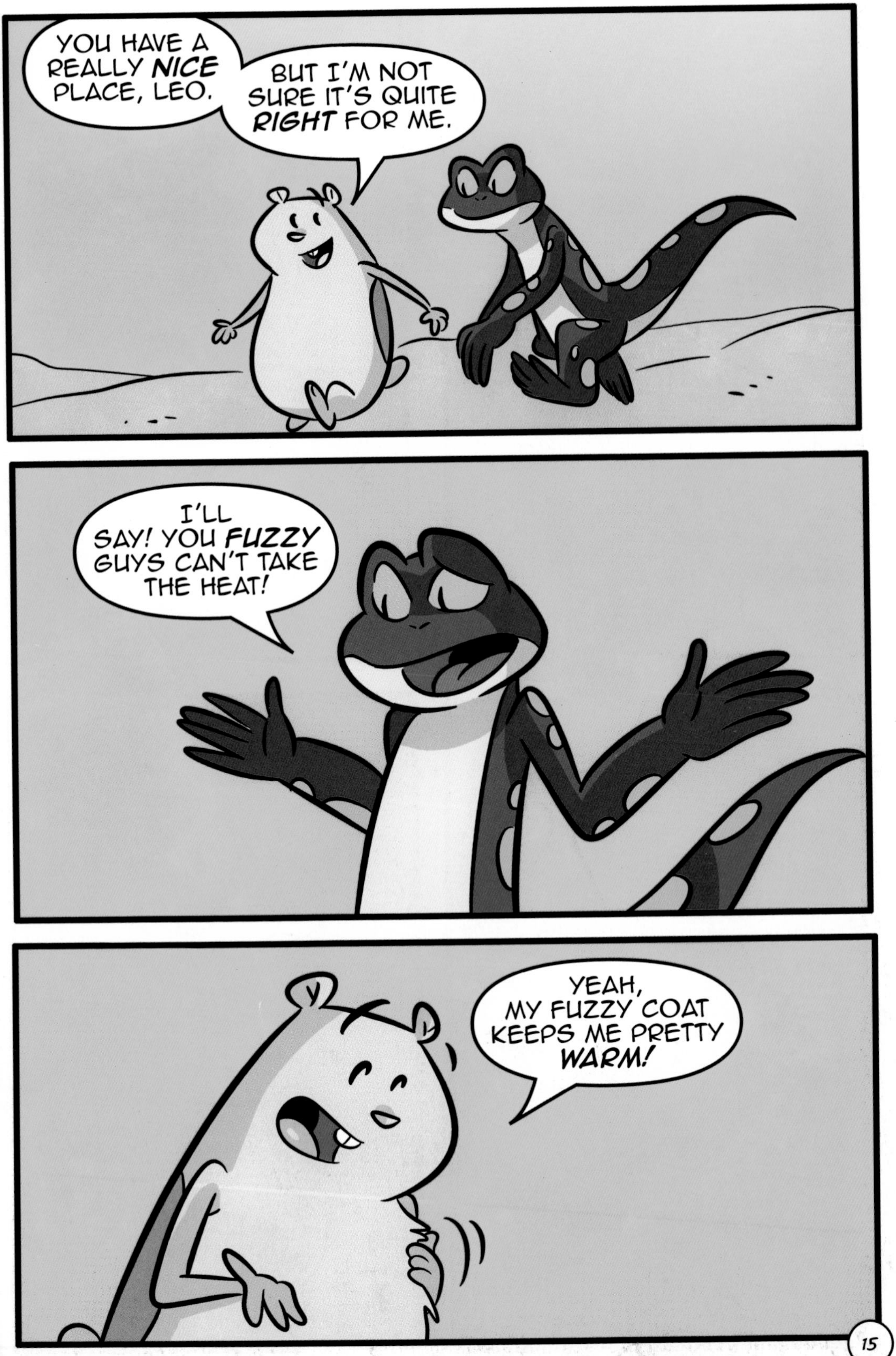
YOU HAVE A REALLY NICE PLACE, LEO.
BUT I'M NOT SURE IT'S QUITE RIGHT FOR ME.
I'LL SAY! YOU FUZZY GUYS CAN'T TAKE THE HEAT!
YEAH, MY FUZZY COAT KEEPS ME PRETTY WARM!

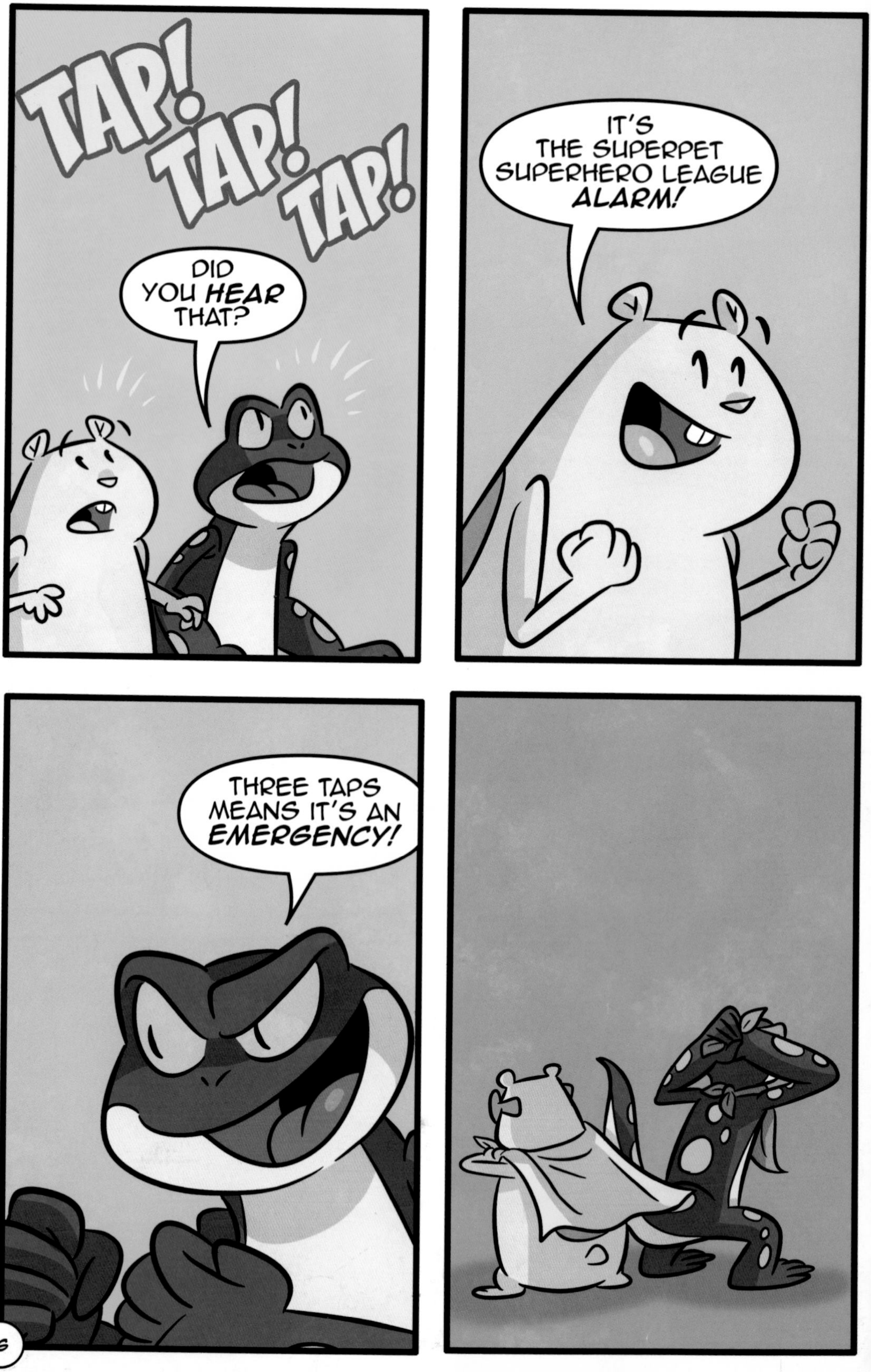
TAP! TAP! TAP!
DID YOU HEAR THAT?
IT'S THE SUPERPET SUPERHERO LEAGUE ALARM!
THREE TAPS MEANS IT'S AN EMERGENCY!

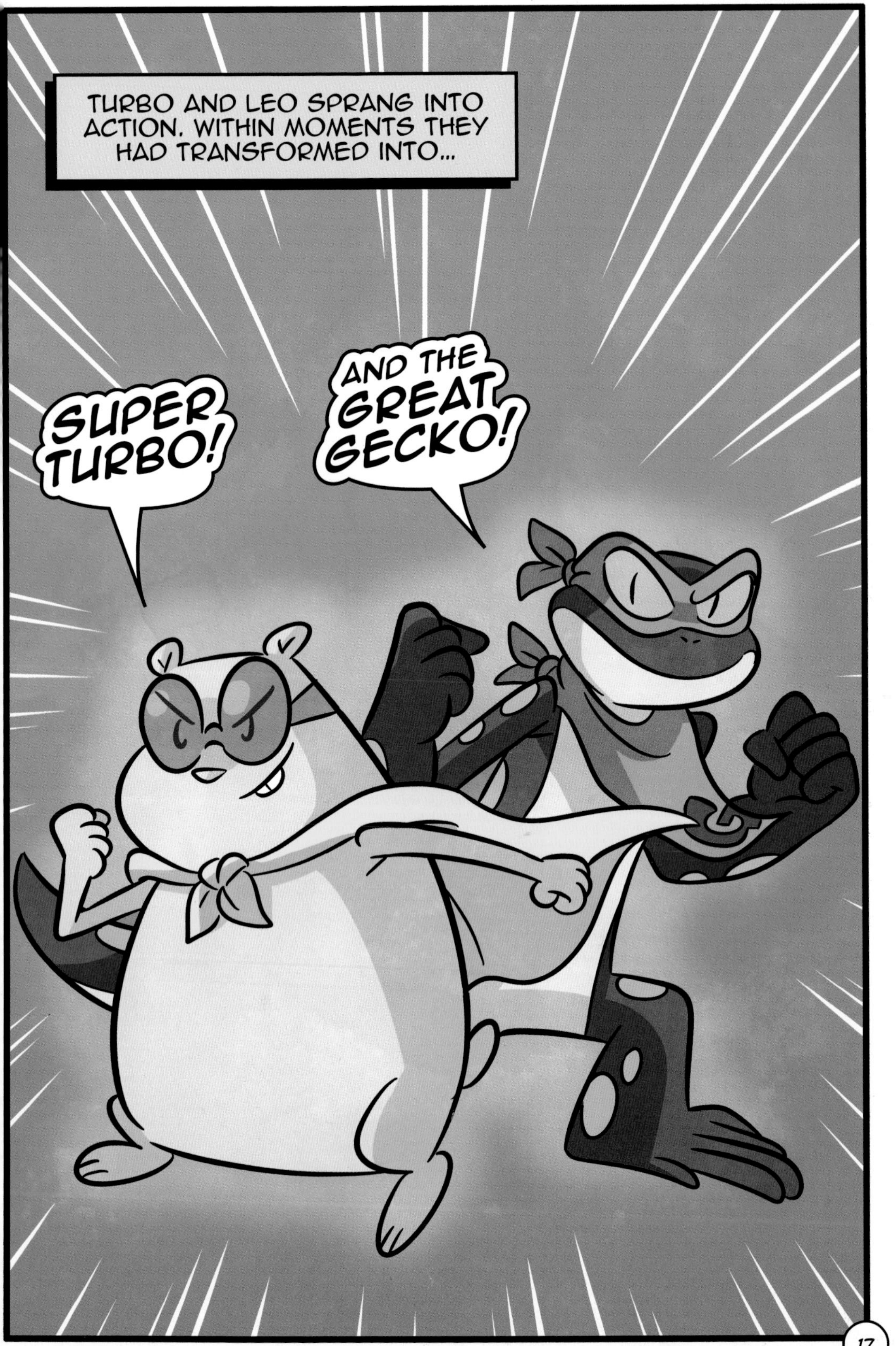
TURBO AND LEO SPRANG INTO ACTION. WITHIN MOMENTS THEY HAD TRANSFORMED INTO...
SUPER TURBO!
AND THE GREAT GECKO!

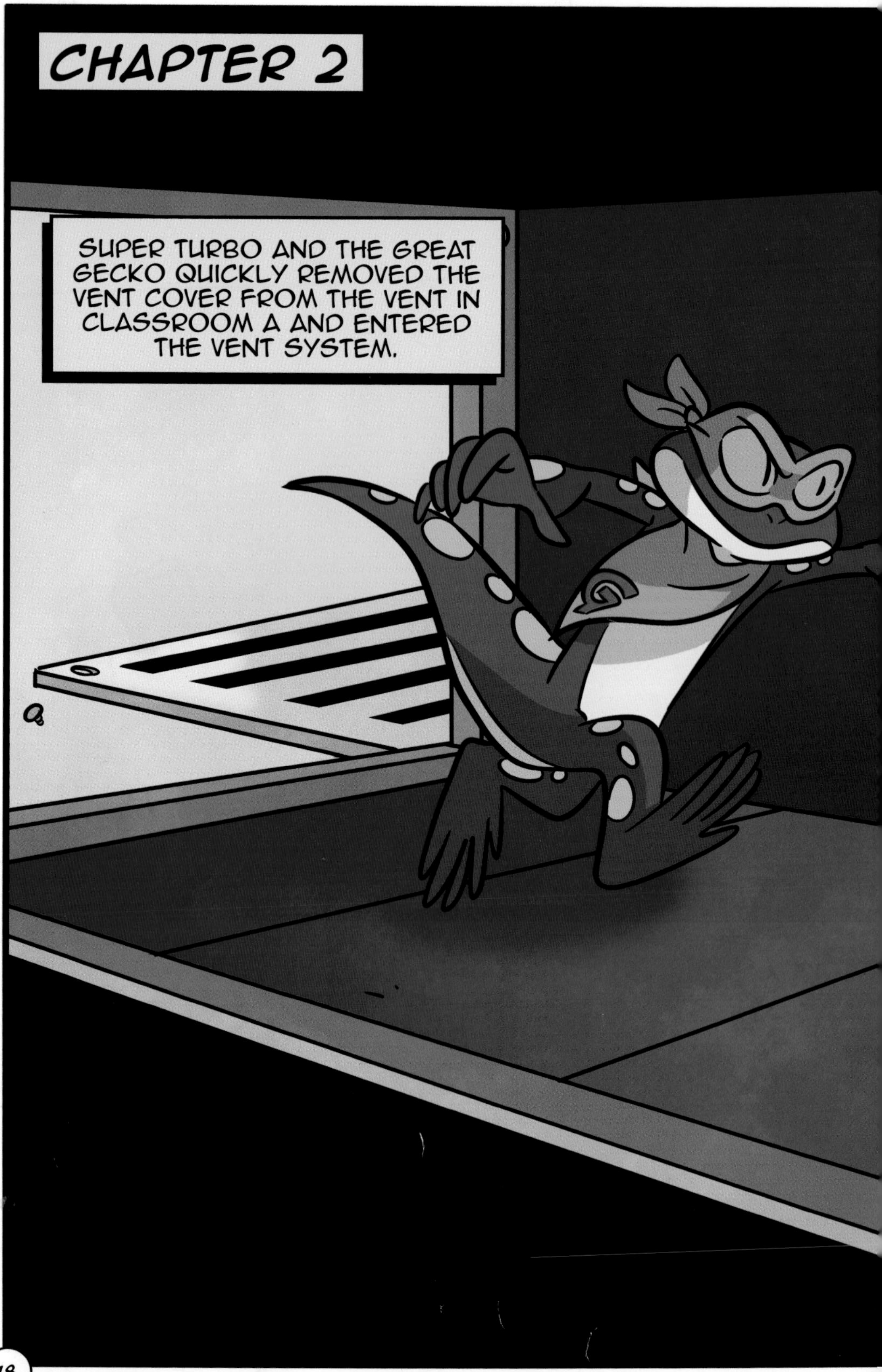
CHAPTER 2
SUPER TURBO AND THE GREAT GECKO QUICKLY REMOVED THE VENT COVER FROM THE VENT IN CLASSROOM A AND ENTERED THE VENT SYSTEM.

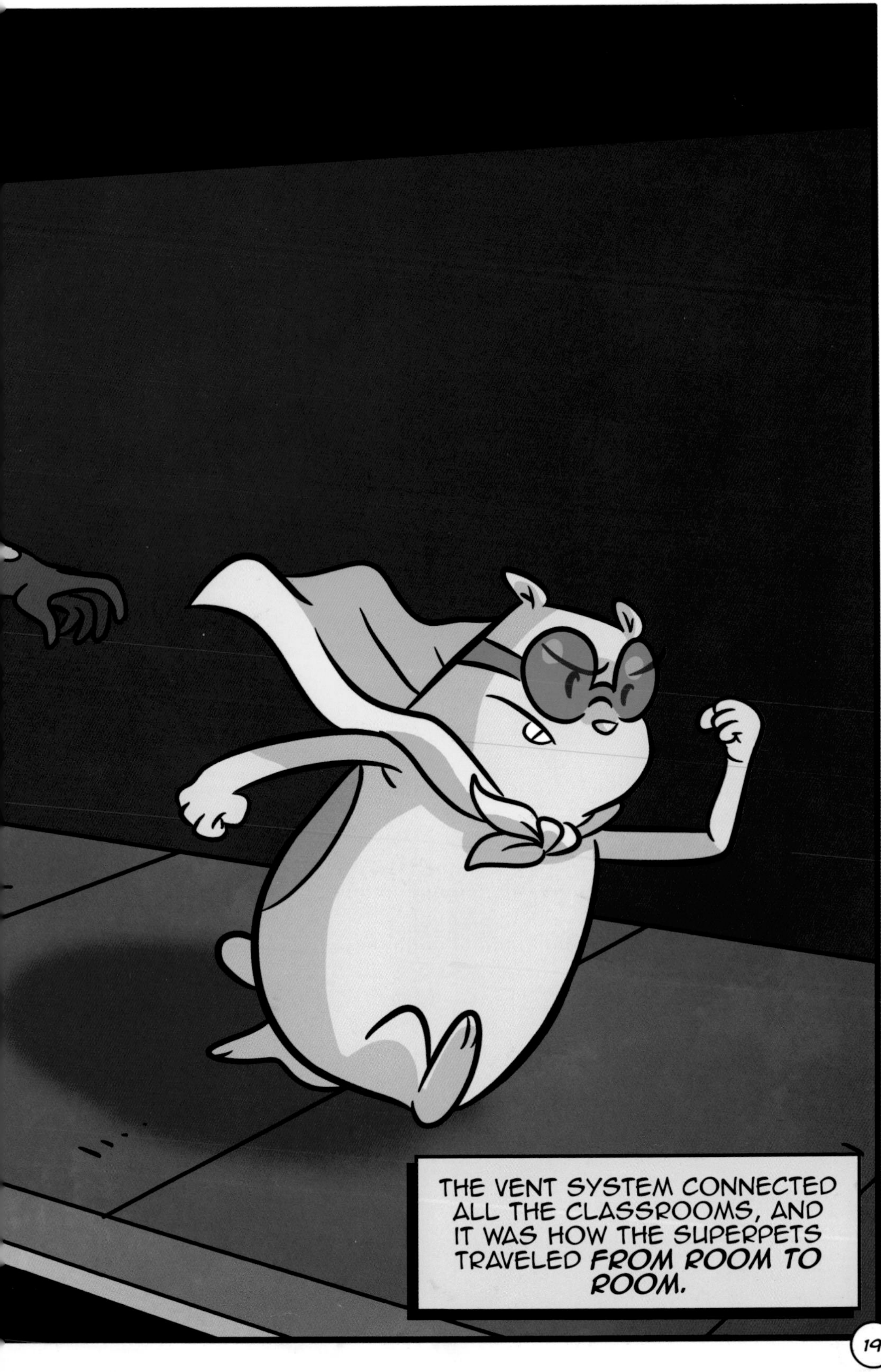
THE VENT SYSTEM CONNECTED ALL THE CLASSROOMS, AND IT WAS HOW THE SUPERPETS TRAVELED *FROM ROOM TO ROOM.*

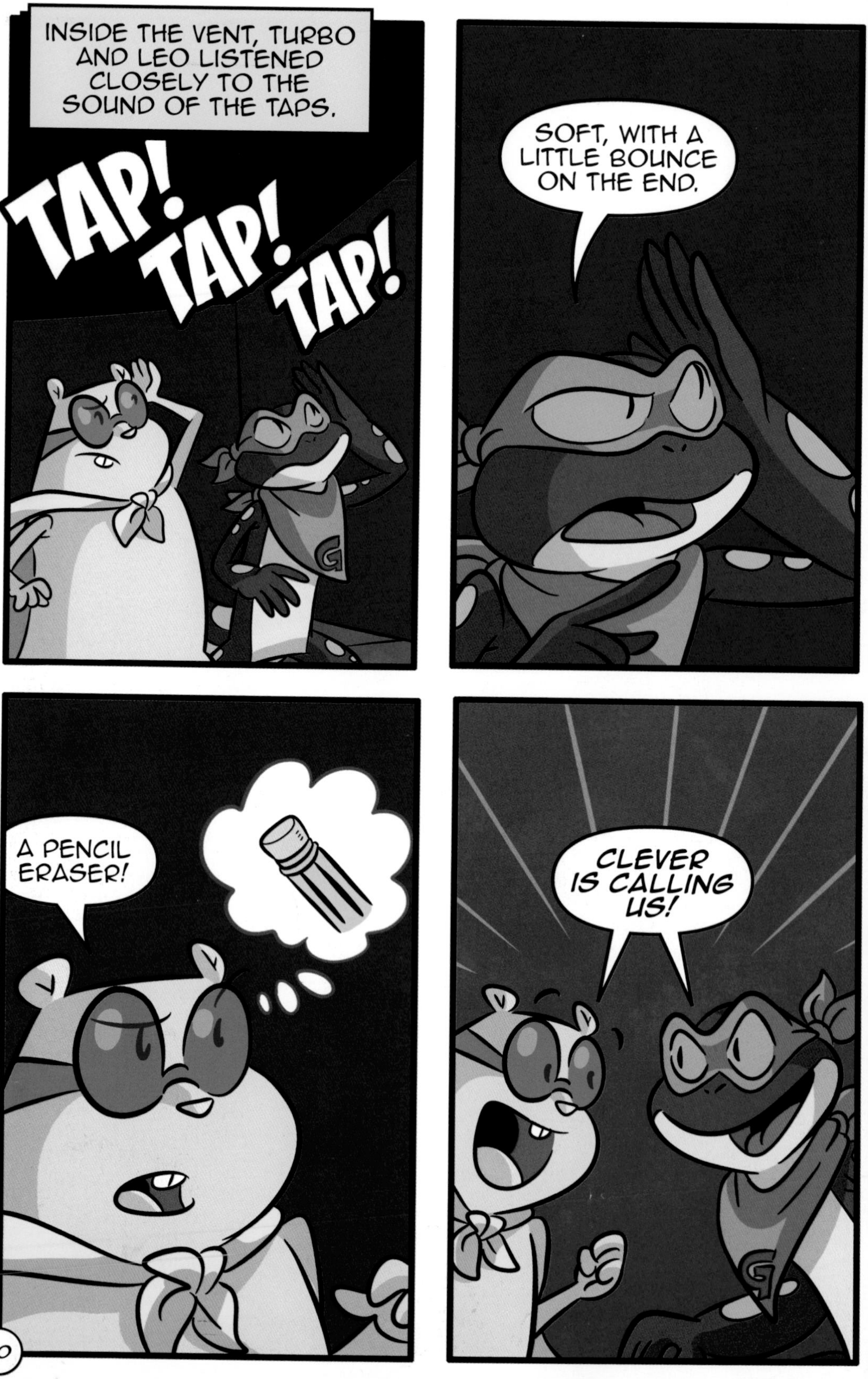
INSIDE THE VENT, TURBO AND LEO LISTENED CLOSELY TO THE SOUND OF THE TAPS.
TAP! TAP! TAP!
SOFT, WITH A LITTLE BOUNCE ON THE END.
A PENCIL ERASER!
CLEVER IS CALLING US!

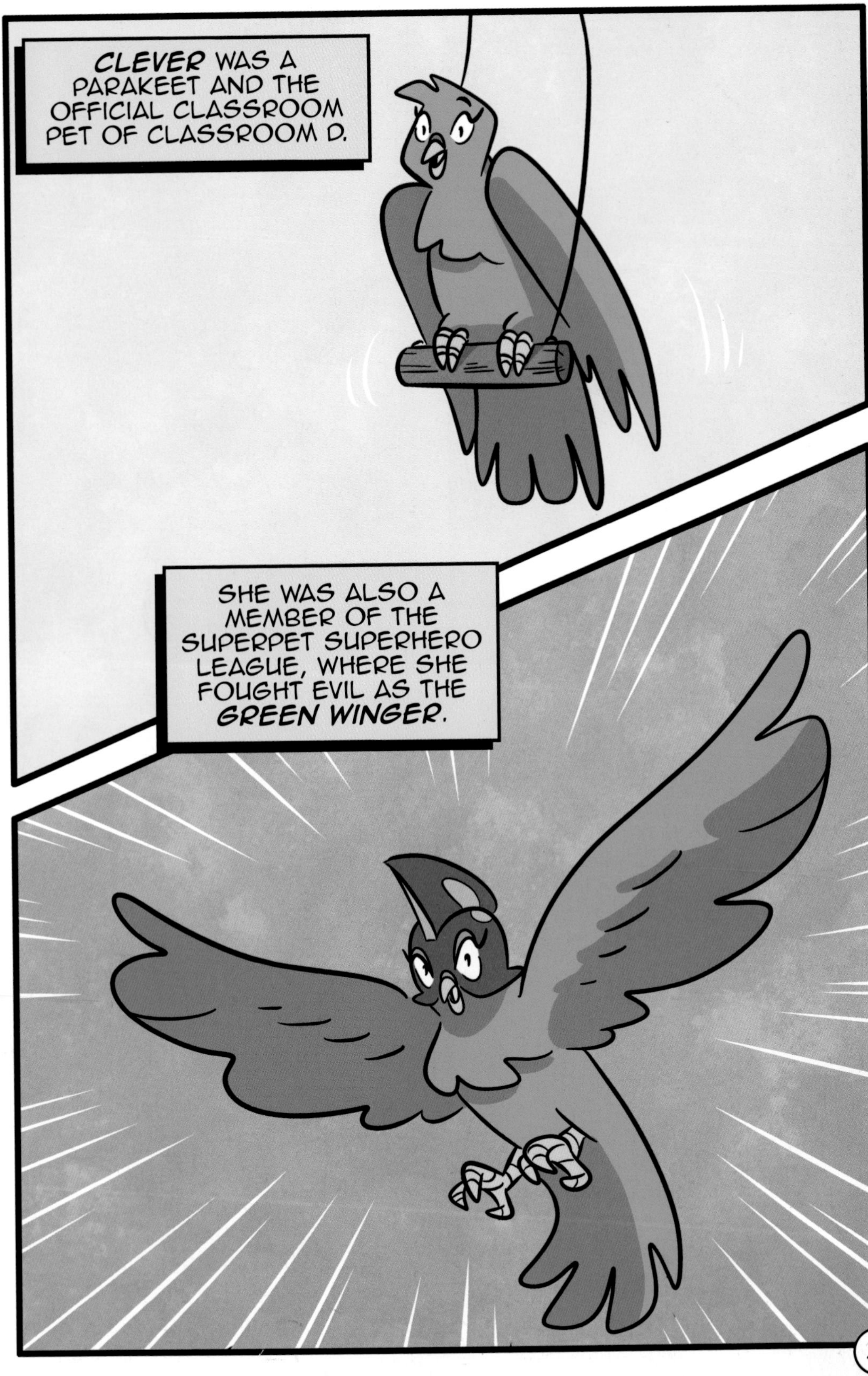
CLEVER WAS A PARAKEET AND THE OFFICIAL CLASSROOM PET OF CLASSROOM D.
SHE WAS ALSO A MEMBER OF THE SUPERPET SUPERHERO LEAGUE, WHERE SHE FOUGHT EVIL AS THE GREEN WINGER.

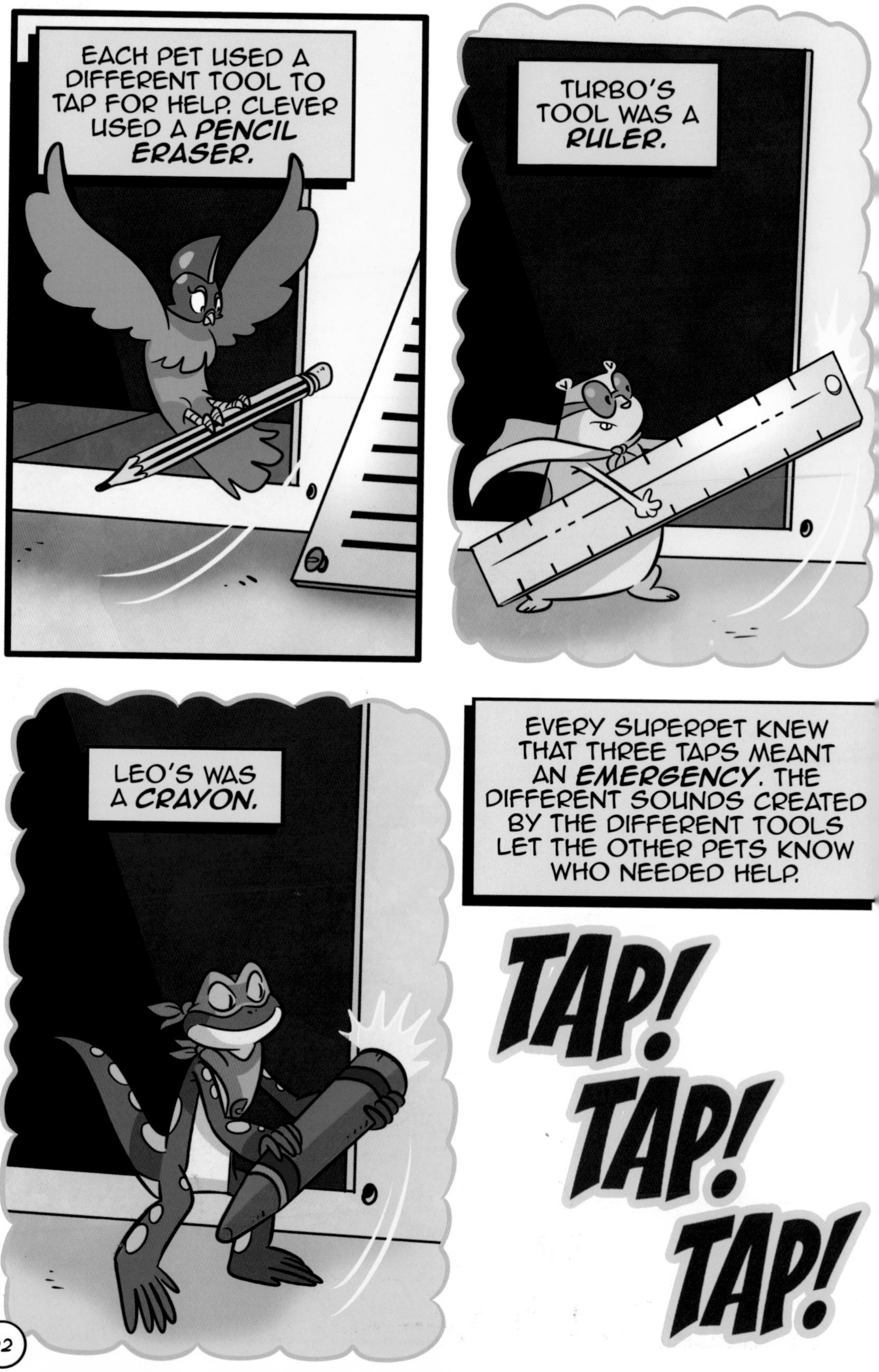
EACH PET USED A DIFFERENT TOOL TO TAP FOR HELP. CLEVER USED A PENCIL ERASER.
TURBO'S TOOL WAS A RULER.
LEO'S WAS A CRAYON.
EVERY SUPERPET KNEW THAT THREE TAPS MEANT AN EMERGENCY. THE DIFFERENT SOUNDS CREATED BY THE DIFFERENT TOOLS LET THE OTHER PETS KNOW WHO NEEDED HELP.
TAP!
TAP!
TAP!

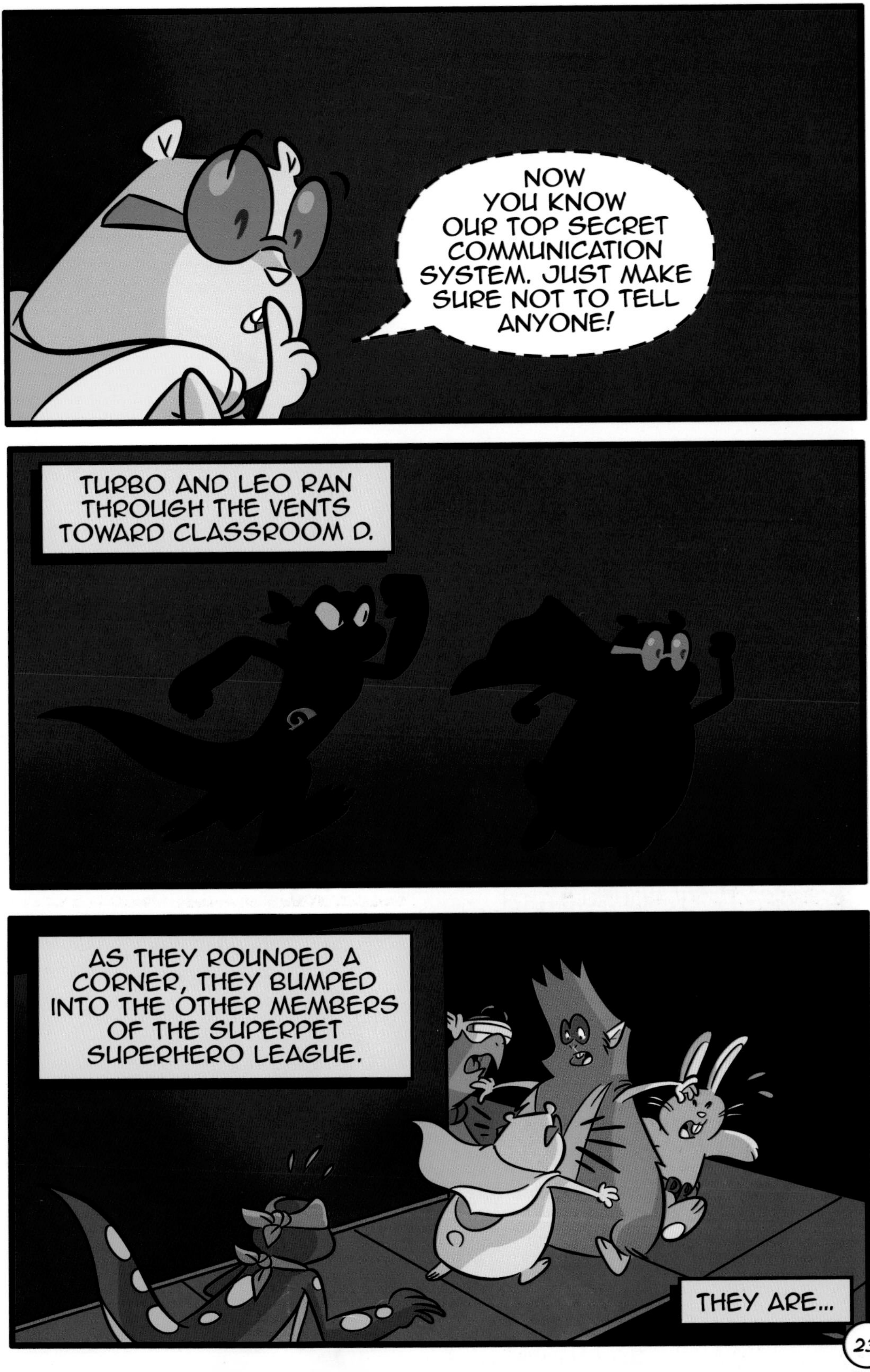
NOW YOU KNOW OUR TOP SECRET COMMUNICATION SYSTEM. JUST MAKE SURE NOT TO TELL ANYONE!
TURBO AND LEO RAN THROUGH THE VENTS TOWARD CLASSROOM D.
AS THEY ROUNDED A CORNER, THEY BUMPED INTO THE OTHER MEMBERS OF THE SUPERPET SUPERHERO LEAGUE.
THEY ARE...

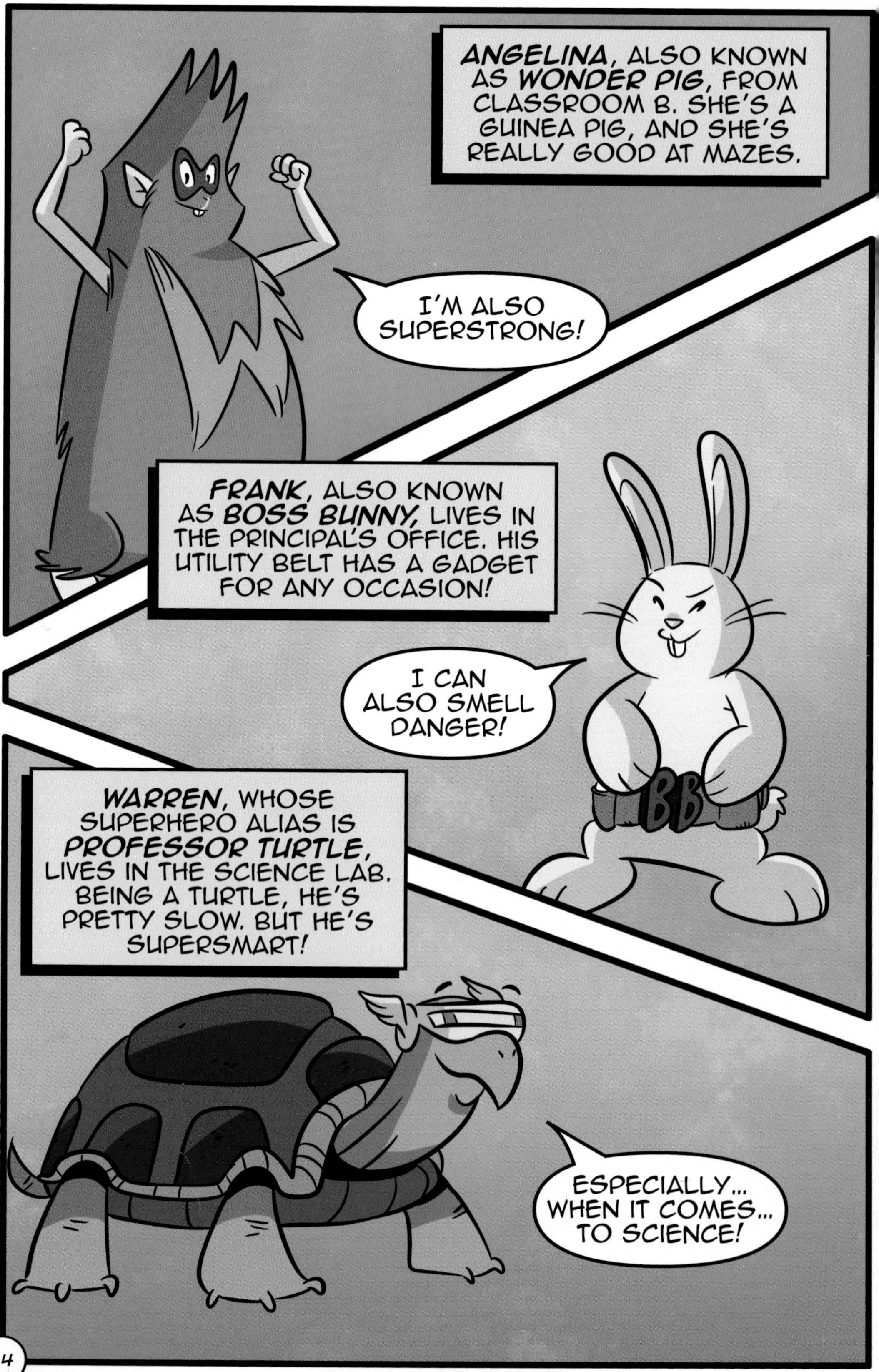
ANGELINA, ALSO KNOWN AS WONDER PIG, FROM CLASSROOM B. SHE'S A GUINEA PIG, AND SHE'S REALLY GOOD AT MAZES.
I'M ALSO SUPERSTRONG!
FRANK, ALSO KNOWN AS BOSS BUNNY, LIVES IN THE PRINCIPAL'S OFFICE. HIS UTILITY BELT HAS A GADGET FOR ANY OCCASION!
I CAN ALSO SMELL DANGER!
BB
WARREN, WHOSE SUPERHERO ALIAS IS PROFESSOR TURTLE, LIVES IN THE SCIENCE LAB. BEING A TURTLE, HE'S PRETTY SLOW. BUT HE'S SUPERSMART!
ESPECIALLY... WHEN IT COMES... TO SCIENCE!

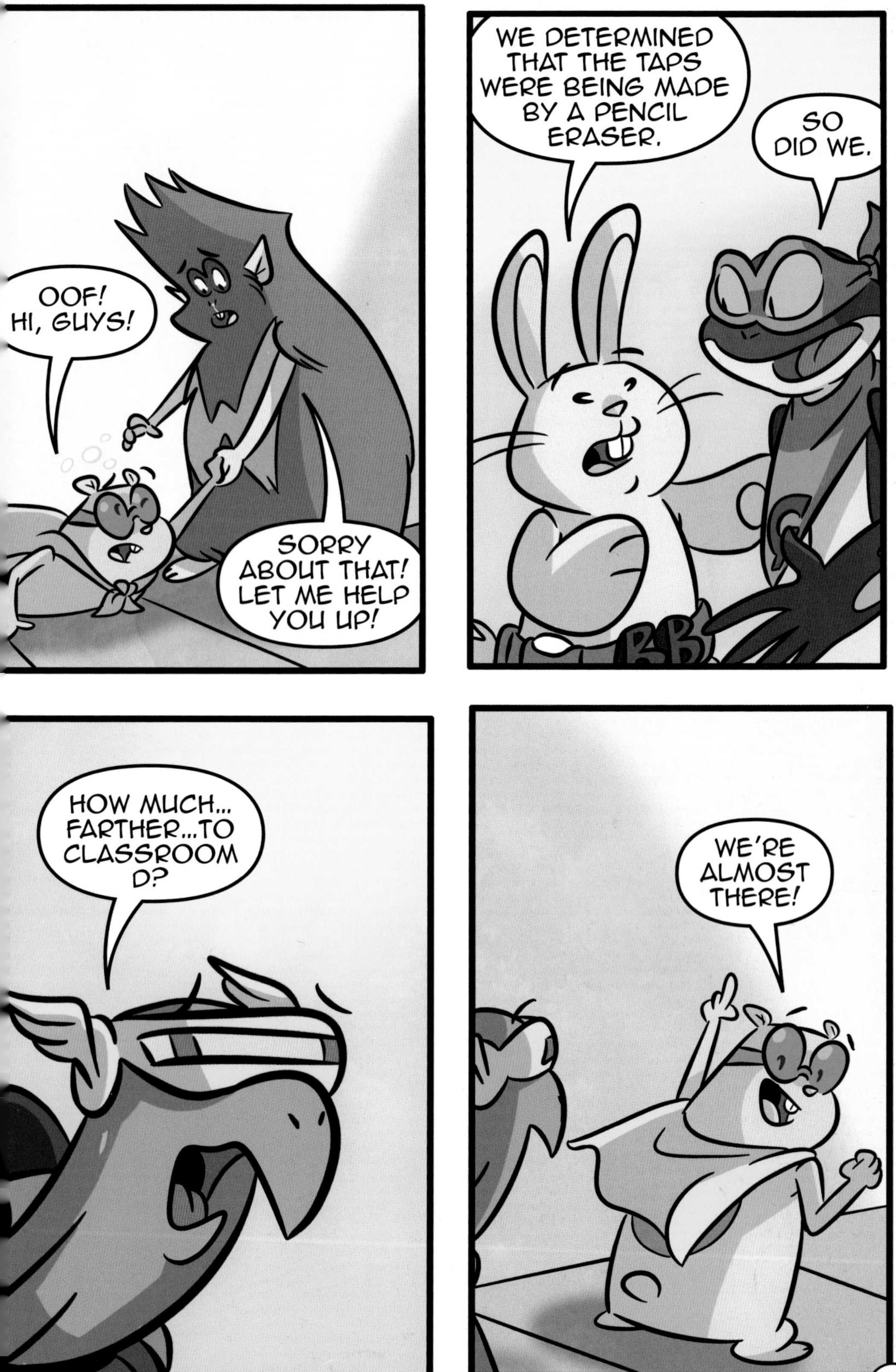

OOF! HI, GUYS!
SORRY ABOUT THAT! LET ME HELP YOU UP!
WE DETERMINED THAT THE TAPS WERE BEING MADE BY A PENCIL ERASER.
SO DID WE.
HOW MUCH... FARTHER...TO CLASSROOM D?
WE'RE ALMOST THERE!

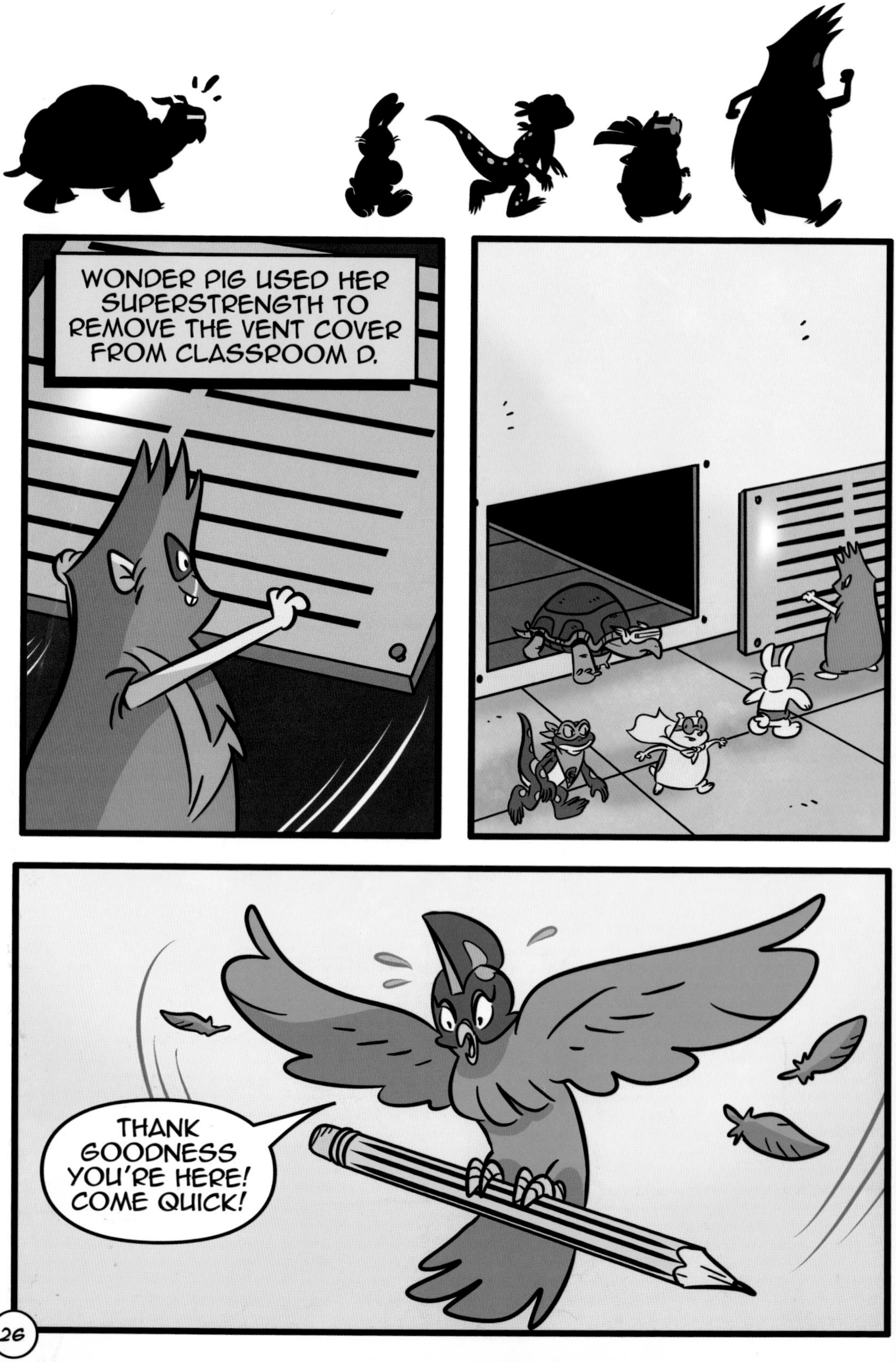
WONDER PIG USED HER SUPERSTRENGTH TO REMOVE THE VENT COVER FROM CLASSROOM D.
THANK GOODNESS YOU'RE HERE! COME QUICK!

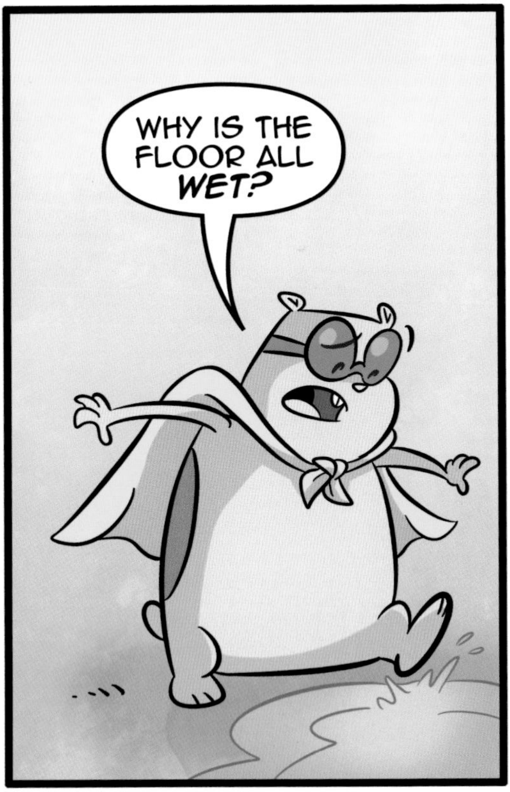
WHY IS THE FLOOR ALL WET?

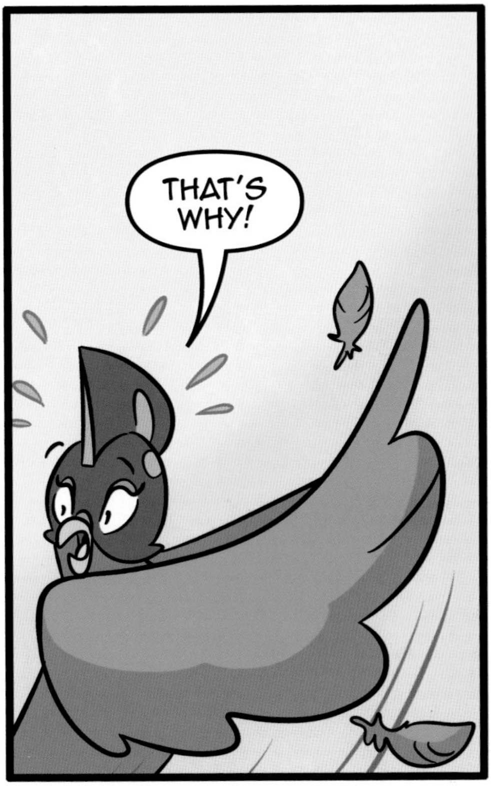
THAT'S WHY!

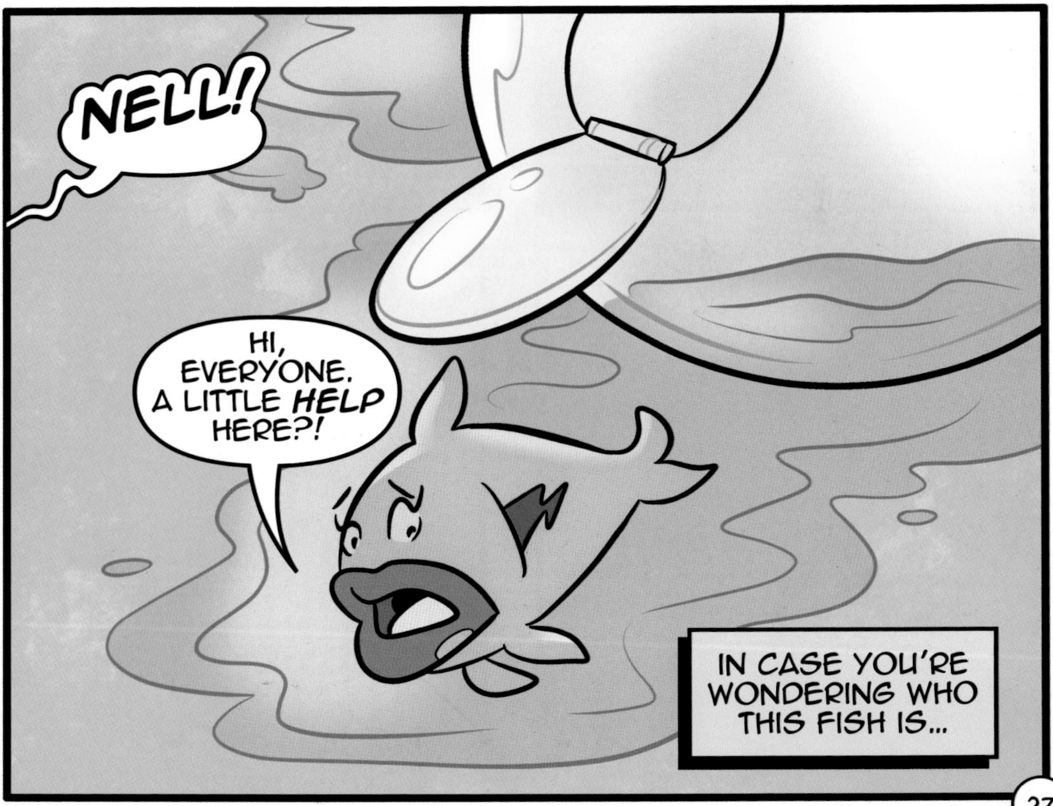
NELL!
HI, EVERYONE. A LITTLE HELP HERE?!
IN CASE YOU'RE WONDERING WHO THIS FISH IS...

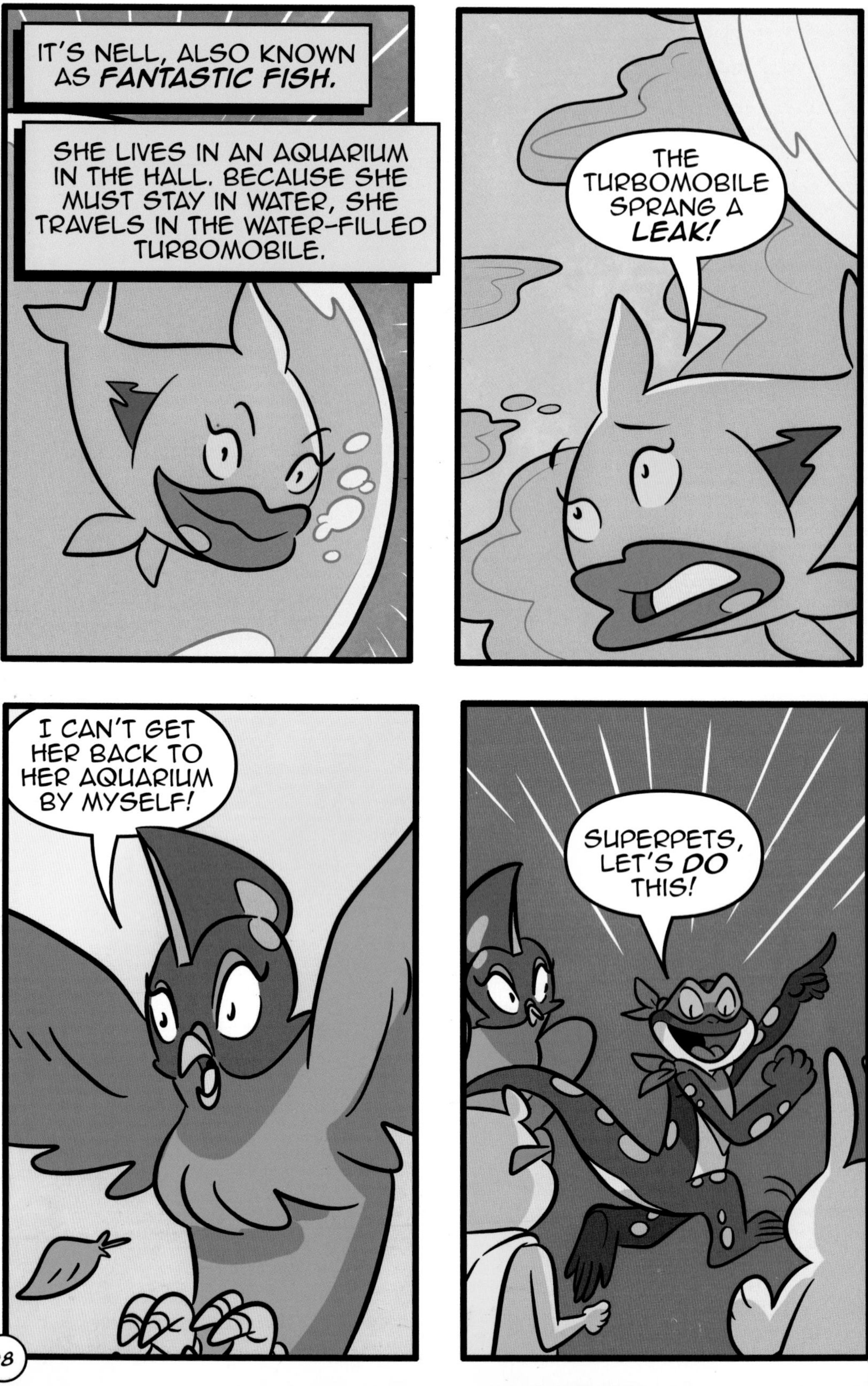
IT'S NELL, ALSO KNOWN AS FANTASTIC FISH.
SHE LIVES IN AN AQUARIUM IN THE HALL. BECAUSE SHE MUST STAY IN WATER, SHE TRAVELS IN THE WATER-FILLED TURBOMOBILE.
THE TURBOMOBILE SPRANG A LEAK!
I CAN'T GET HER BACK TO HER AQUARIUM BY MYSELF!
SUPERPETS, LET'S DO THIS!

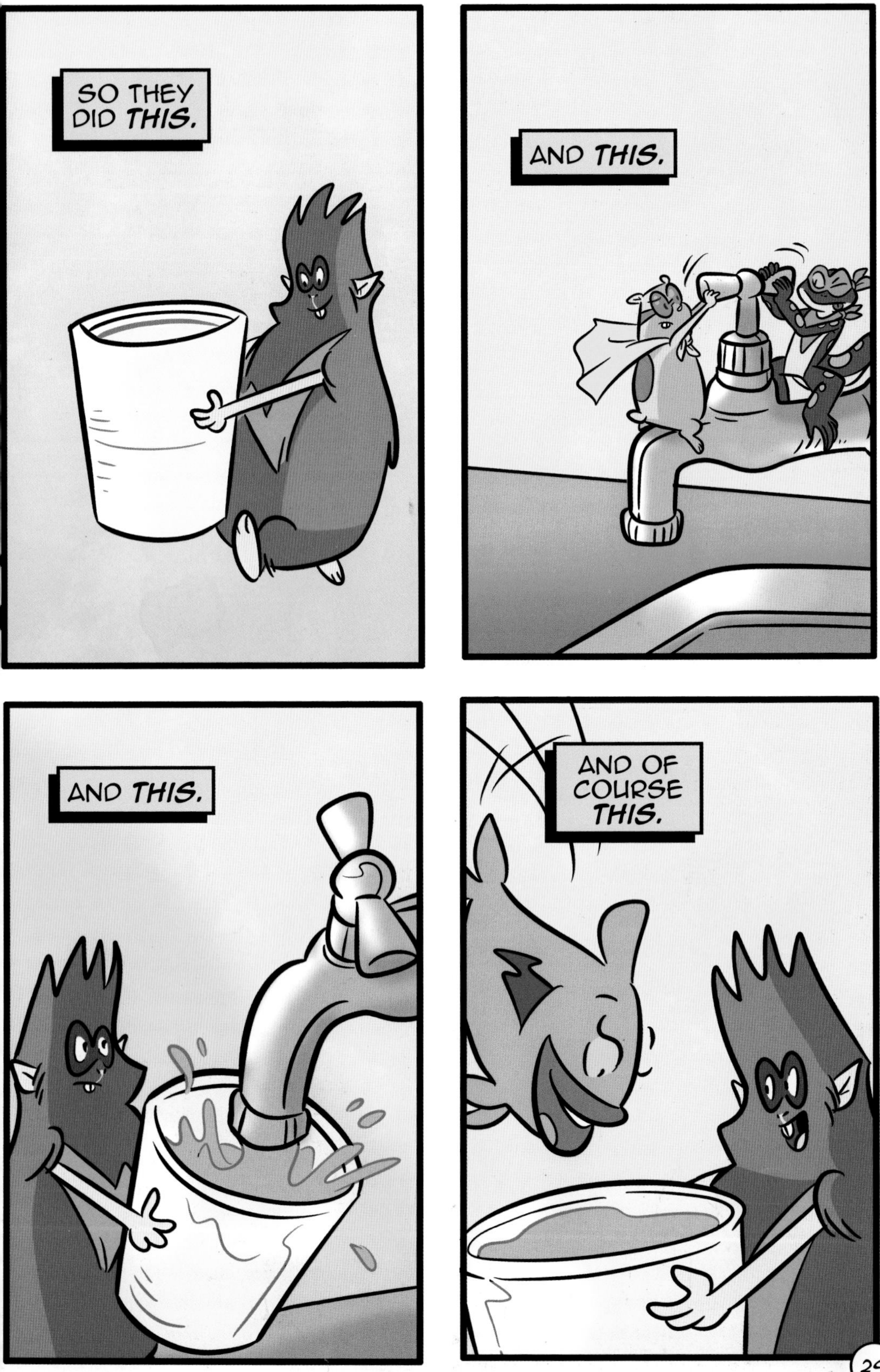

SO THEY DID THIS.
AND THIS.
AND THIS.
AND OF COURSE THIS.

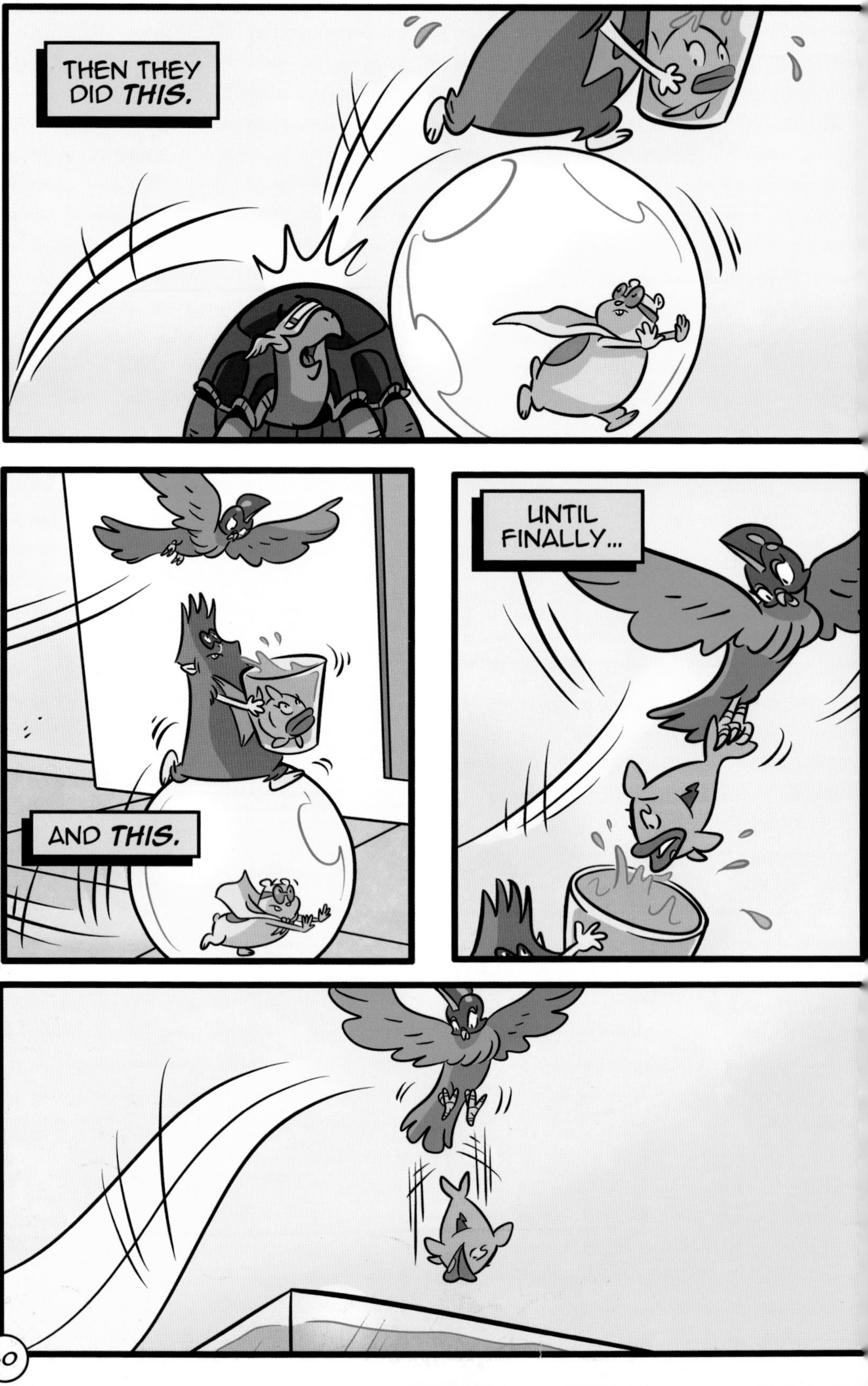
THEN THEY DID *THIS.*
AND *THIS.*
UNTIL FINALLY...

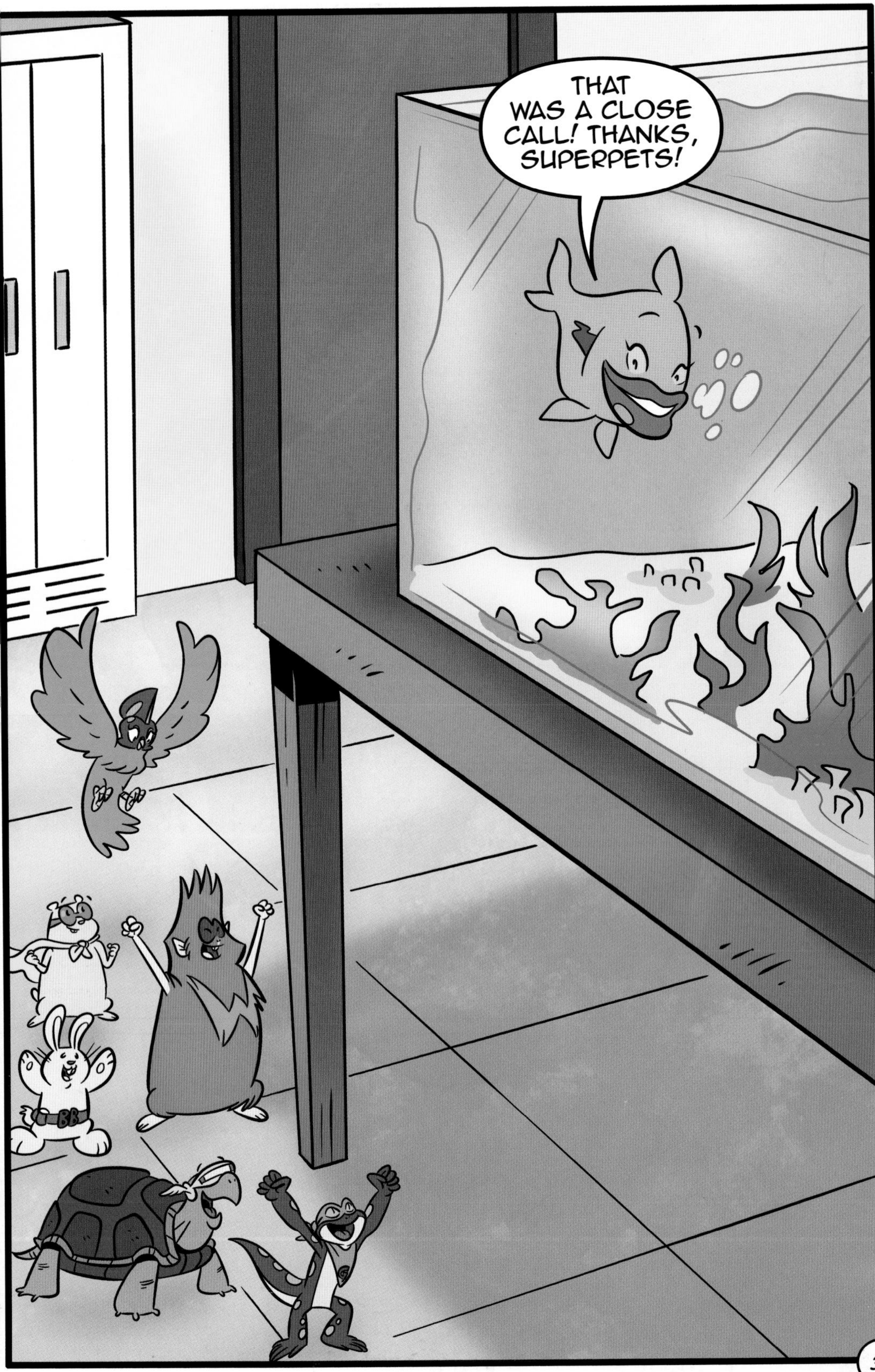
THAT WAS A CLOSE CALL! THANKS, SUPERPETS!

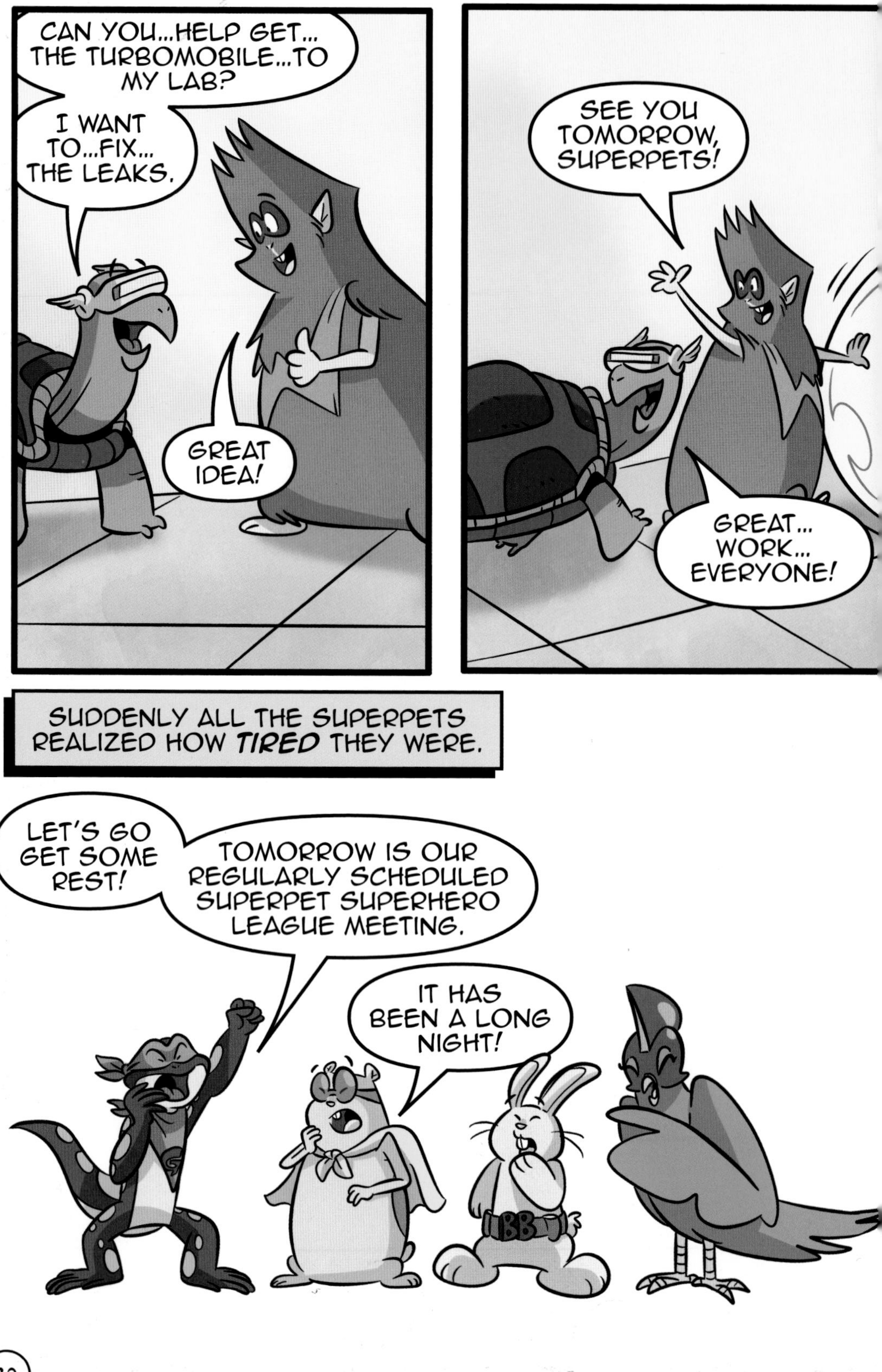
CAN YOU...HELP GET... THE TURBOMOBILE...TO MY LAB?
I WANT TO...FIX... THE LEAKS.
GREAT IDEA!
SEE YOU TOMORROW, SUPERPETS!
GREAT... WORK... EVERYONE!
SUDDENLY ALL THE SUPERPETS REALIZED HOW *TIRED* THEY WERE.
LET'S GO GET SOME REST!
TOMORROW IS OUR REGULARLY SCHEDULED SUPERPET SUPERHERO LEAGUE MEETING.
IT HAS BEEN A LONG NIGHT!
BB

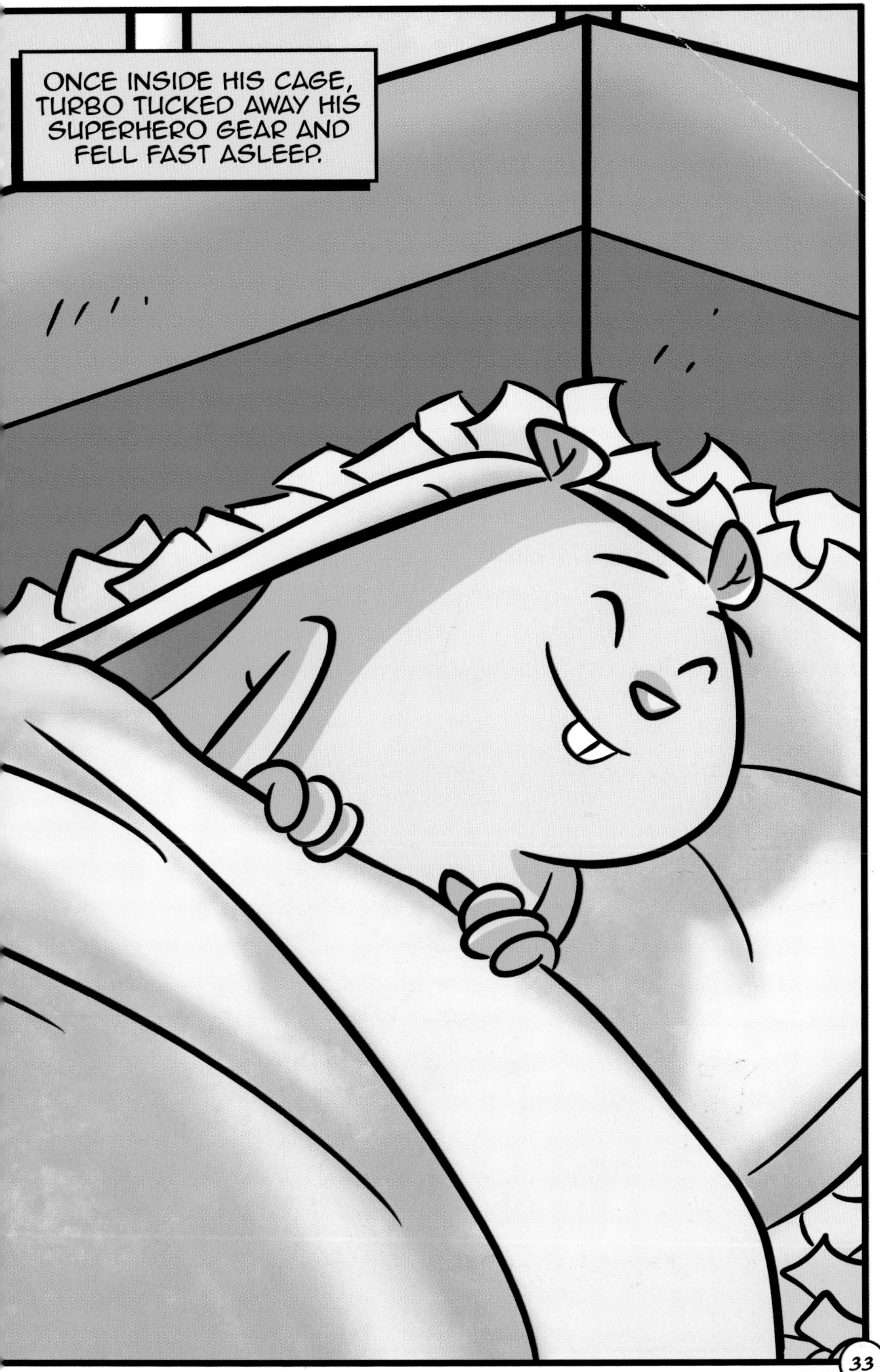
ONCE INSIDE HIS CAGE, TURBO TUCKED AWAY HIS SUPERHERO GEAR AND FELL FAST ASLEEP.

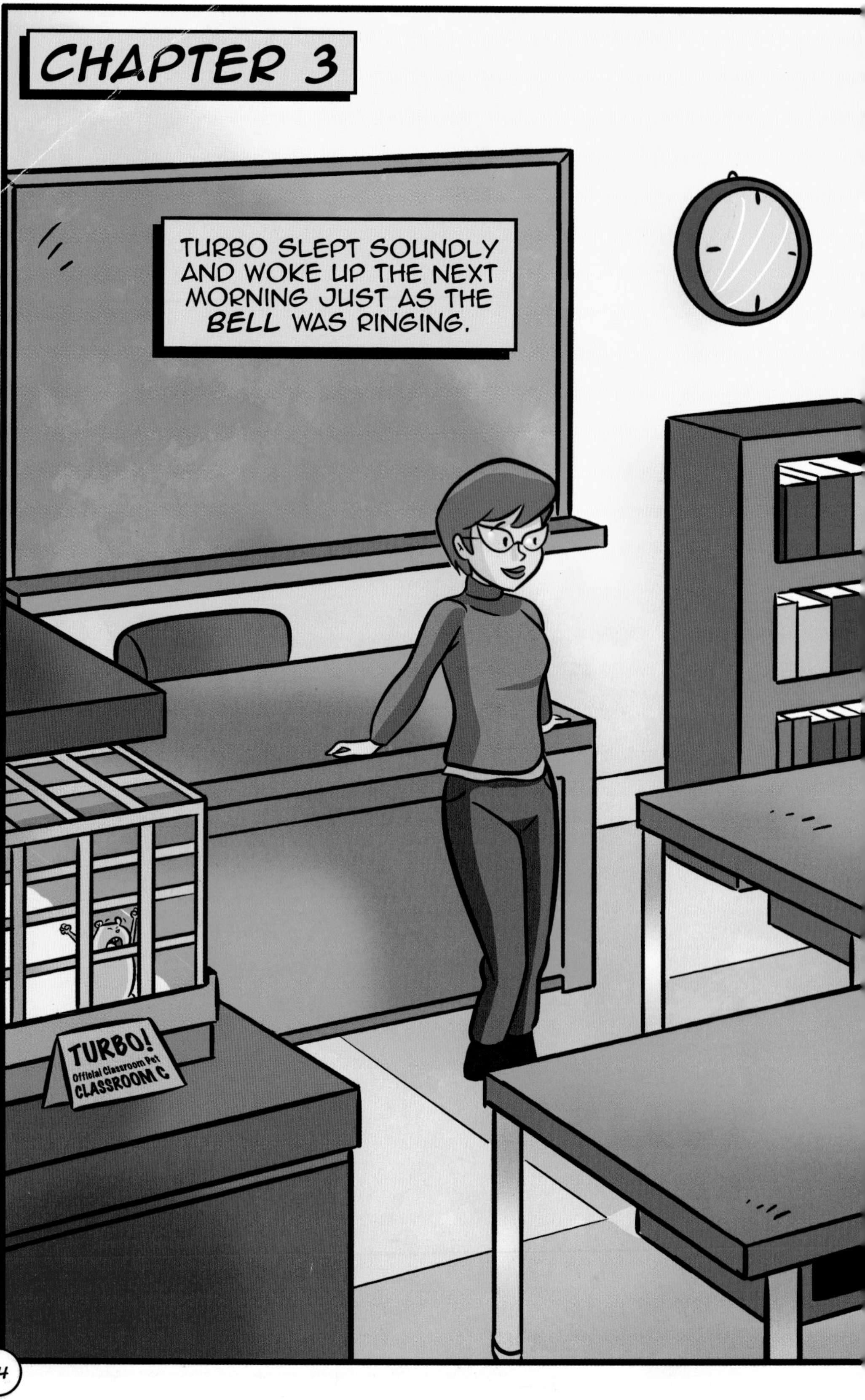
CHAPTER 3
TURBO SLEPT SOUNDLY AND WOKE UP THE NEXT MORNING JUST AS THE BELL WAS RINGING.
TURBO!
Official Classroom Pet
CLASSROOM C

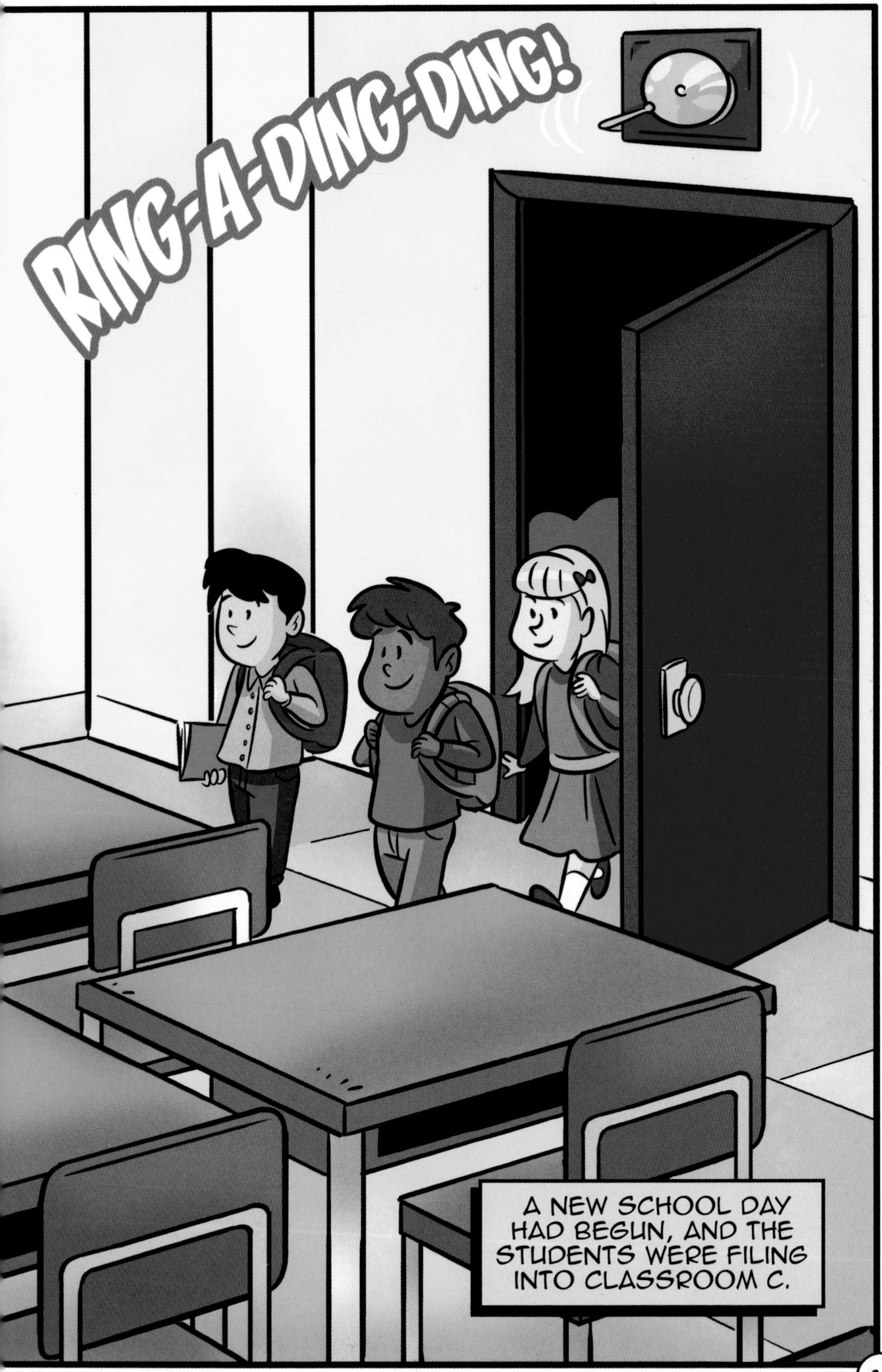
RING-A-DING-DING!
A NEW SCHOOL DAY HAD BEGUN, AND THE STUDENTS WERE FILING INTO CLASSROOM C.

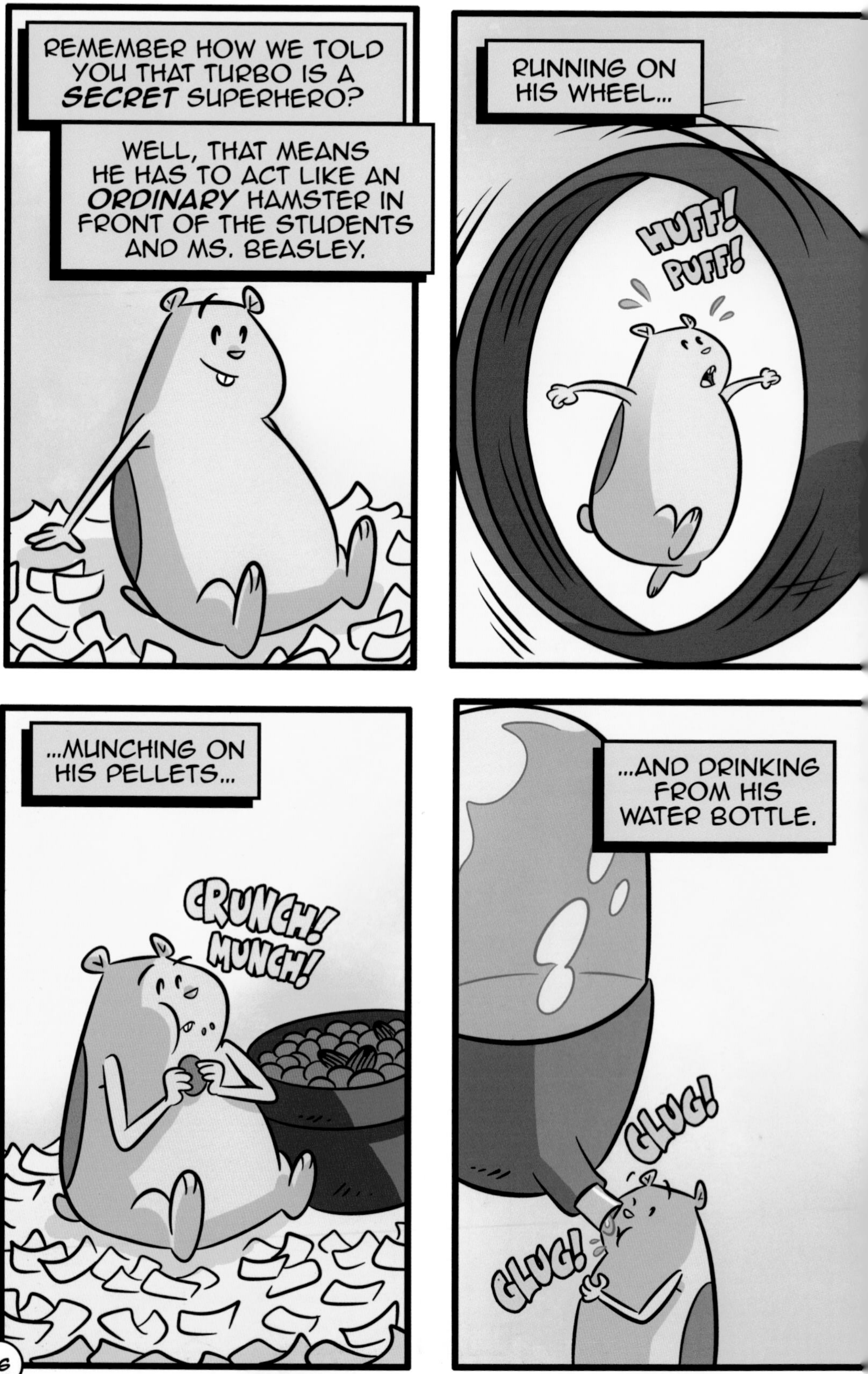
REMEMBER HOW WE TOLD YOU THAT TURBO IS A SECRET SUPERHERO?
WELL, THAT MEANS HE HAS TO ACT LIKE AN ORDINARY HAMSTER IN FRONT OF THE STUDENTS AND MS. BEASLEY.
RUNNING ON HIS WHEEL...
HUFF! PUFF!
...MUNCHING ON HIS PELLETS...
CRUNCH! MUNCH!
...AND DRINKING FROM HIS WATER BOTTLE.
GLUG! GLUG!

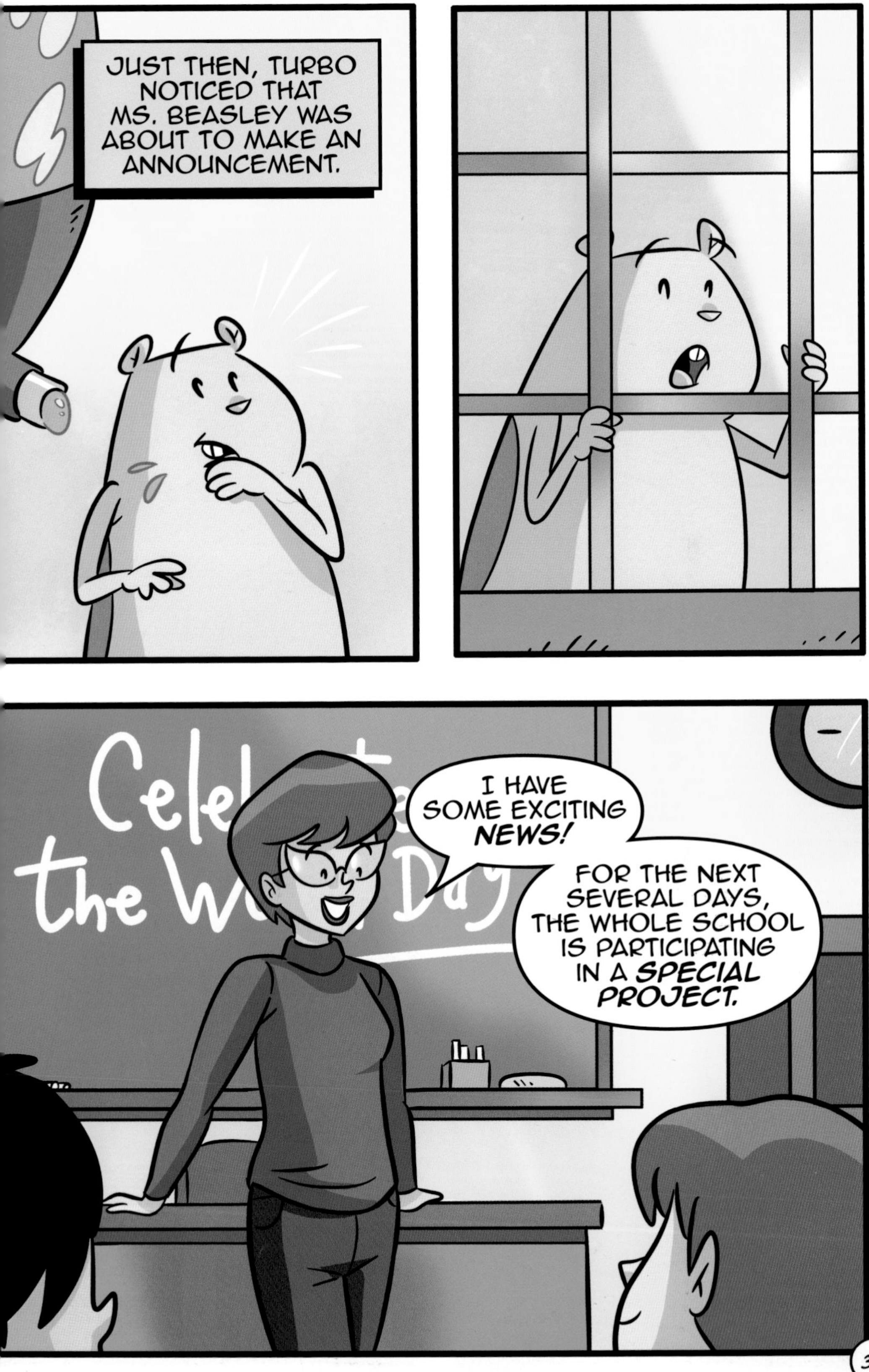
JUST THEN, TURBO NOTICED THAT MS. BEASLEY WAS ABOUT TO MAKE AN ANNOUNCEMENT.
Celeb... the W... Day
I HAVE SOME EXCITING NEWS!
FOR THE NEXT SEVERAL DAYS, THE WHOLE SCHOOL IS PARTICIPATING IN A SPECIAL PROJECT.

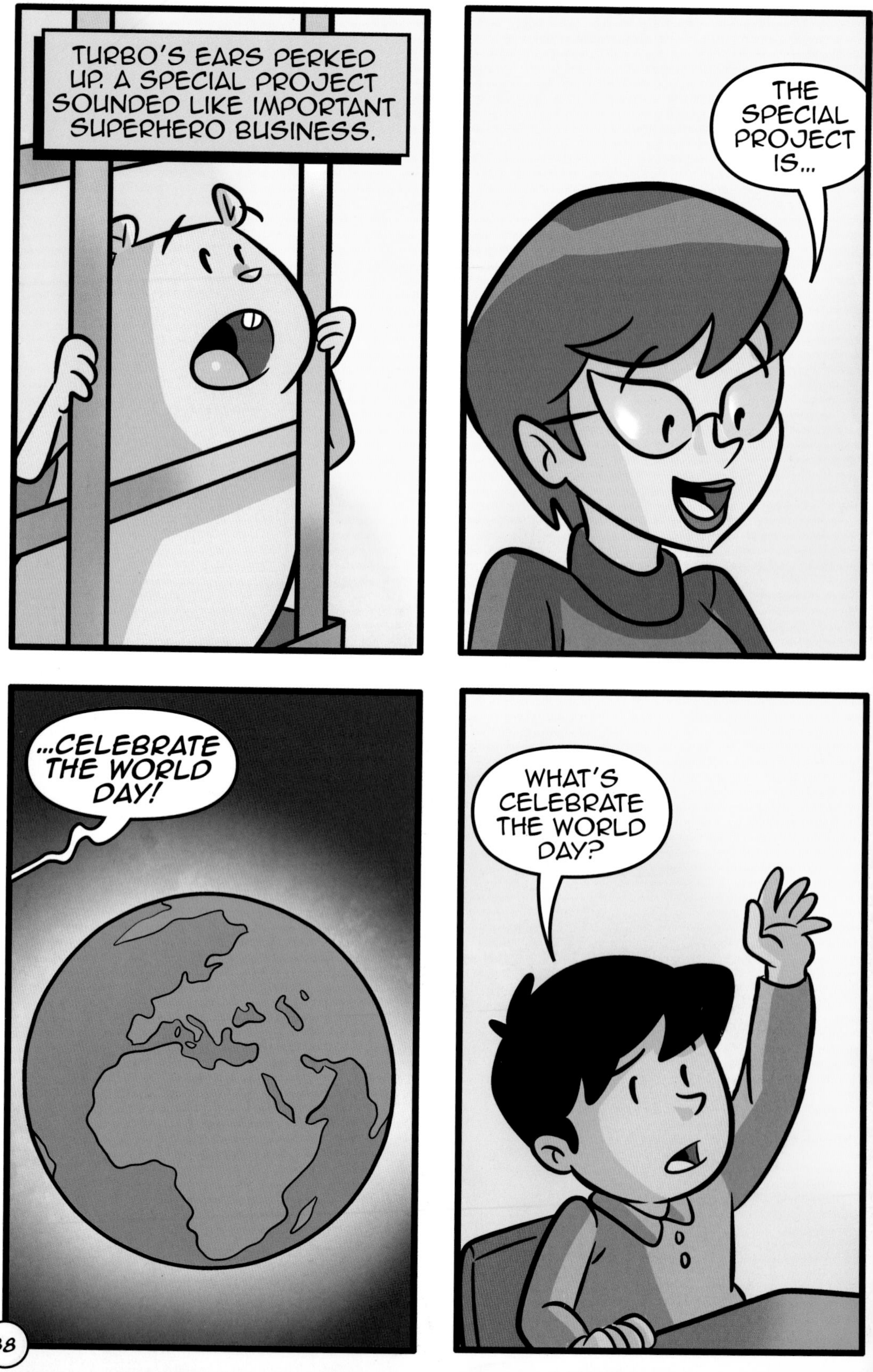
TURBO'S EARS PERKED UP. A SPECIAL PROJECT SOUNDED LIKE IMPORTANT SUPERHERO BUSINESS.
THE SPECIAL PROJECT IS...
...CELEBRATE THE WORLD DAY!
WHAT'S CELEBRATE THE WORLD DAY?

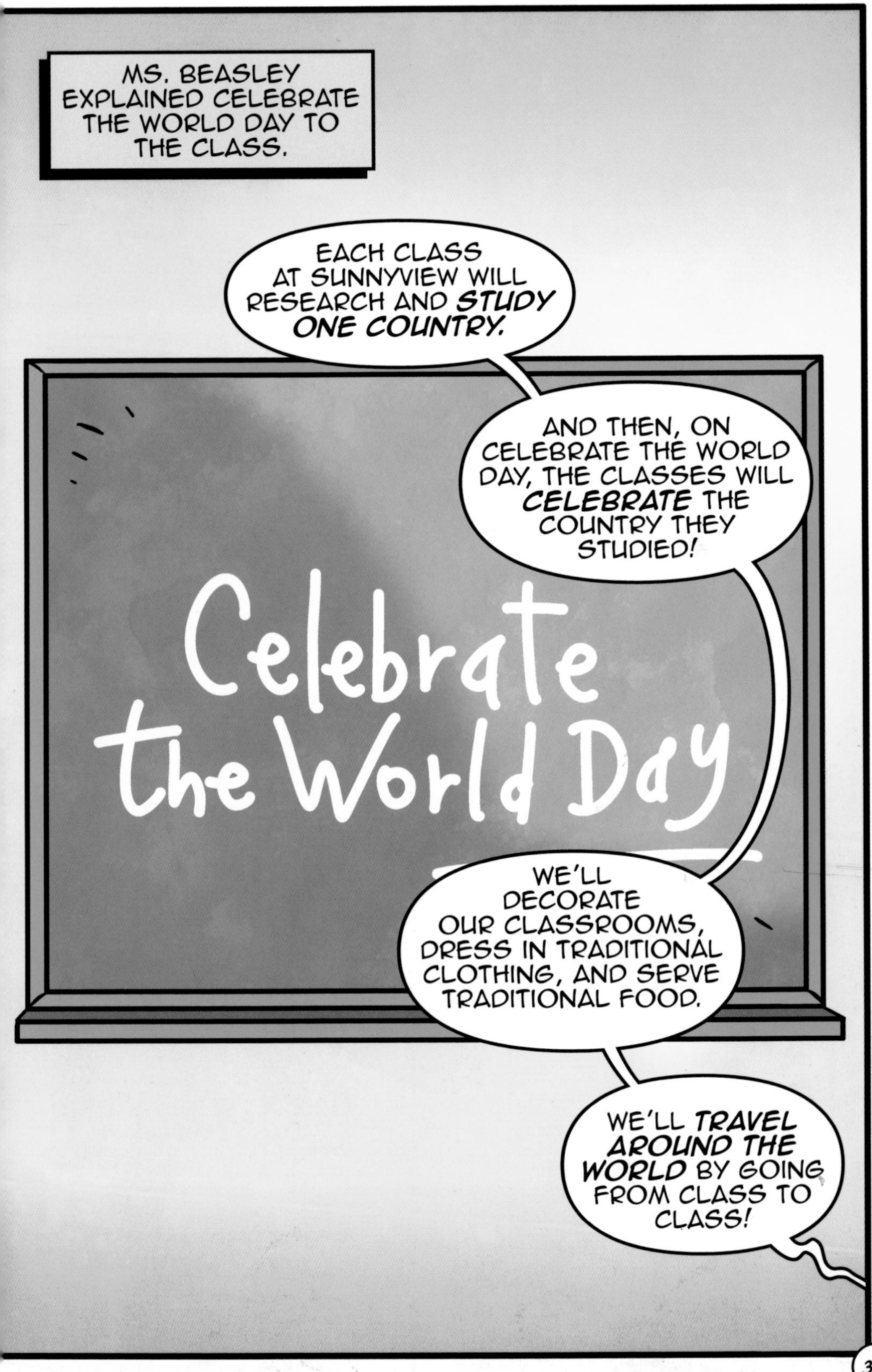
MS. BEASLEY EXPLAINED CELEBRATE THE WORLD DAY TO THE CLASS.
EACH CLASS AT SUNNYVIEW WILL RESEARCH AND STUDY ONE COUNTRY.
AND THEN, ON CELEBRATE THE WORLD DAY, THE CLASSES WILL CELEBRATE THE COUNTRY THEY STUDIED!
Celebrate the World Day
WE'LL DECORATE OUR CLASSROOMS, DRESS IN TRADITIONAL CLOTHING, AND SERVE TRADITIONAL FOOD.
WE'LL TRAVEL AROUND THE WORLD BY GOING FROM CLASS TO CLASS!

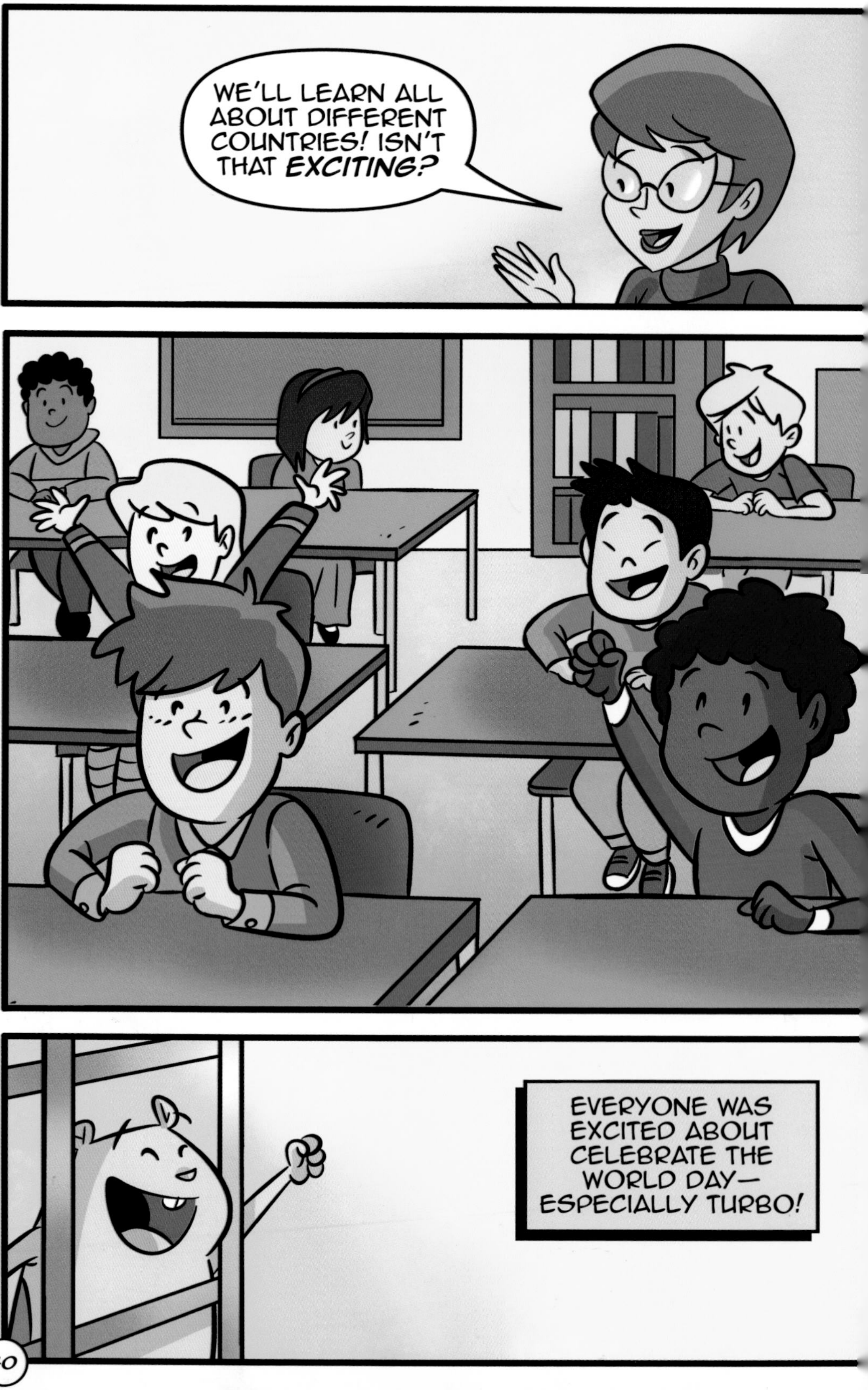
WE'LL LEARN ALL ABOUT DIFFERENT COUNTRIES! ISN'T THAT *EXCITING?*
EVERYONE WAS EXCITED ABOUT CELEBRATE THE WORLD DAY—ESPECIALLY TURBO!

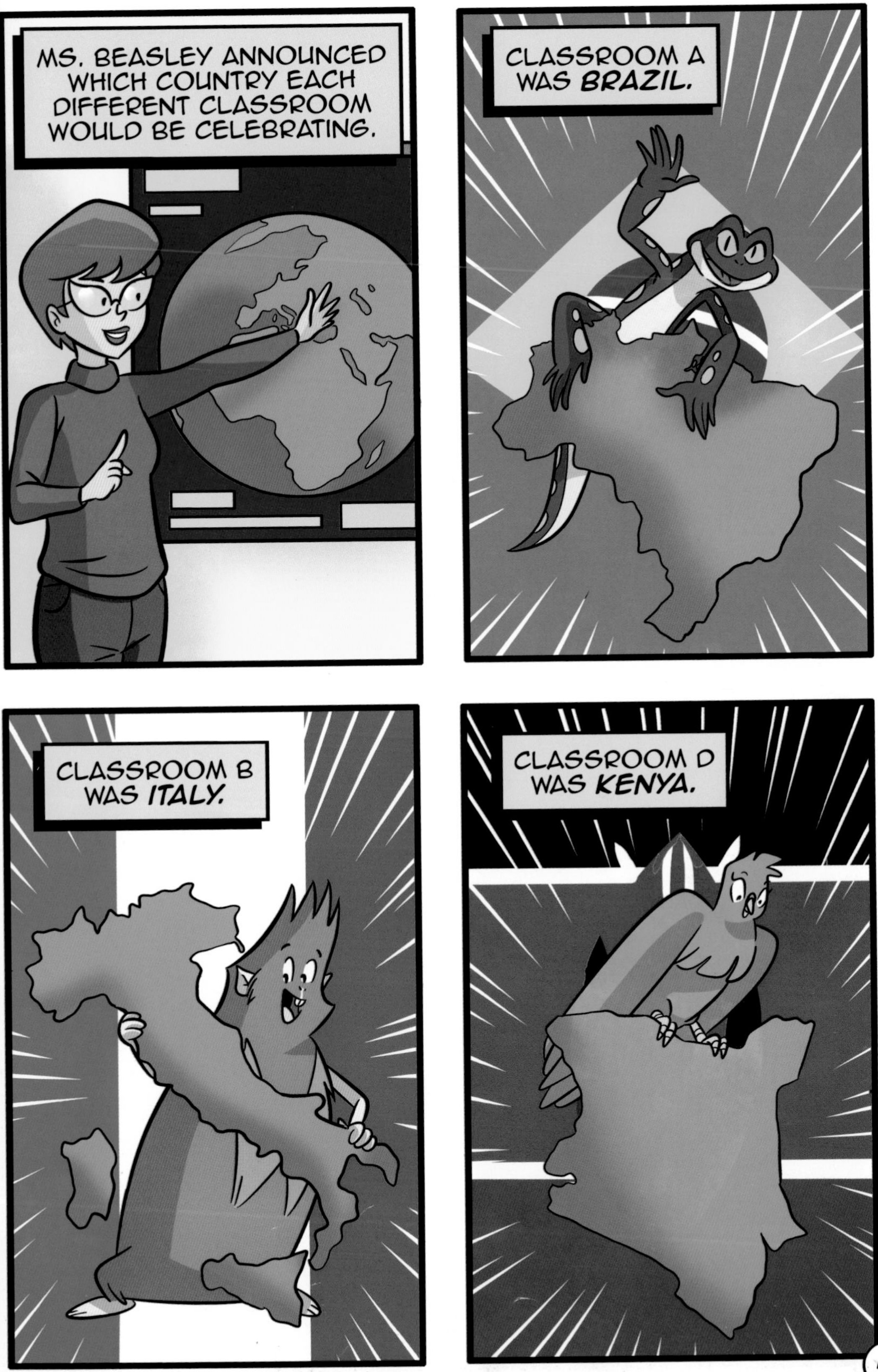
MS. BEASLEY ANNOUNCED WHICH COUNTRY EACH DIFFERENT CLASSROOM WOULD BE CELEBRATING.
CLASSROOM A WAS BRAZIL.
CLASSROOM B WAS ITALY.
CLASSROOM D WAS KENYA.

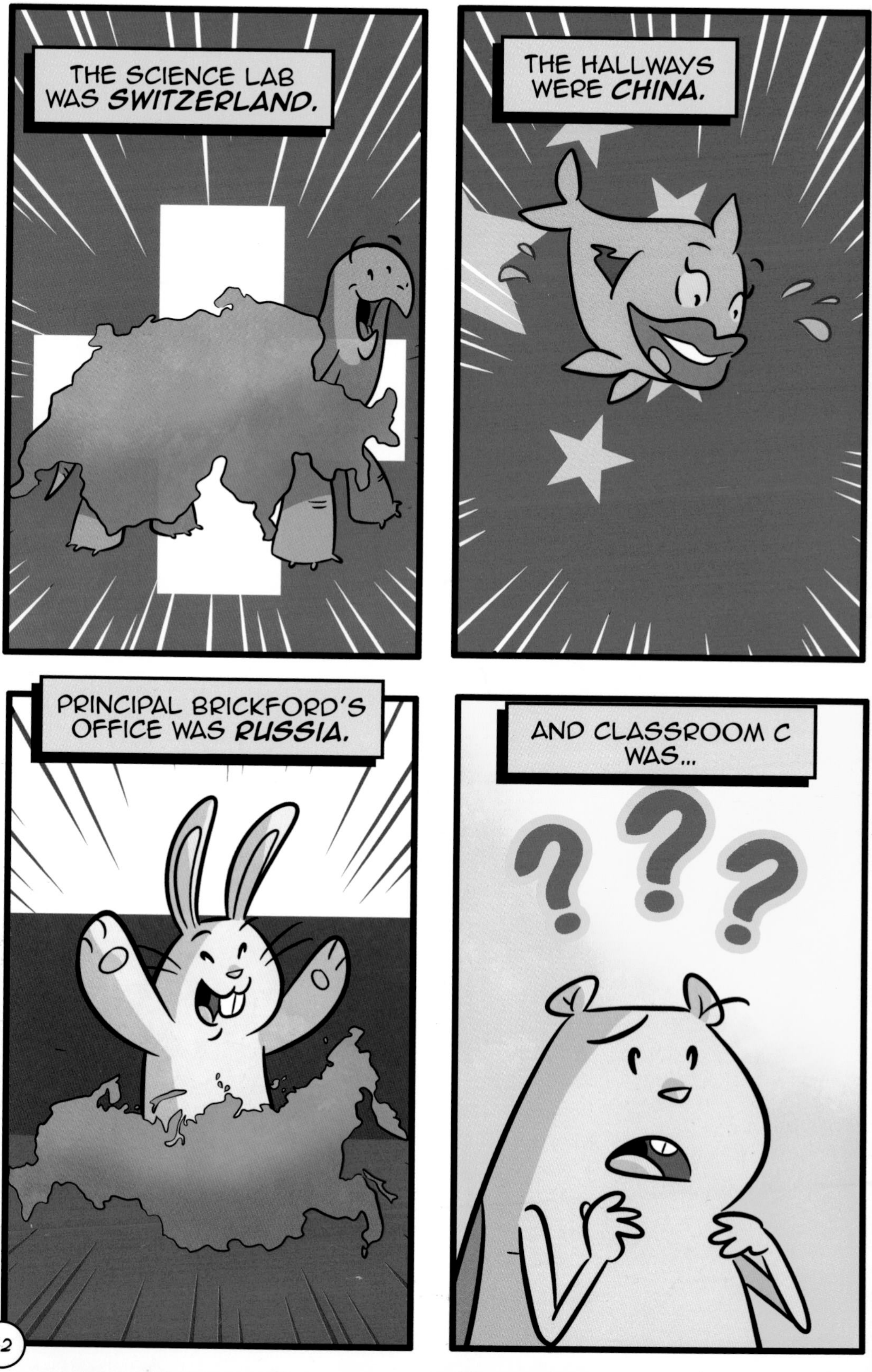
THE SCIENCE LAB WAS SWITZERLAND.
THE HALLWAYS WERE CHINA.
PRINCIPAL BRICKFORD'S OFFICE WAS RUSSIA.
AND CLASSROOM C WAS...

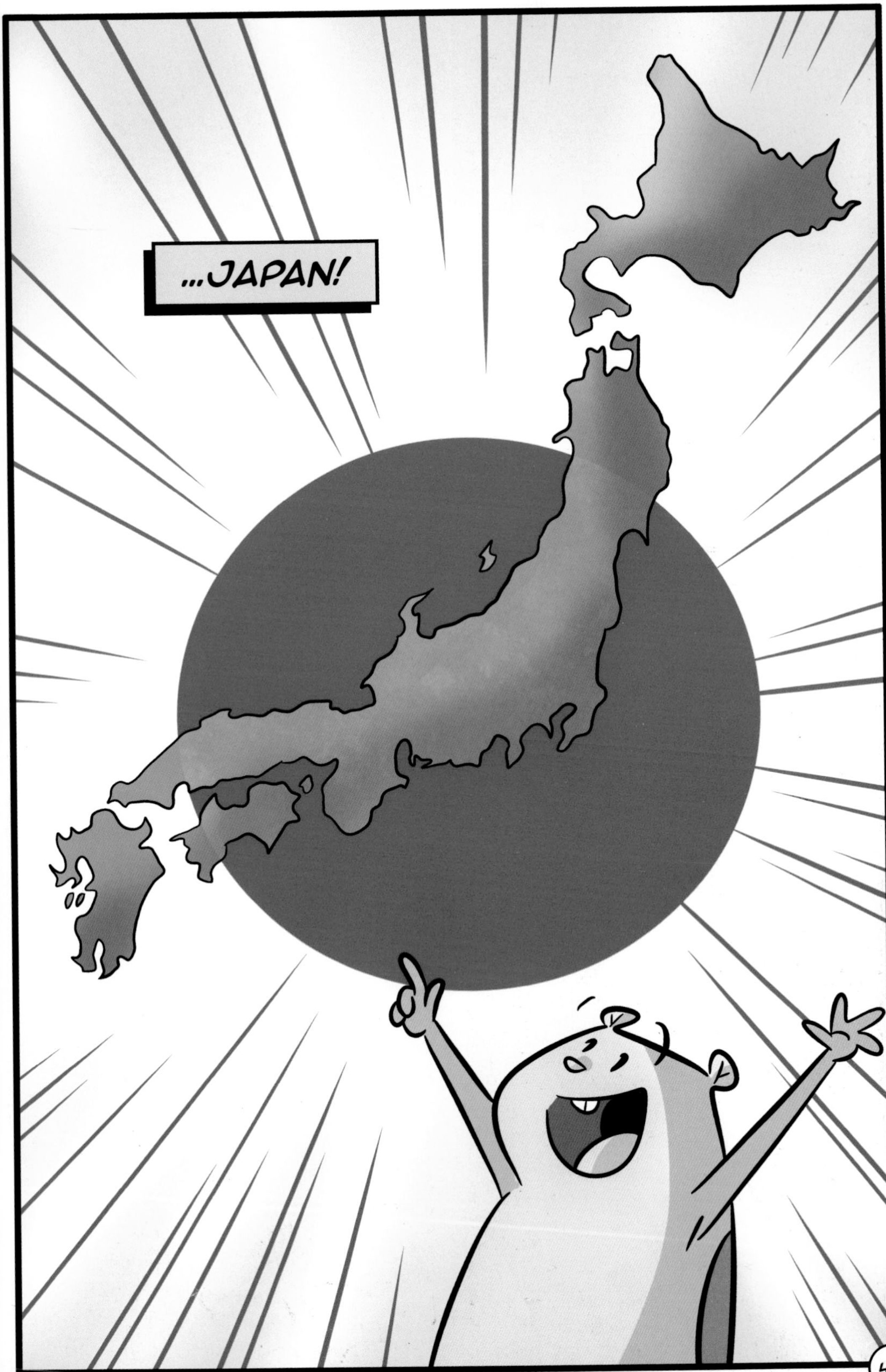
...JAPAN!

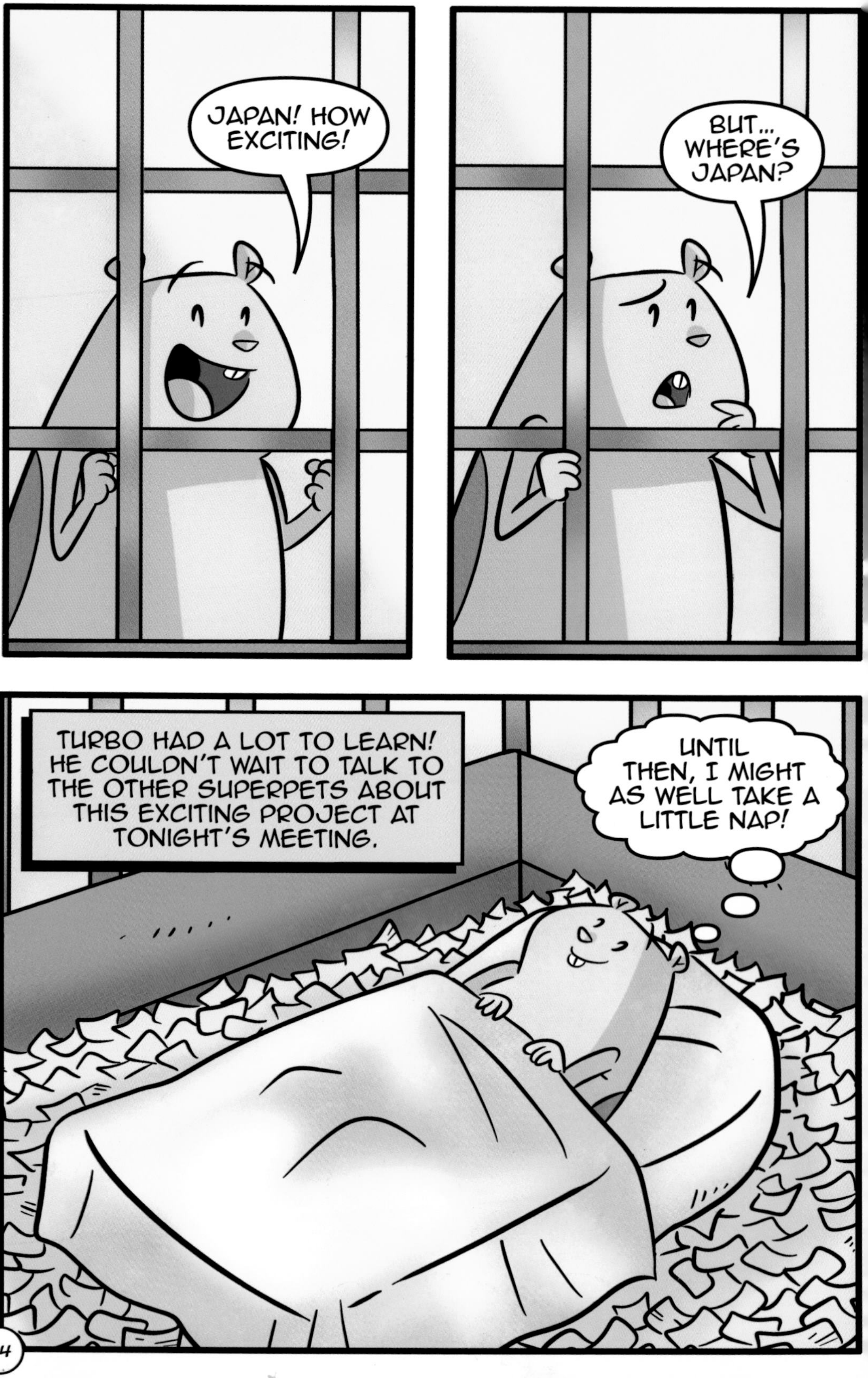
JAPAN! HOW EXCITING!
BUT... WHERE'S JAPAN?
TURBO HAD A LOT TO LEARN! HE COULDN'T WAIT TO TALK TO THE OTHER SUPERPETS ABOUT THIS EXCITING PROJECT AT TONIGHT'S MEETING.
UNTIL THEN, I MIGHT AS WELL TAKE A LITTLE NAP!

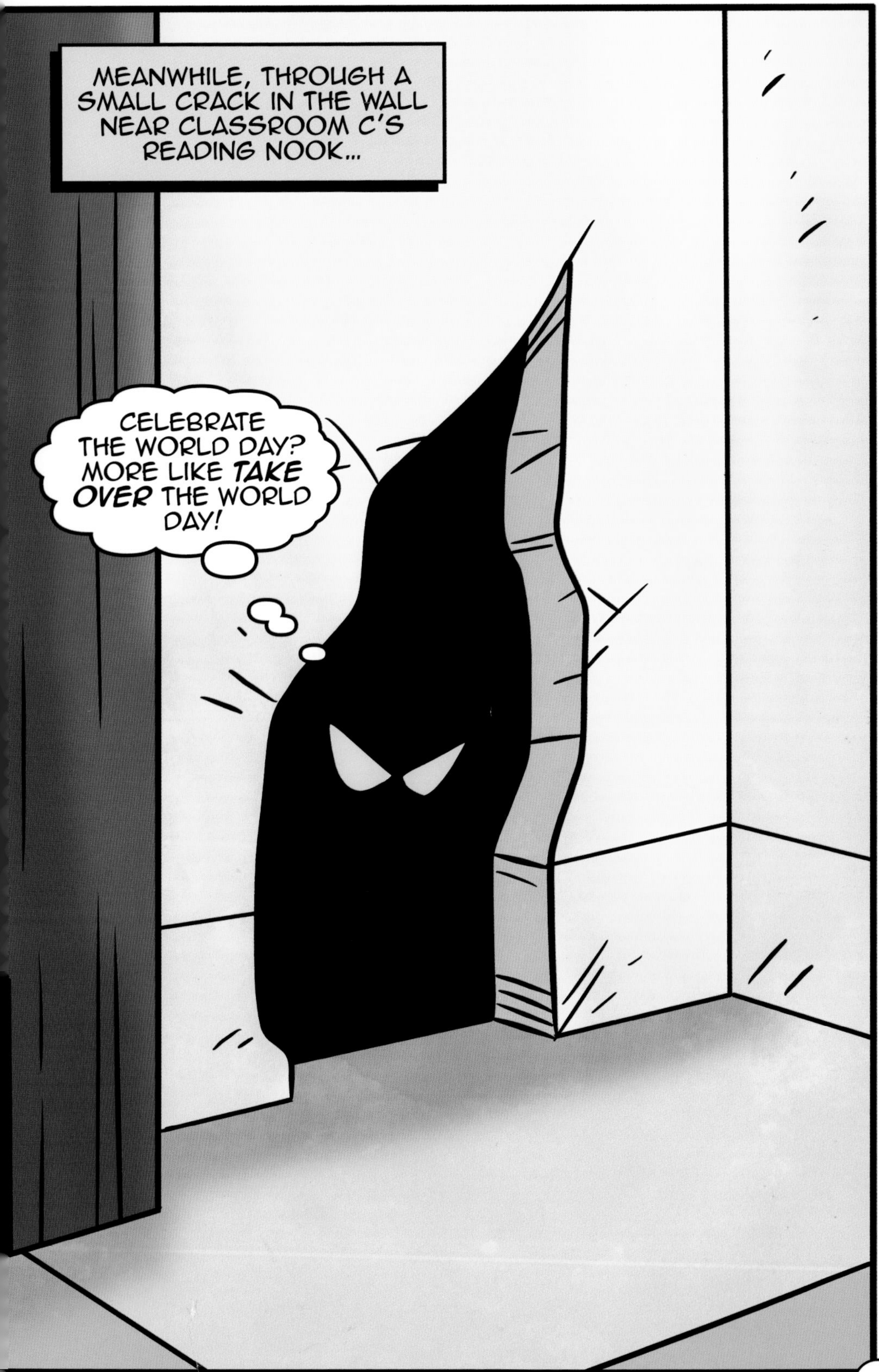
MEANWHILE, THROUGH A SMALL CRACK IN THE WALL NEAR CLASSROOM C'S READING NOOK...
CELEBRATE THE WORLD DAY? MORE LIKE ***TAKE OVER*** THE WORLD DAY!

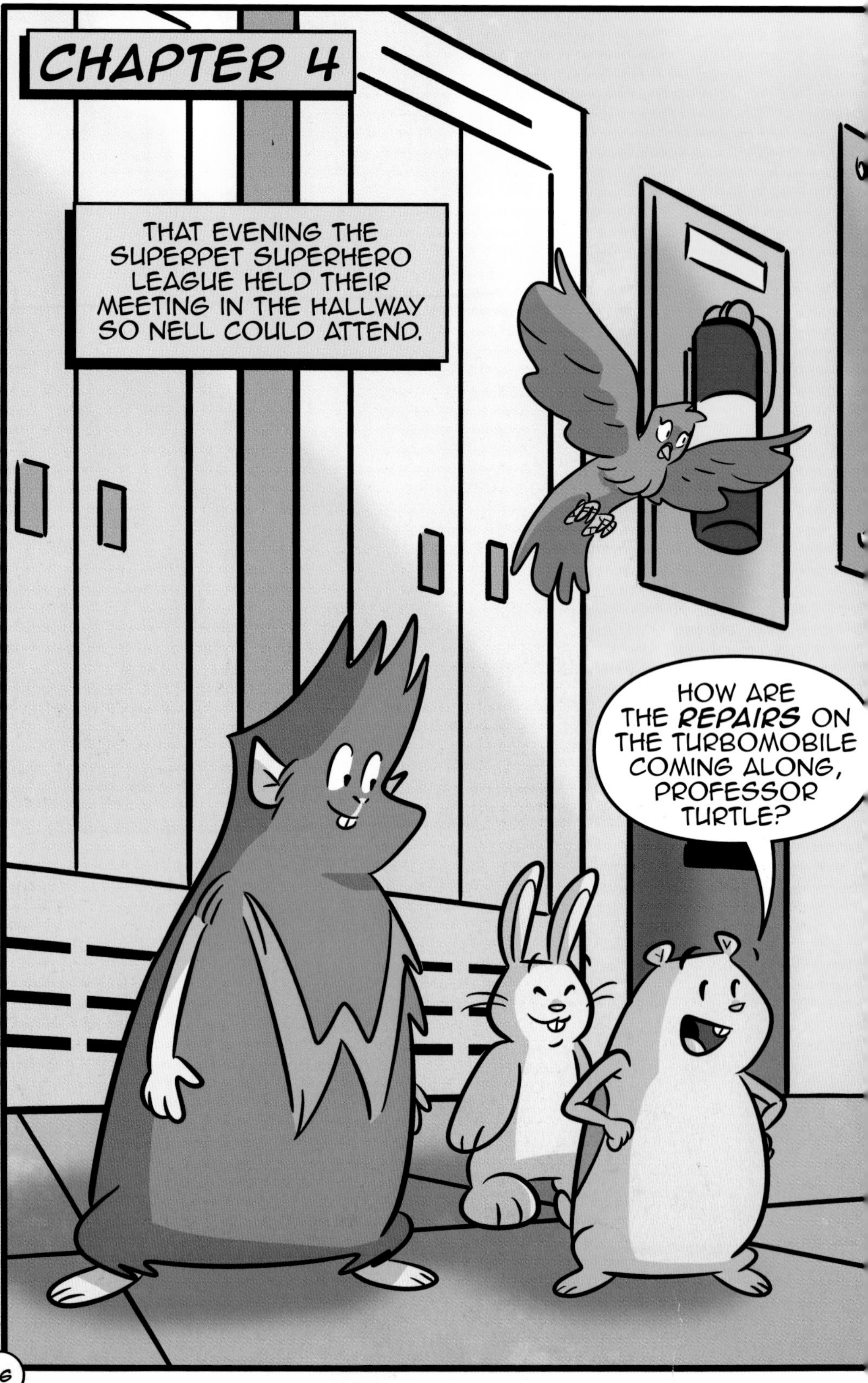
CHAPTER 4
THAT EVENING THE SUPERPET SUPERHERO LEAGUE HELD THEIR MEETING IN THE HALLWAY SO NELL COULD ATTEND.
HOW ARE THE **REPAIRS** ON THE TURBOMOBILE COMING ALONG, PROFESSOR TURTLE?

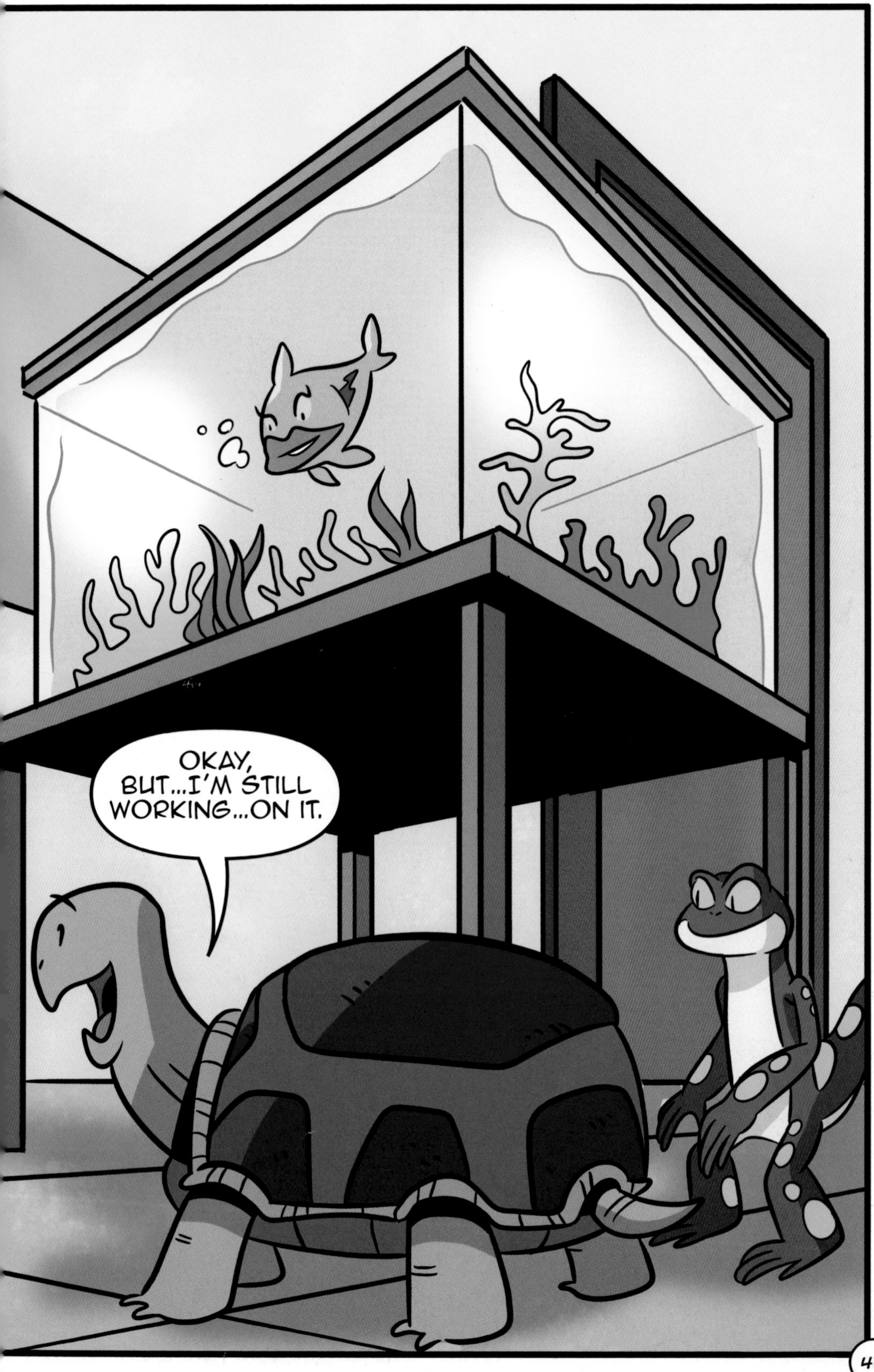
OKAY, BUT...I'M STILL WORKING...ON IT.

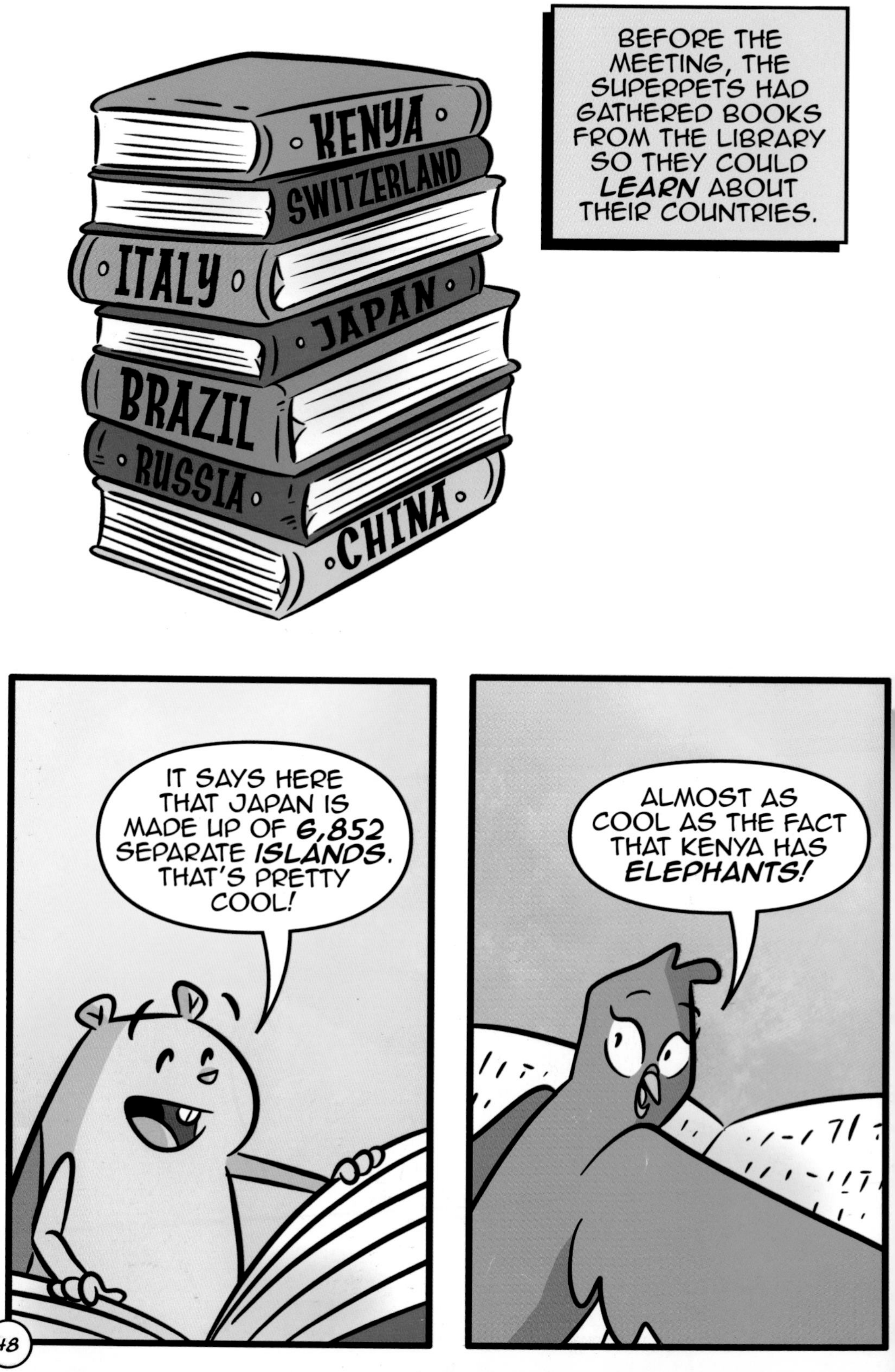
BEFORE THE MEETING, THE SUPERPETS HAD GATHERED BOOKS FROM THE LIBRARY SO THEY COULD LEARN ABOUT THEIR COUNTRIES.
KENYA
SWITZERLAND
ITALY
JAPAN
BRAZIL
RUSSIA
CHINA
IT SAYS HERE THAT JAPAN IS MADE UP OF 6,852 SEPARATE ISLANDS. THAT'S PRETTY COOL!
ALMOST AS COOL AS THE FACT THAT KENYA HAS ELEPHANTS!

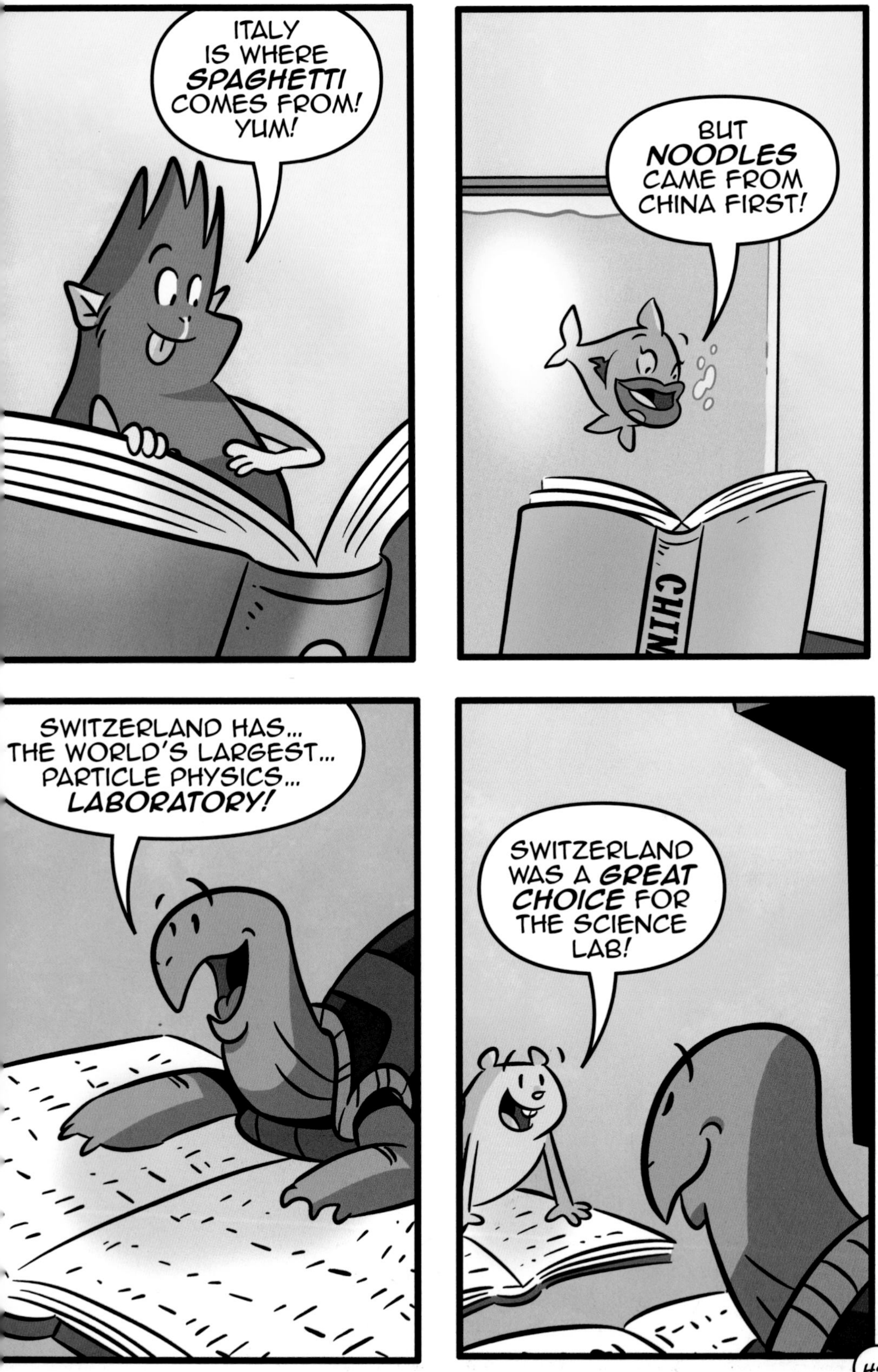
ITALY IS WHERE SPAGHETTI COMES FROM! YUM!
BUT NOODLES CAME FROM CHINA FIRST!
CHIN
SWITZERLAND HAS... THE WORLD'S LARGEST... PARTICLE PHYSICS... LABORATORY!
SWITZERLAND WAS A GREAT CHOICE FOR THE SCIENCE LAB!

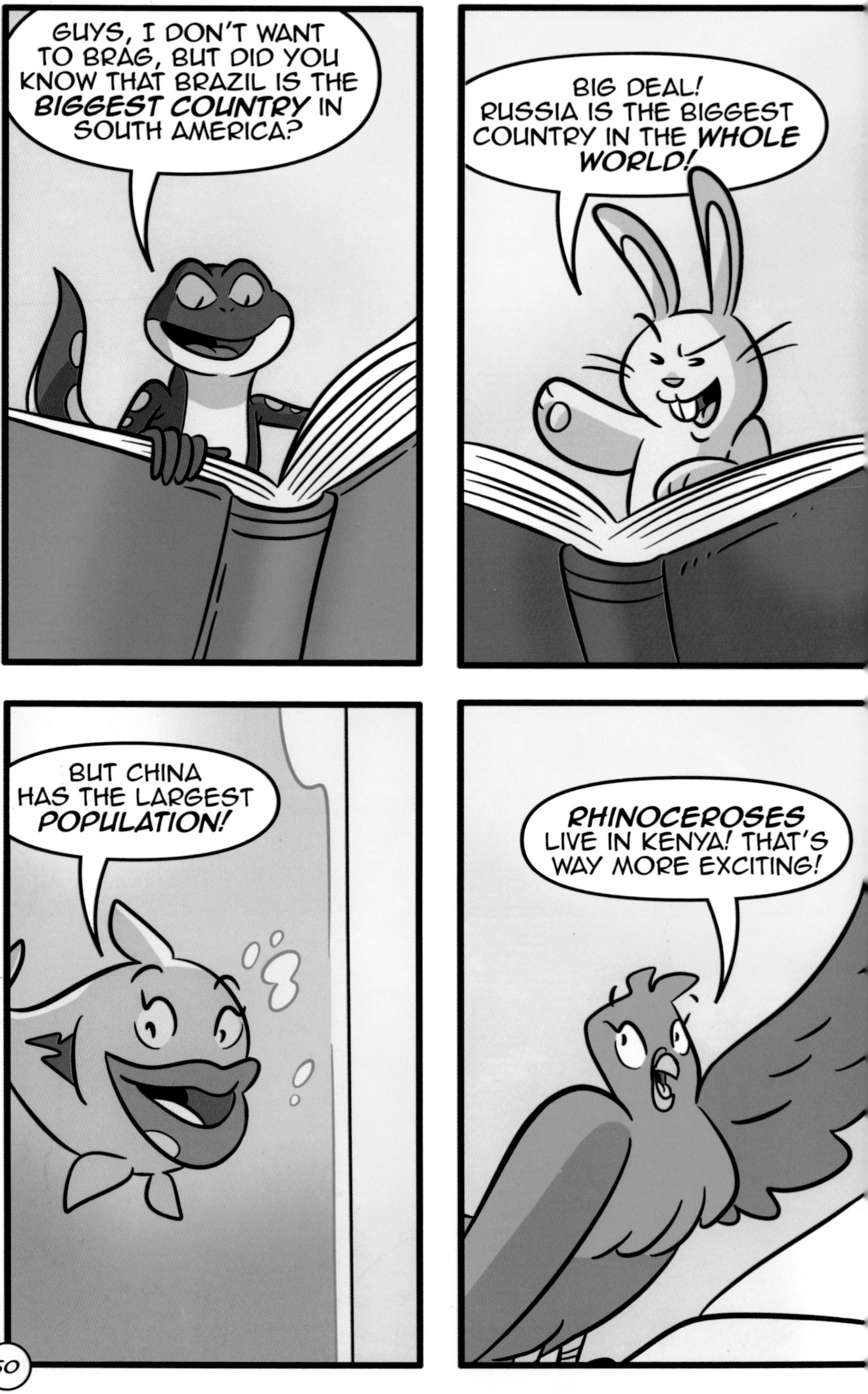
GUYS, I DON'T WANT TO BRAG, BUT DID YOU KNOW THAT BRAZIL IS THE BIGGEST COUNTRY IN SOUTH AMERICA?
BIG DEAL! RUSSIA IS THE BIGGEST COUNTRY IN THE WHOLE WORLD!
BUT CHINA HAS THE LARGEST POPULATION!
RHINOCEROSES LIVE IN KENYA! THAT'S WAY MORE EXCITING!

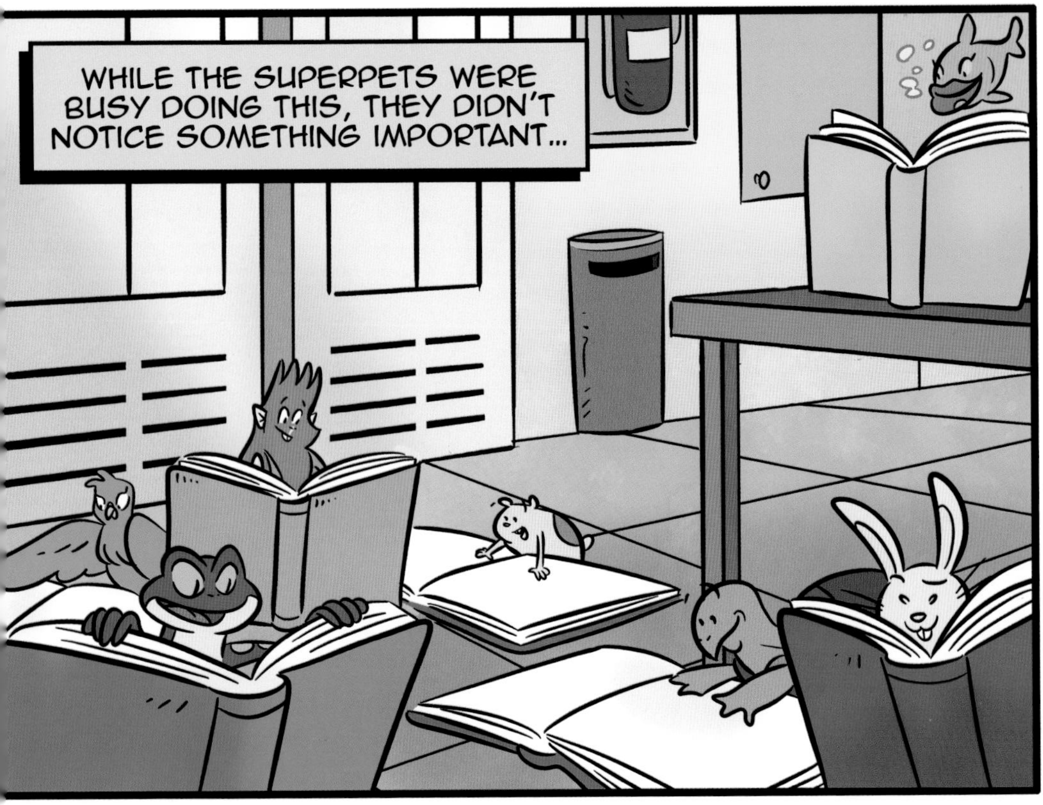
WHILE THE SUPERPETS WERE BUSY DOING THIS, THEY DIDN'T NOTICE SOMETHING IMPORTANT...

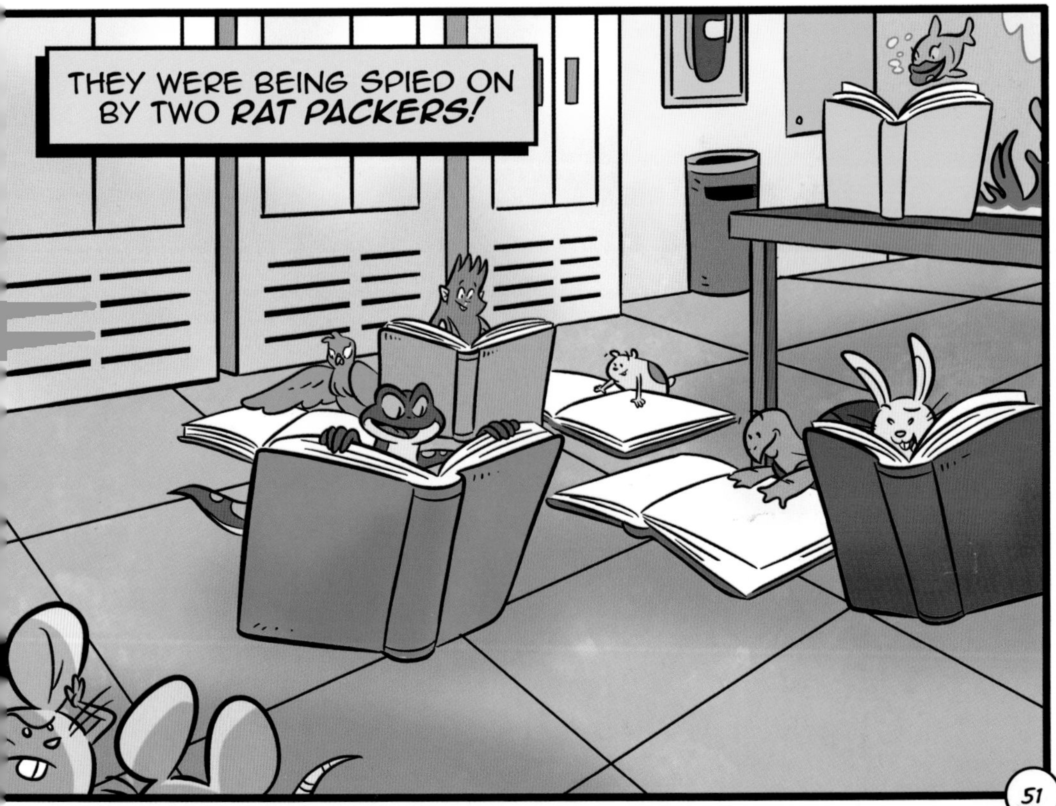
THEY WERE BEING SPIED ON BY TWO *RAT PACKERS!*

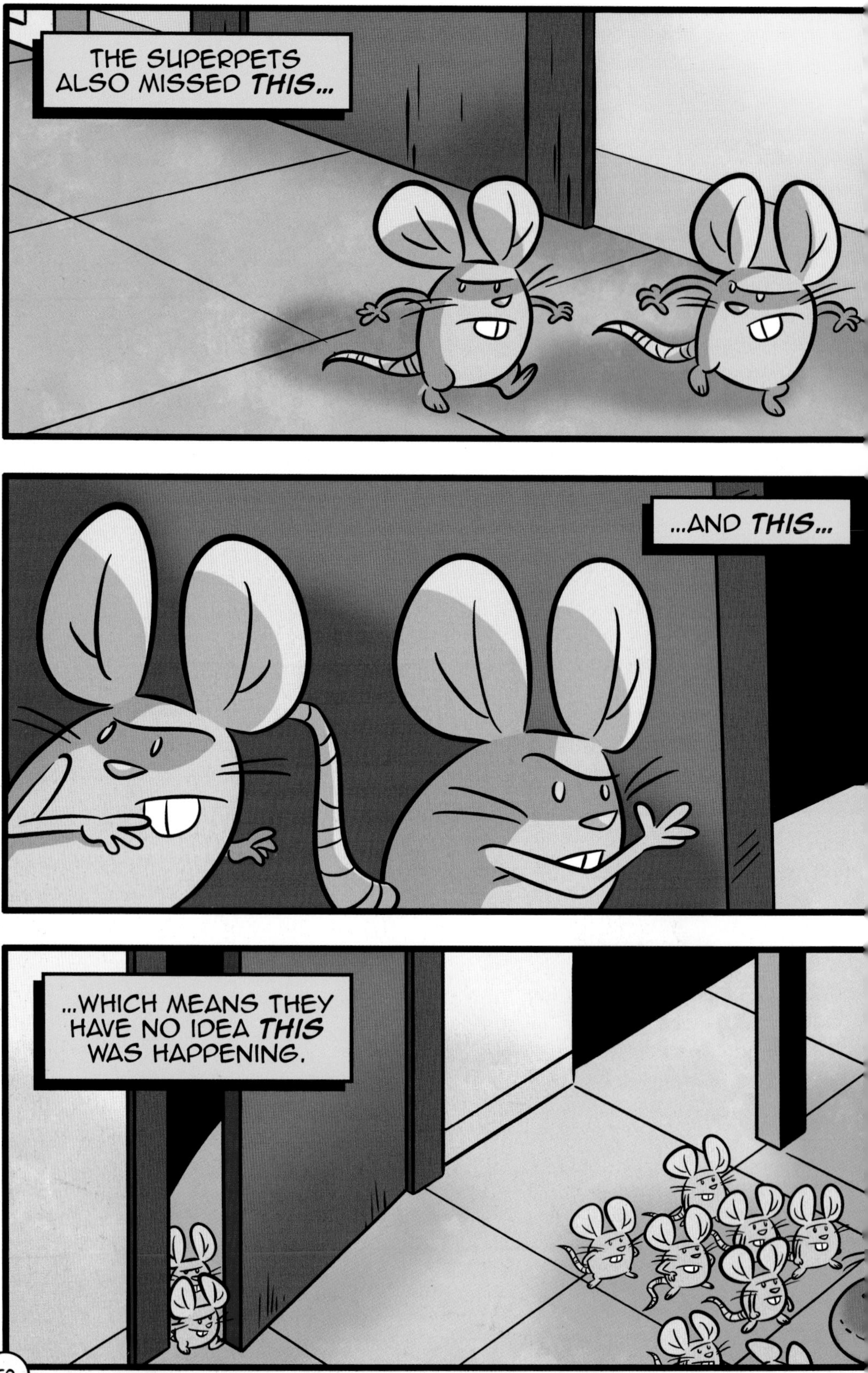
THE SUPERPETS ALSO MISSED THIS...
...AND THIS...
...WHICH MEANS THEY HAVE NO IDEA THIS WAS HAPPENING.

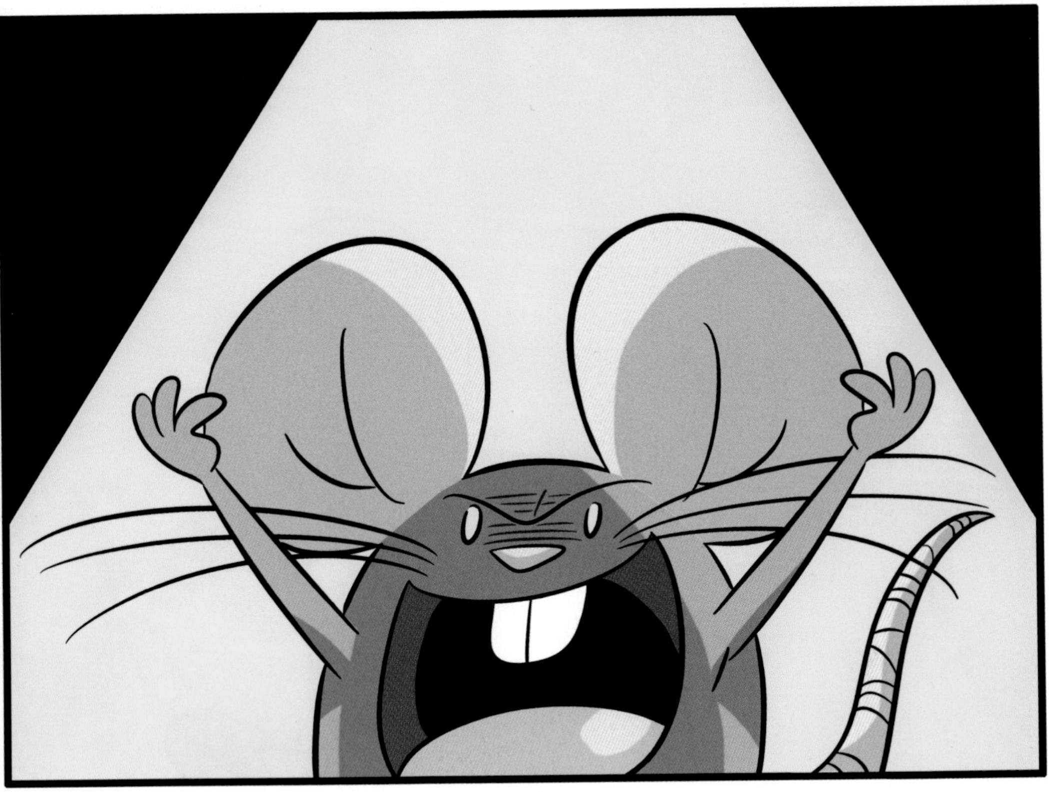

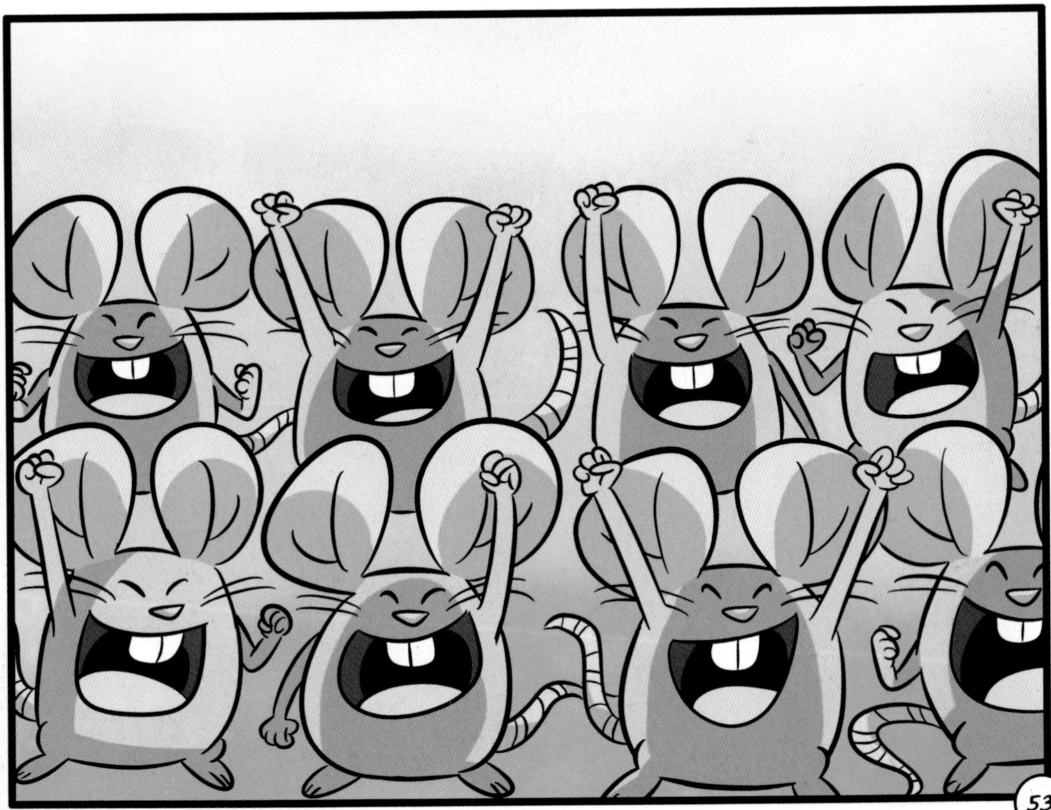

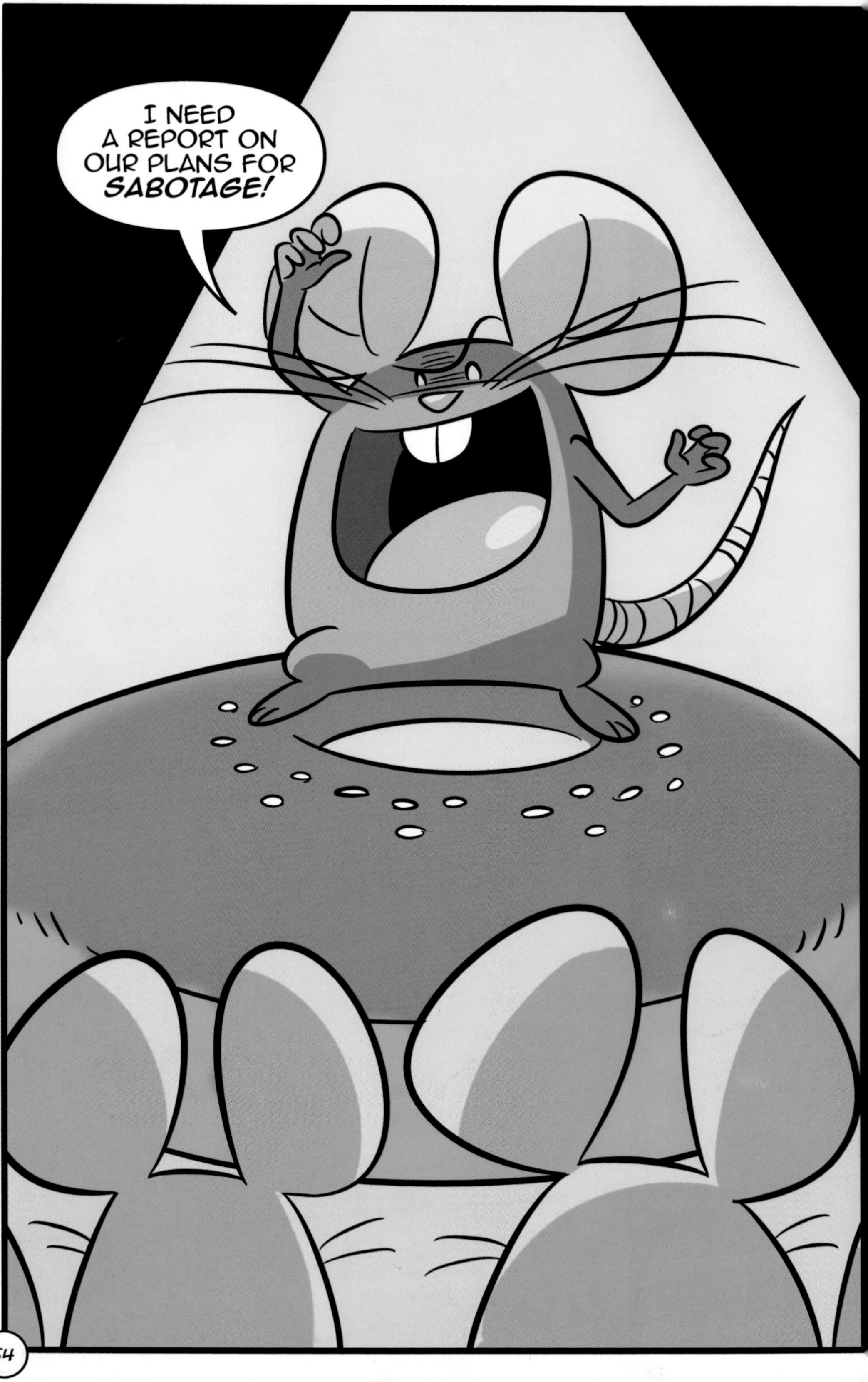
I NEED A REPORT ON OUR PLANS FOR *SABOTAGE!*

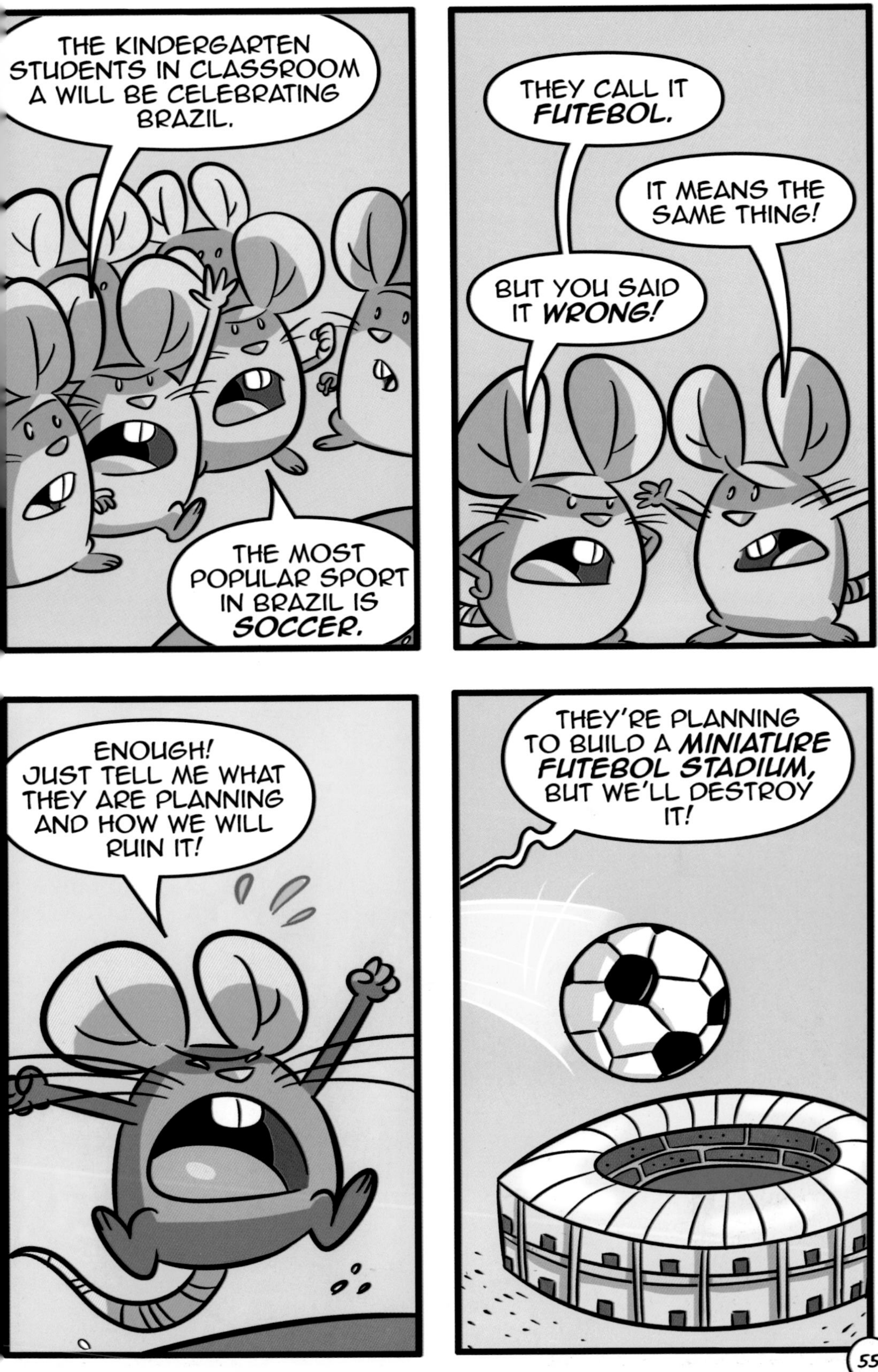
THE KINDERGARTEN STUDENTS IN CLASSROOM A WILL BE CELEBRATING BRAZIL.
THE MOST POPULAR SPORT IN BRAZIL IS *SOCCER.*
THEY CALL IT *FUTEBOL.*
BUT YOU SAID IT *WRONG!*
IT MEANS THE SAME THING!
ENOUGH! JUST TELL ME WHAT THEY ARE PLANNING AND HOW WE WILL RUIN IT!
THEY'RE PLANNING TO BUILD A *MINIATURE FUTEBOL STADIUM,* BUT WE'LL DESTROY IT!

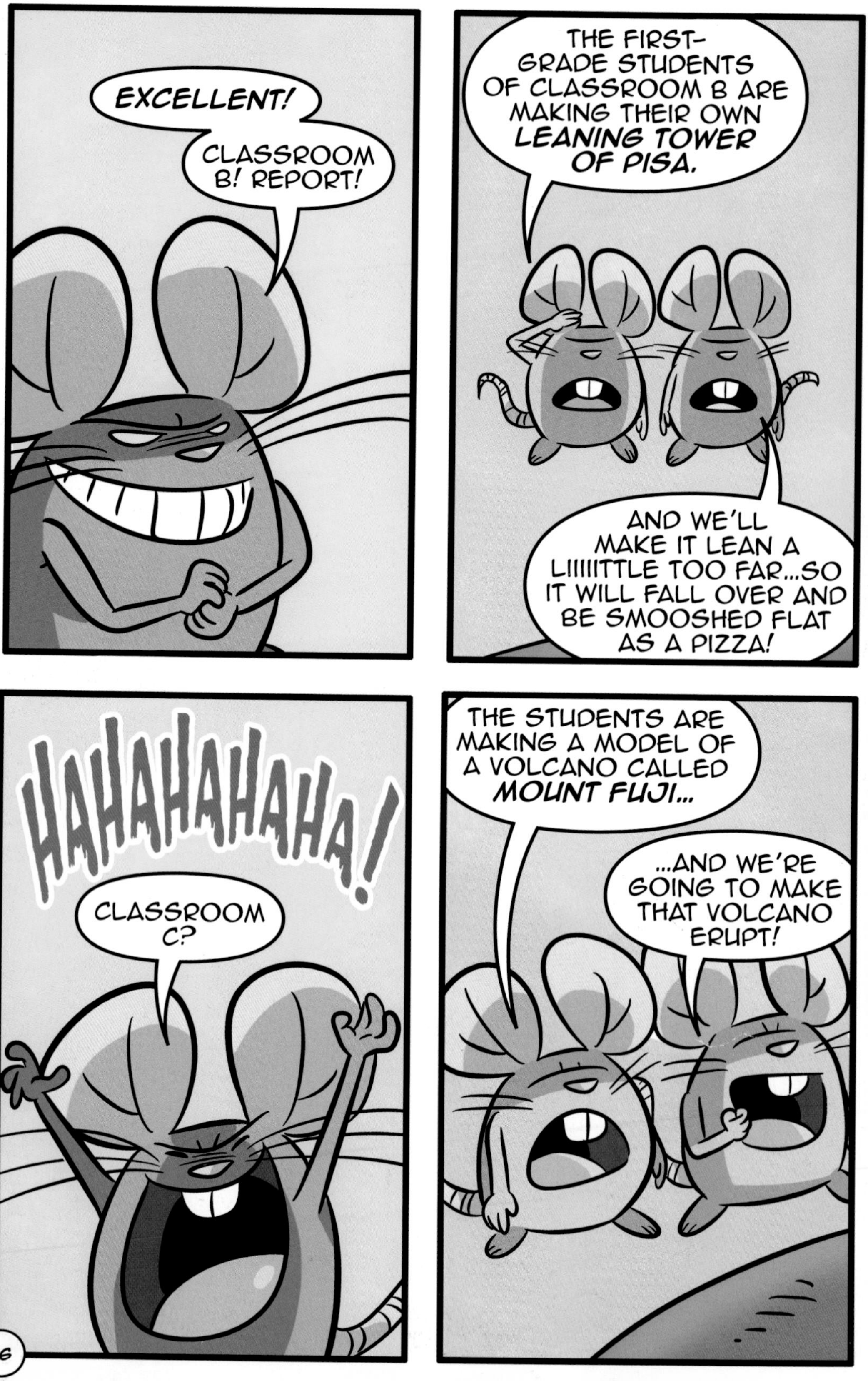
EXCELLENT!
CLASSROOM B! REPORT!
THE FIRST-GRADE STUDENTS OF CLASSROOM B ARE MAKING THEIR OWN LEANING TOWER OF PISA.
AND WE'LL MAKE IT LEAN A LIIIIITTLE TOO FAR...SO IT WILL FALL OVER AND BE SMOOSHED FLAT AS A PIZZA!
HAHAHAHAHAHA!
CLASSROOM C?
THE STUDENTS ARE MAKING A MODEL OF A VOLCANO CALLED MOUNT FUJI...
...AND WE'RE GOING TO MAKE THAT VOLCANO ERUPT!

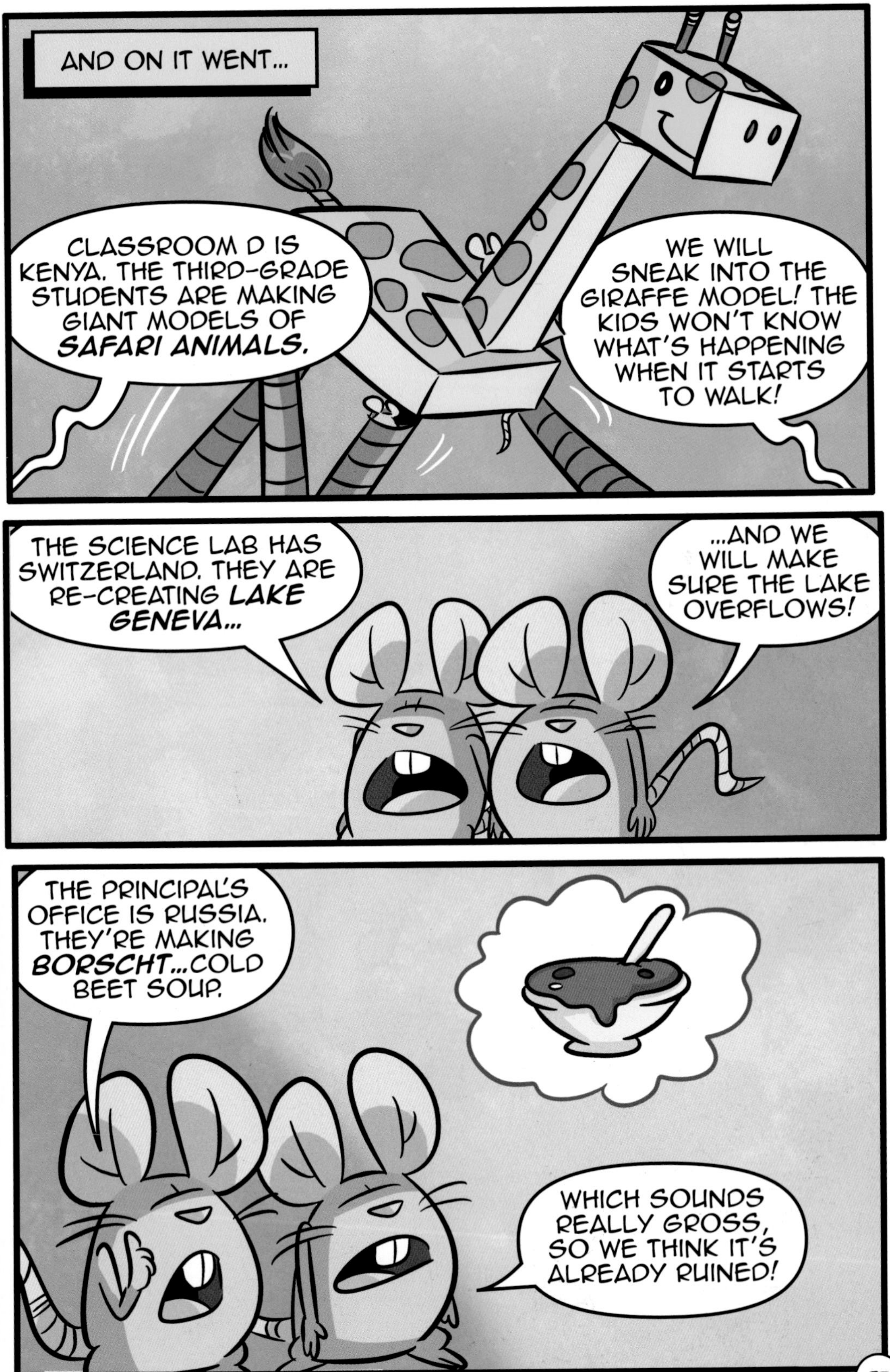
AND ON IT WENT...
CLASSROOM D IS KENYA. THE THIRD-GRADE STUDENTS ARE MAKING GIANT MODELS OF SAFARI ANIMALS.
WE WILL SNEAK INTO THE GIRAFFE MODEL! THE KIDS WON'T KNOW WHAT'S HAPPENING WHEN IT STARTS TO WALK!
THE SCIENCE LAB HAS SWITZERLAND. THEY ARE RE-CREATING LAKE GENEVA...
...AND WE WILL MAKE SURE THE LAKE OVERFLOWS!
THE PRINCIPAL'S OFFICE IS RUSSIA. THEY'RE MAKING BORSCHT...COLD BEET SOUP.
WHICH SOUNDS REALLY GROSS, SO WE THINK IT'S ALREADY RUINED!

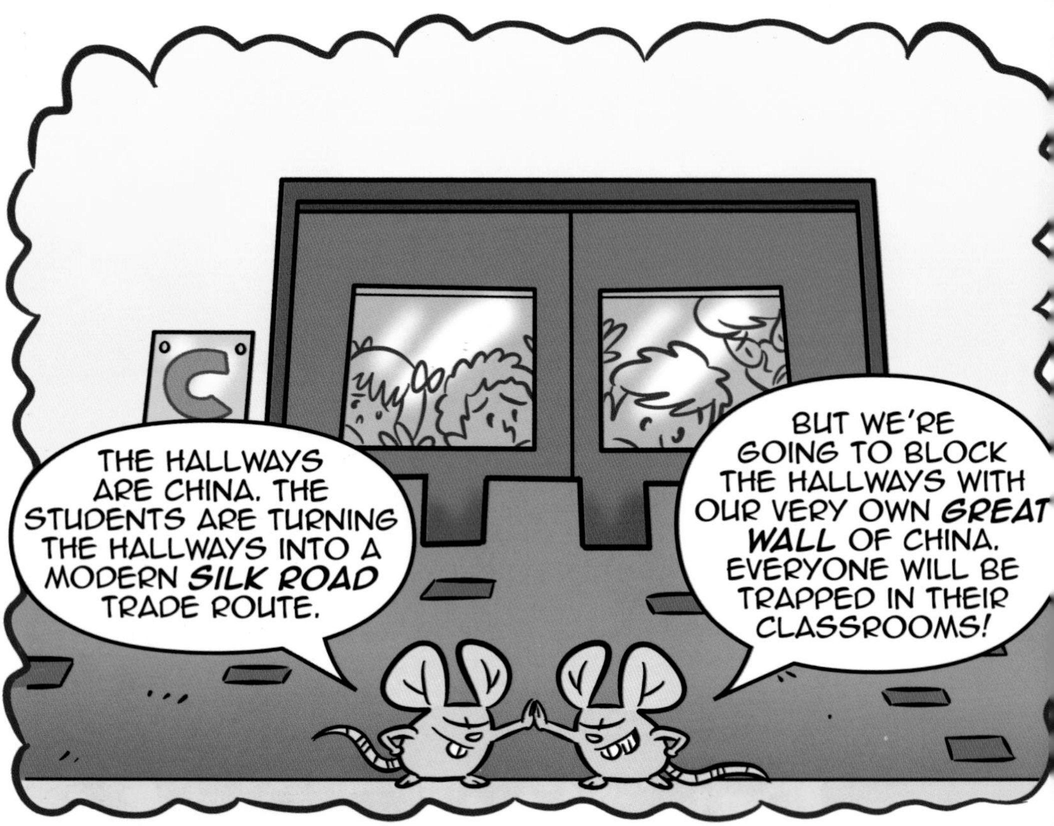
THE HALLWAYS ARE CHINA. THE STUDENTS ARE TURNING THE HALLWAYS INTO A MODERN SILK ROAD TRADE ROUTE.
BUT WE'RE GOING TO BLOCK THE HALLWAYS WITH OUR VERY OWN GREAT WALL OF CHINA. EVERYONE WILL BE TRAPPED IN THEIR CLASSROOMS!

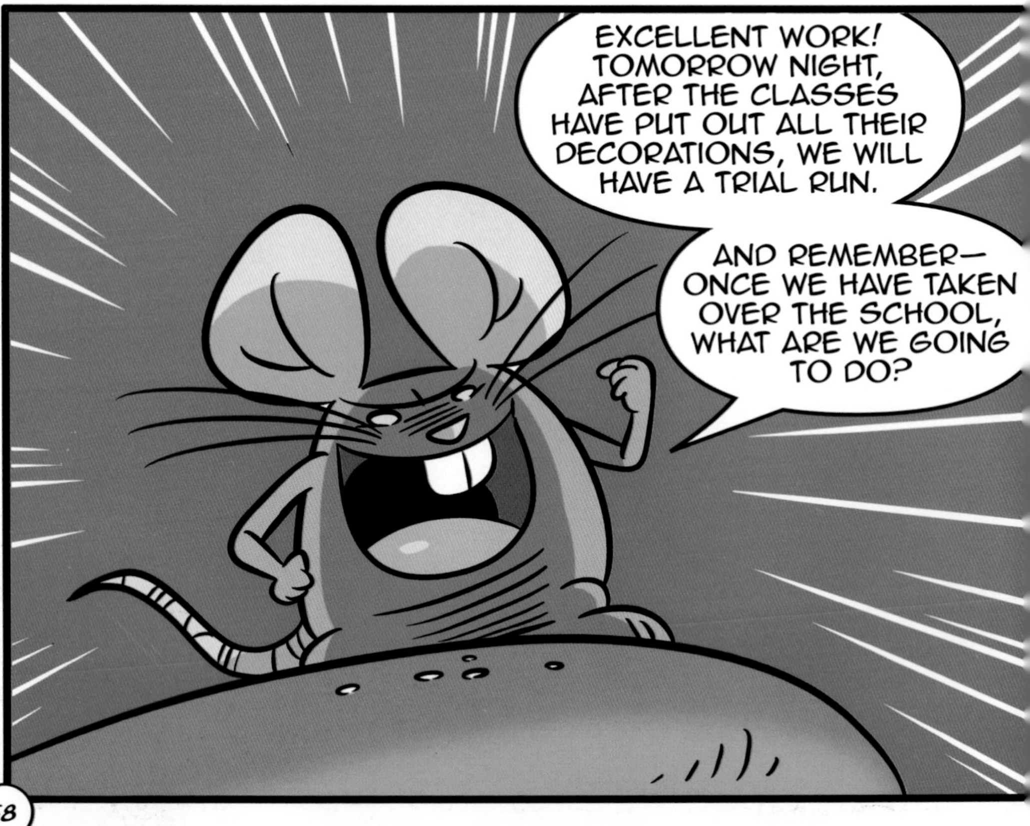
EXCELLENT WORK! TOMORROW NIGHT, AFTER THE CLASSES HAVE PUT OUT ALL THEIR DECORATIONS, WE WILL HAVE A TRIAL RUN.
AND REMEMBER— ONCE WE HAVE TAKEN OVER THE SCHOOL, WHAT ARE WE GOING TO DO?

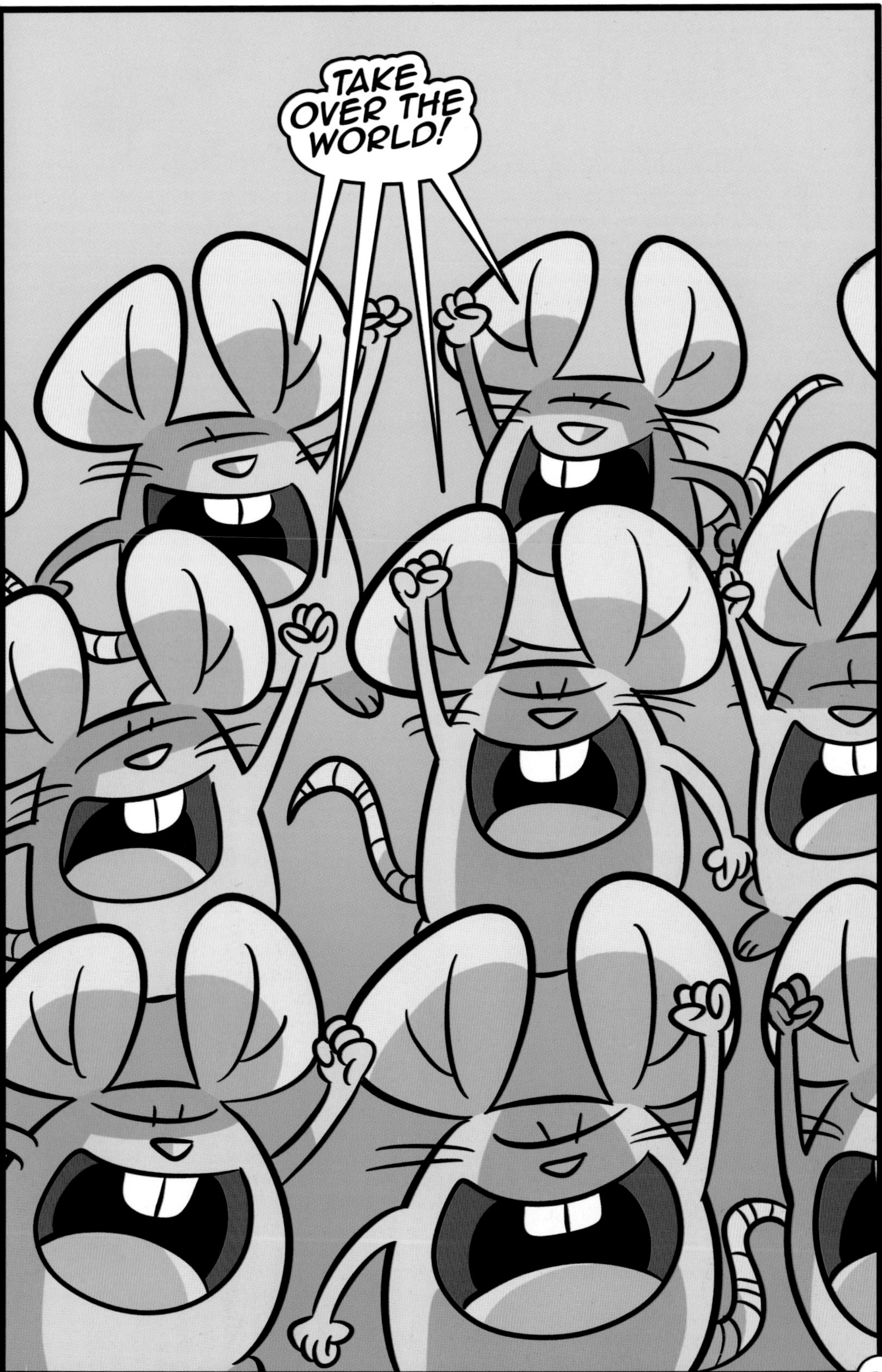
TAKE OVER THE WORLD!

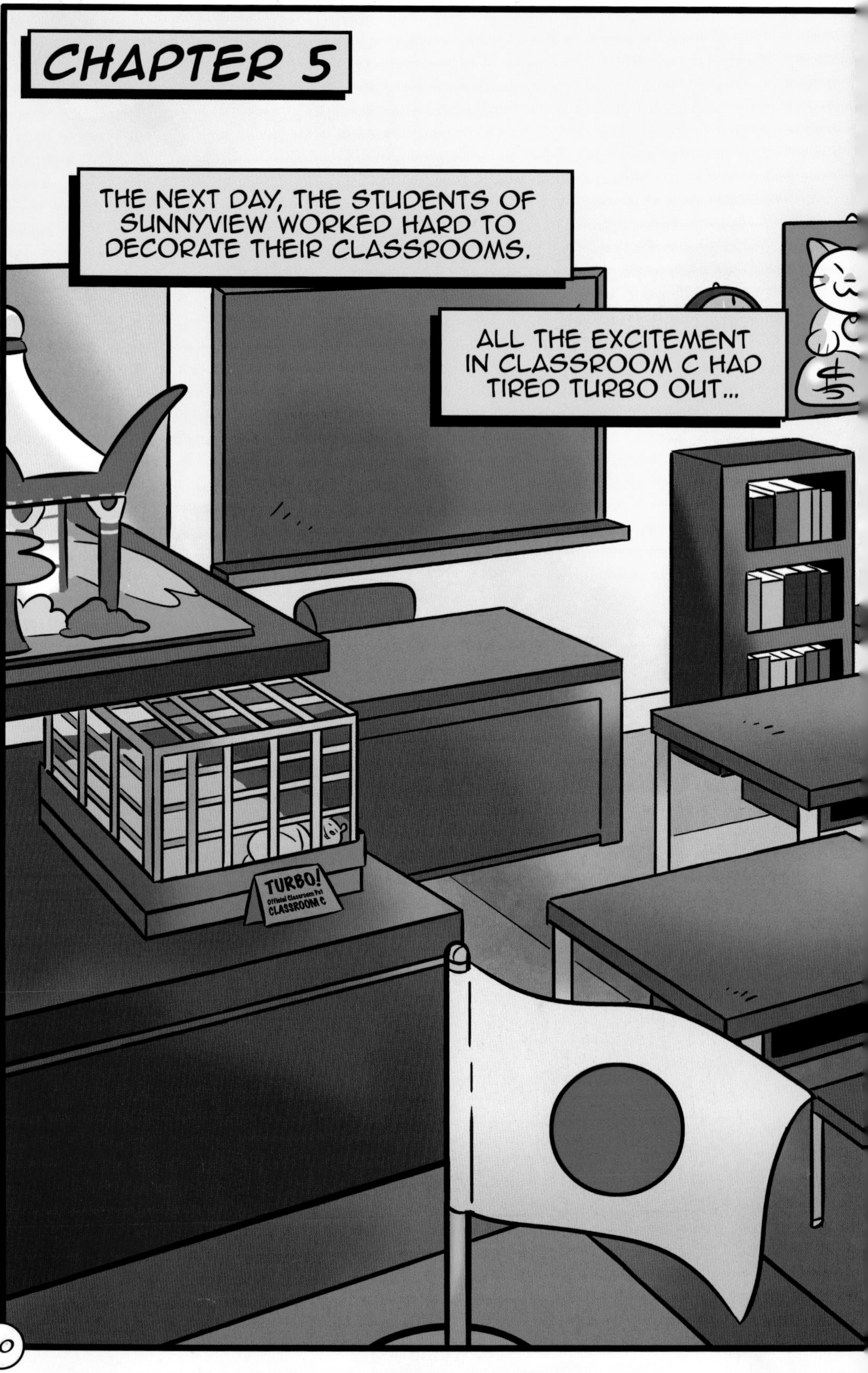
CHAPTER 5
THE NEXT DAY, THE STUDENTS OF SUNNYVIEW WORKED HARD TO DECORATE THEIR CLASSROOMS.
ALL THE EXCITEMENT IN CLASSROOM C HAD TIRED TURBO OUT...
TURBO!
Official Classroom Pet
CLASSROOM C

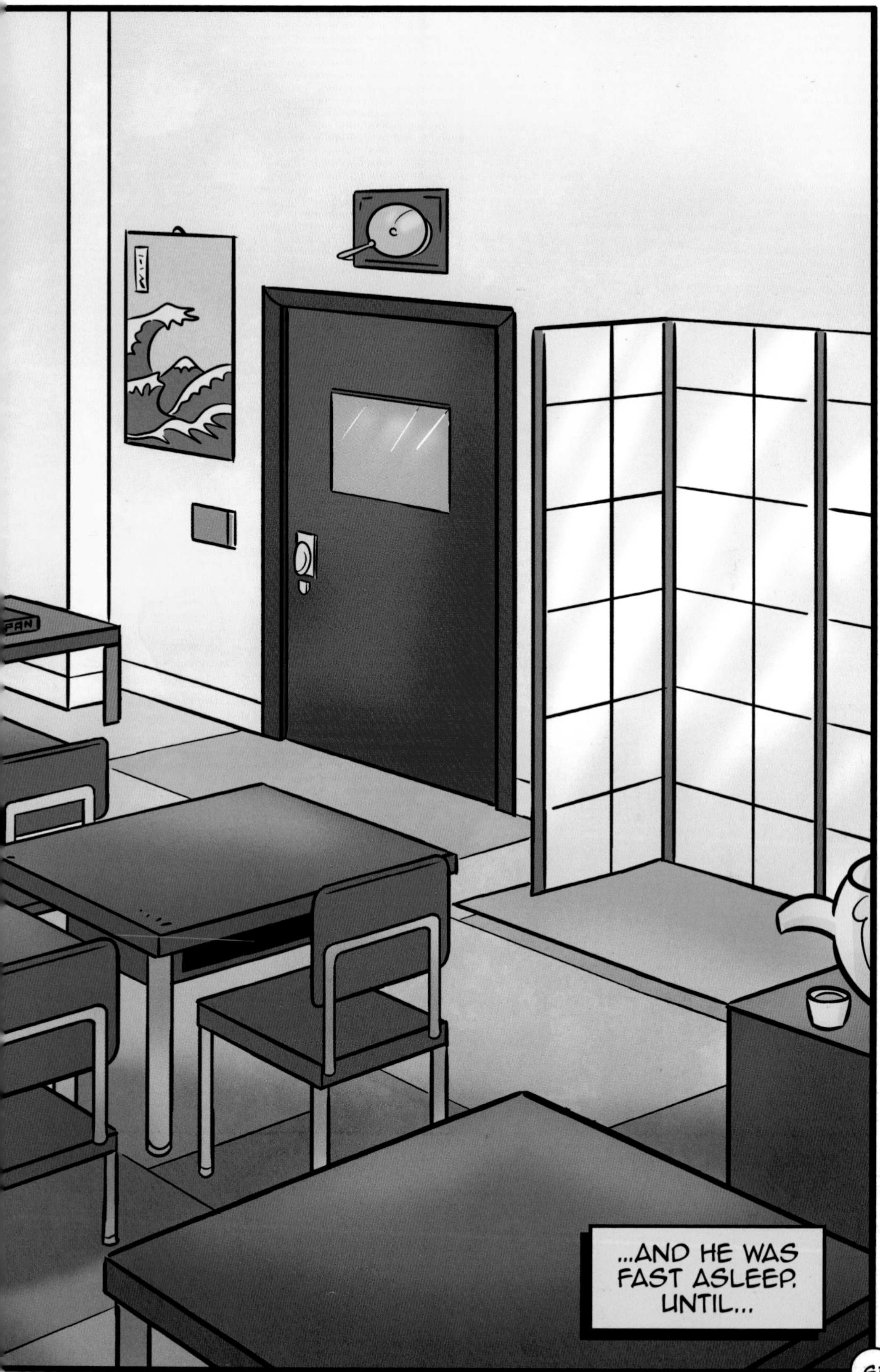
...AND HE WAS FAST ASLEEP. UNTIL...

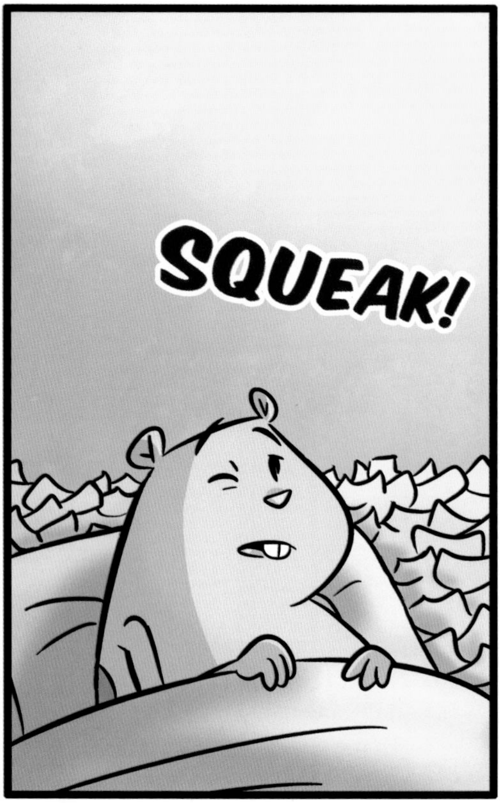
SQUEAK!

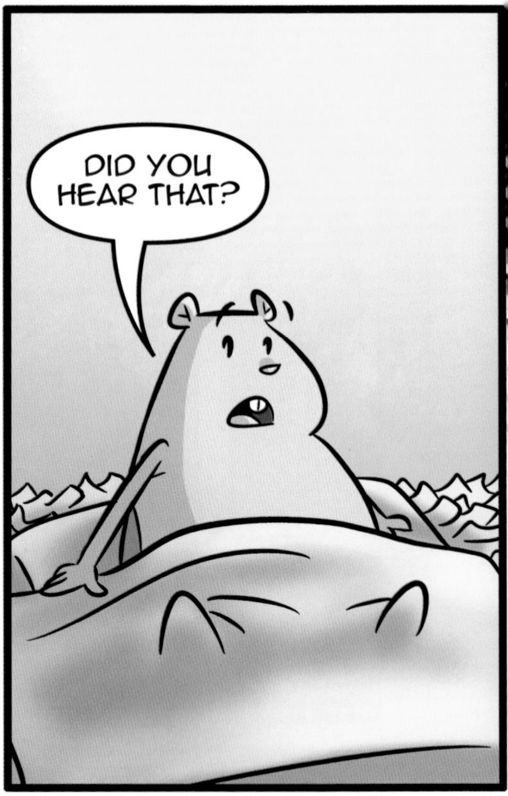
DID YOU HEAR THAT?

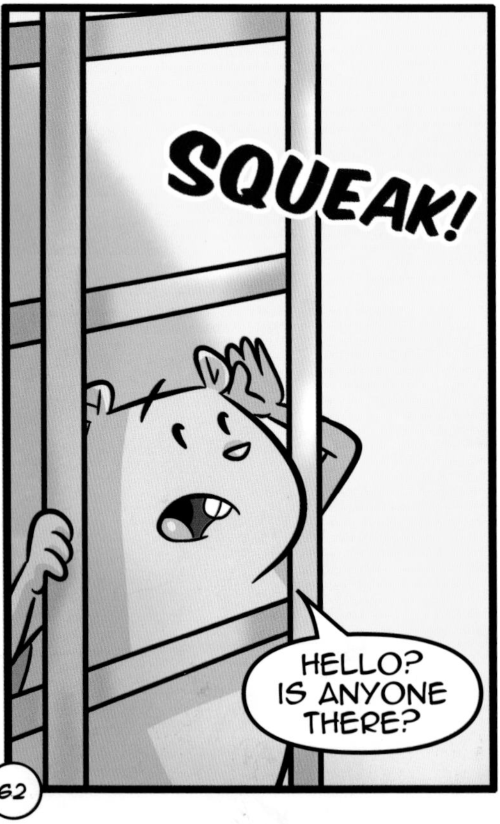
SQUEAK!
HELLO? IS ANYONE THERE?

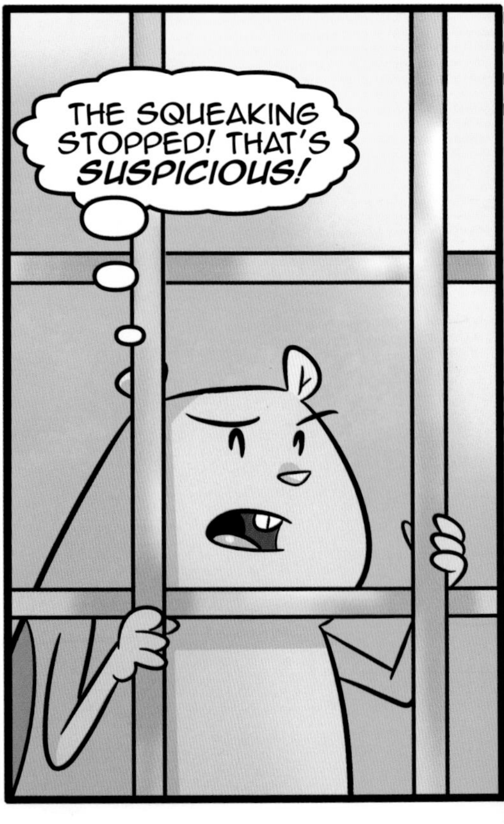
THE SQUEAKING STOPPED! THAT'S *SUSPICIOUS!*

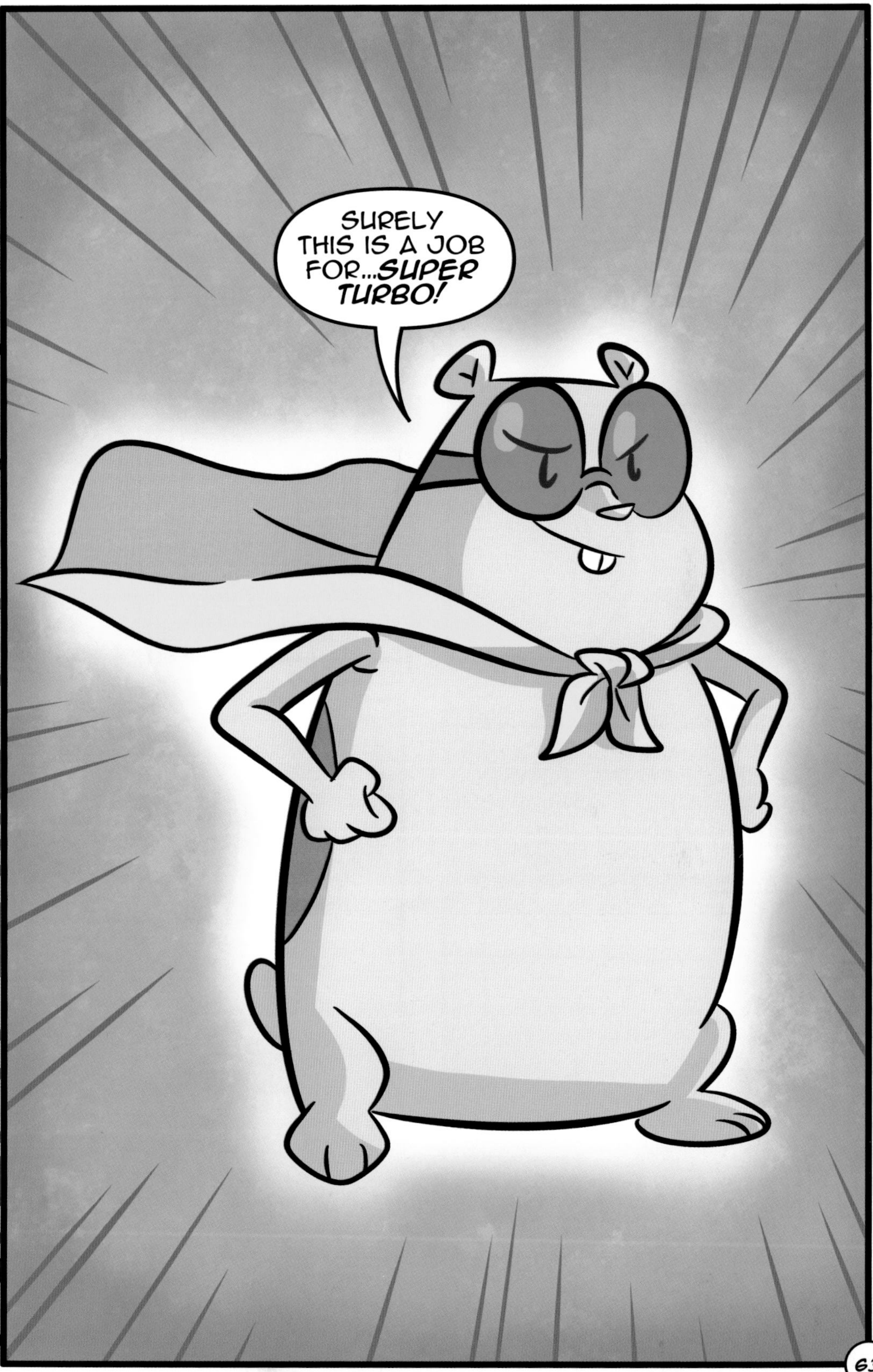
SURELY THIS IS A JOB FOR...SUPER TURBO!

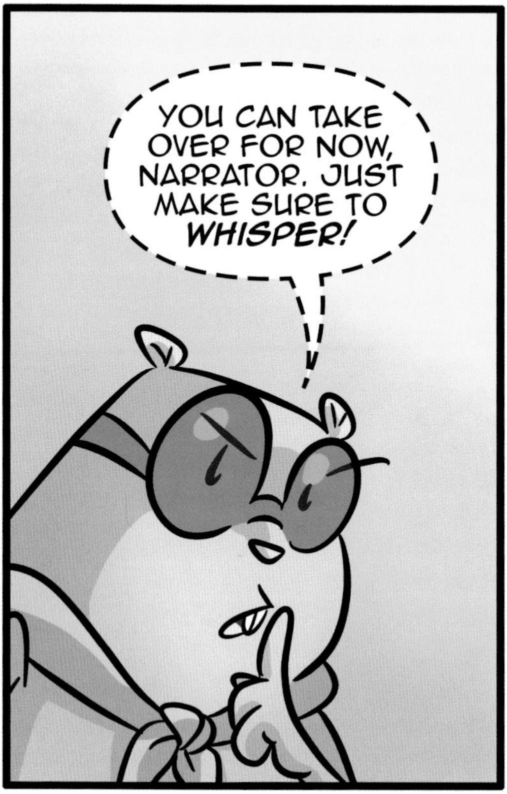
YOU CAN TAKE OVER FOR NOW, NARRATOR. JUST MAKE SURE TO *WHISPER!*

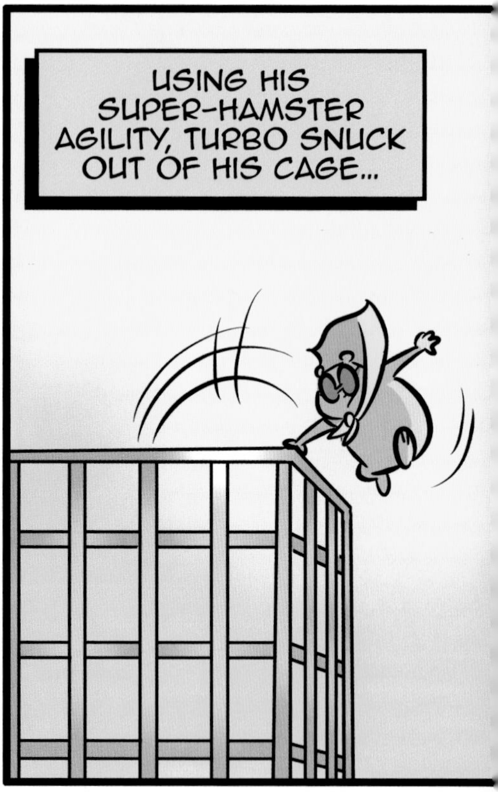
USING HIS SUPER-HAMSTER AGILITY, TURBO SNUCK OUT OF HIS CAGE...

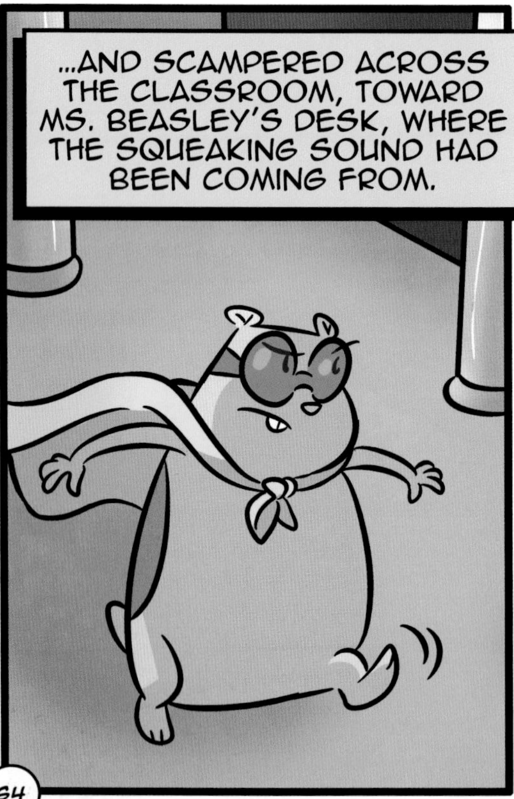
...AND SCAMPERED ACROSS THE CLASSROOM, TOWARD MS. BEASLEY'S DESK, WHERE THE SQUEAKING SOUND HAD BEEN COMING FROM.

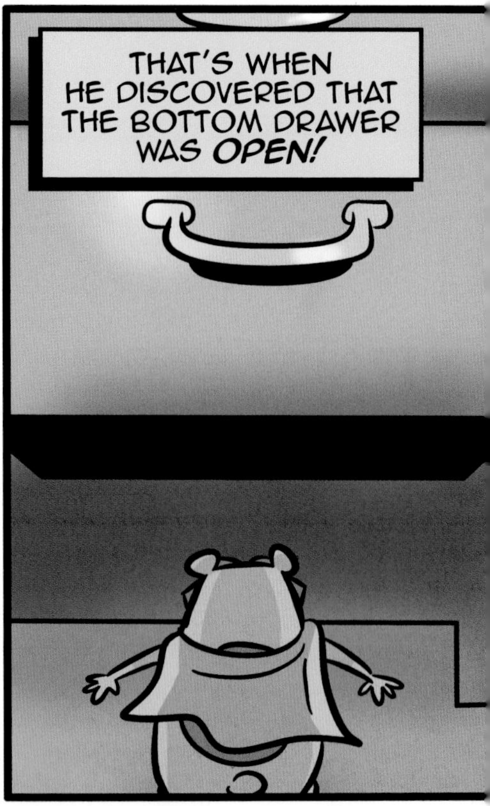
THAT'S WHEN HE DISCOVERED THAT THE BOTTOM DRAWER WAS *OPEN!*

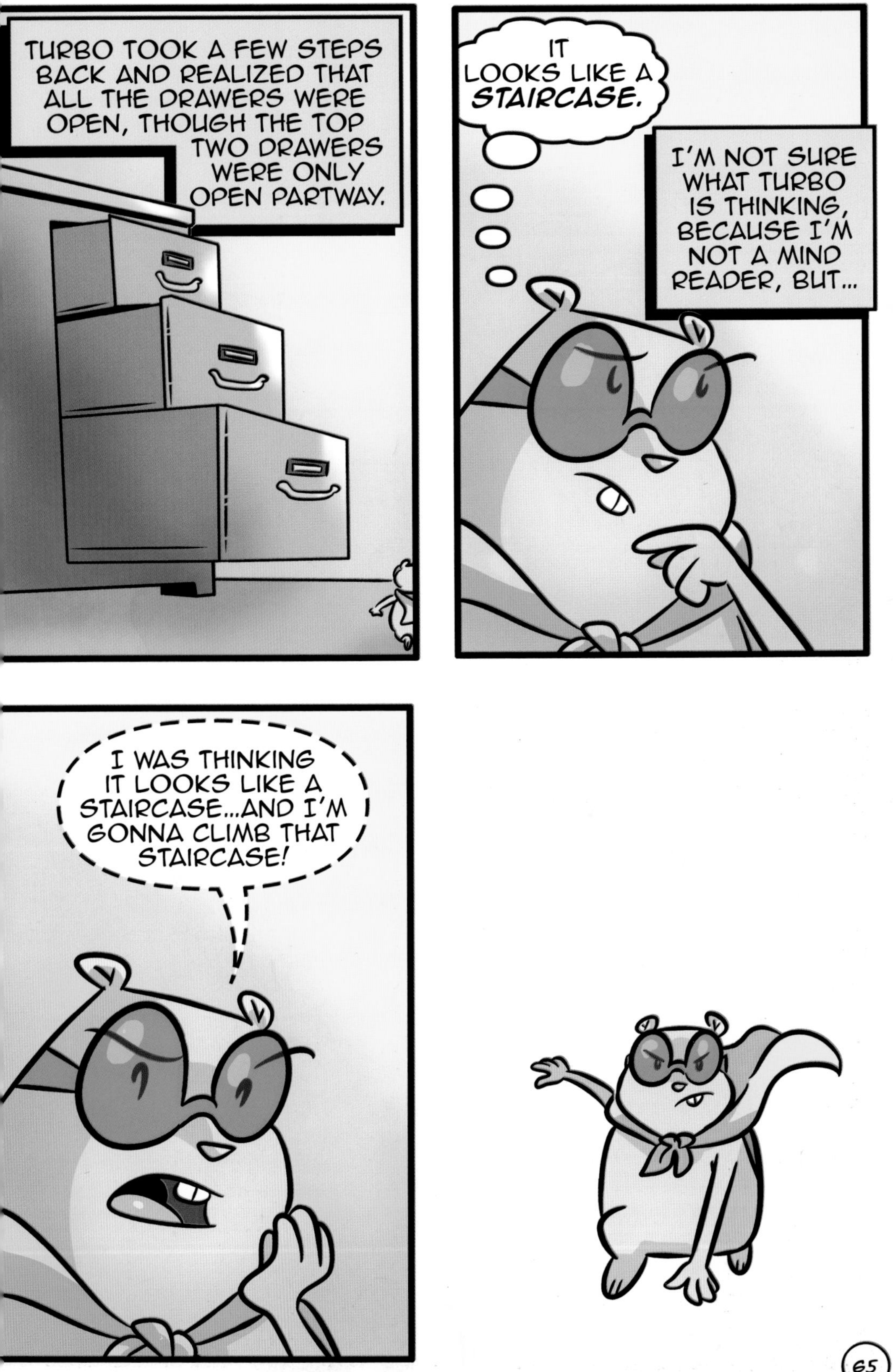

TURBO TOOK A FEW STEPS BACK AND REALIZED THAT ALL THE DRAWERS WERE OPEN, THOUGH THE TOP TWO DRAWERS WERE ONLY OPEN PARTWAY.
IT LOOKS LIKE A *STAIRCASE.*
I'M NOT SURE WHAT TURBO IS THINKING, BECAUSE I'M NOT A MIND READER, BUT...
I WAS THINKING IT LOOKS LIKE A STAIRCASE...AND I'M GONNA CLIMB THAT STAIRCASE!

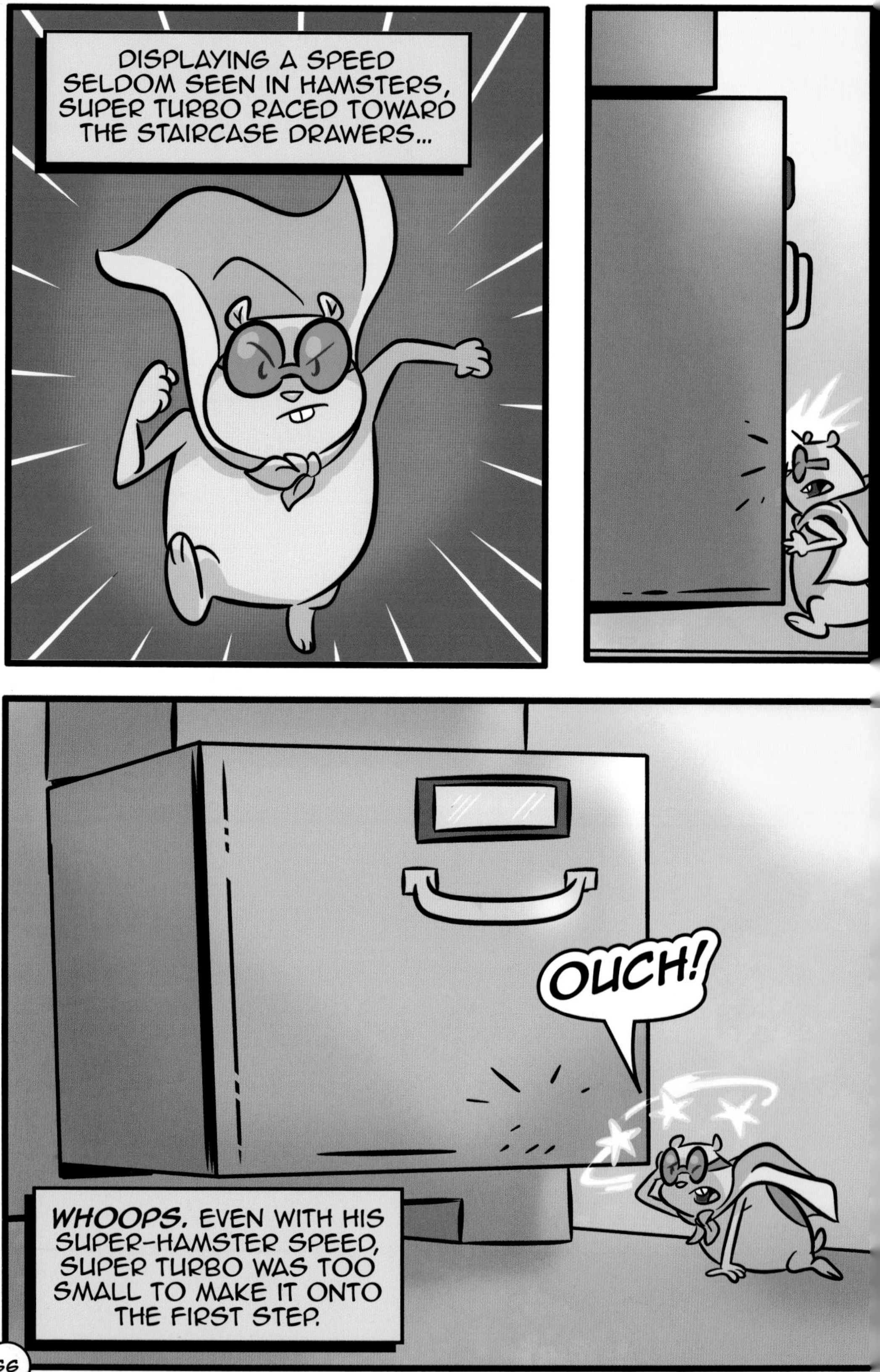
DISPLAYING A SPEED SELDOM SEEN IN HAMSTERS, SUPER TURBO RACED TOWARD THE STAIRCASE DRAWERS...
OUCH!
WHOOPS. EVEN WITH HIS SUPER-HAMSTER SPEED, SUPER TURBO WAS TOO SMALL TO MAKE IT ONTO THE FIRST STEP.

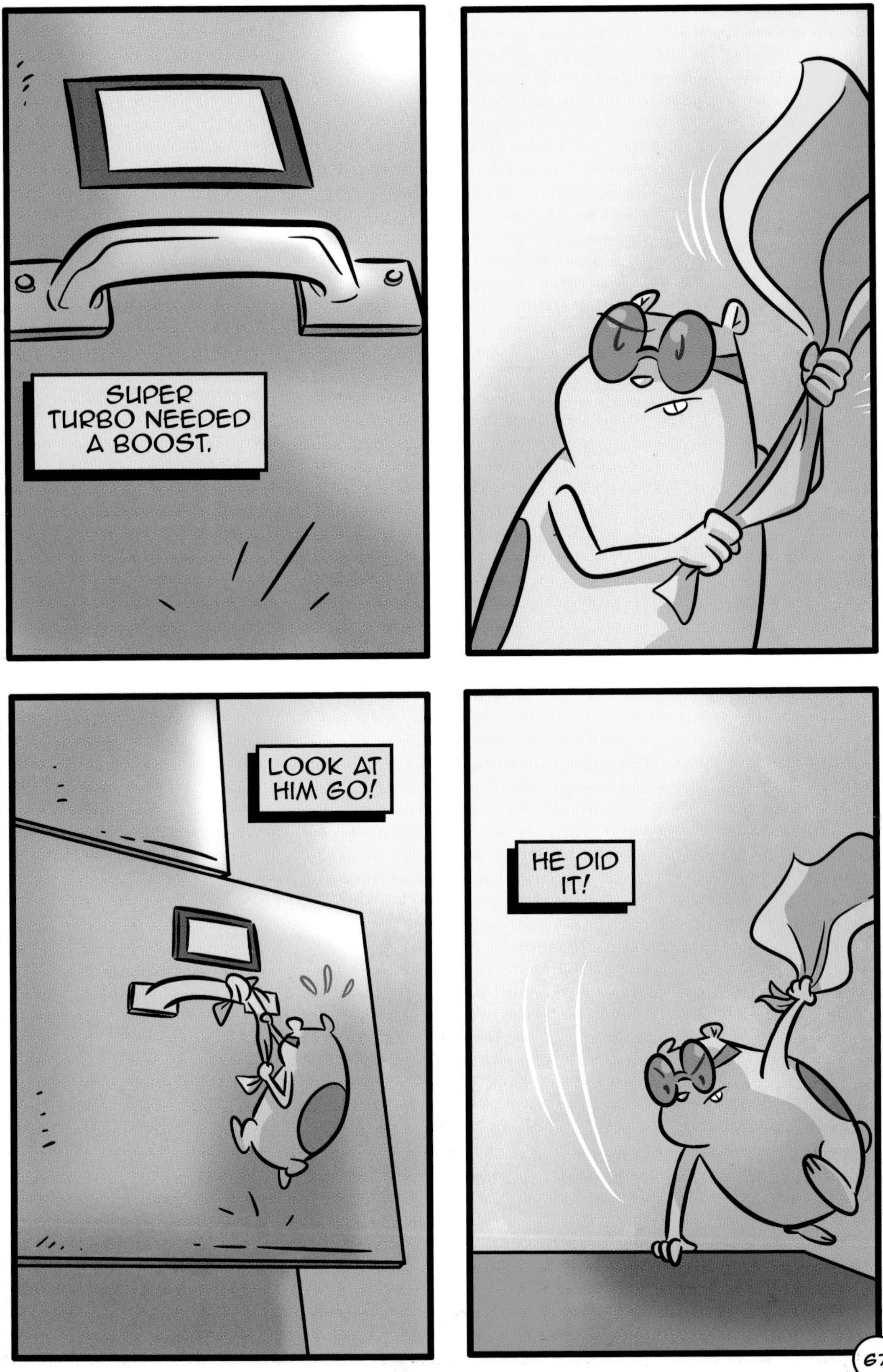
SUPER TURBO NEEDED A BOOST.
LOOK AT HIM GO!
HE DID IT!

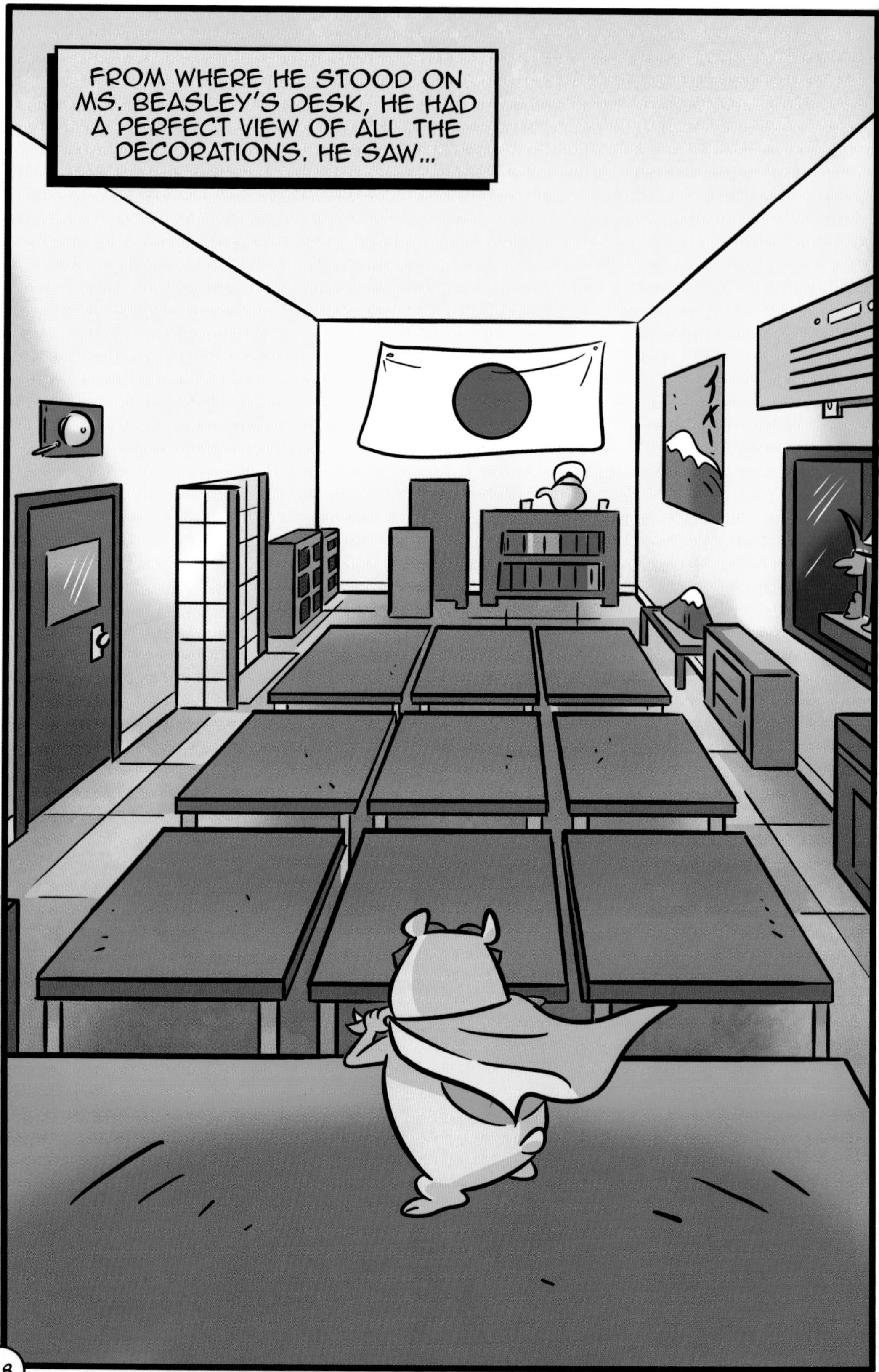
FROM WHERE HE STOOD ON MS. BEASLEY'S DESK, HE HAD A PERFECT VIEW OF ALL THE DECORATIONS. HE SAW...

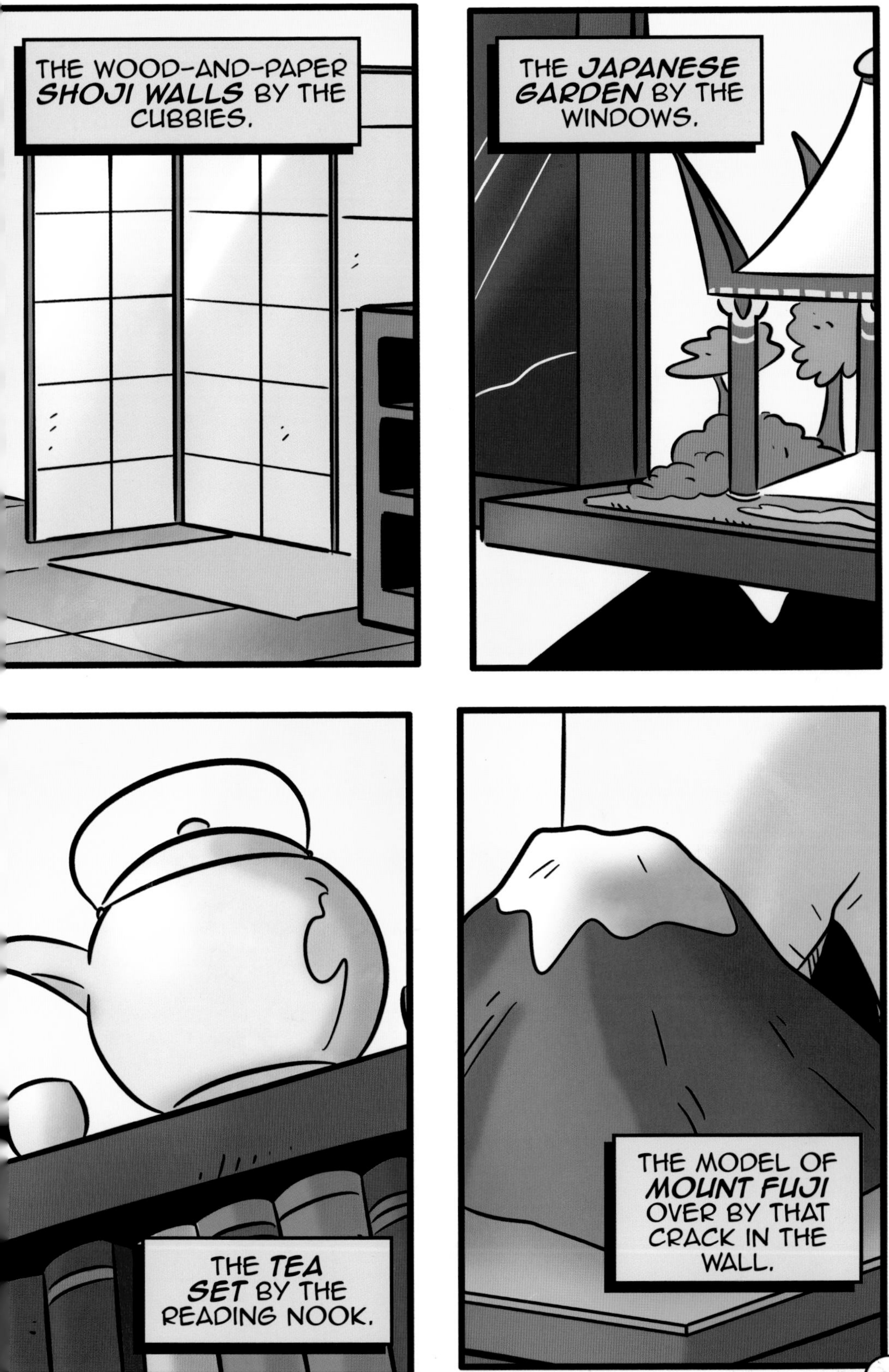
THE WOOD-AND-PAPER SHOJI WALLS BY THE CUBBIES.
THE JAPANESE GARDEN BY THE WINDOWS.
THE TEA SET BY THE READING NOOK.
THE MODEL OF MOUNT FUJI OVER BY THAT CRACK IN THE WALL.

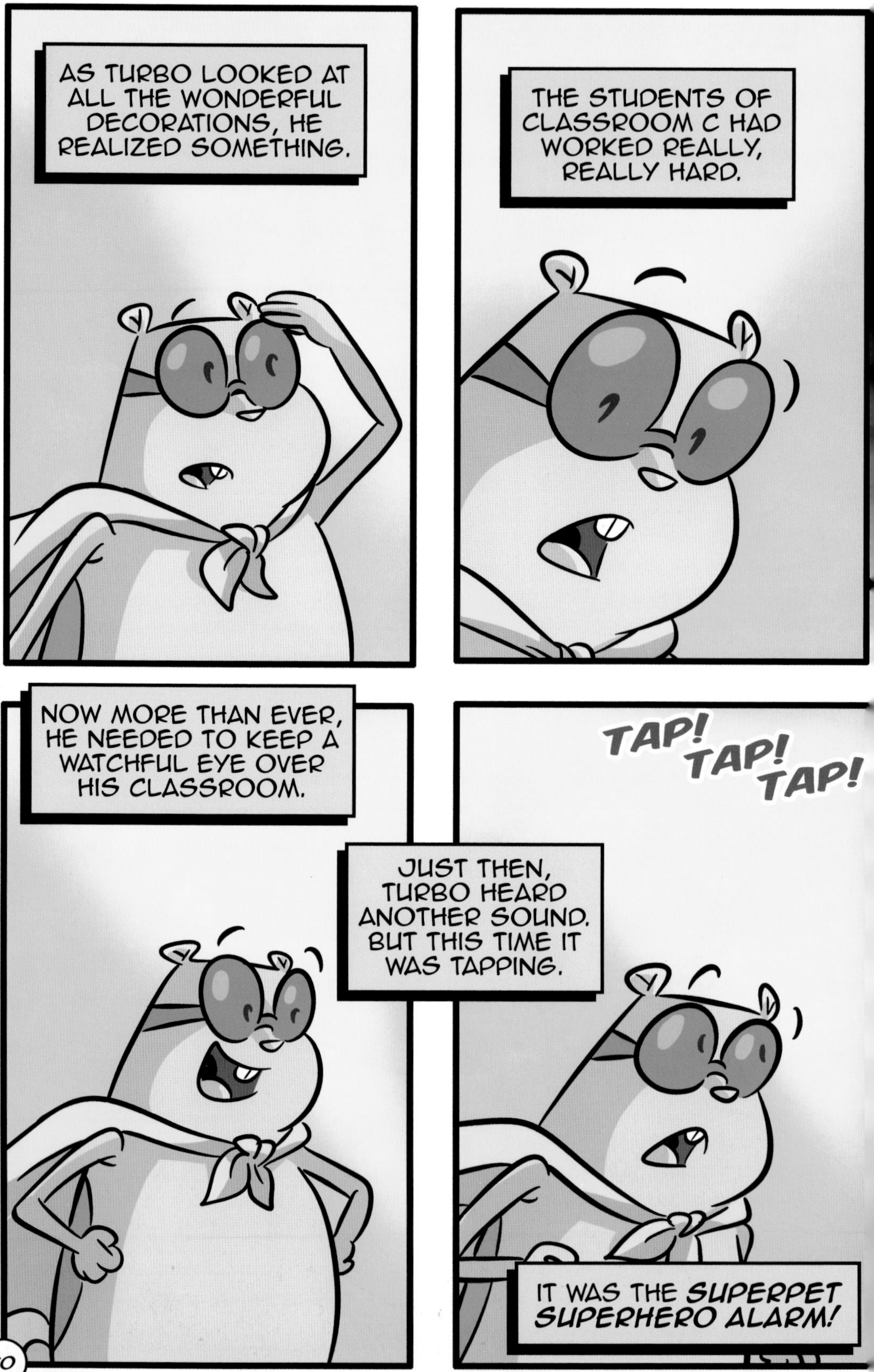
AS TURBO LOOKED AT ALL THE WONDERFUL DECORATIONS, HE REALIZED SOMETHING.
THE STUDENTS OF CLASSROOM C HAD WORKED REALLY, REALLY HARD.
NOW MORE THAN EVER, HE NEEDED TO KEEP A WATCHFUL EYE OVER HIS CLASSROOM.
TAP! TAP! TAP!
JUST THEN, TURBO HEARD ANOTHER SOUND. BUT THIS TIME IT WAS TAPPING.
IT WAS THE SUPERPET SUPERHERO ALARM!

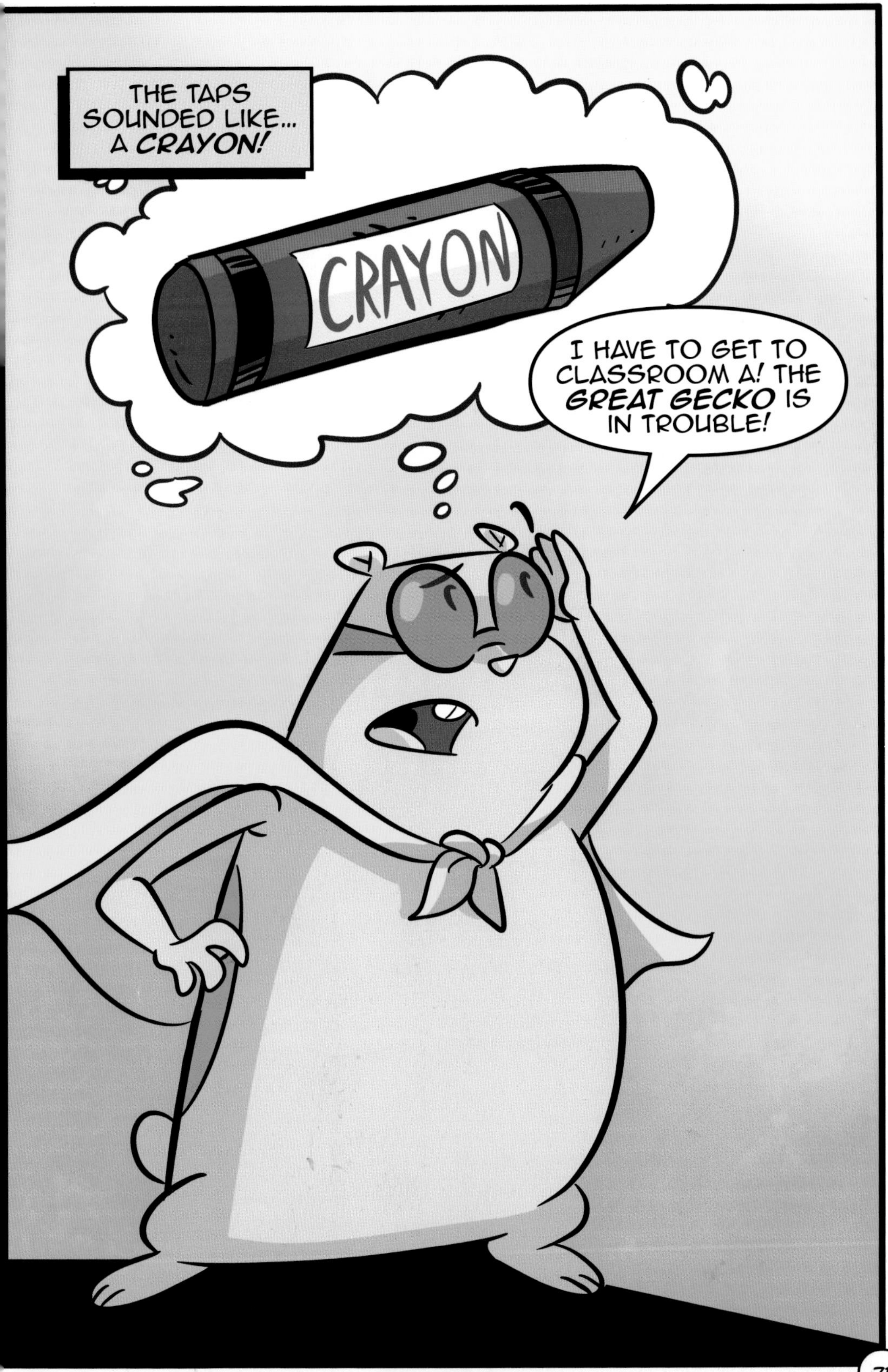
THE TAPS SOUNDED LIKE... A CRAYON!
CRAYON
I HAVE TO GET TO CLASSROOM A! THE GREAT GECKO IS IN TROUBLE!

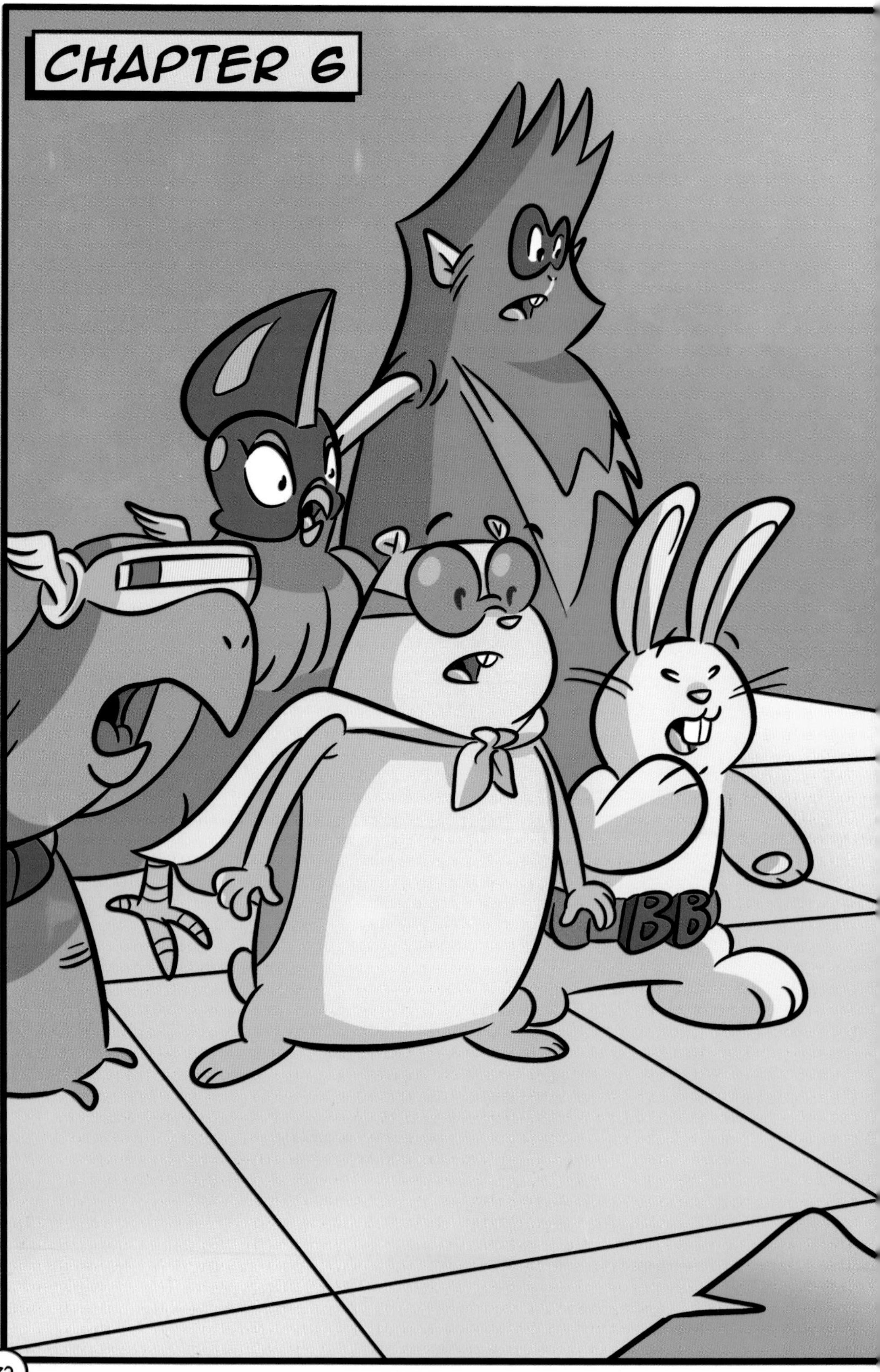
CHAPTER 6
BB

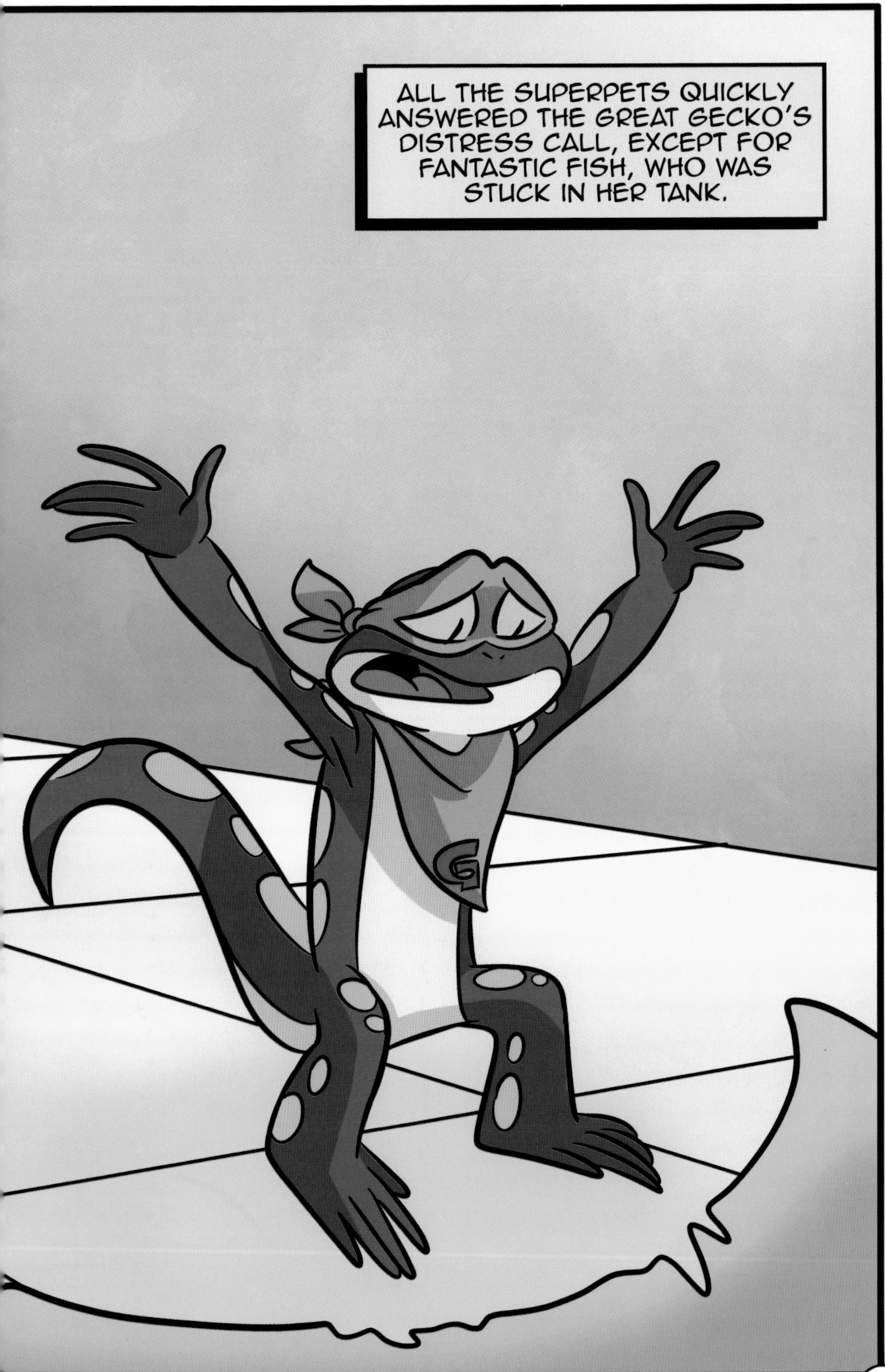
ALL THE SUPERPETS QUICKLY ANSWERED THE GREAT GECKO'S DISTRESS CALL, EXCEPT FOR FANTASTIC FISH, WHO WAS STUCK IN HER TANK.

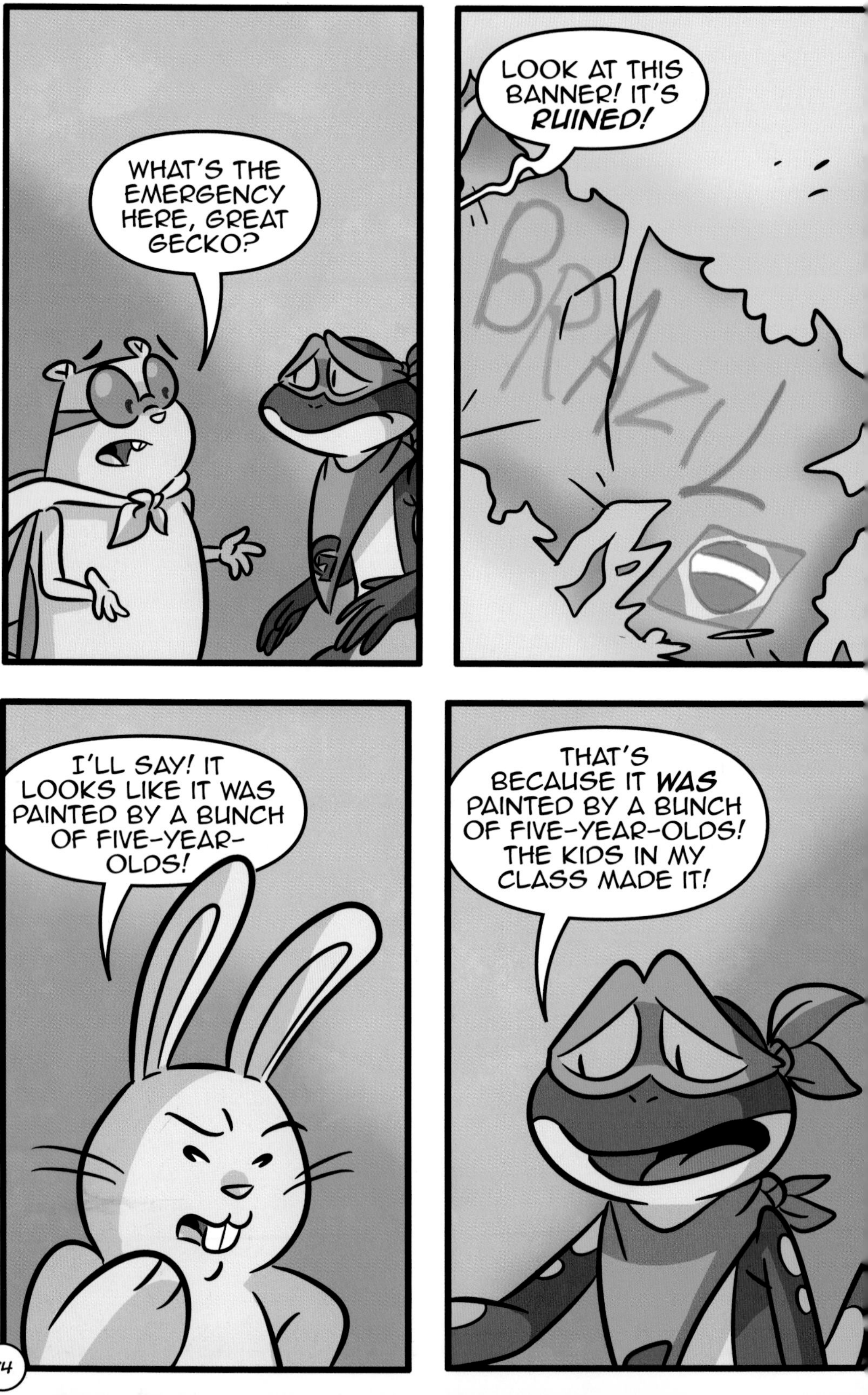
WHAT'S THE EMERGENCY HERE, GREAT GECKO?
LOOK AT THIS BANNER! IT'S RUINED!
BRAZIL
I'LL SAY! IT LOOKS LIKE IT WAS PAINTED BY A BUNCH OF FIVE-YEAR-OLDS!
THAT'S BECAUSE IT WAS PAINTED BY A BUNCH OF FIVE-YEAR-OLDS! THE KIDS IN MY CLASS MADE IT!

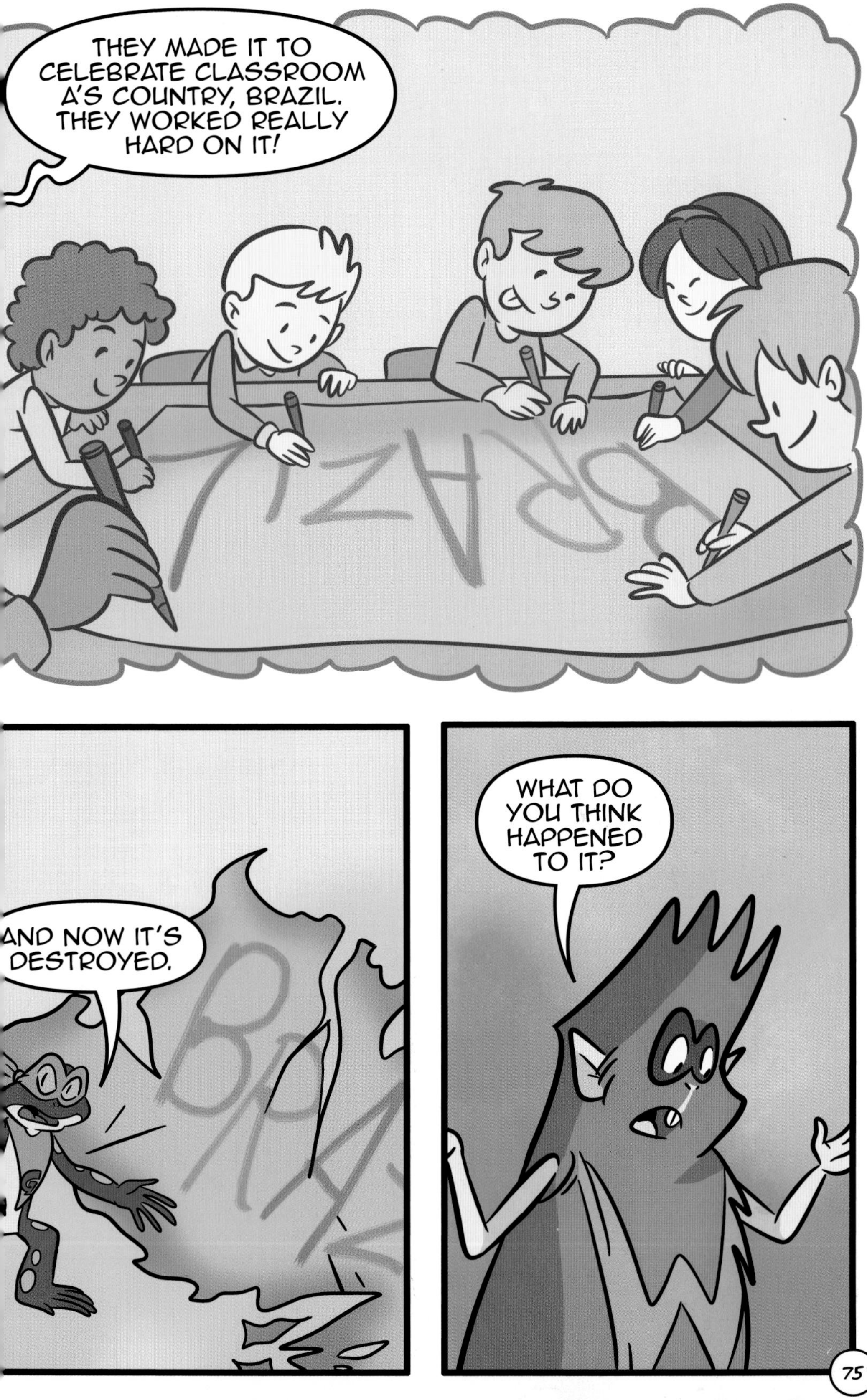
THEY MADE IT TO CELEBRATE CLASSROOM A'S COUNTRY, BRAZIL. THEY WORKED REALLY HARD ON IT!
AND NOW IT'S DESTROYED.
WHAT DO YOU THINK HAPPENED TO IT?

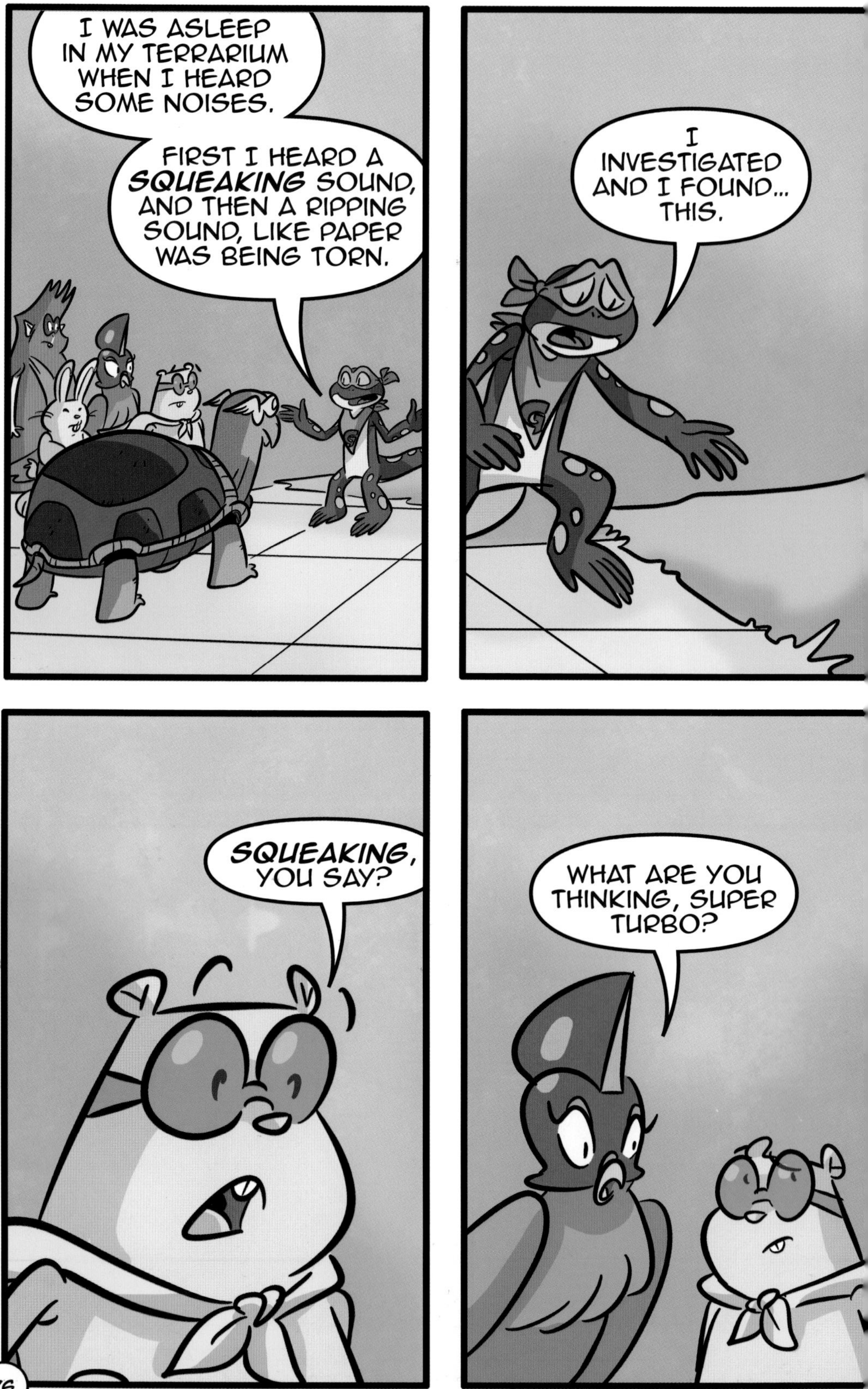
I WAS ASLEEP IN MY TERRARIUM WHEN I HEARD SOME NOISES.
FIRST I HEARD A *SQUEAKING* SOUND, AND THEN A RIPPING SOUND, LIKE PAPER WAS BEING TORN.
I INVESTIGATED AND I FOUND... THIS.
SQUEAKING, YOU SAY?
WHAT ARE YOU THINKING, SUPER TURBO?

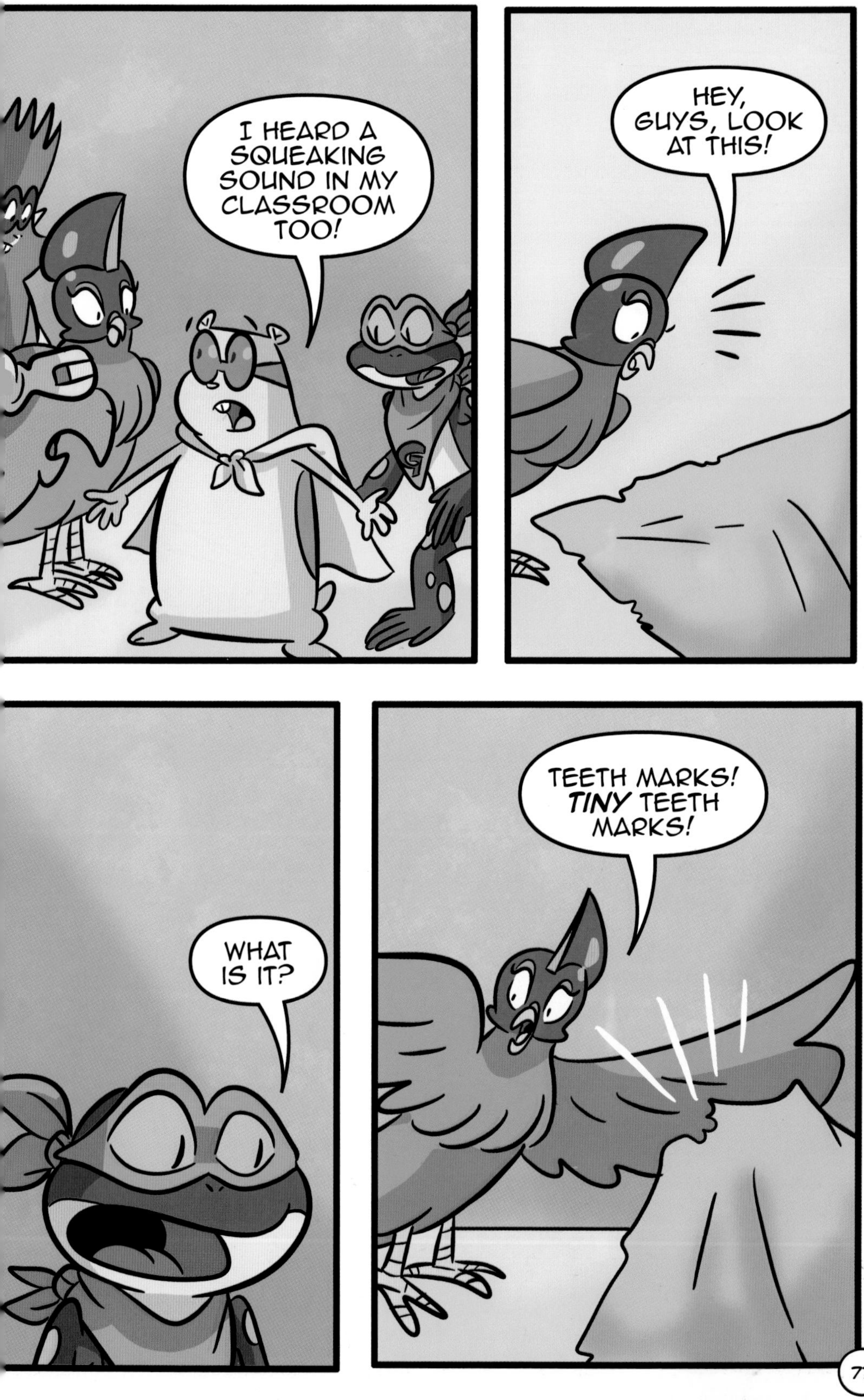
I HEARD A SQUEAKING SOUND IN MY CLASSROOM TOO!
HEY, GUYS, LOOK AT THIS!
WHAT IS IT?
TEETH MARKS! *TINY* TEETH MARKS!

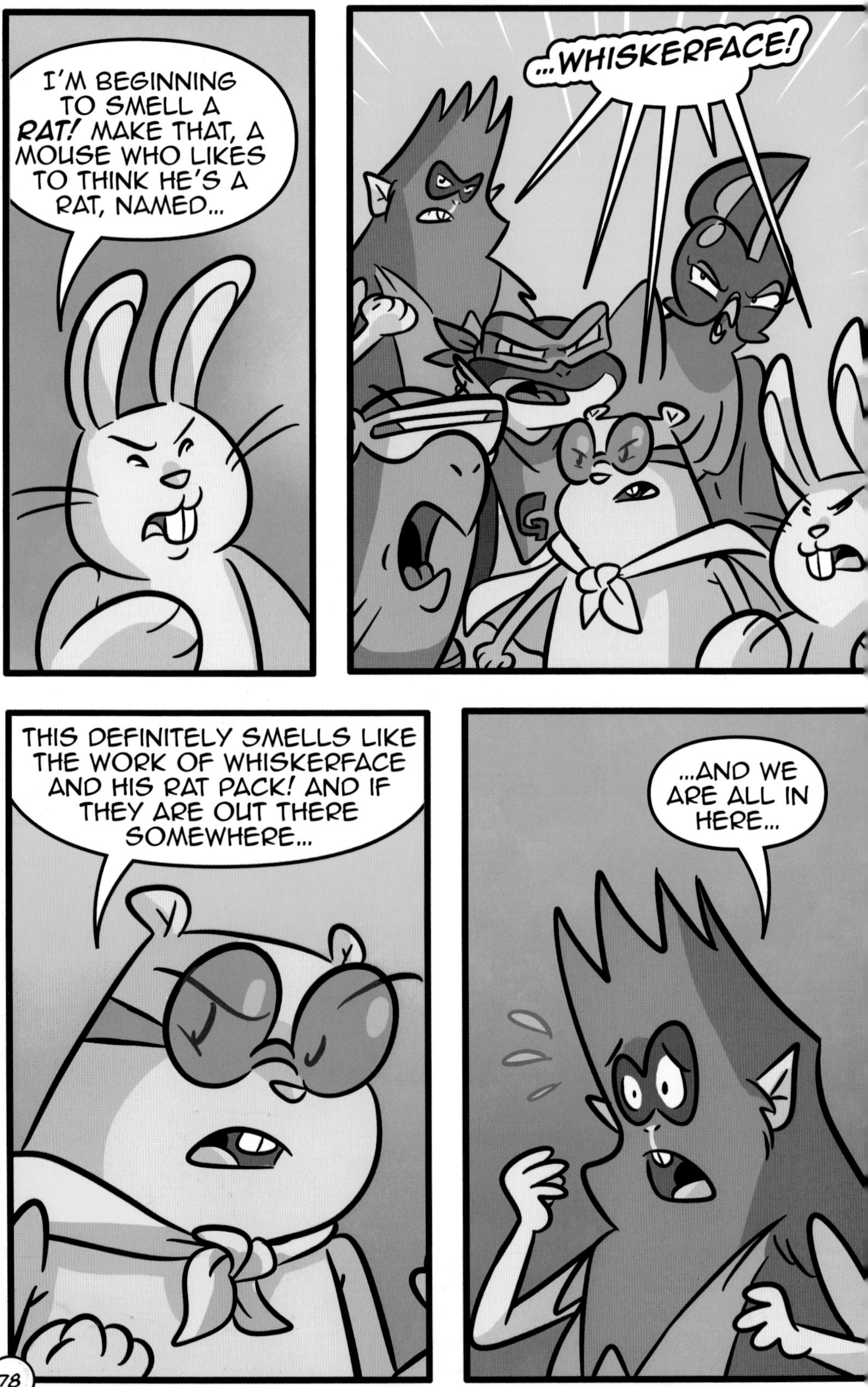
I'M BEGINNING TO SMELL A RAT! MAKE THAT, A MOUSE WHO LIKES TO THINK HE'S A RAT, NAMED...
...WHISKERFACE!
THIS DEFINITELY SMELLS LIKE THE WORK OF WHISKERFACE AND HIS RAT PACK! AND IF THEY ARE OUT THERE SOMEWHERE...
...AND WE ARE ALL IN HERE...

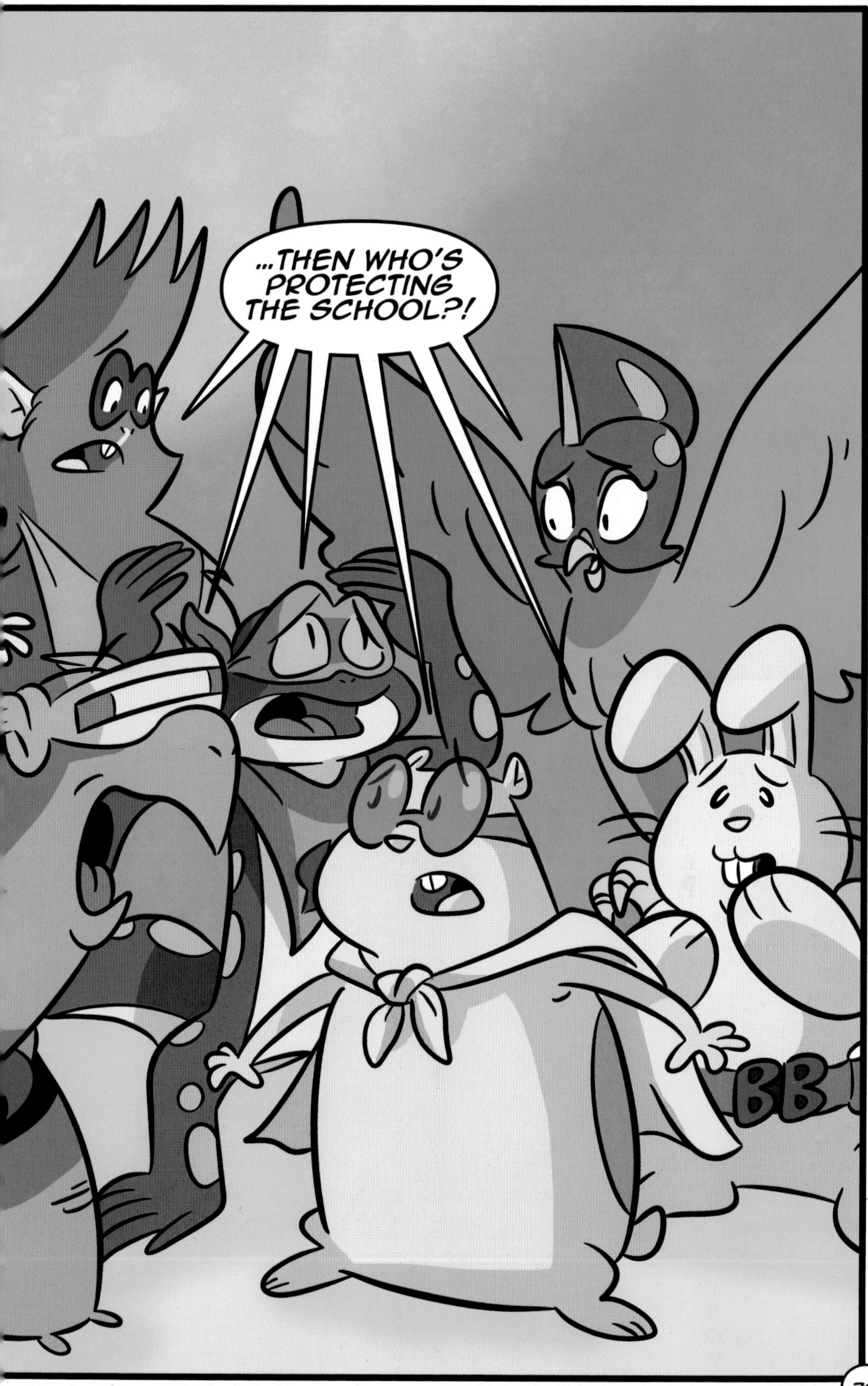
...THEN WHO'S PROTECTING THE SCHOOL?!
BB

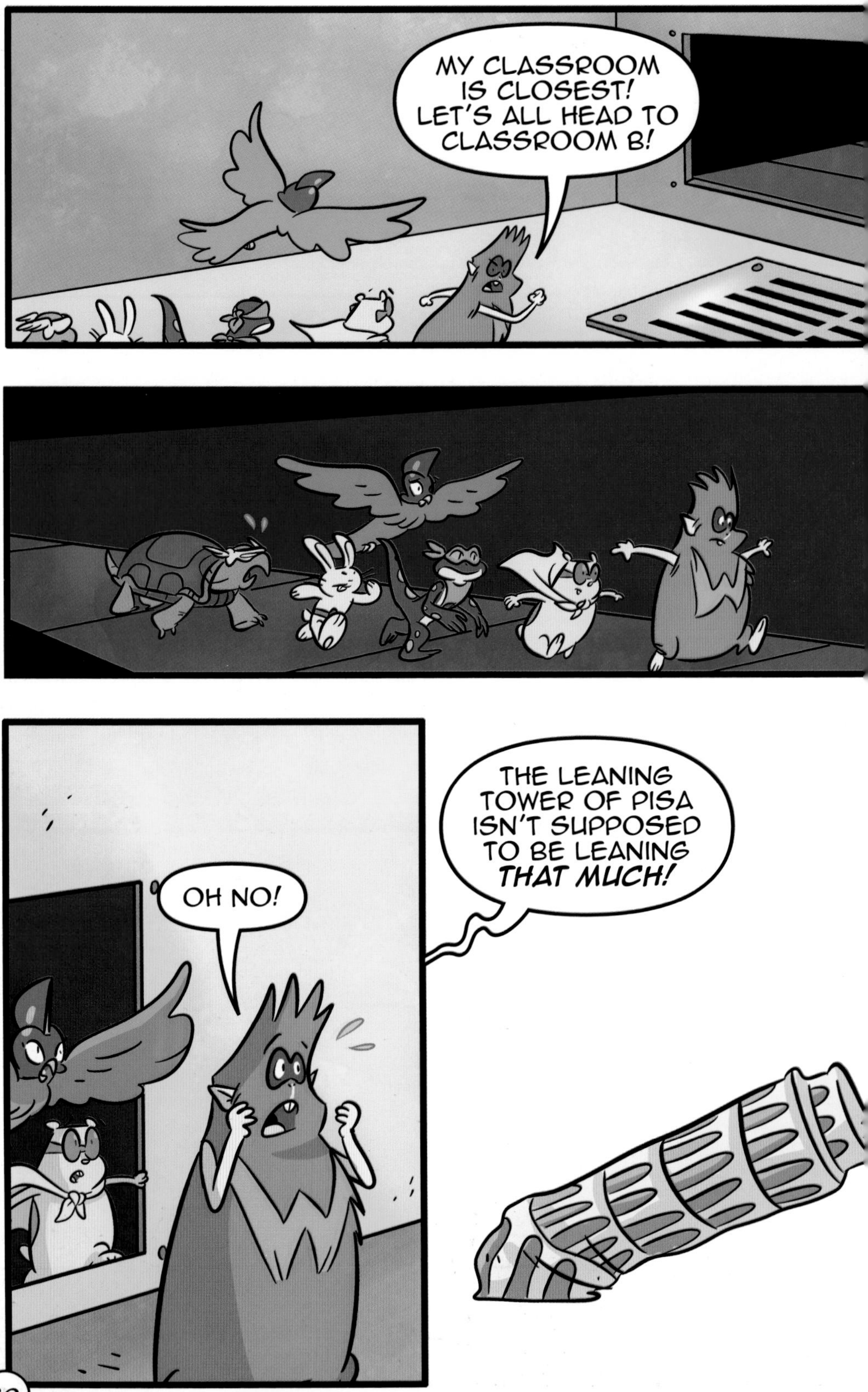
MY CLASSROOM IS CLOSEST! LET'S ALL HEAD TO CLASSROOM B!
OH NO!
THE LEANING TOWER OF PISA ISN'T SUPPOSED TO BE LEANING *THAT MUCH!*

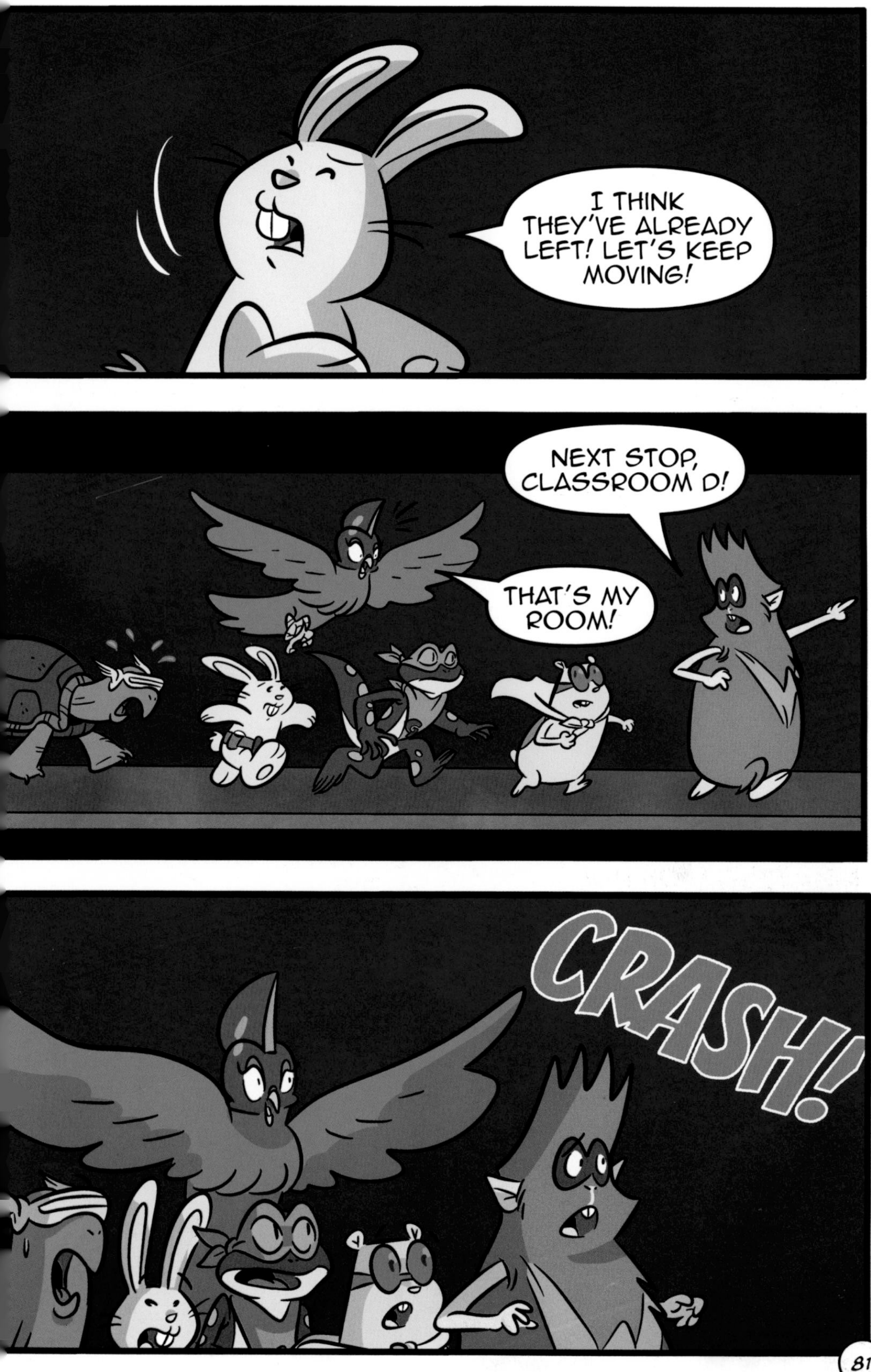
I THINK THEY'VE ALREADY LEFT! LET'S KEEP MOVING!
NEXT STOP, CLASSROOM D!
THAT'S MY ROOM!
CRASH!

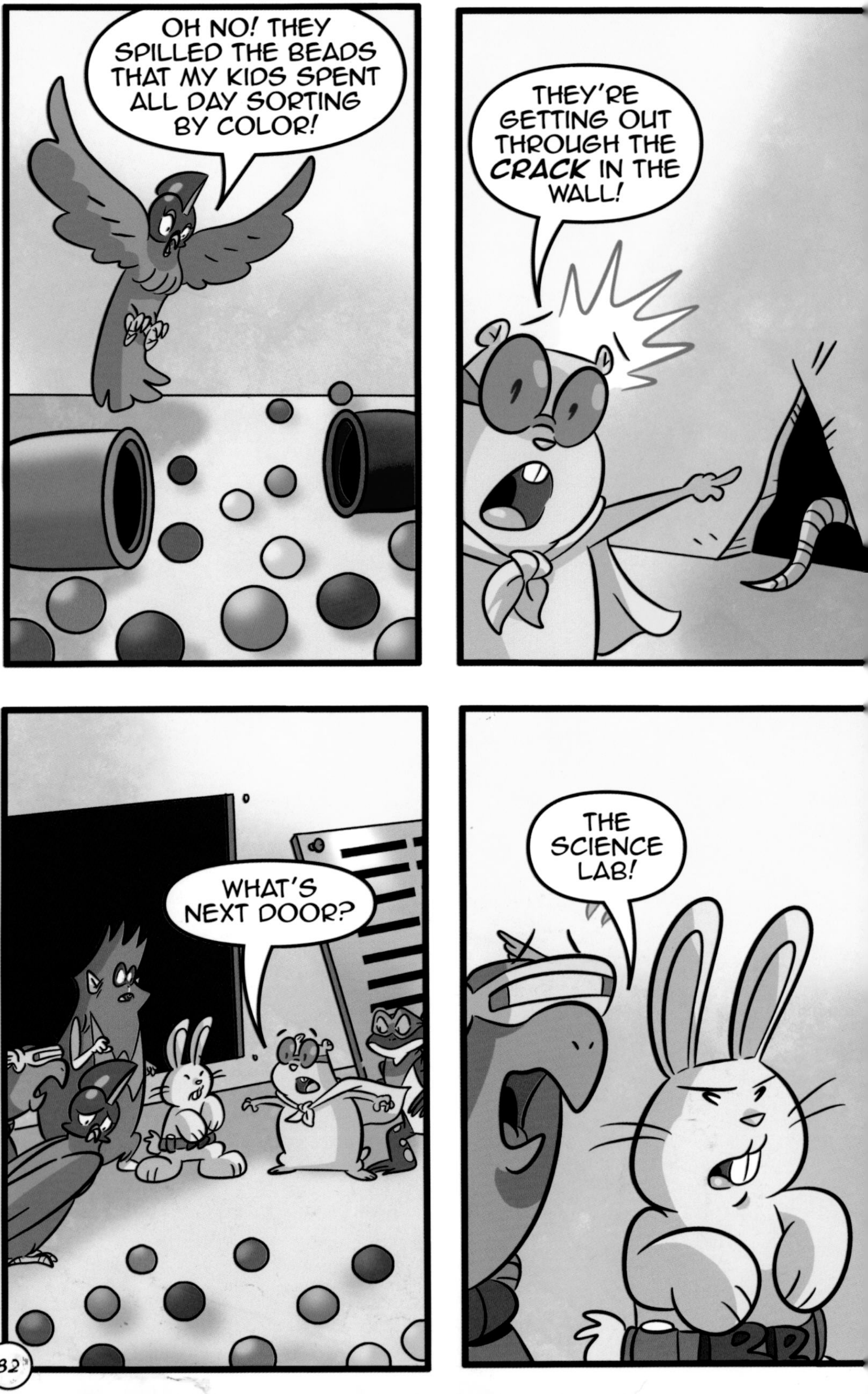
OH NO! THEY SPILLED THE BEADS THAT MY KIDS SPENT ALL DAY SORTING BY COLOR!
THEY'RE GETTING OUT THROUGH THE CRACK IN THE WALL!
WHAT'S NEXT DOOR?
THE SCIENCE LAB!

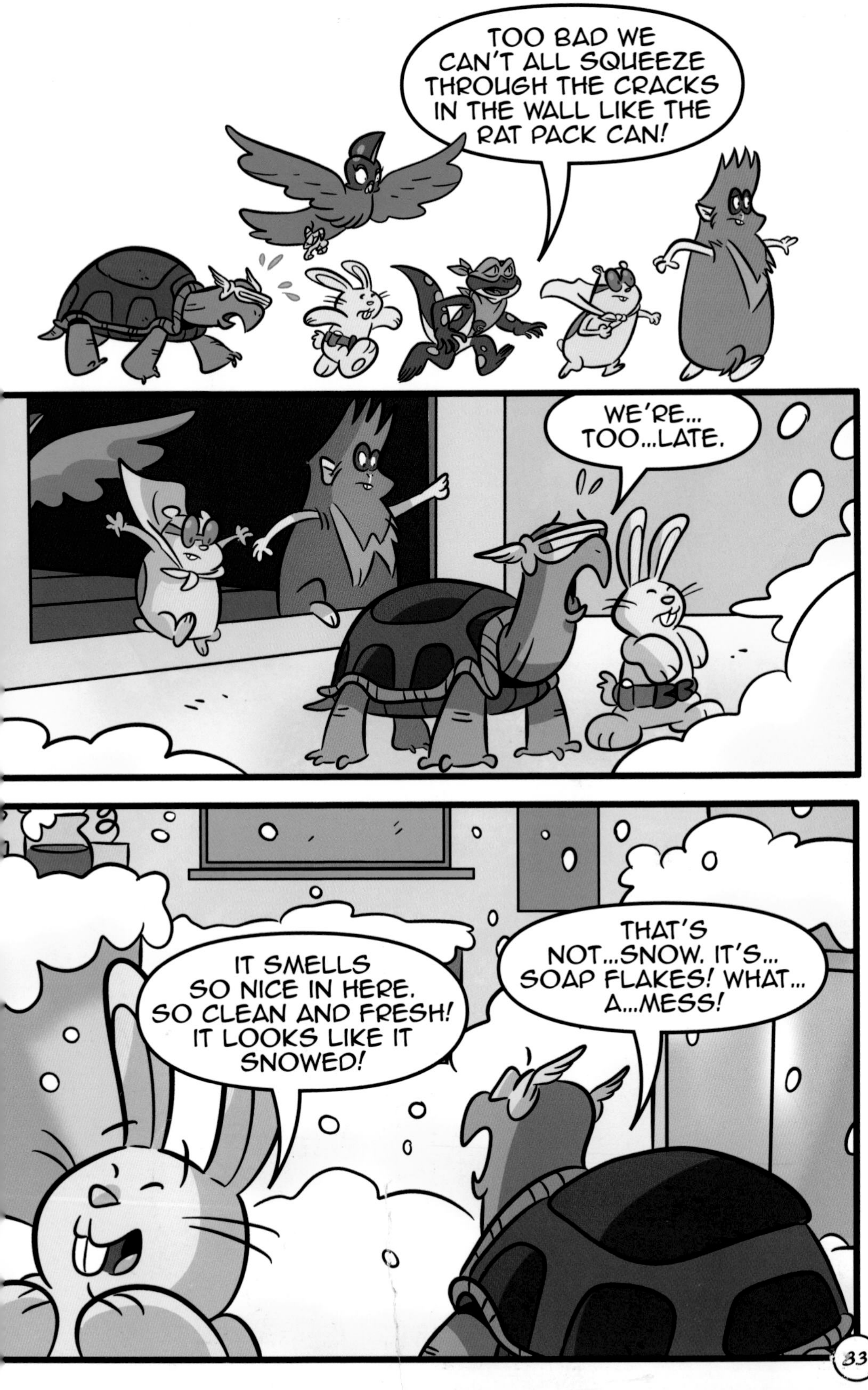
TOO BAD WE CAN'T ALL SQUEEZE THROUGH THE CRACKS IN THE WALL LIKE THE RAT PACK CAN!
WE'RE... TOO...LATE.
IT SMELLS SO NICE IN HERE. SO CLEAN AND FRESH! IT LOOKS LIKE IT SNOWED!
THAT'S NOT...SNOW. IT'S... SOAP FLAKES! WHAT... A...MESS!

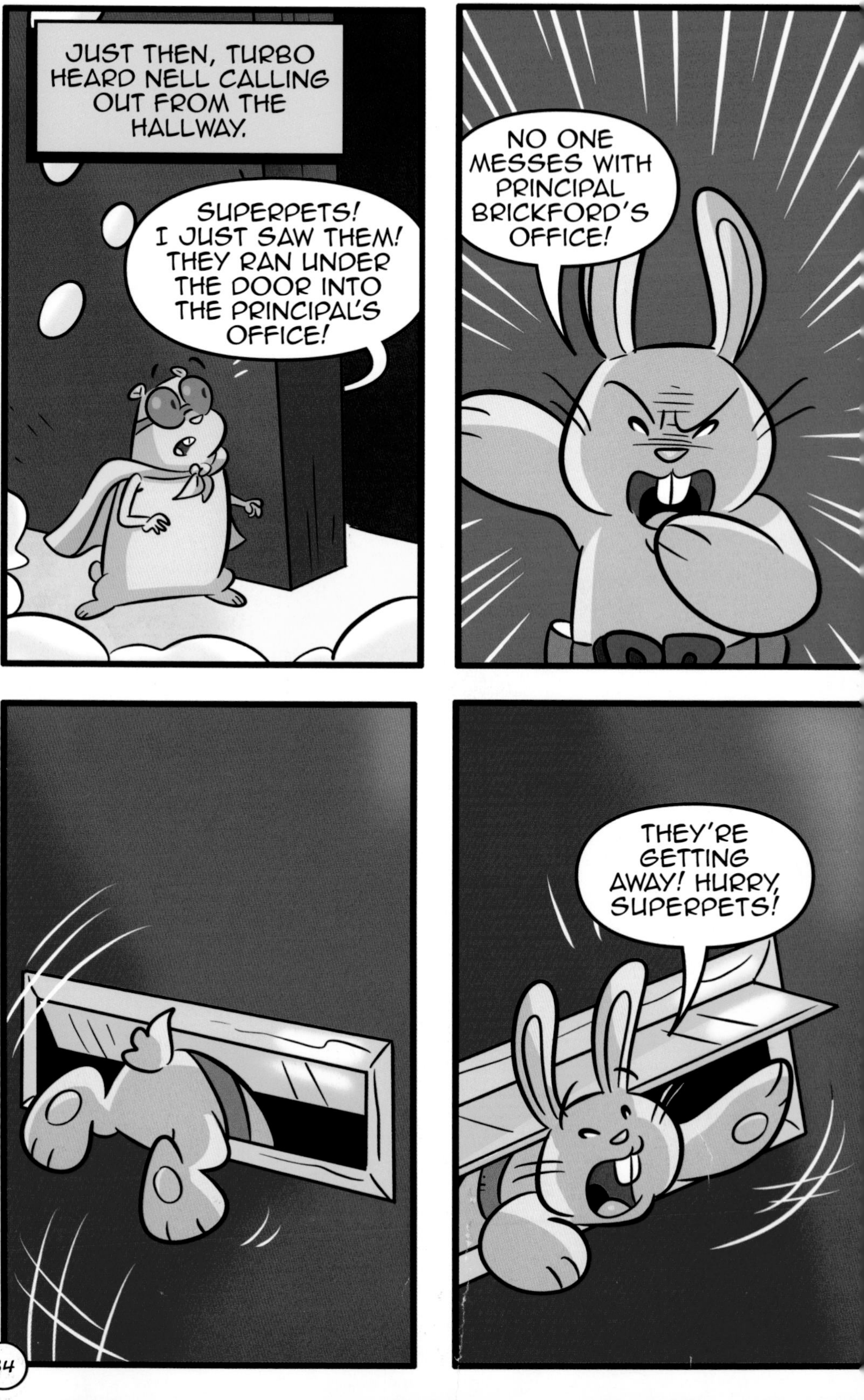

JUST THEN, TURBO HEARD NELL CALLING OUT FROM THE HALLWAY.
SUPERPETS! I JUST SAW THEM! THEY RAN UNDER THE DOOR INTO THE PRINCIPAL'S OFFICE!
NO ONE MESSES WITH PRINCIPAL BRICKFORD'S OFFICE!
THEY'RE GETTING AWAY! HURRY, SUPERPETS!

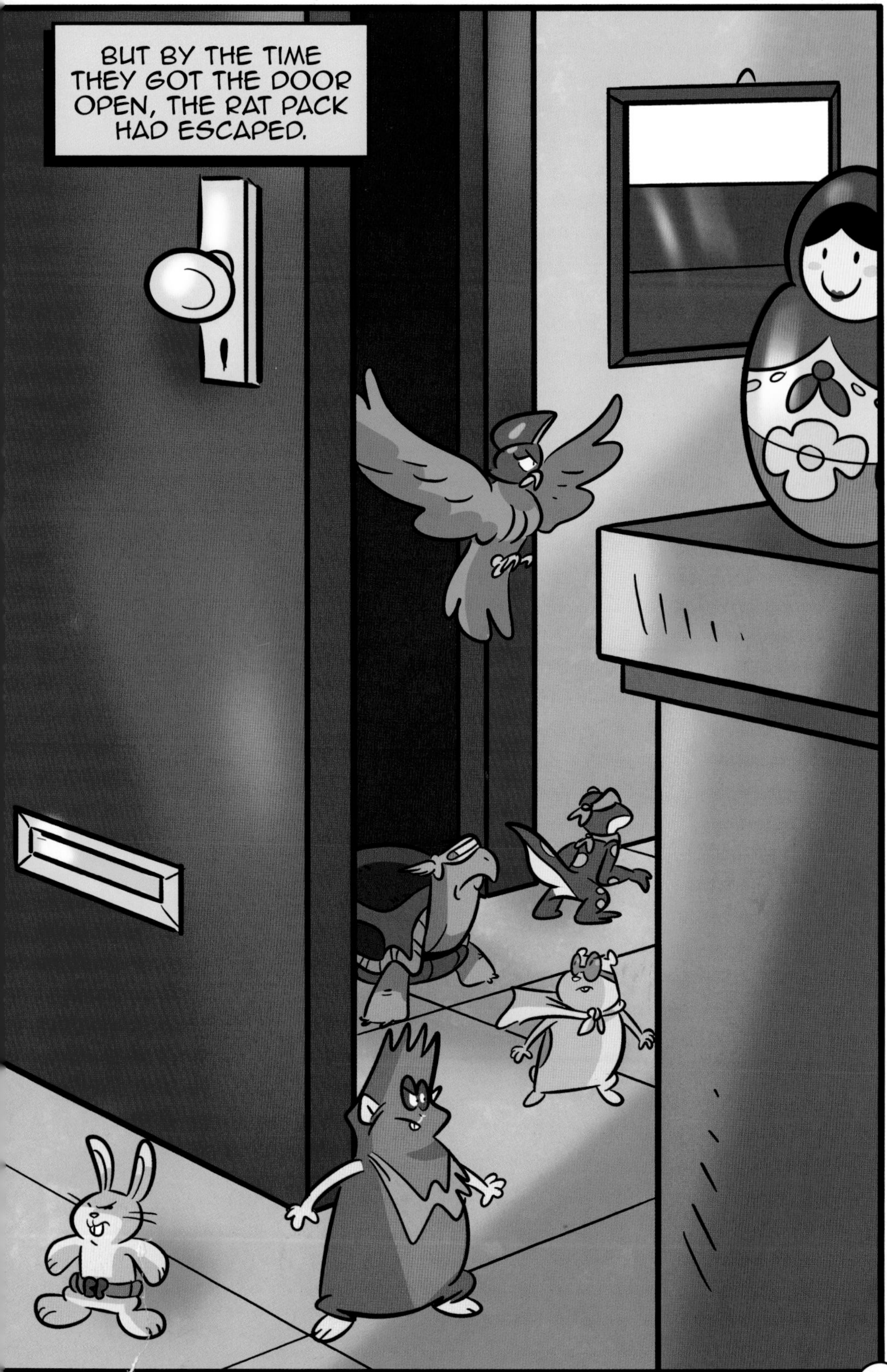
BUT BY THE TIME THEY GOT THE DOOR OPEN, THE RAT PACK HAD ESCAPED.

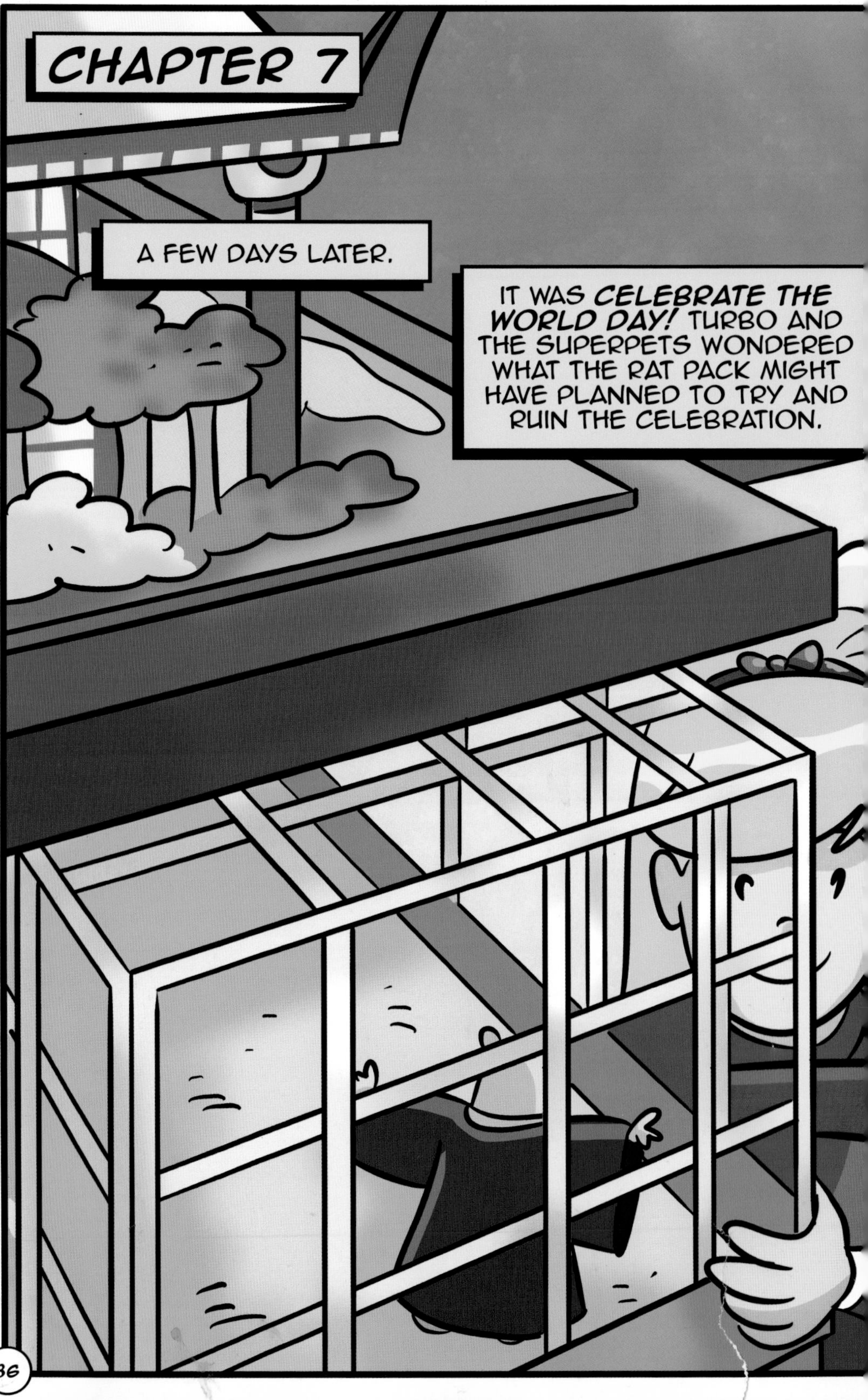
CHAPTER 7
A FEW DAYS LATER.
IT WAS CELEBRATE THE WORLD DAY! TURBO AND THE SUPERPETS WONDERED WHAT THE RAT PACK MIGHT HAVE PLANNED TO TRY AND RUIN THE CELEBRATION.

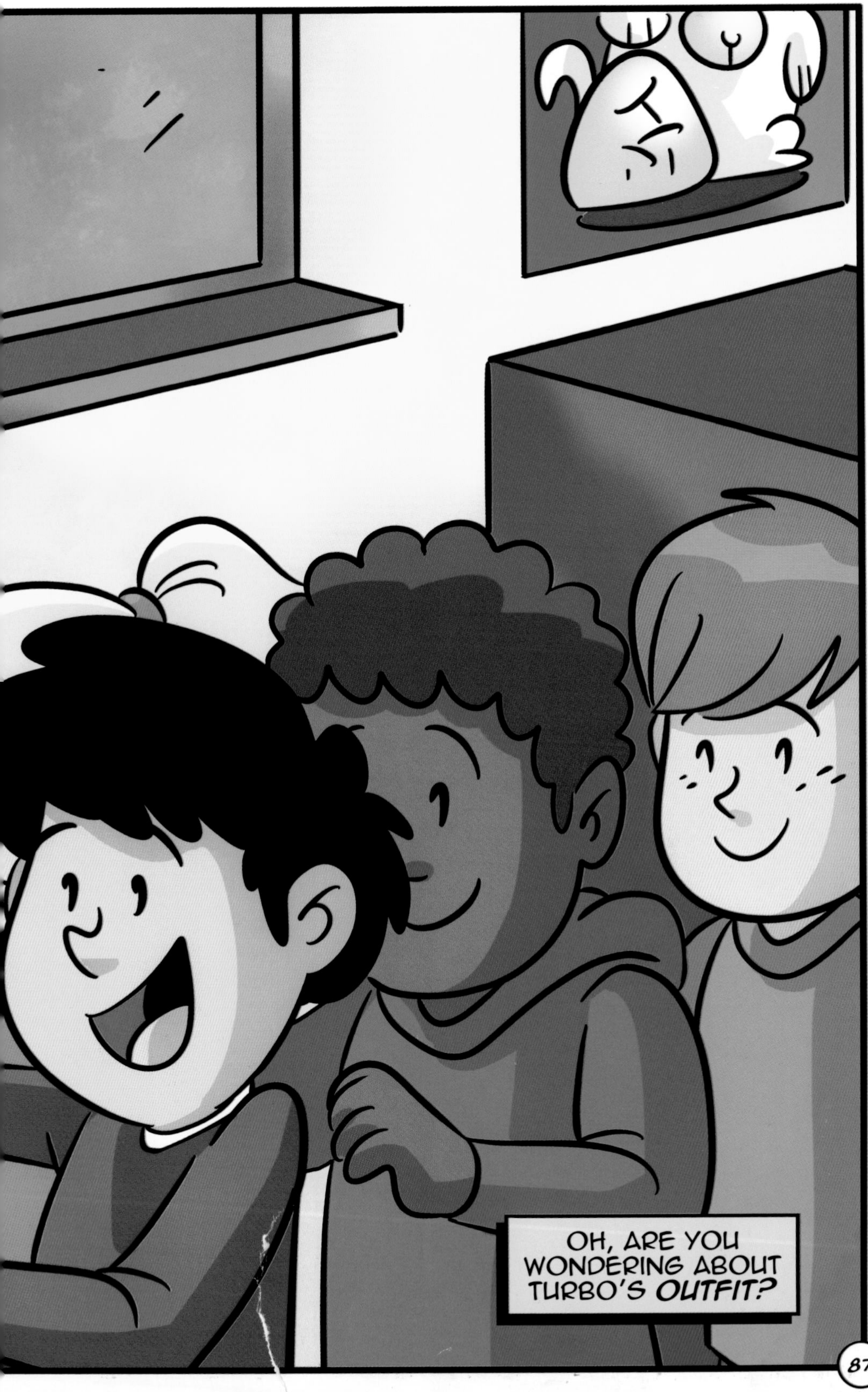
OH, ARE YOU WONDERING ABOUT TURBO'S *OUTFIT?*

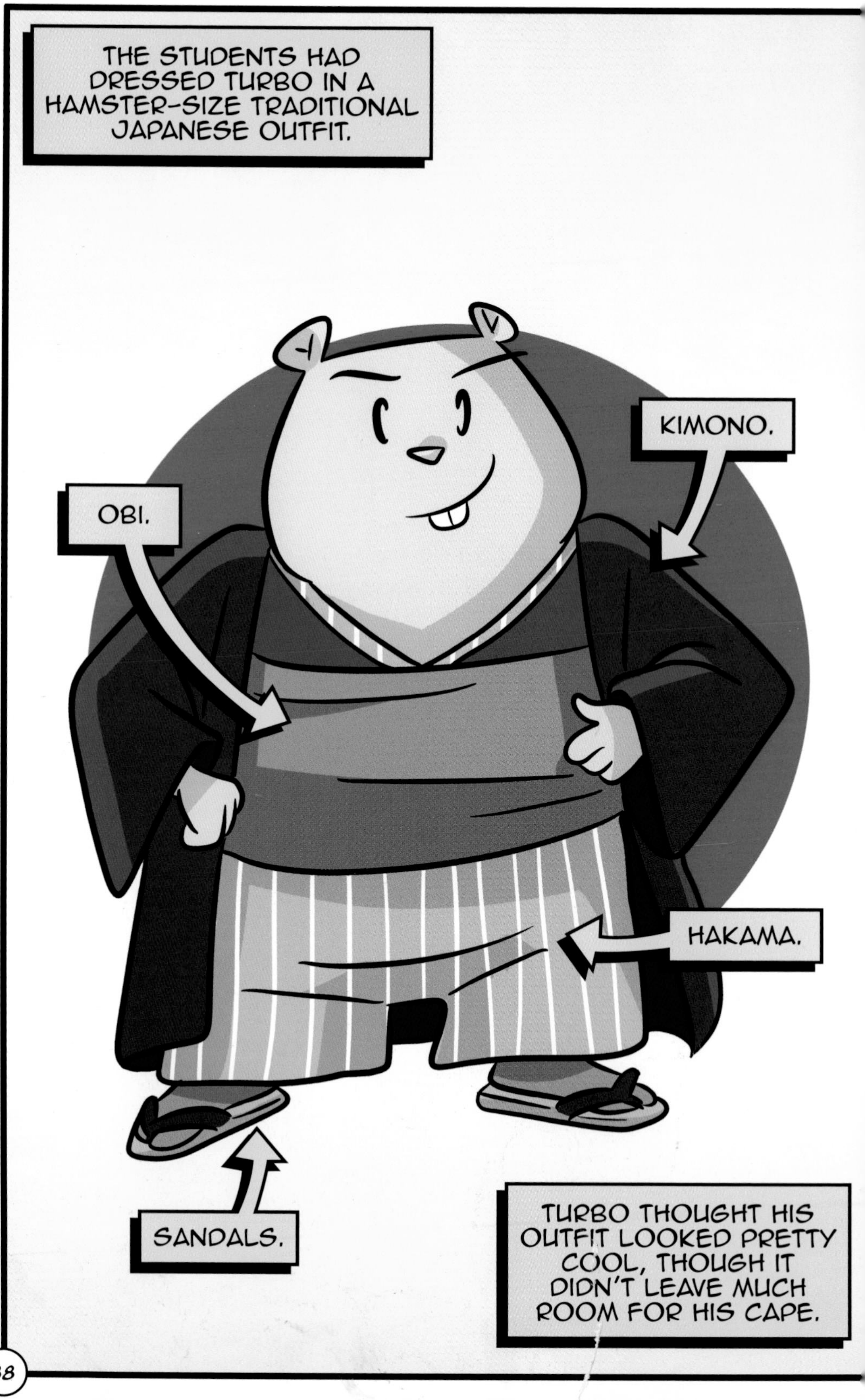
THE STUDENTS HAD DRESSED TURBO IN A HAMSTER-SIZE TRADITIONAL JAPANESE OUTFIT.
KIMONO.
OBI.
HAKAMA.
SANDALS.
TURBO THOUGHT HIS OUTFIT LOOKED PRETTY COOL, THOUGH IT DIDN'T LEAVE MUCH ROOM FOR HIS CAPE.

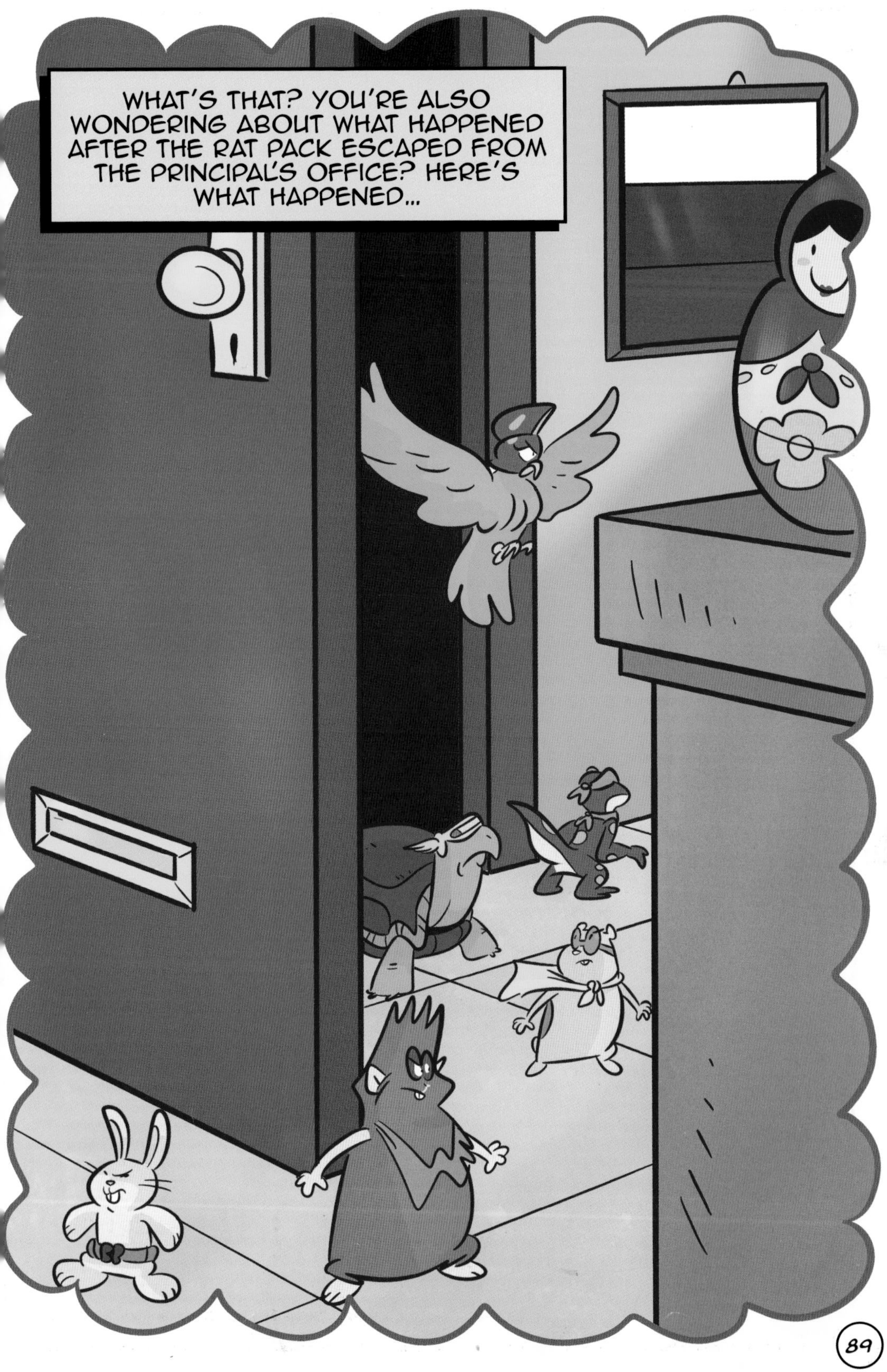
WHAT'S THAT? YOU'RE ALSO WONDERING ABOUT WHAT HAPPENED AFTER THE RAT PACK ESCAPED FROM THE PRINCIPAL'S OFFICE? HERE'S WHAT HAPPENED...

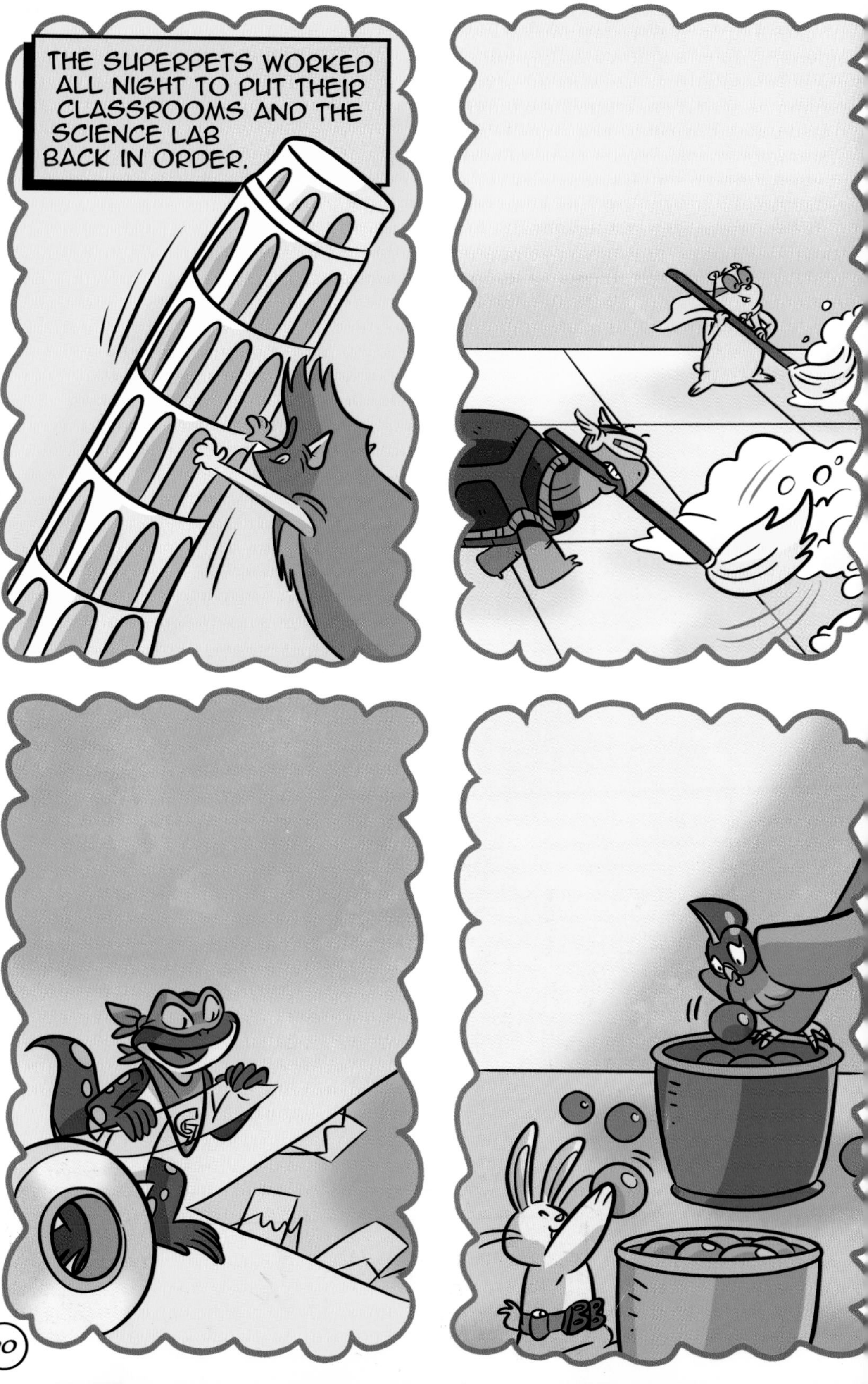
THE SUPERPETS WORKED ALL NIGHT TO PUT THEIR CLASSROOMS AND THE SCIENCE LAB BACK IN ORDER.

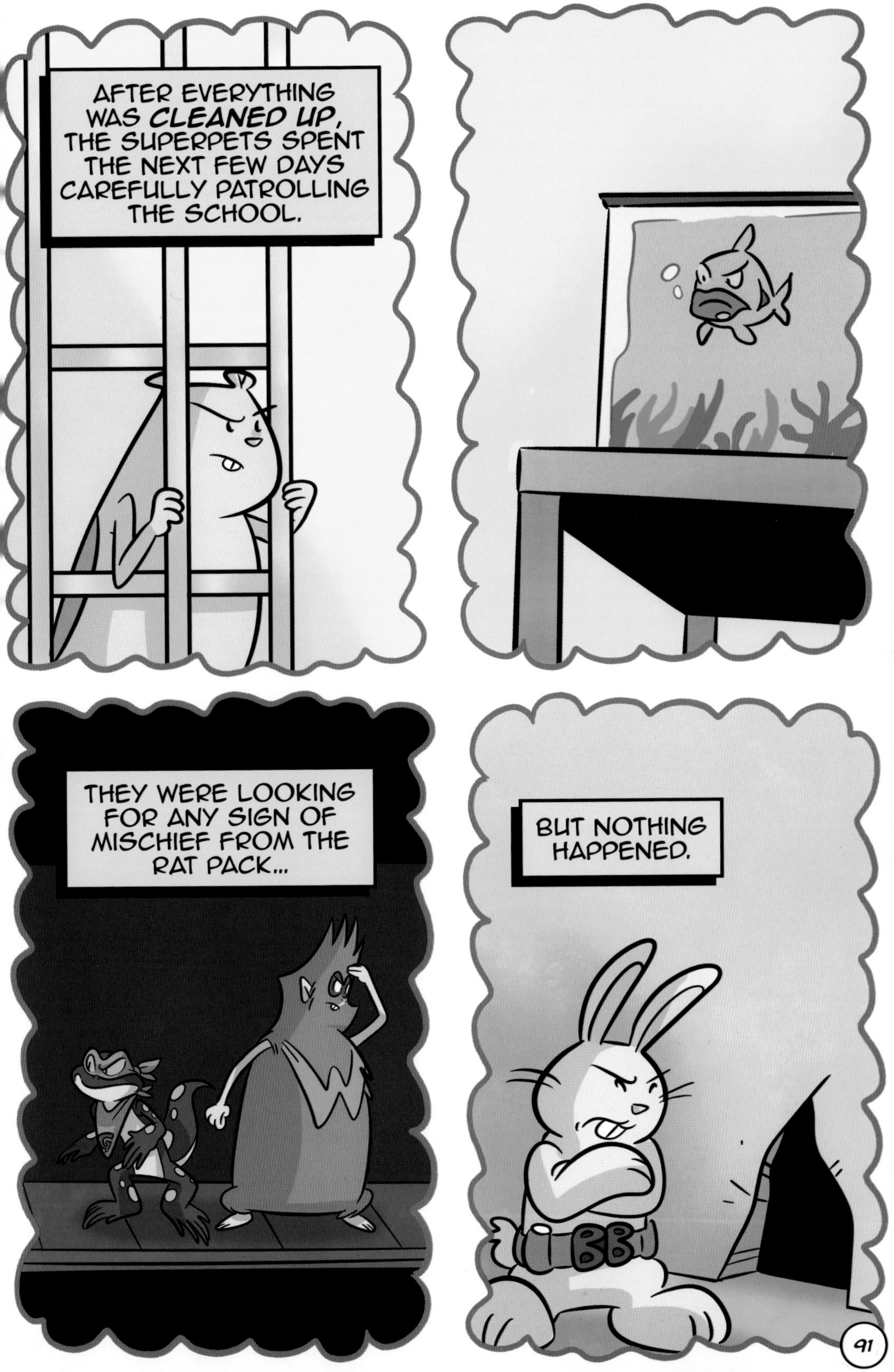
AFTER EVERYTHING WAS CLEANED UP, THE SUPERPETS SPENT THE NEXT FEW DAYS CAREFULLY PATROLLING THE SCHOOL.
THEY WERE LOOKING FOR ANY SIGN OF MISCHIEF FROM THE RAT PACK...
BUT NOTHING HAPPENED.
BB

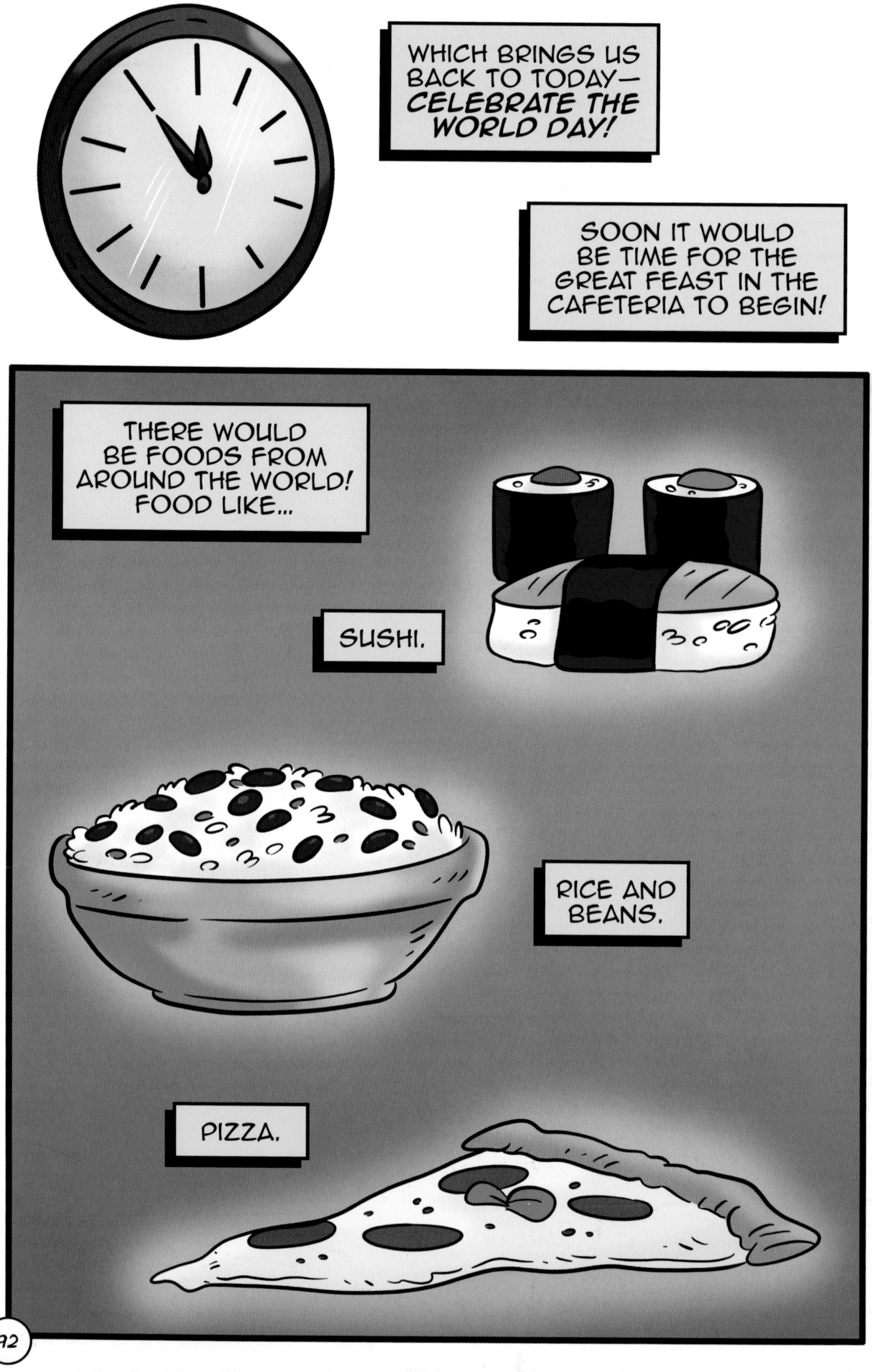

WHICH BRINGS US BACK TO TODAY—*CELEBRATE THE WORLD DAY!*
SOON IT WOULD BE TIME FOR THE GREAT FEAST IN THE CAFETERIA TO BEGIN!
THERE WOULD BE FOODS FROM AROUND THE WORLD! FOOD LIKE...
SUSHI.
RICE AND BEANS.
PIZZA.

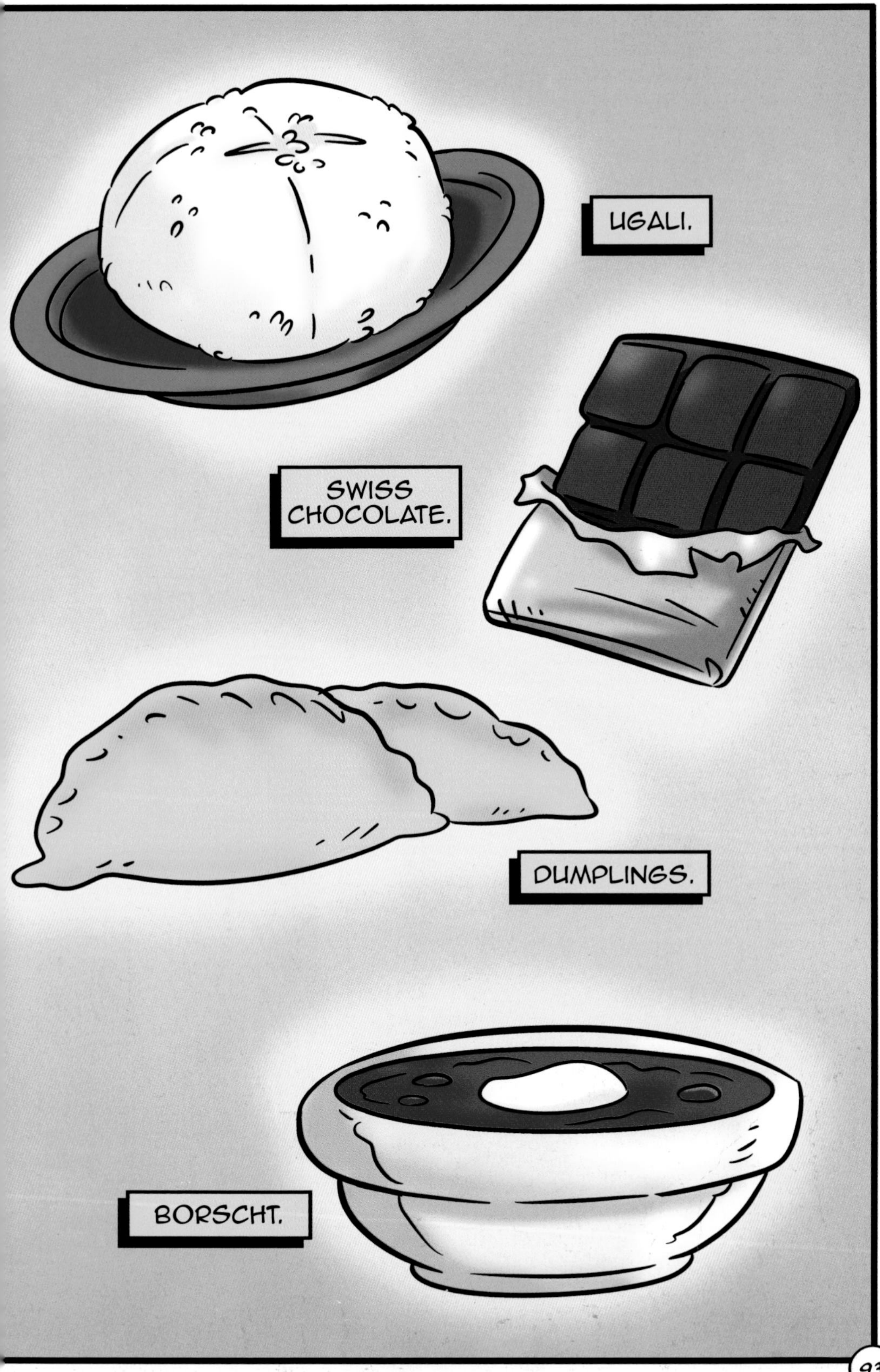
UGALI.
SWISS CHOCOLATE.
DUMPLINGS.
BORSCHT.

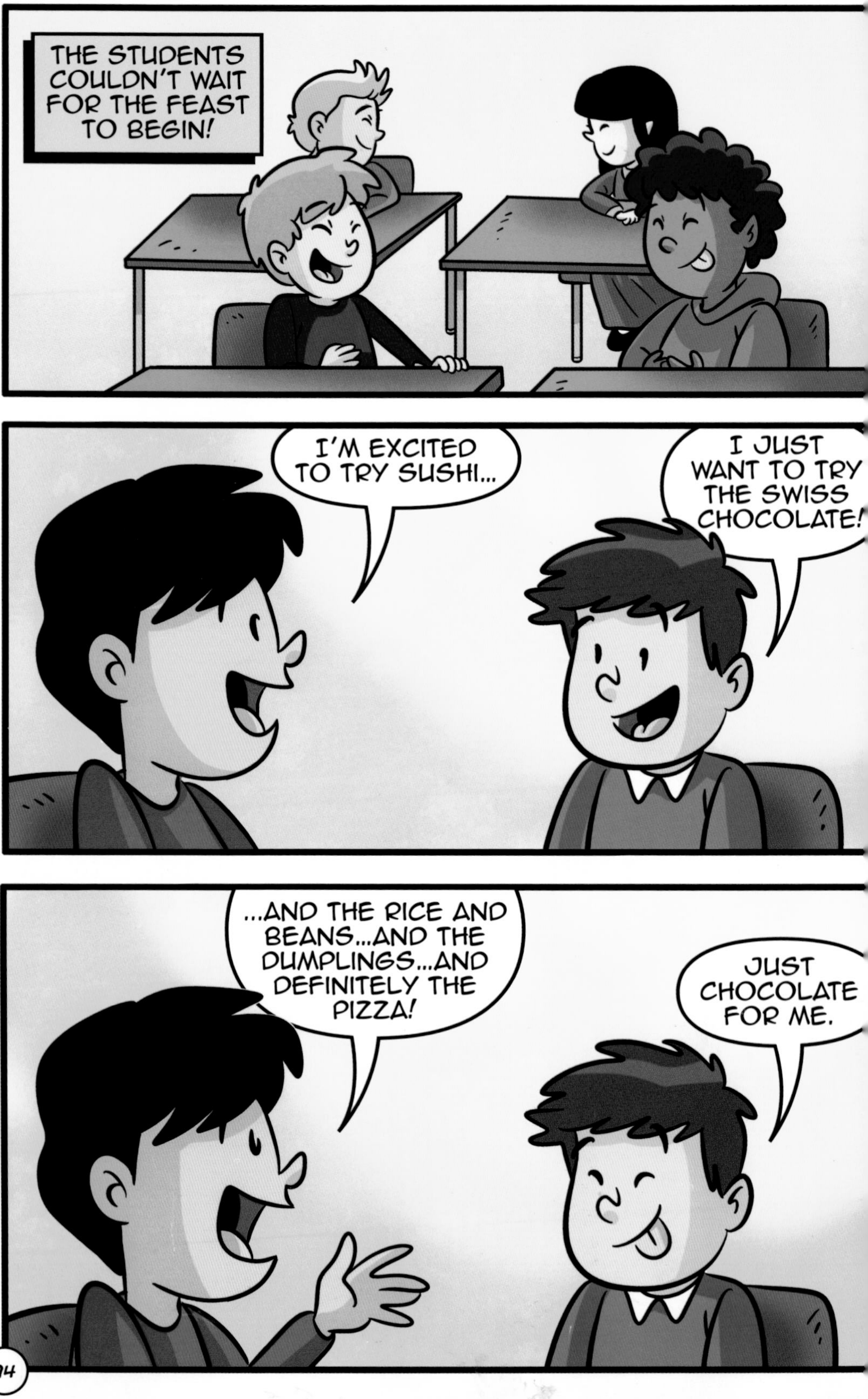
THE STUDENTS COULDN'T WAIT FOR THE FEAST TO BEGIN!
I'M EXCITED TO TRY SUSHI...
I JUST WANT TO TRY THE SWISS CHOCOLATE!
...AND THE RICE AND BEANS...AND THE DUMPLINGS...AND DEFINITELY THE PIZZA!
JUST CHOCOLATE FOR ME.

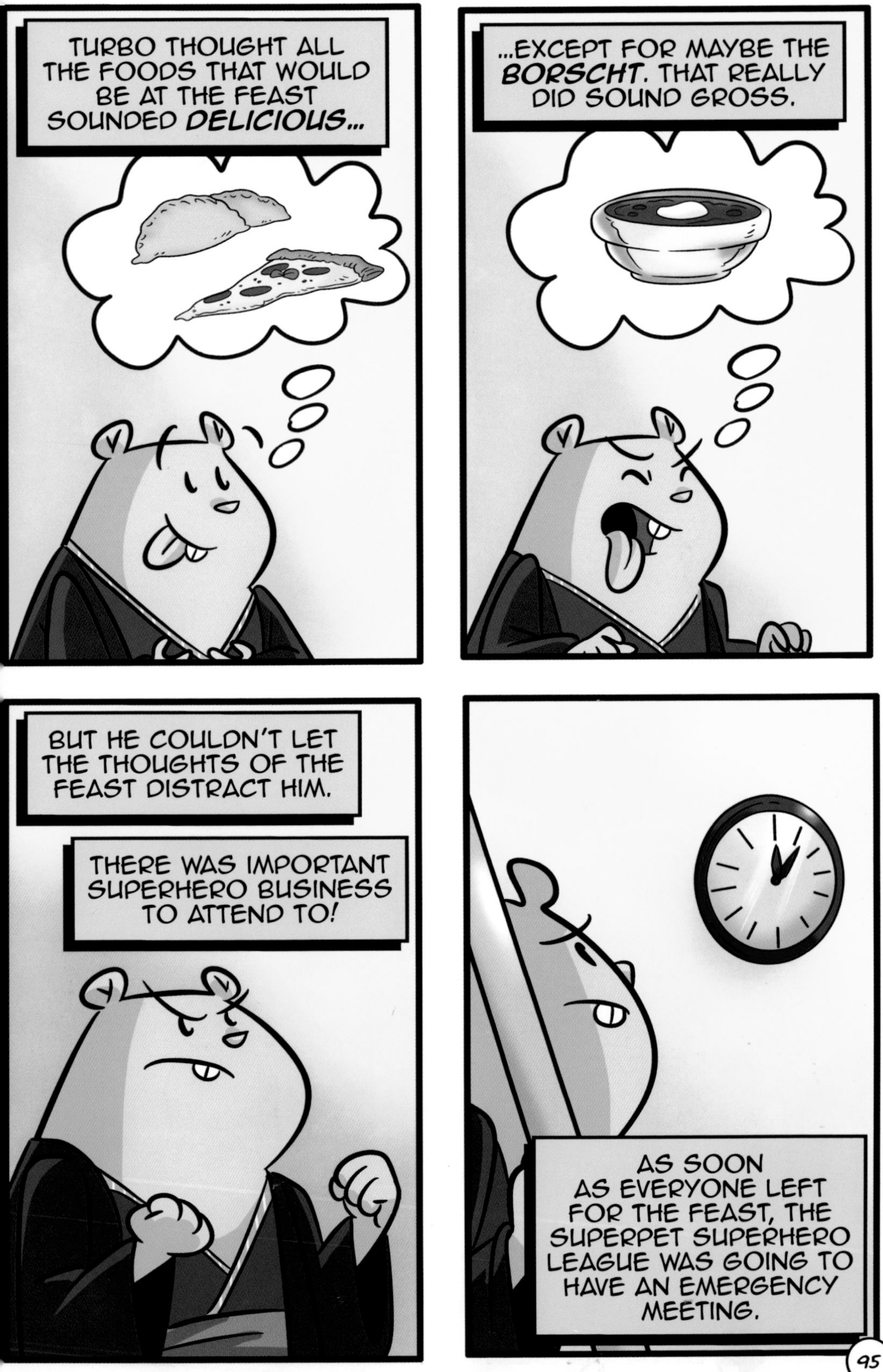
TURBO THOUGHT ALL THE FOODS THAT WOULD BE AT THE FEAST SOUNDED DELICIOUS...
...EXCEPT FOR MAYBE THE BORSCHT. THAT REALLY DID SOUND GROSS.
BUT HE COULDN'T LET THE THOUGHTS OF THE FEAST DISTRACT HIM.
THERE WAS IMPORTANT SUPERHERO BUSINESS TO ATTEND TO!
AS SOON AS EVERYONE LEFT FOR THE FEAST, THE SUPERPET SUPERHERO LEAGUE WAS GOING TO HAVE AN EMERGENCY MEETING.

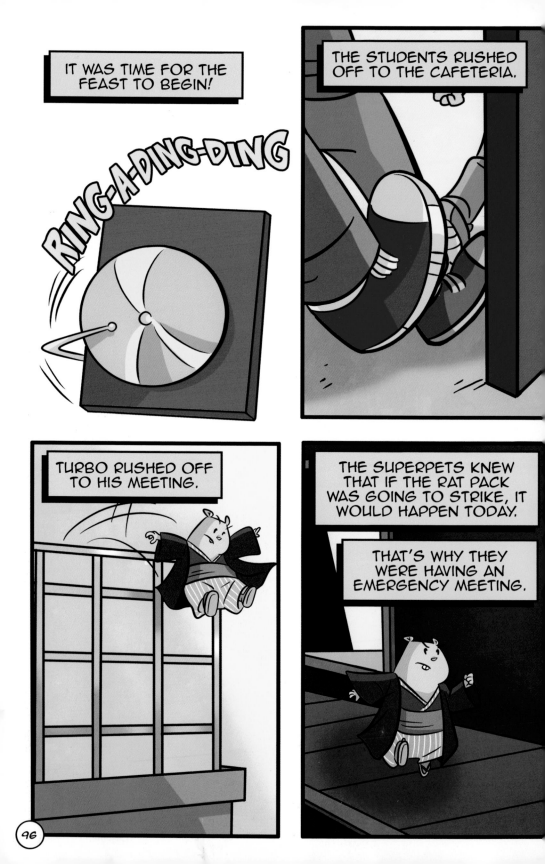

IT WAS TIME FOR THE FEAST TO BEGIN!

RING-A-DING-DING

THE STUDENTS RUSHED OFF TO THE CAFETERIA.

TURBO RUSHED OFF TO HIS MEETING.

THE SUPERPETS KNEW THAT IF THE RAT PACK WAS GOING TO STRIKE, IT WOULD HAPPEN TODAY.

THAT'S WHY THEY WERE HAVING AN EMERGENCY MEETING.

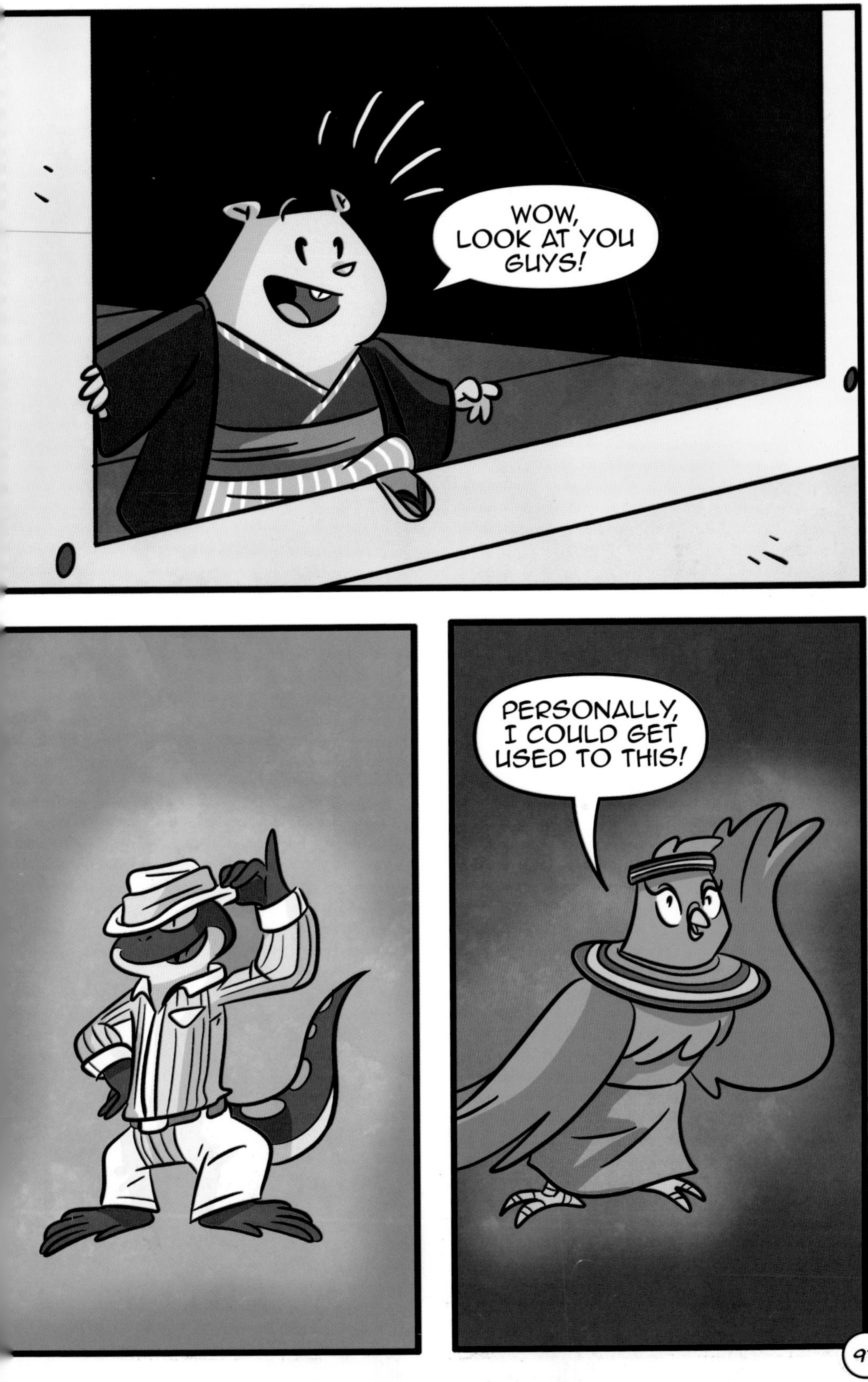
WOW, LOOK AT YOU GUYS!
PERSONALLY, I COULD GET USED TO THIS!

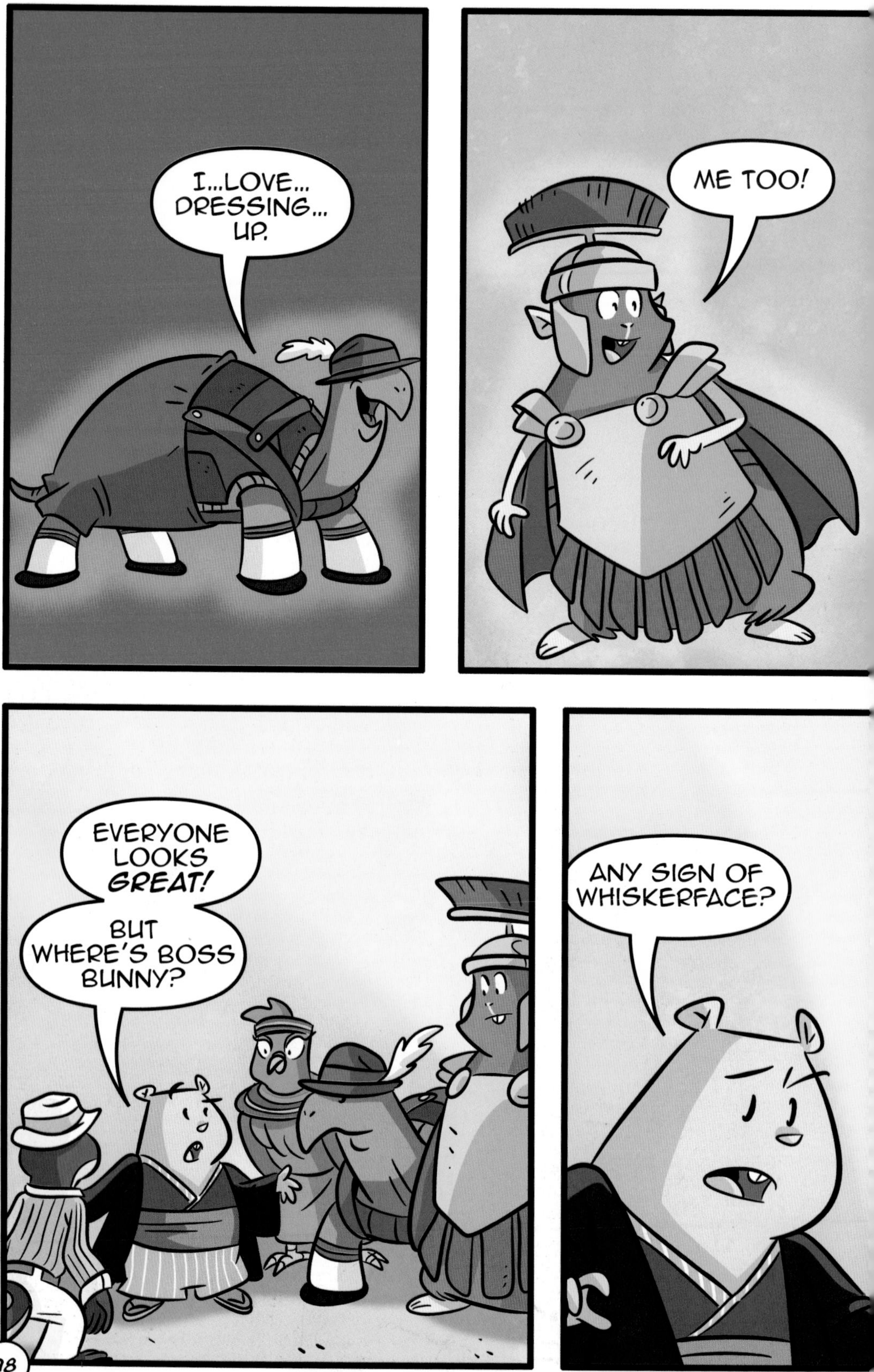
I...LOVE... DRESSING... UP.
ME TOO!
EVERYONE LOOKS *GREAT!*
BUT WHERE'S BOSS BUNNY?
ANY SIGN OF WHISKERFACE?

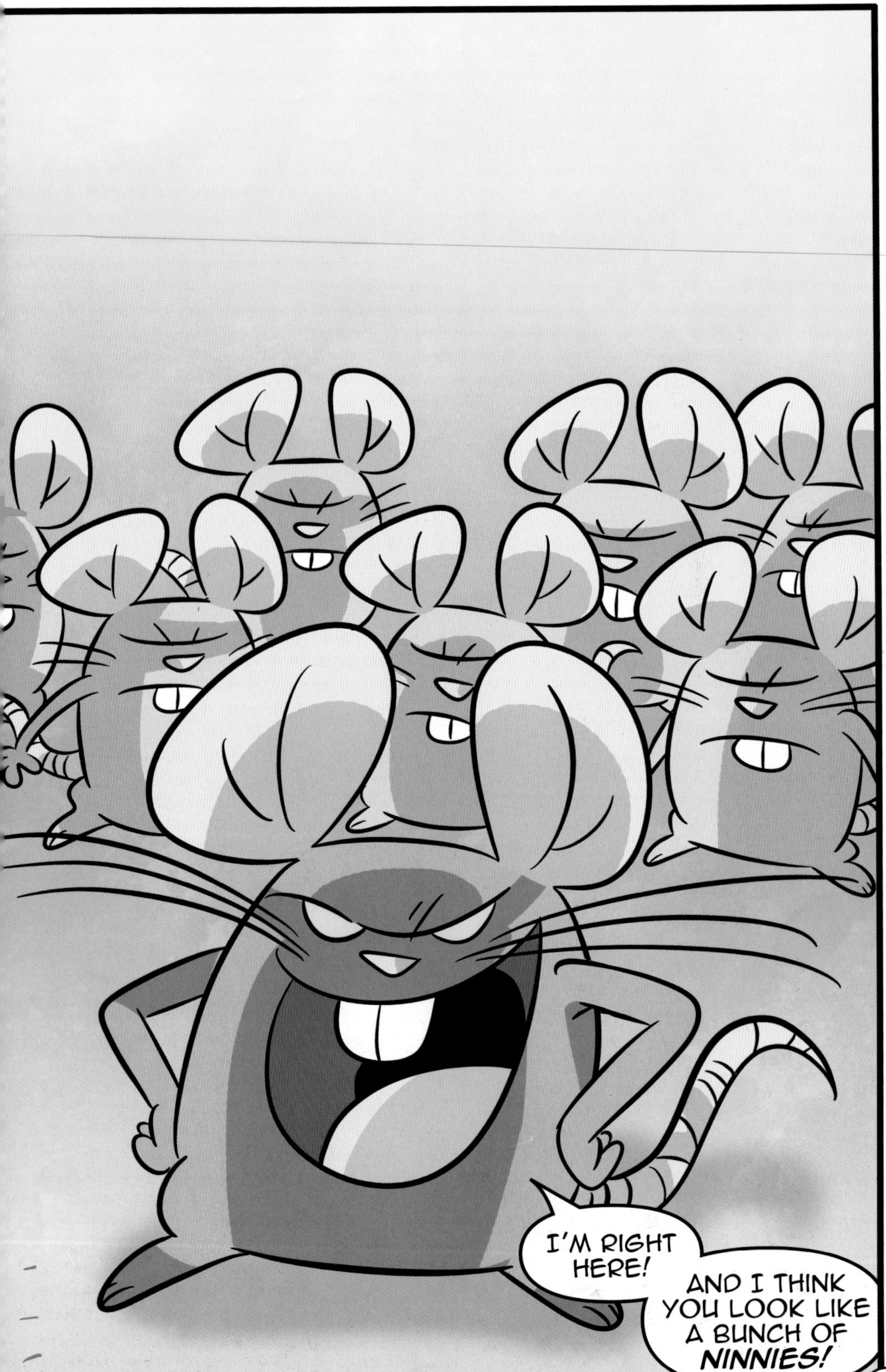
I'M RIGHT HERE!
AND I THINK YOU LOOK LIKE A BUNCH OF *NINNIES!*

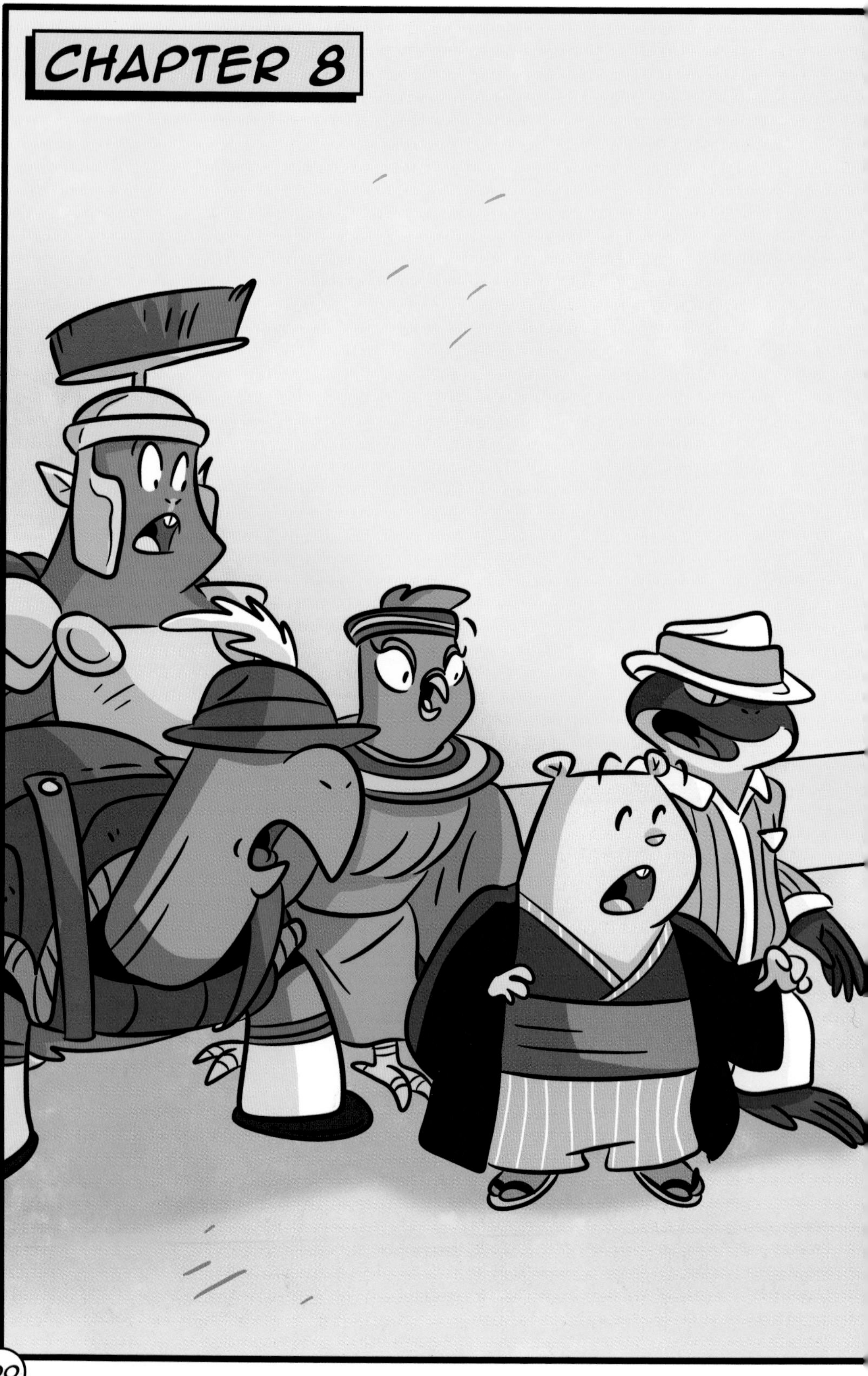
CHAPTER 8

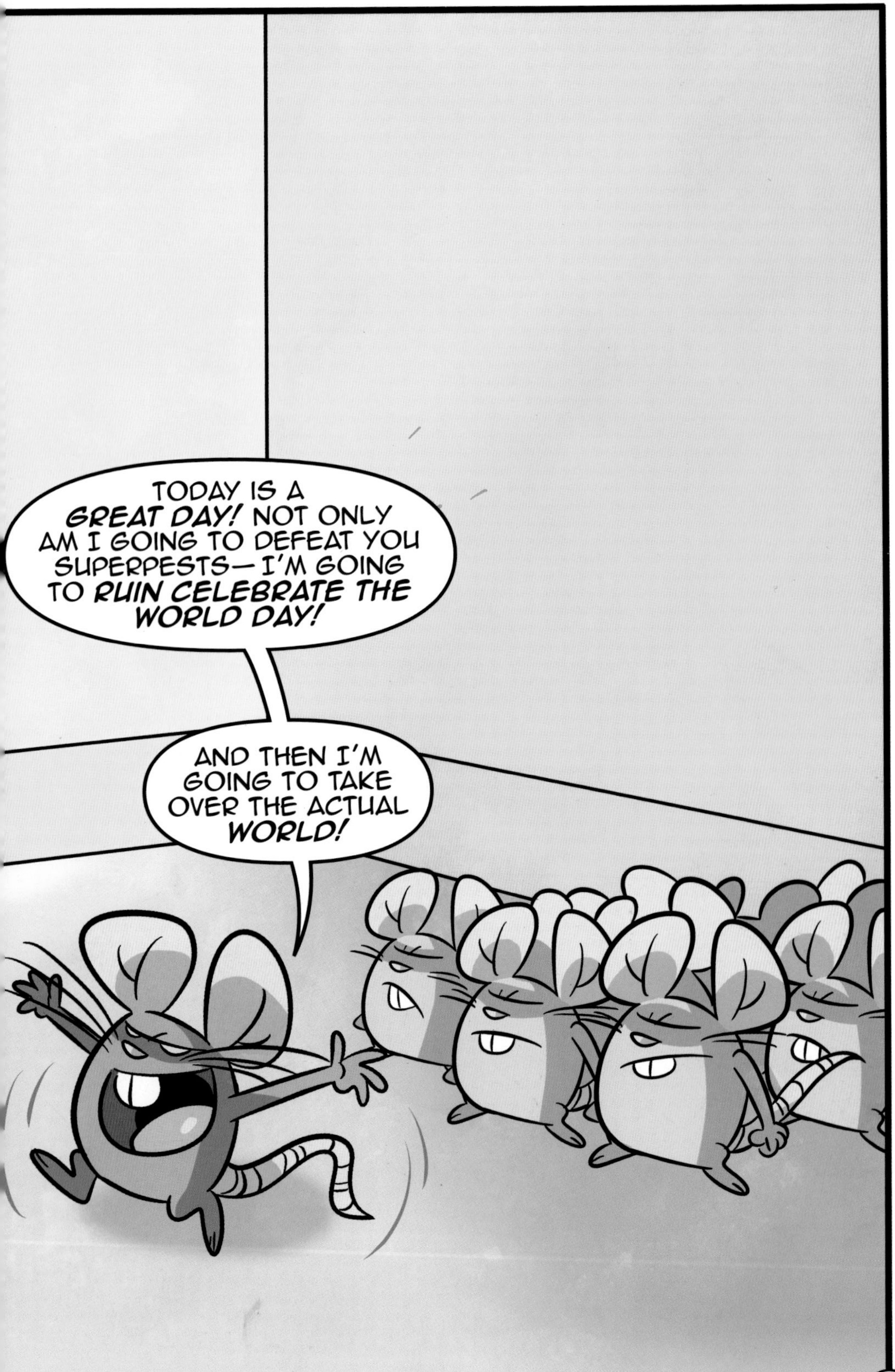
TODAY IS A GREAT DAY! NOT ONLY AM I GOING TO DEFEAT YOU SUPERPESTS—I'M GOING TO RUIN CELEBRATE THE WORLD DAY!
AND THEN I'M GOING TO TAKE OVER THE ACTUAL WORLD!

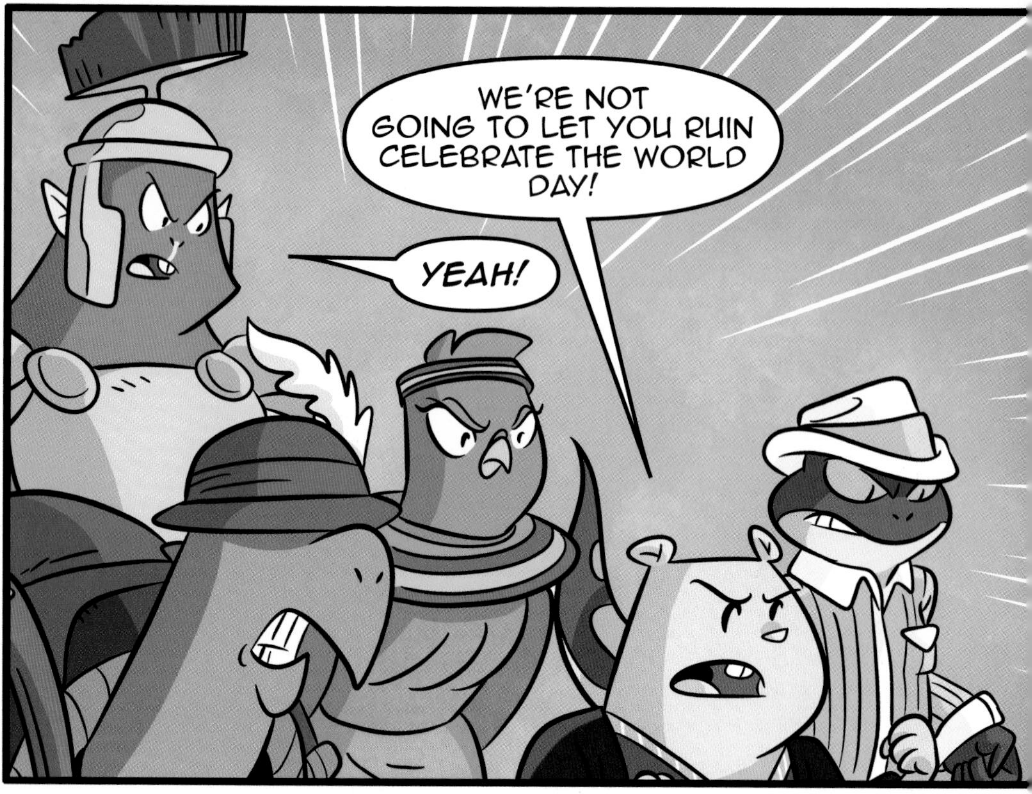
WE'RE NOT GOING TO LET YOU RUIN CELEBRATE THE WORLD DAY!
YEAH!

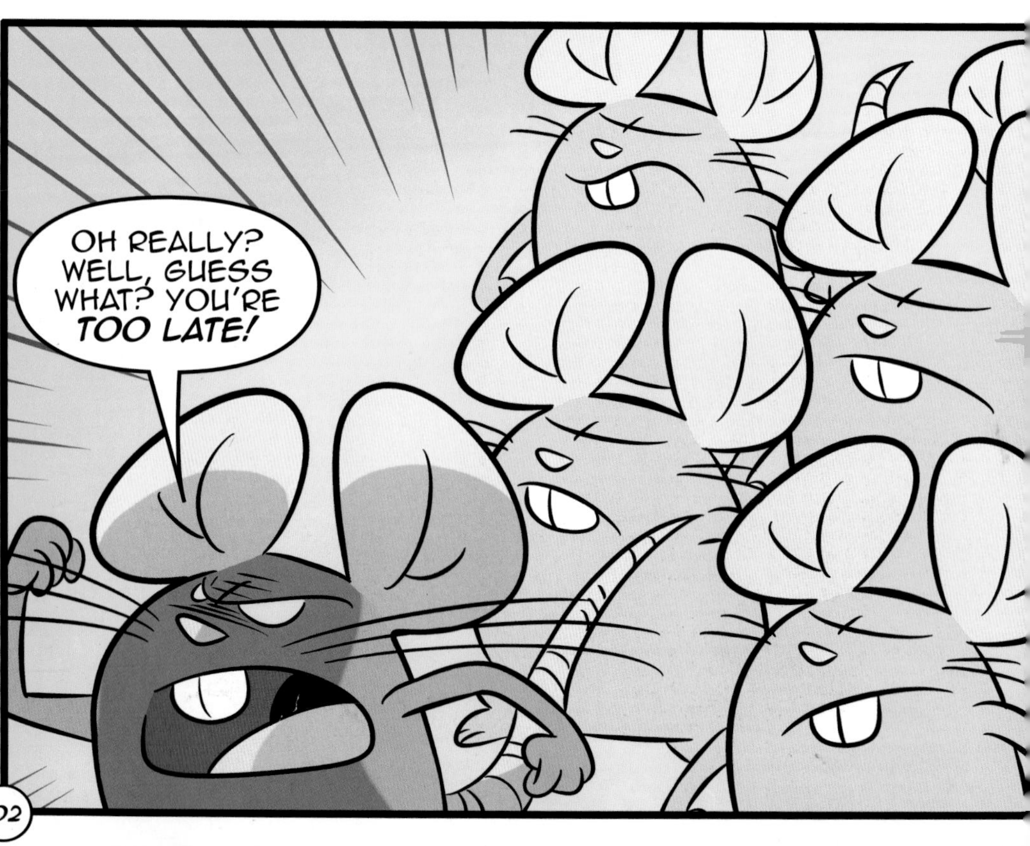
OH REALLY? WELL, GUESS WHAT? YOU'RE *TOO LATE!*

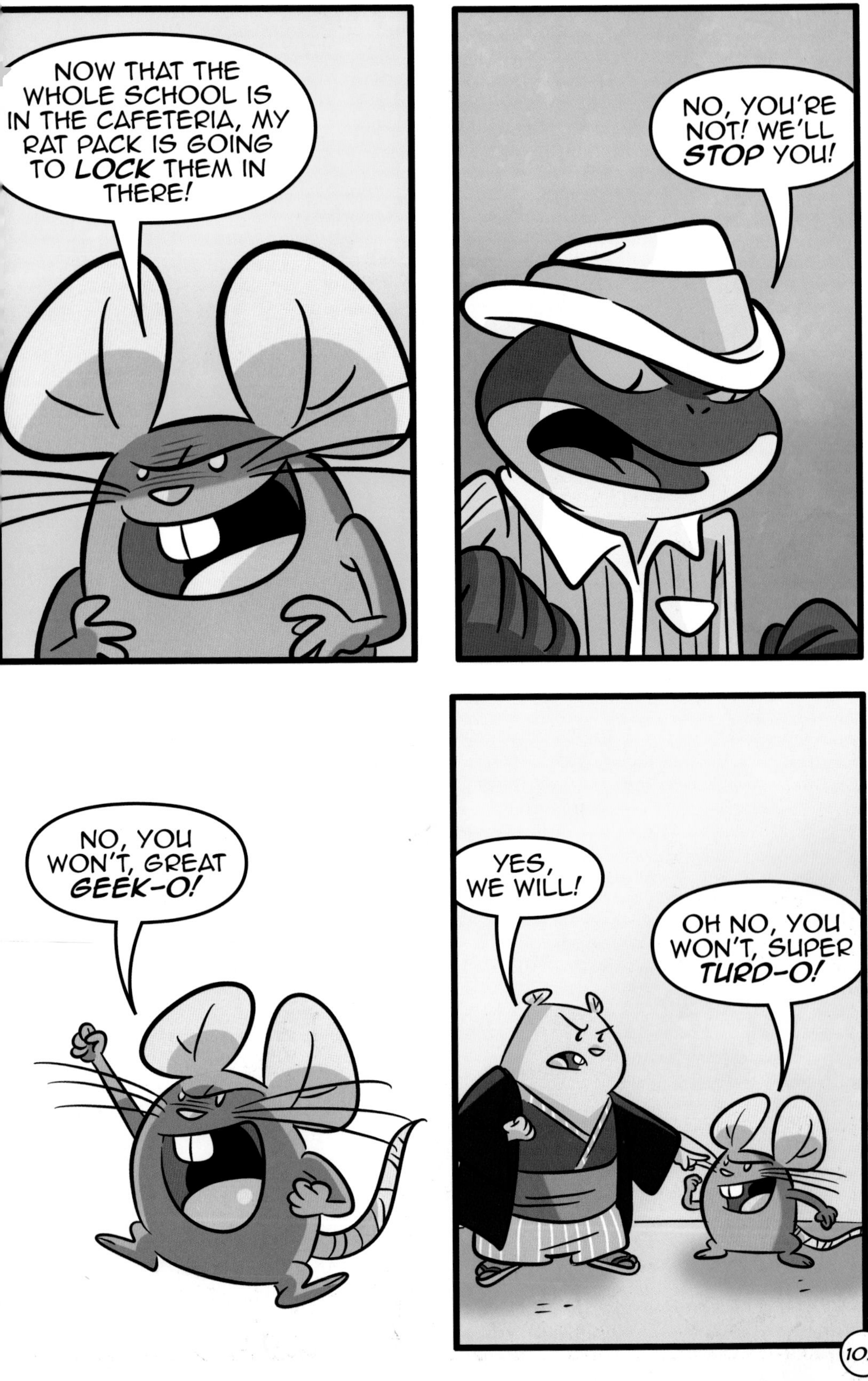
NOW THAT THE WHOLE SCHOOL IS IN THE CAFETERIA, MY RAT PACK IS GOING TO LOCK THEM IN THERE!
NO, YOU'RE NOT! WE'LL STOP YOU!
NO, YOU WON'T, GREAT GEEK-O!
YES, WE WILL!
OH NO, YOU WON'T, SUPER TURD-O!

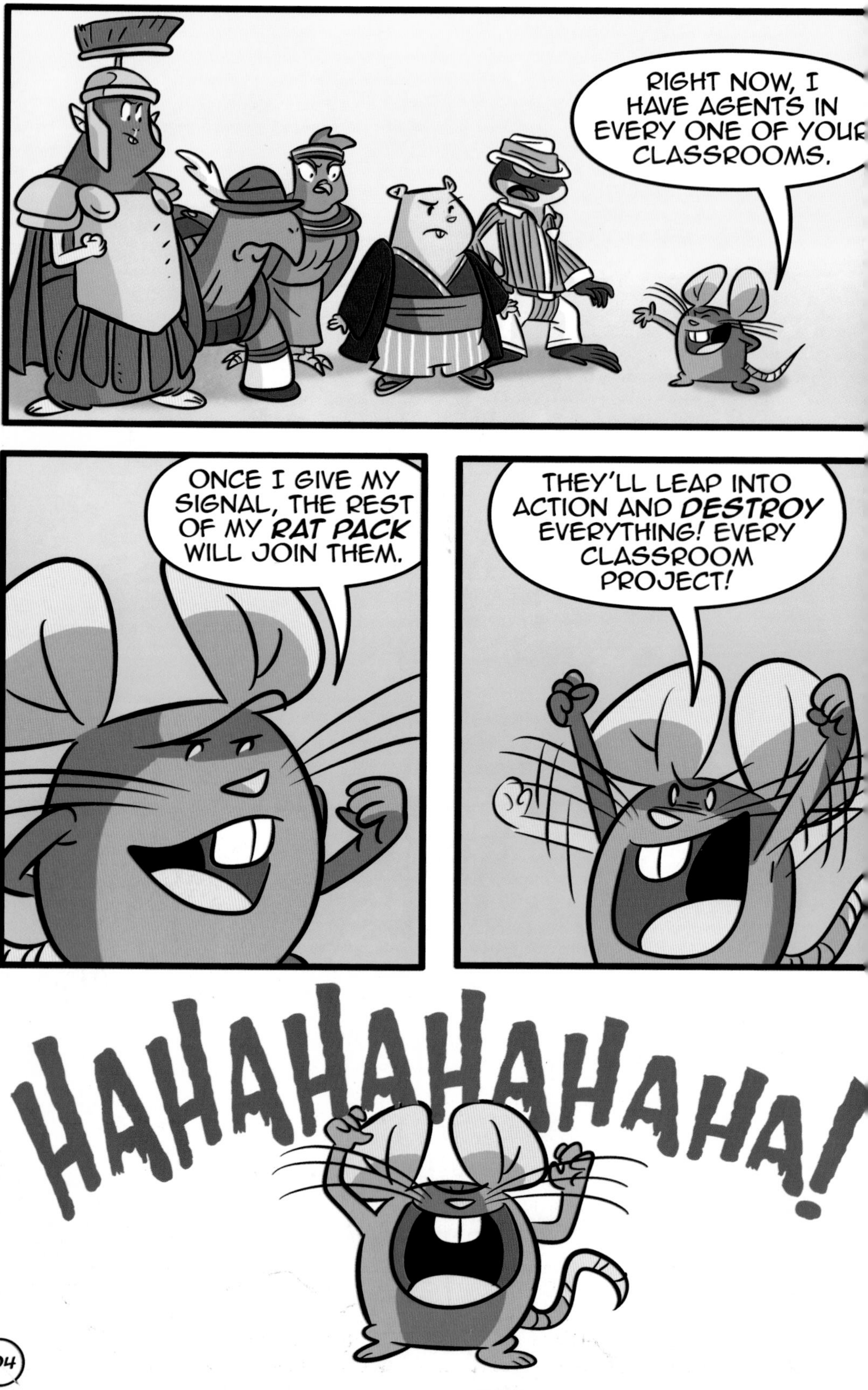
RIGHT NOW, I HAVE AGENTS IN EVERY ONE OF YOUR CLASSROOMS.
ONCE I GIVE MY SIGNAL, THE REST OF MY *RAT PACK* WILL JOIN THEM.
THEY'LL LEAP INTO ACTION AND *DESTROY* EVERYTHING! EVERY CLASSROOM PROJECT!
HAHAHAHAHAHAHA!

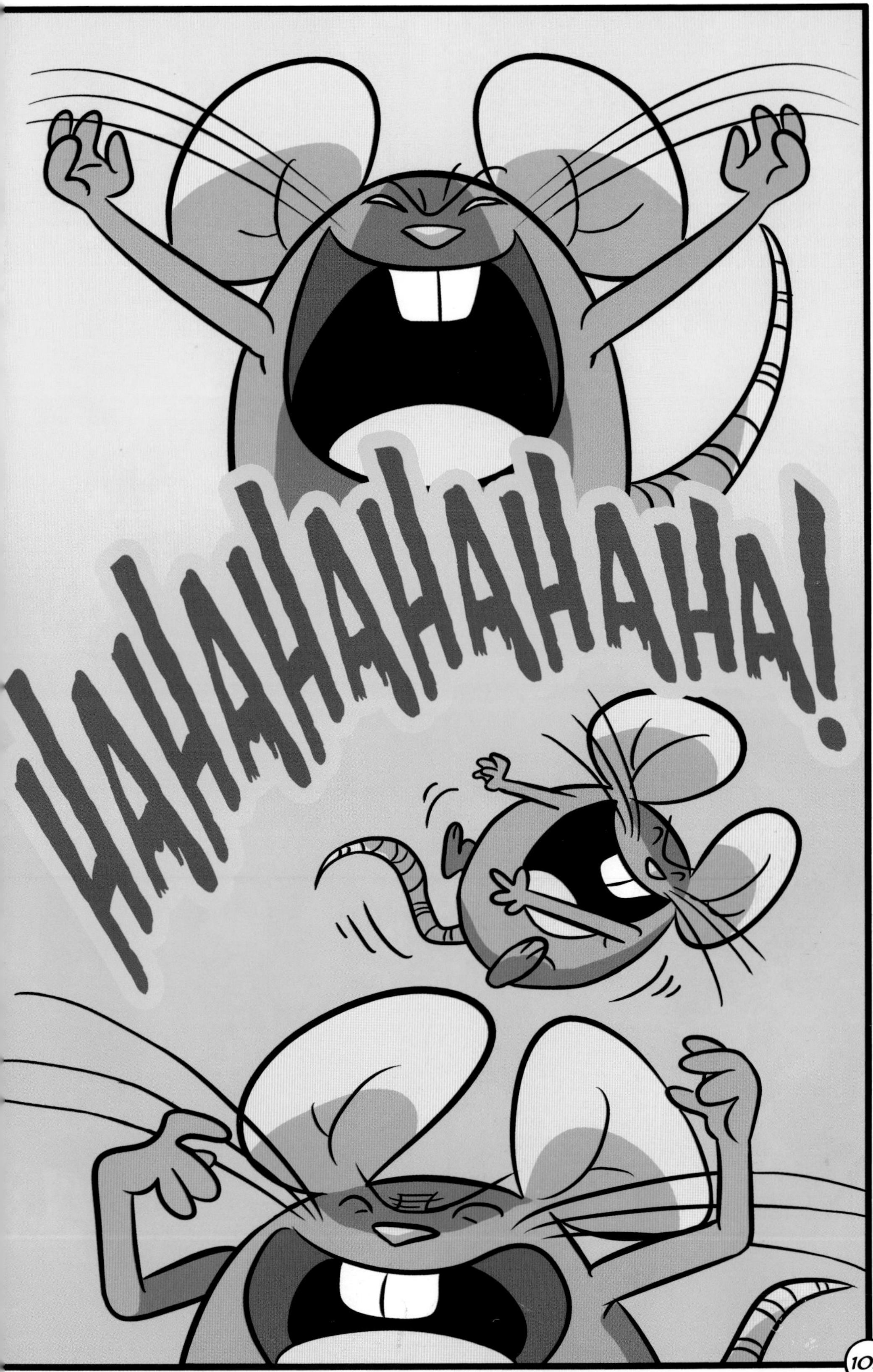
HAHAHAHAHAHAHAHA!

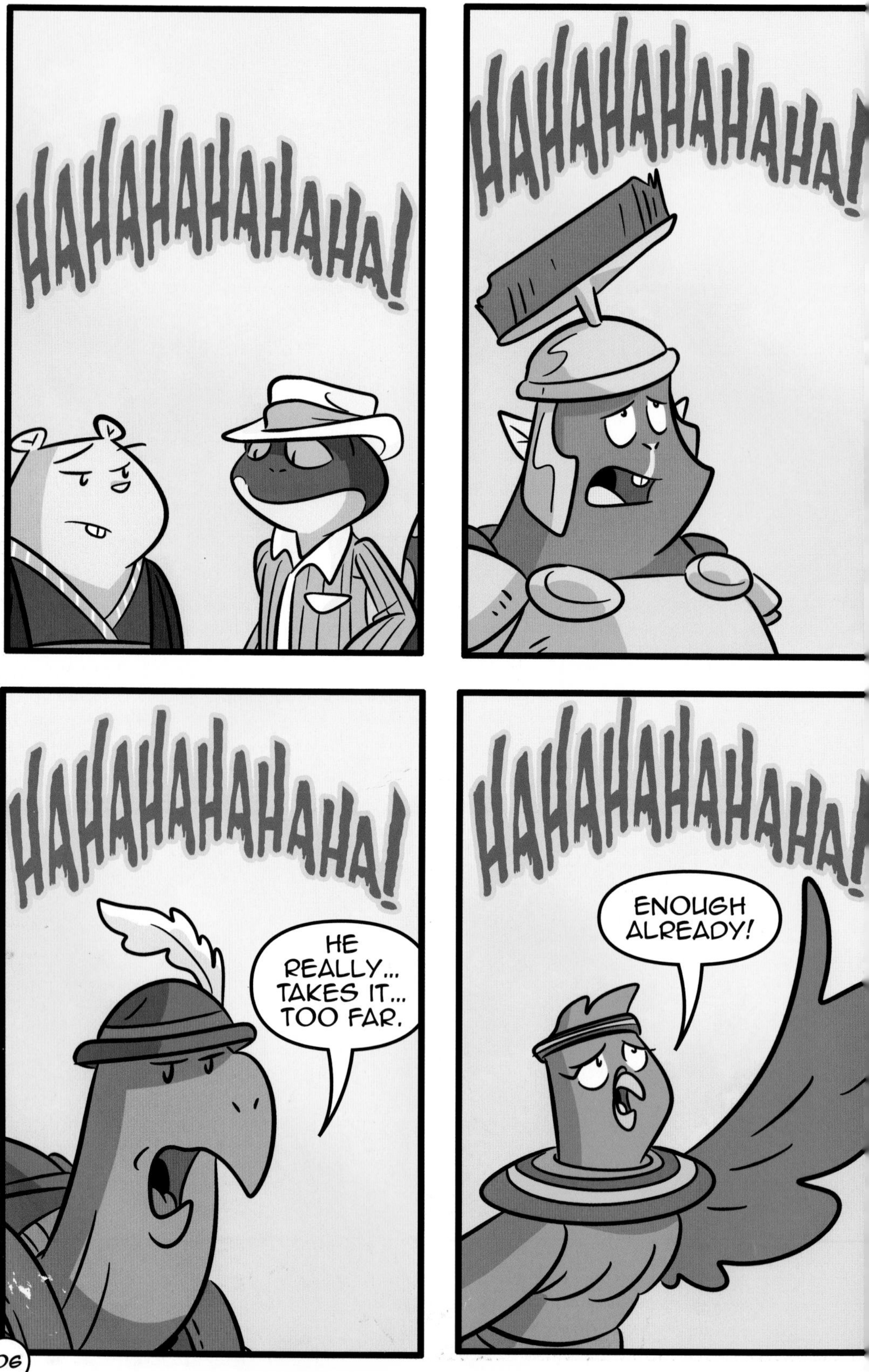
HAHAHAHAHAHAHA!
HAHAHAHAHAHAHA!
HAHAHAHAHAHAHA!
HE REALLY... TAKES IT... TOO FAR.
HAHAHAHAHAHAHA!
ENOUGH ALREADY!

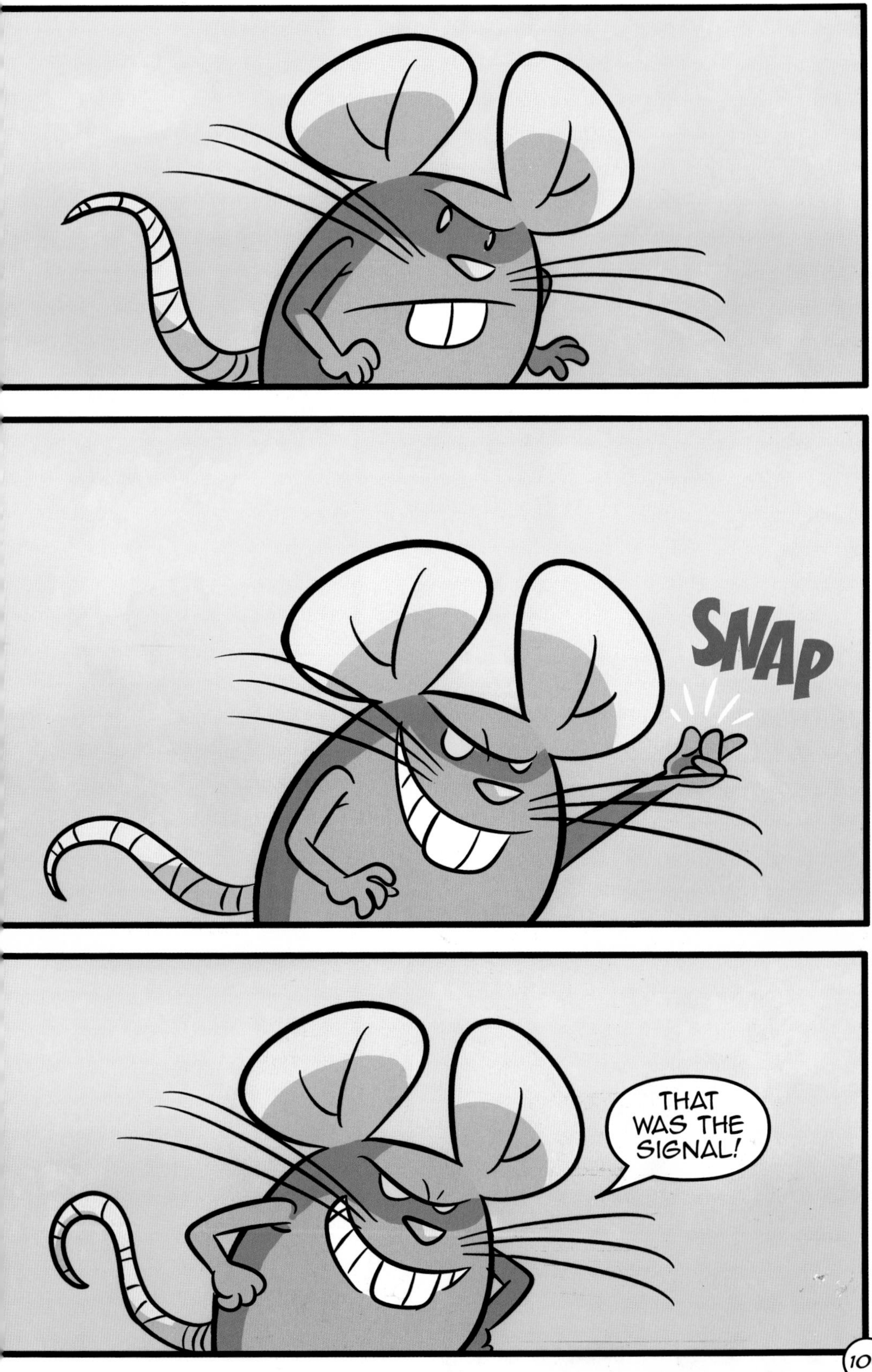
SNAP
THAT WAS THE SIGNAL!

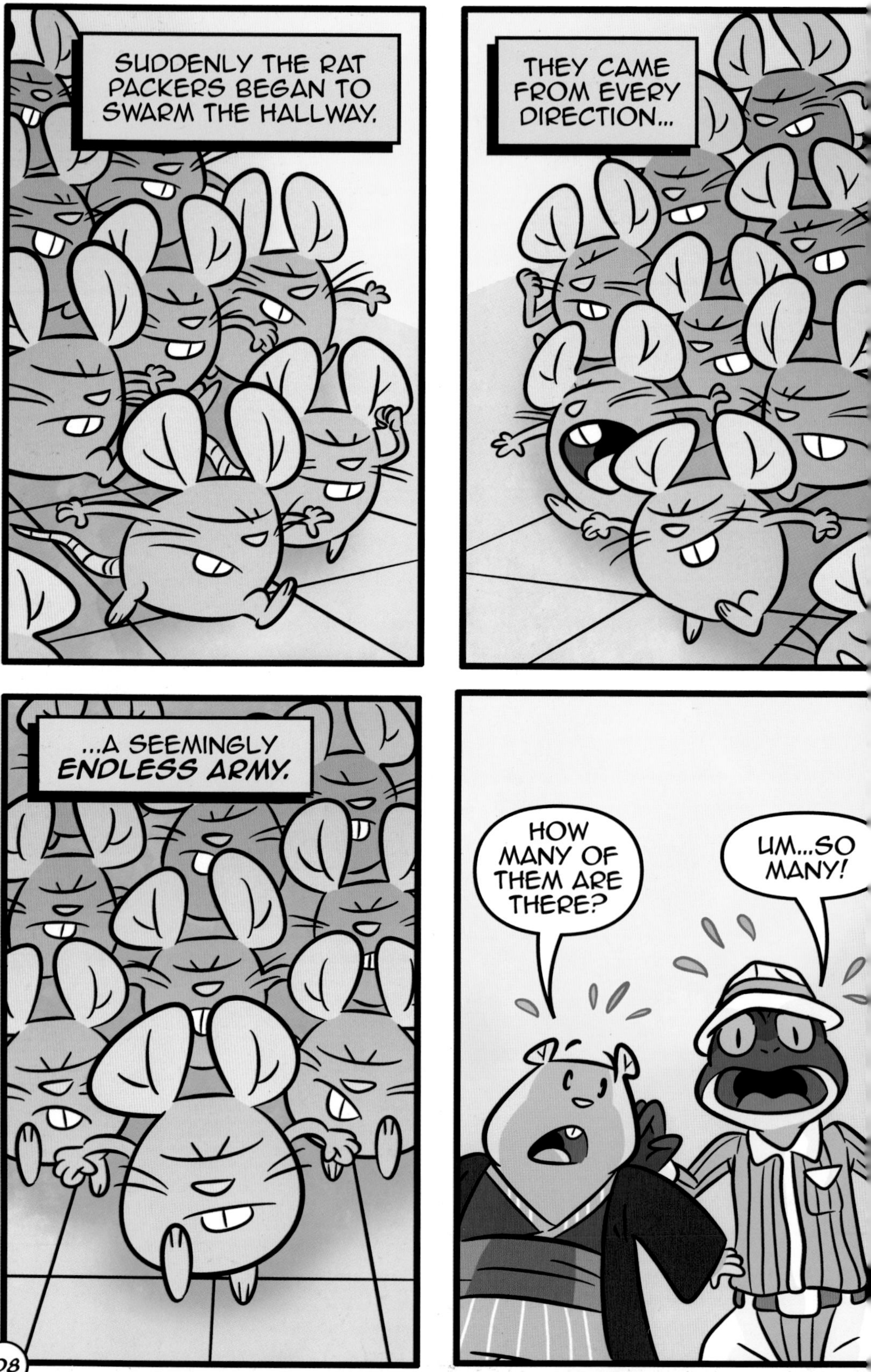
SUDDENLY THE RAT PACKERS BEGAN TO SWARM THE HALLWAY.
THEY CAME FROM EVERY DIRECTION...
...A SEEMINGLY ENDLESS ARMY.
HOW MANY OF THEM ARE THERE?
UM...SO MANY!

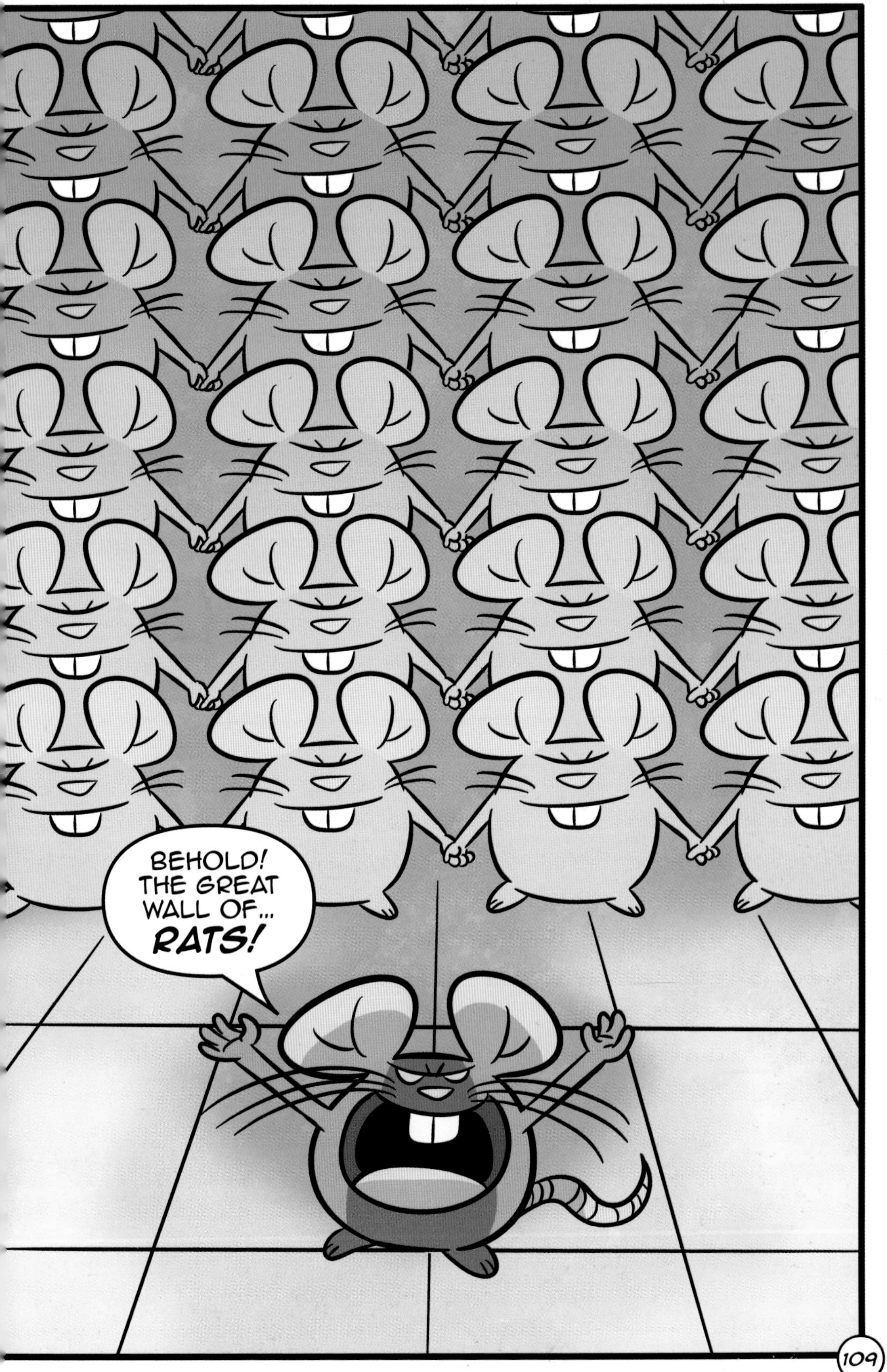
BEHOLD! THE GREAT WALL OF... RATS!

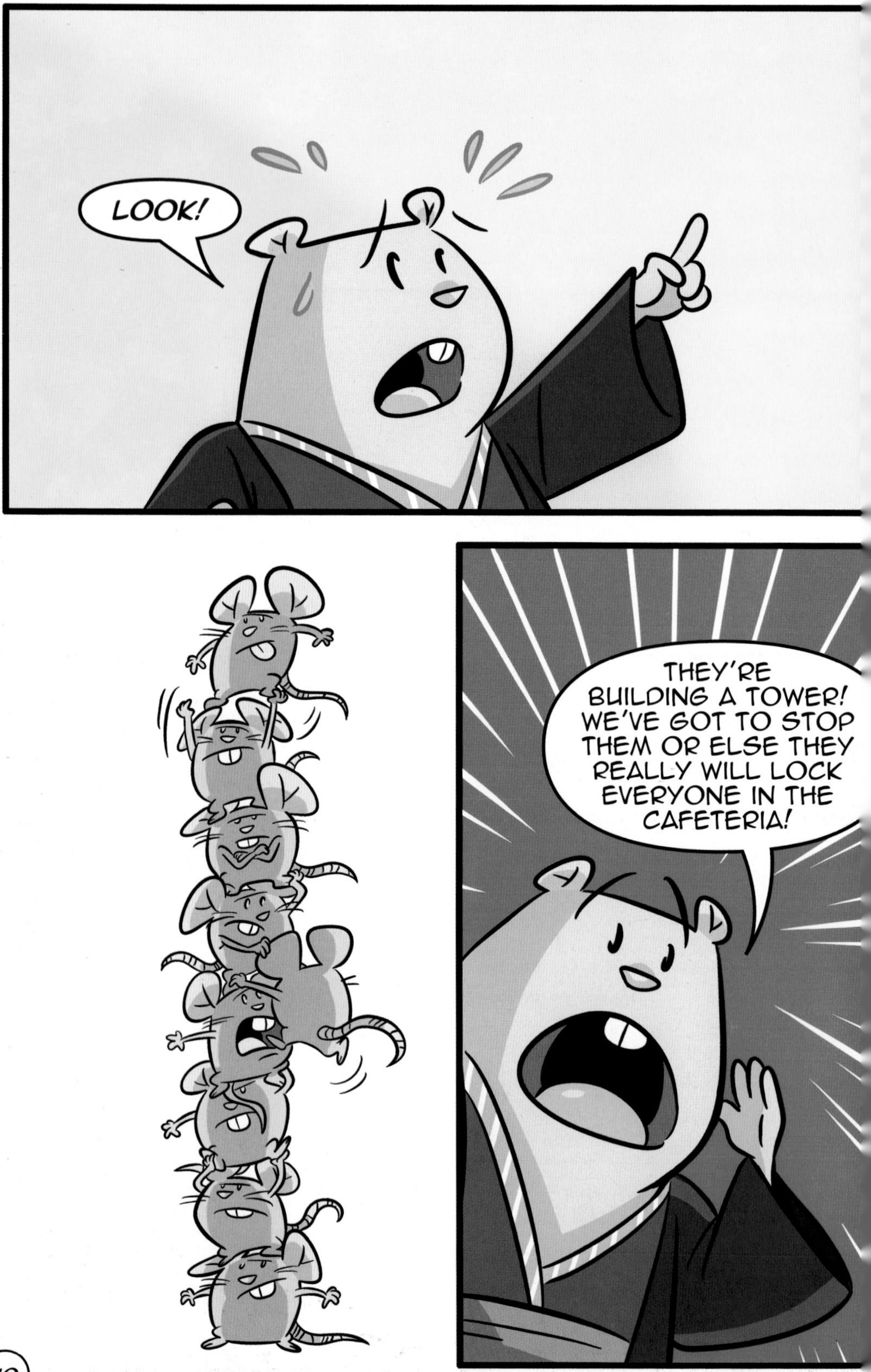
LOOK!
THEY'RE BUILDING A TOWER! WE'VE GOT TO STOP THEM OR ELSE THEY REALLY WILL LOCK EVERYONE IN THE CAFETERIA!

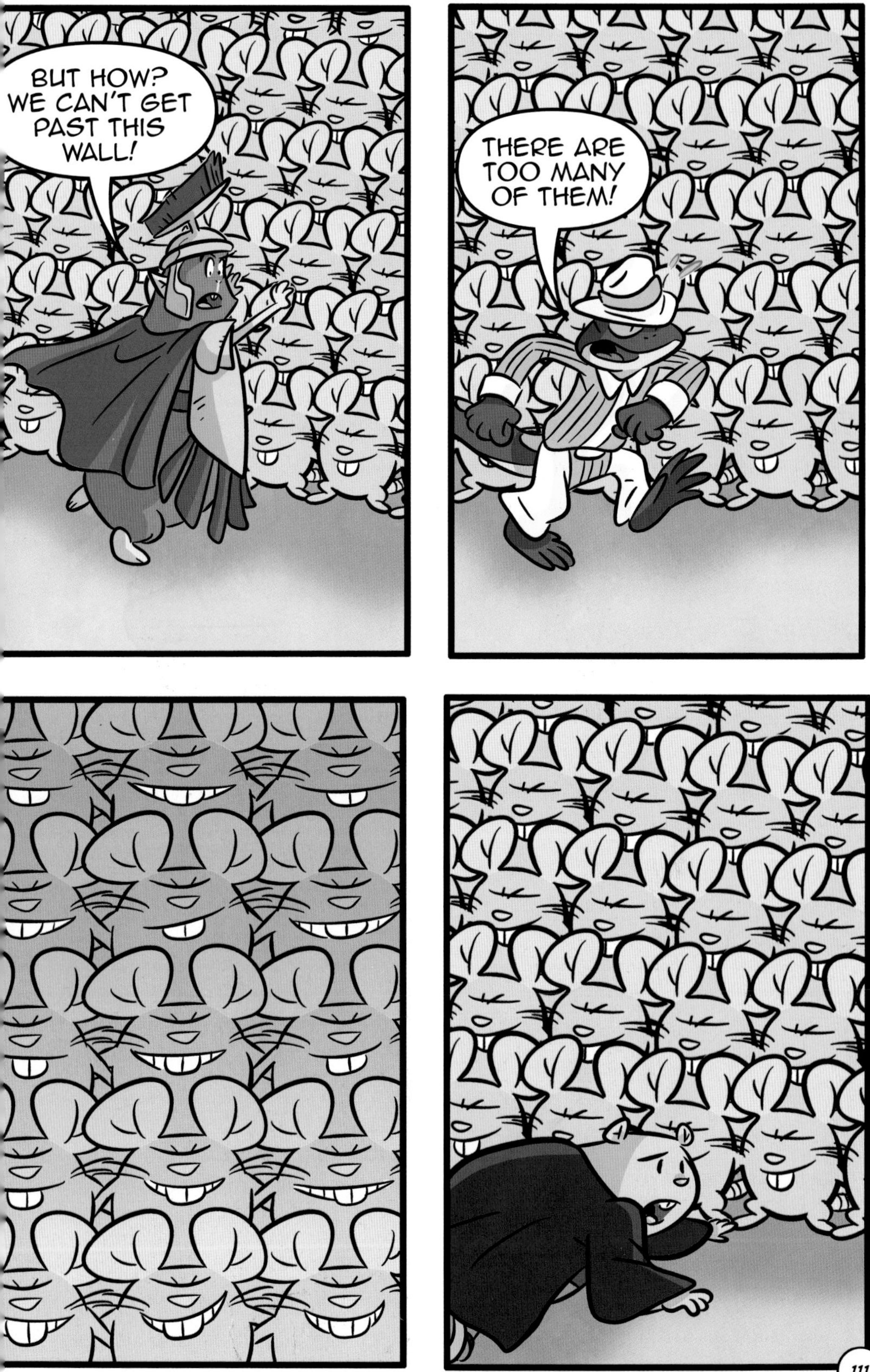
BUT HOW? WE CAN'T GET PAST THIS WALL!
THERE ARE TOO MANY OF THEM!

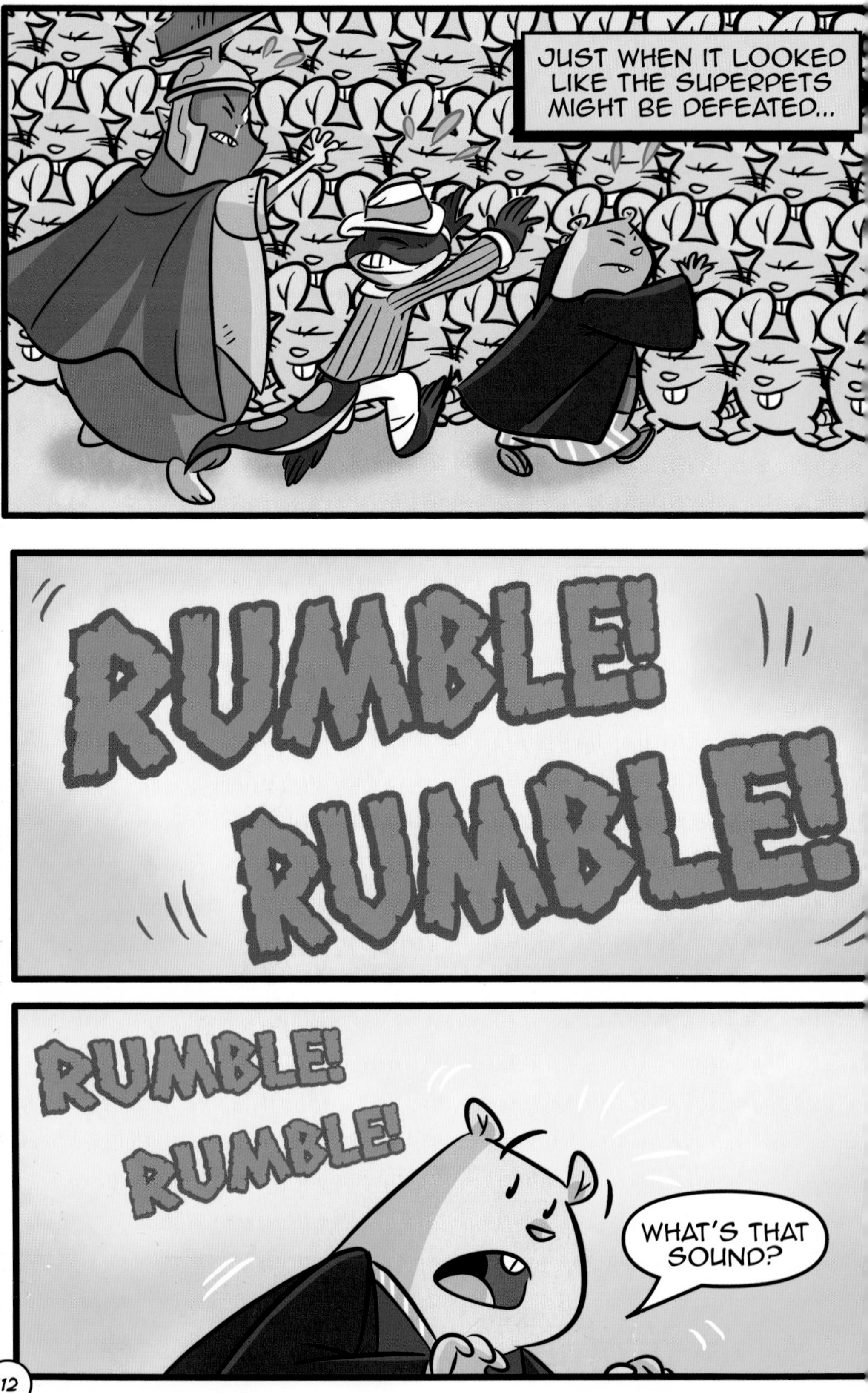
JUST WHEN IT LOOKED LIKE THE SUPERPETS MIGHT BE DEFEATED...
RUMBLE! RUMBLE!
RUMBLE! RUMBLE!
WHAT'S THAT SOUND?

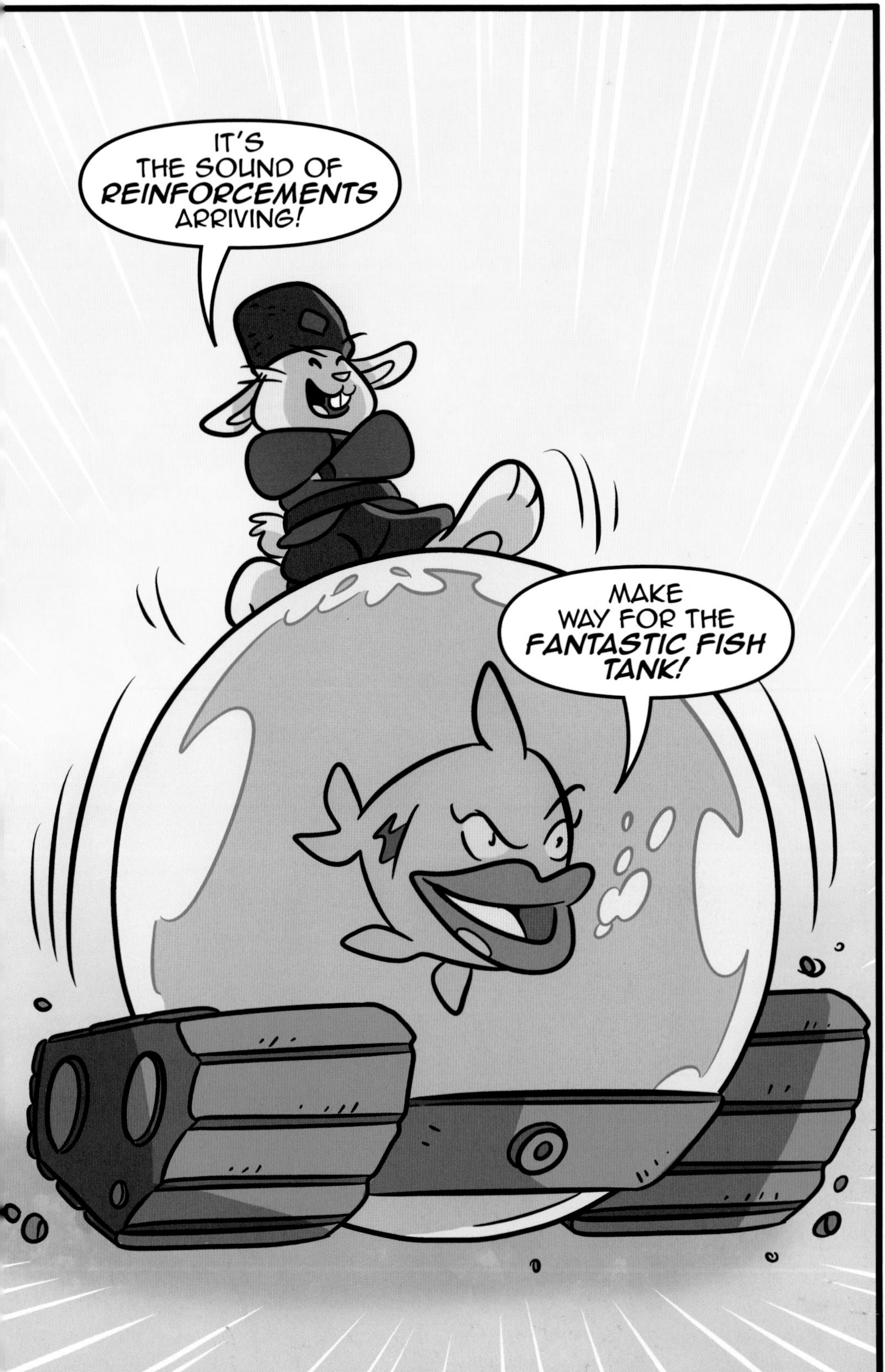
IT'S THE SOUND OF REINFORCEMENTS ARRIVING!
MAKE WAY FOR THE FANTASTIC FISH TANK!

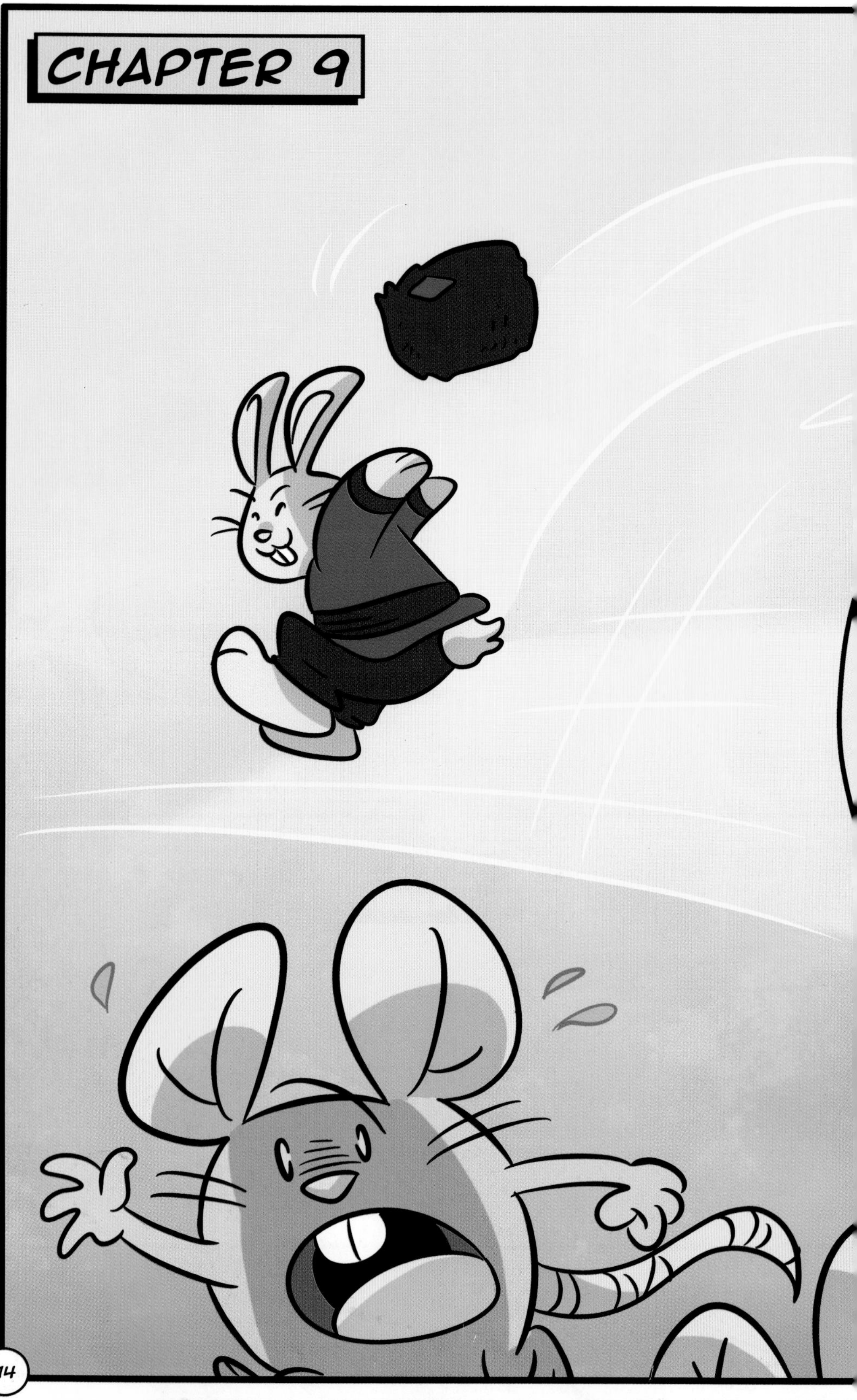
CHAPTER 9

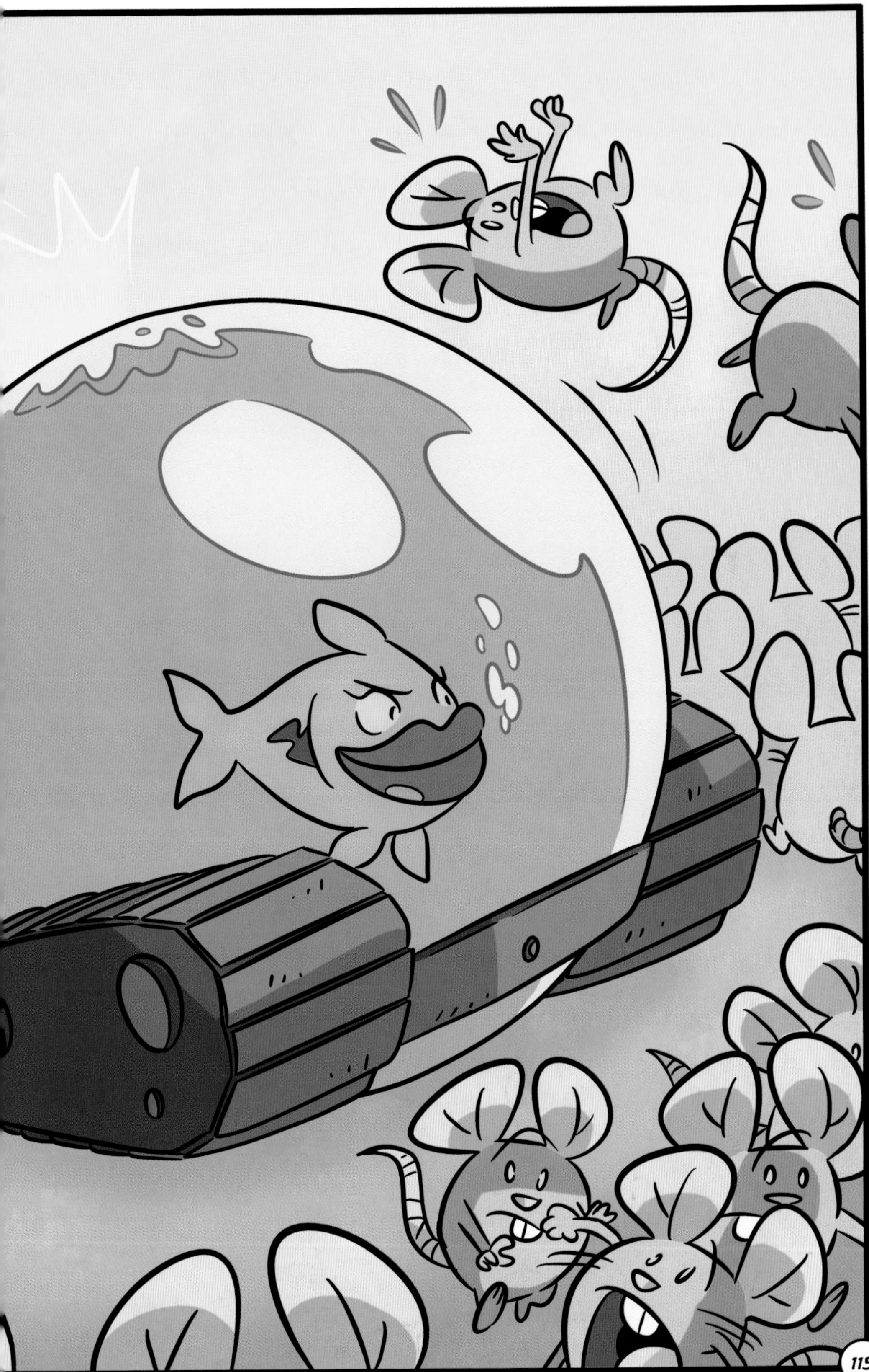

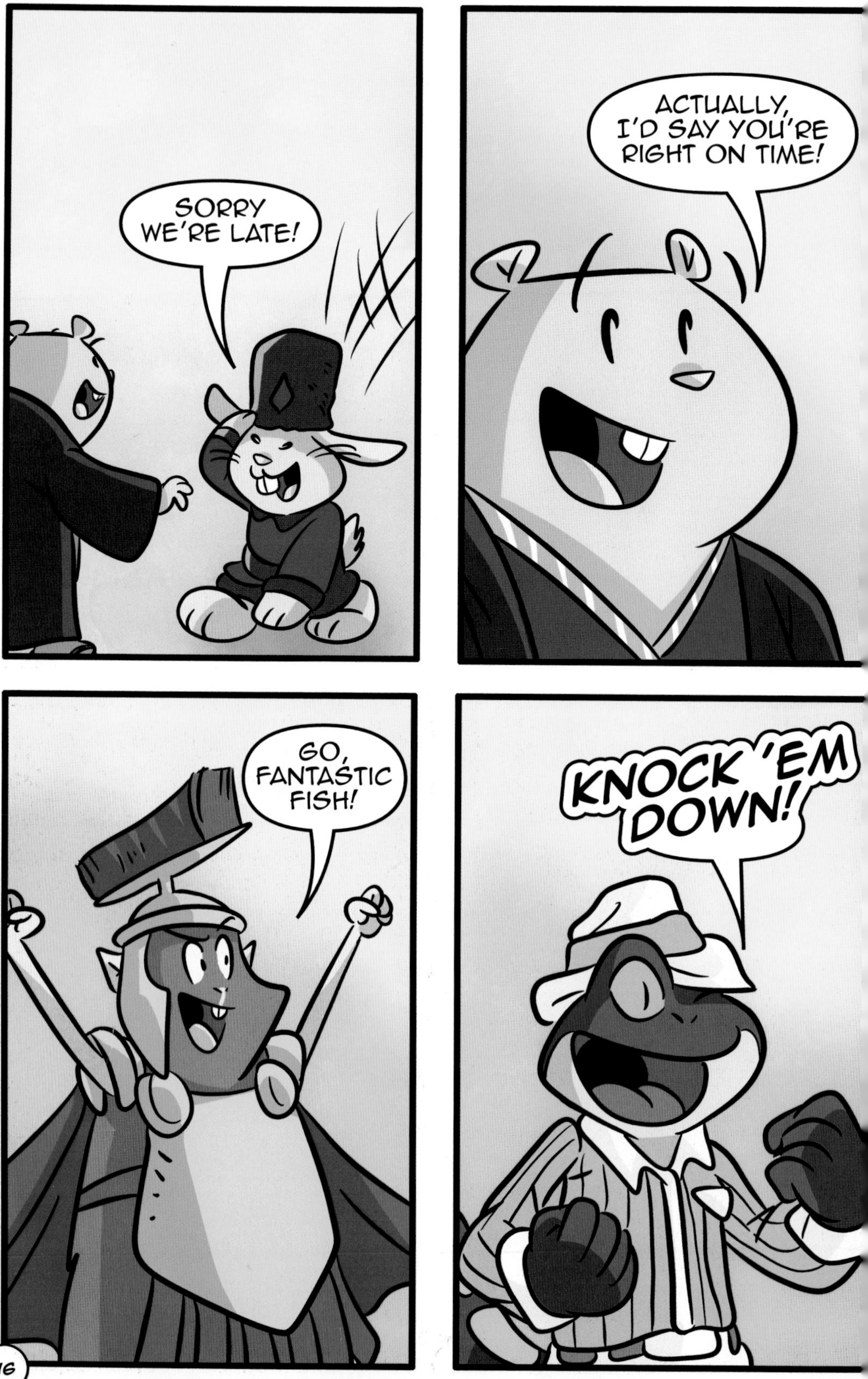
SORRY WE'RE LATE!
ACTUALLY, I'D SAY YOU'RE RIGHT ON TIME!
GO, FANTASTIC FISH!
KNOCK 'EM DOWN!

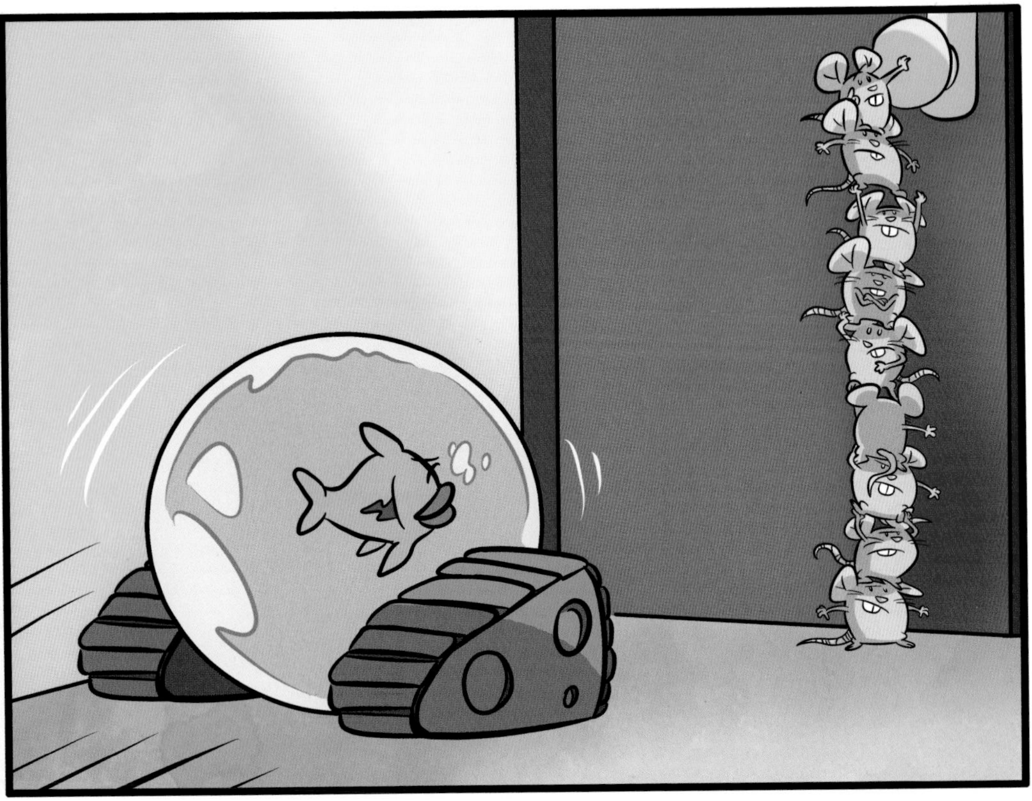

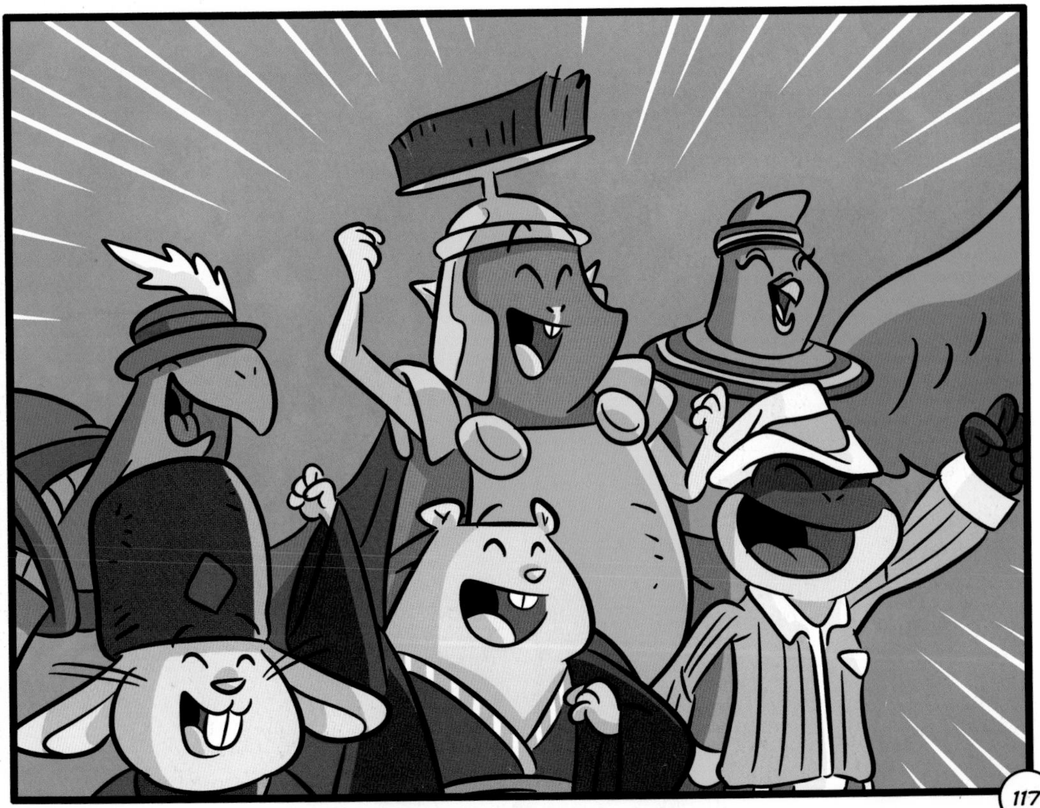

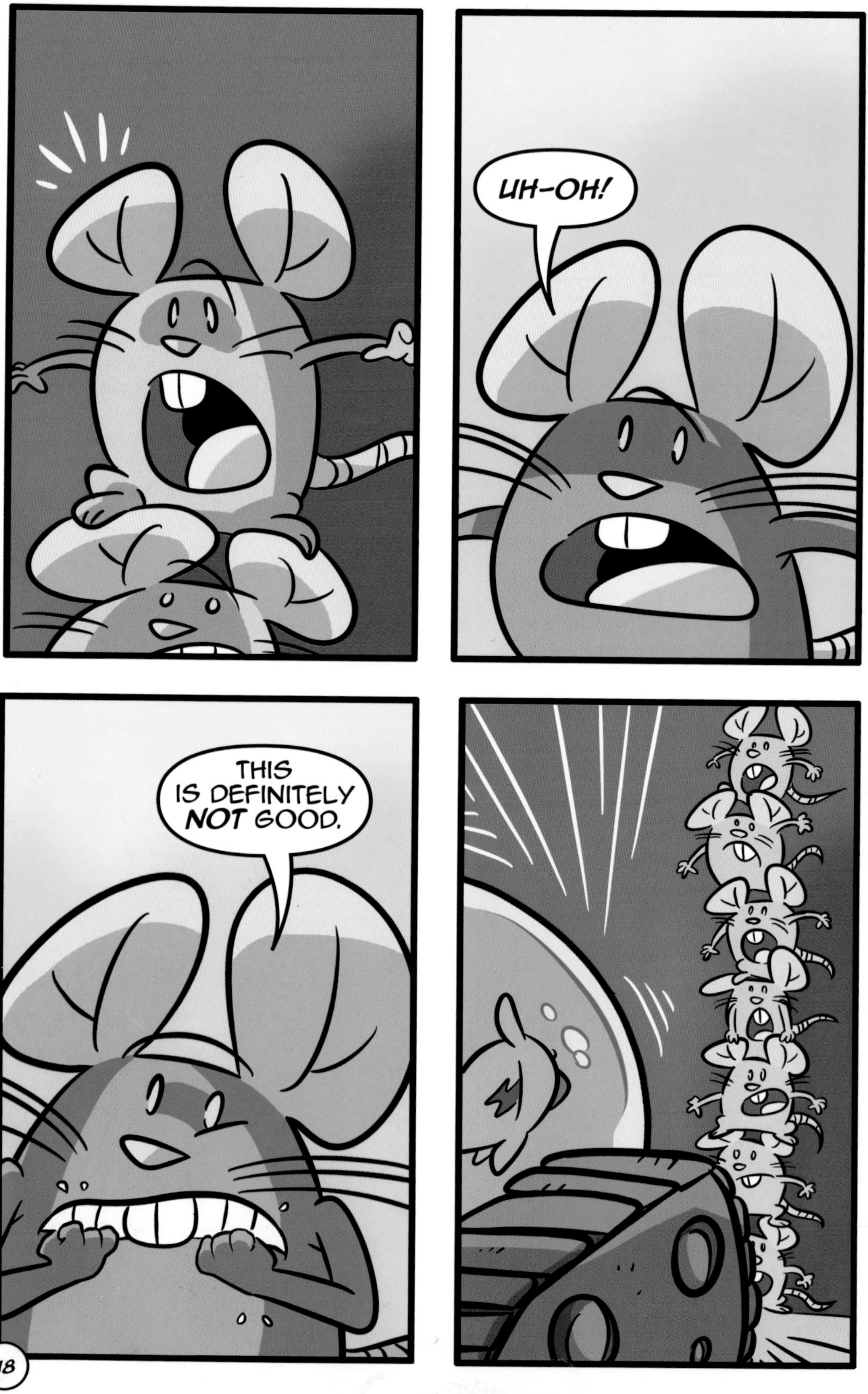
UH-OH!
THIS IS DEFINITELY NOT GOOD.

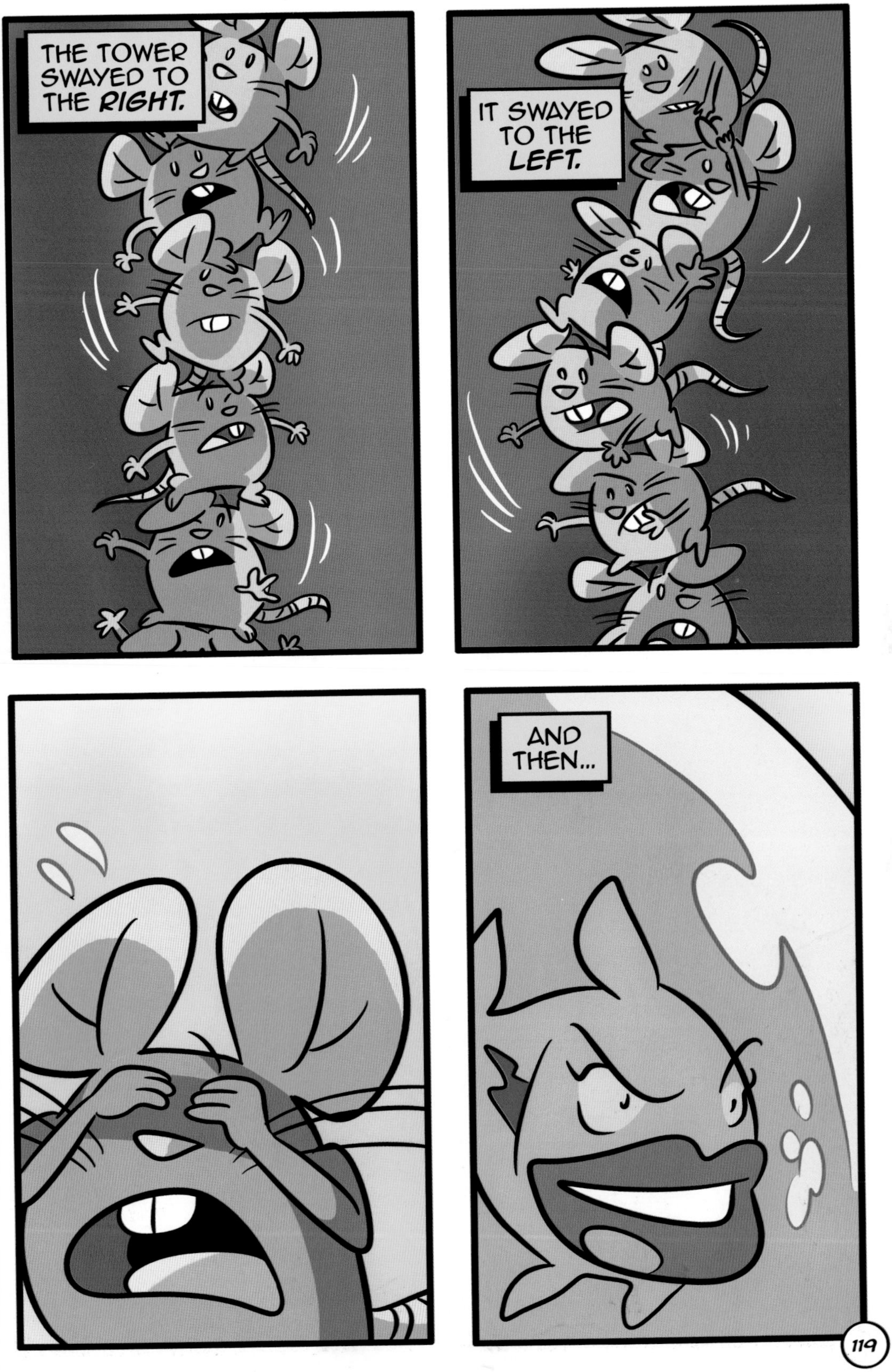
THE TOWER SWAYED TO THE *RIGHT.*
IT SWAYED TO THE *LEFT.*
AND THEN...

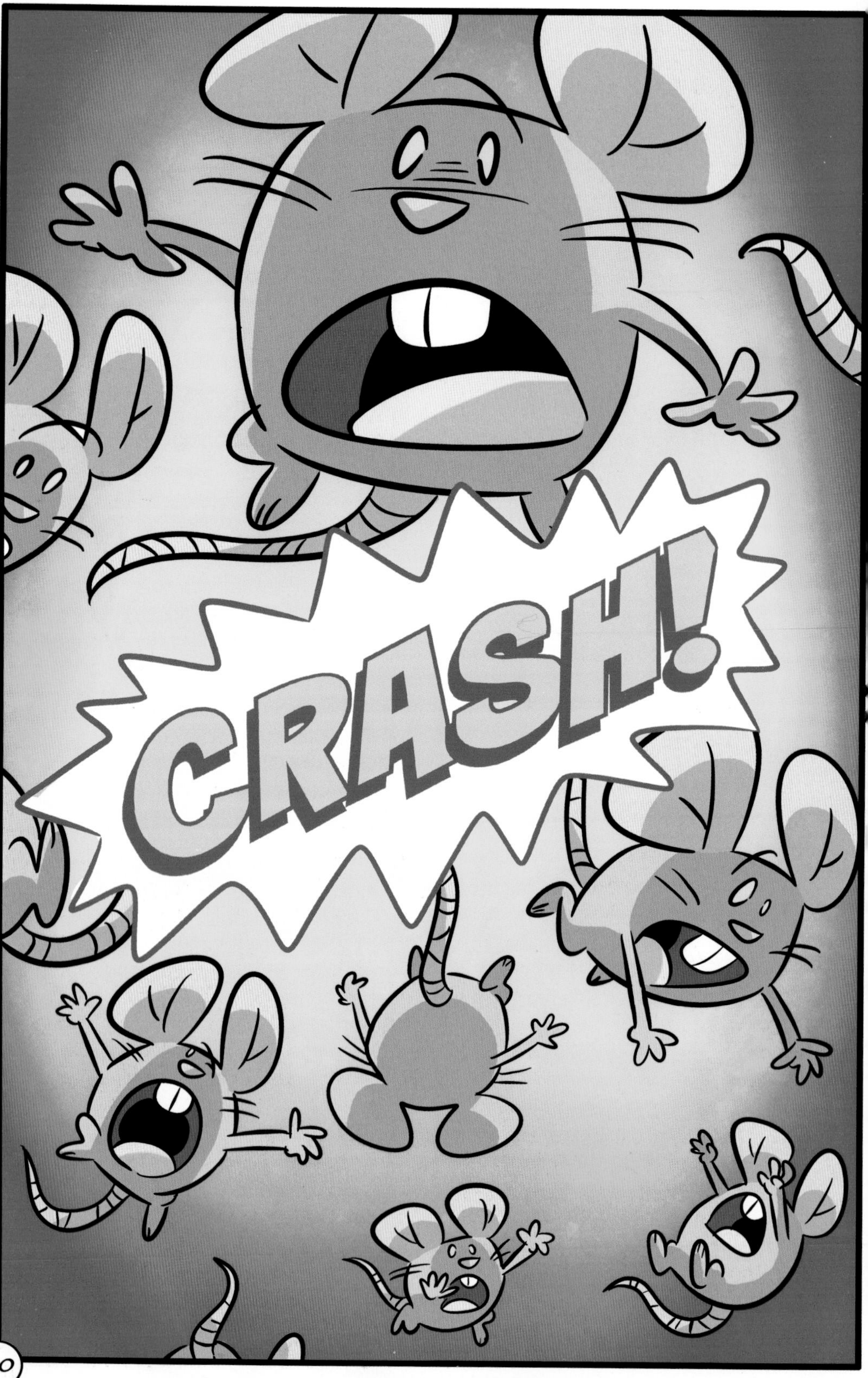
CRASH!

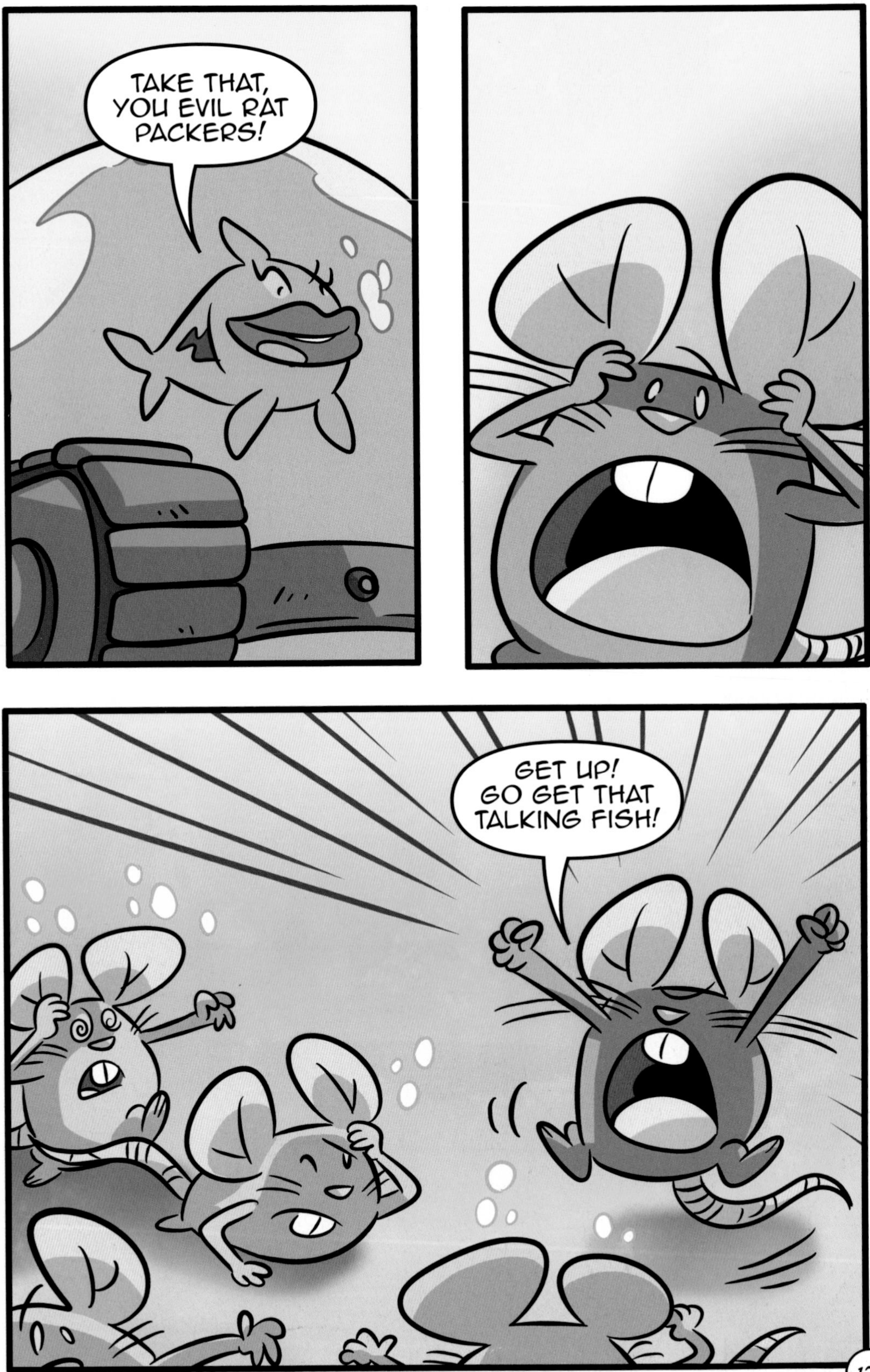
TAKE THAT, YOU EVIL RAT PACKERS!
GET UP! GO GET THAT TALKING FISH!

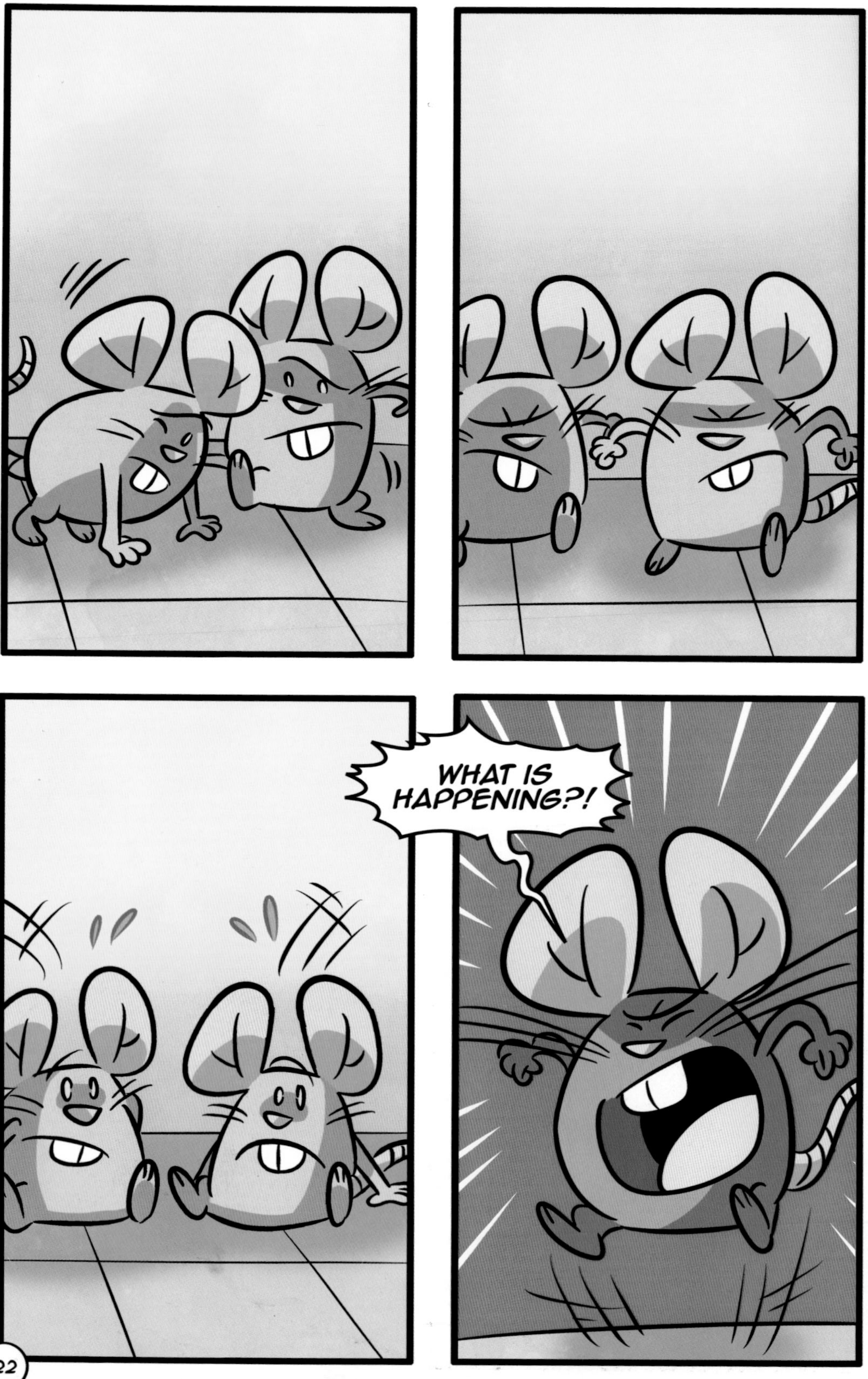
WHAT IS HAPPENING?!

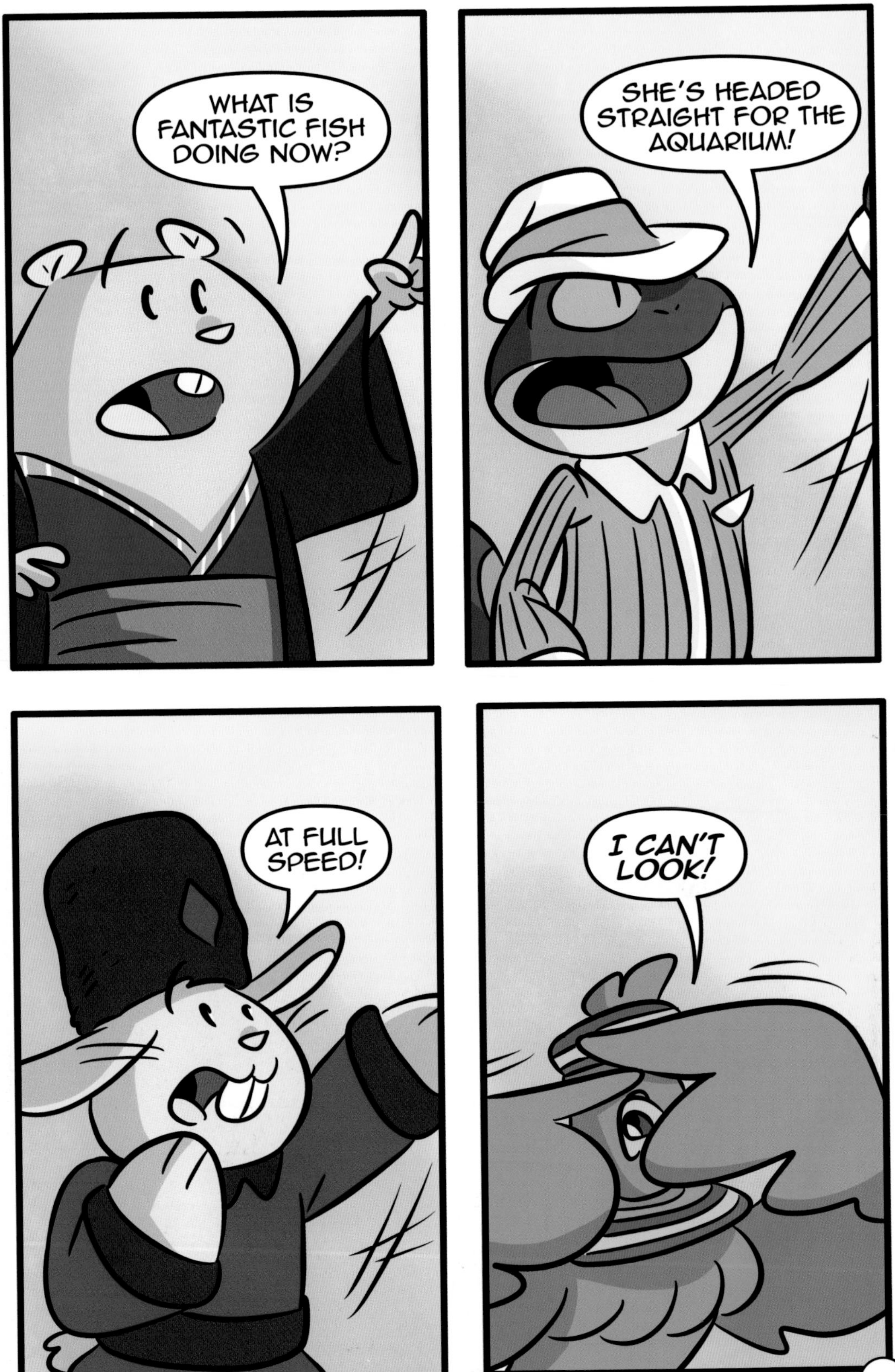
WHAT IS FANTASTIC FISH DOING NOW?
SHE'S HEADED STRAIGHT FOR THE AQUARIUM!
AT FULL SPEED!
I CAN'T LOOK!

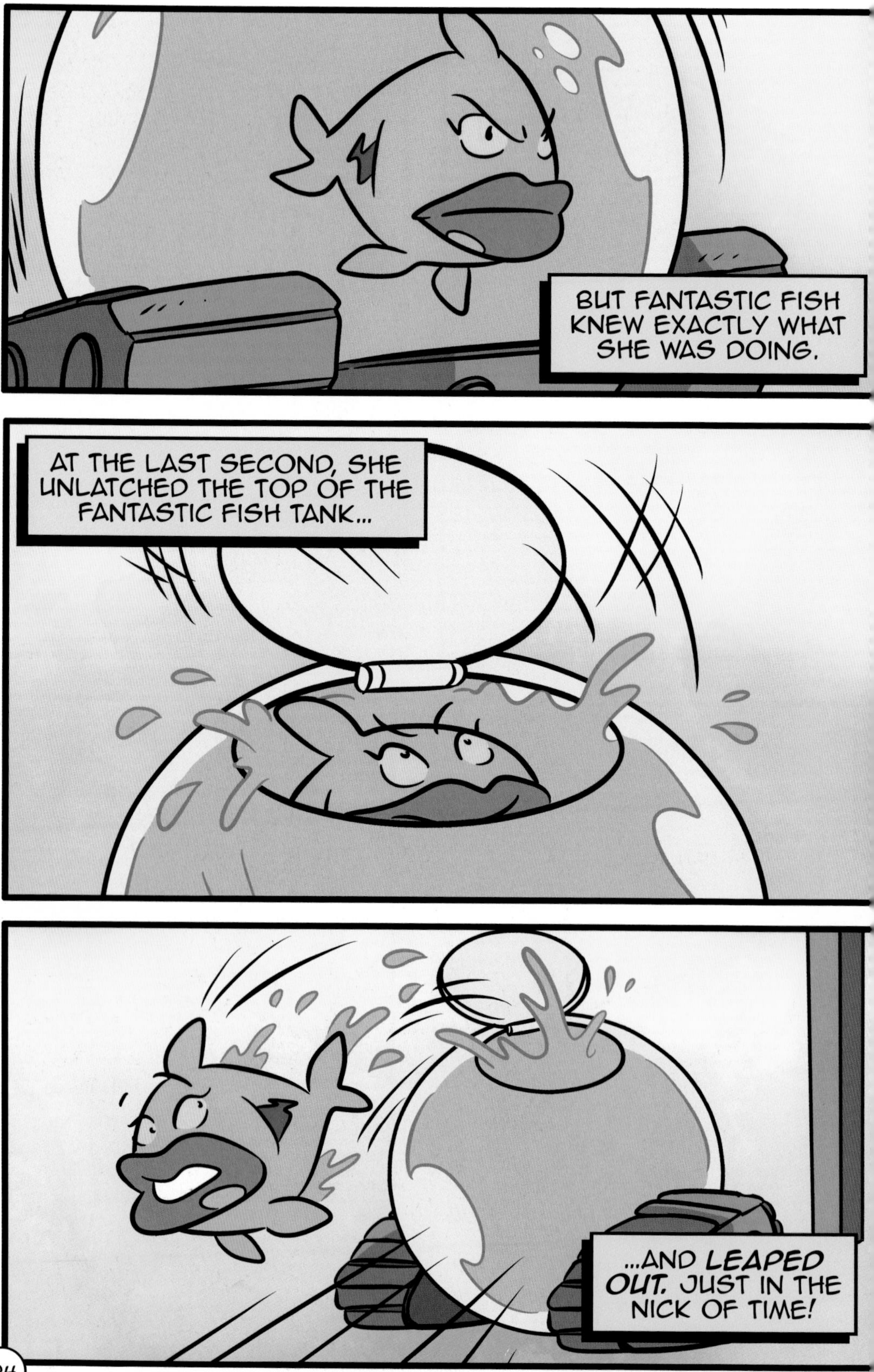
BUT FANTASTIC FISH KNEW EXACTLY WHAT SHE WAS DOING.
AT THE LAST SECOND, SHE UNLATCHED THE TOP OF THE FANTASTIC FISH TANK...
...AND LEAPED OUT. JUST IN THE NICK OF TIME!

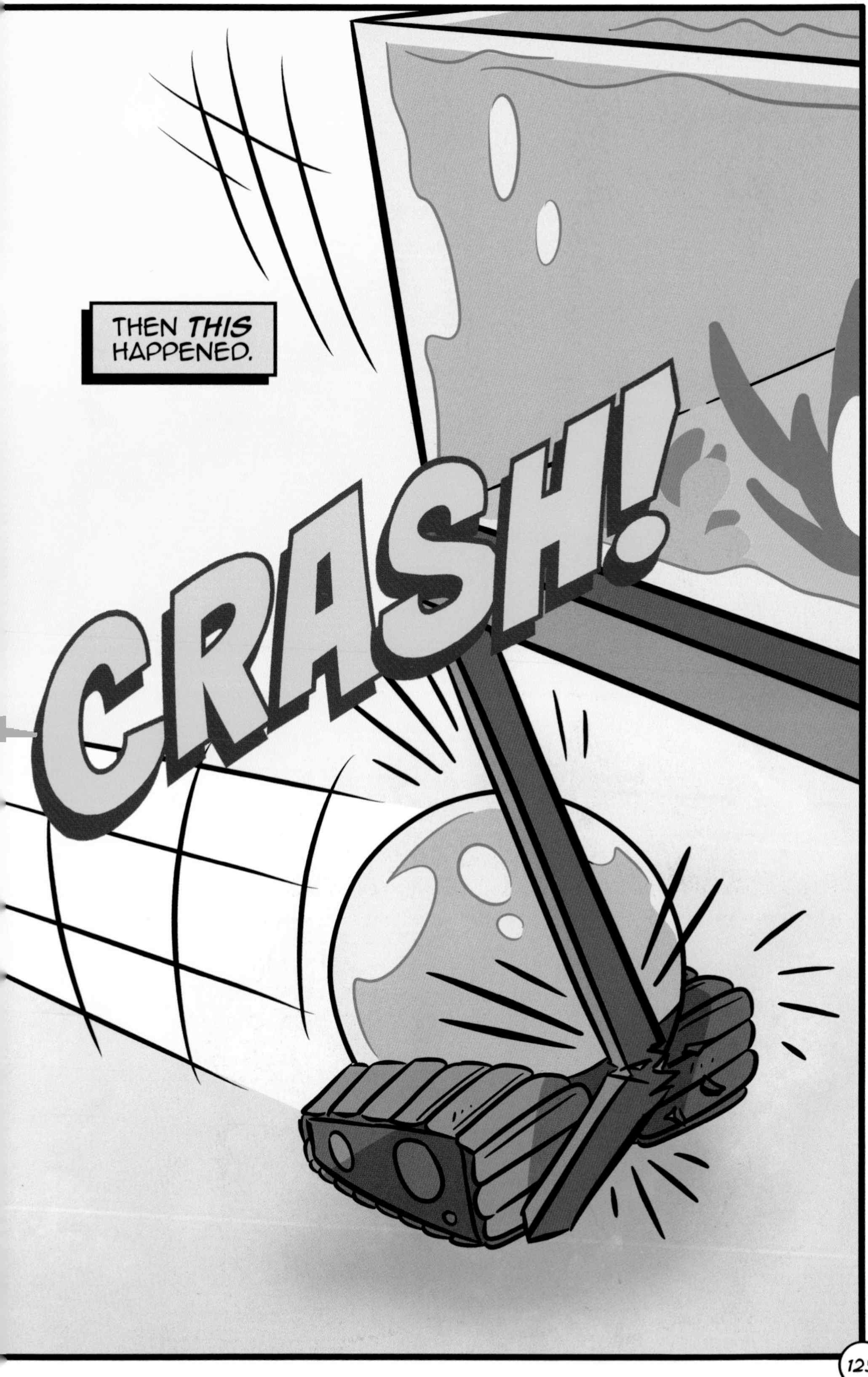
THEN *THIS* HAPPENED.
CRASH!

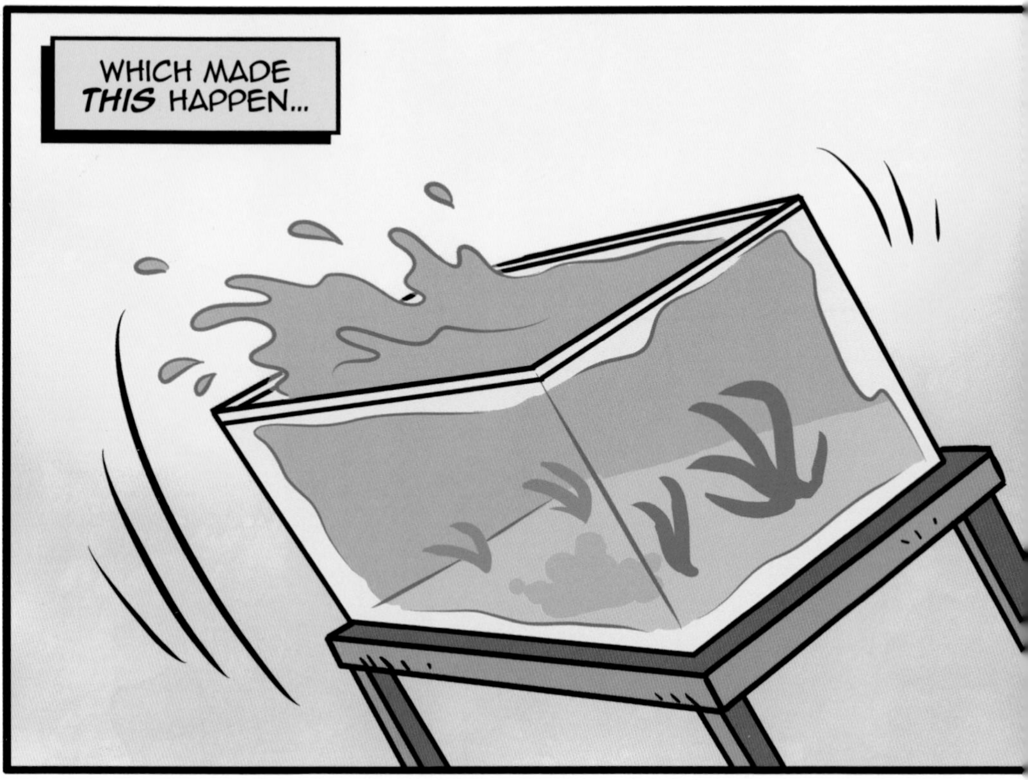
WHICH MADE THIS HAPPEN...

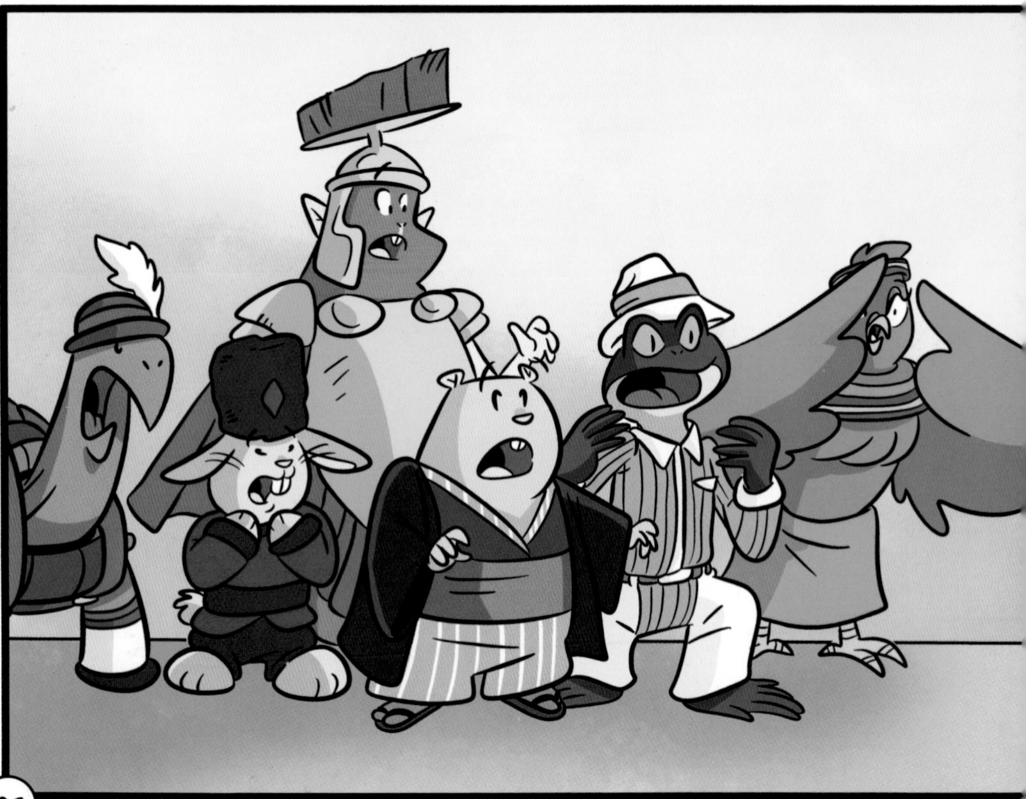

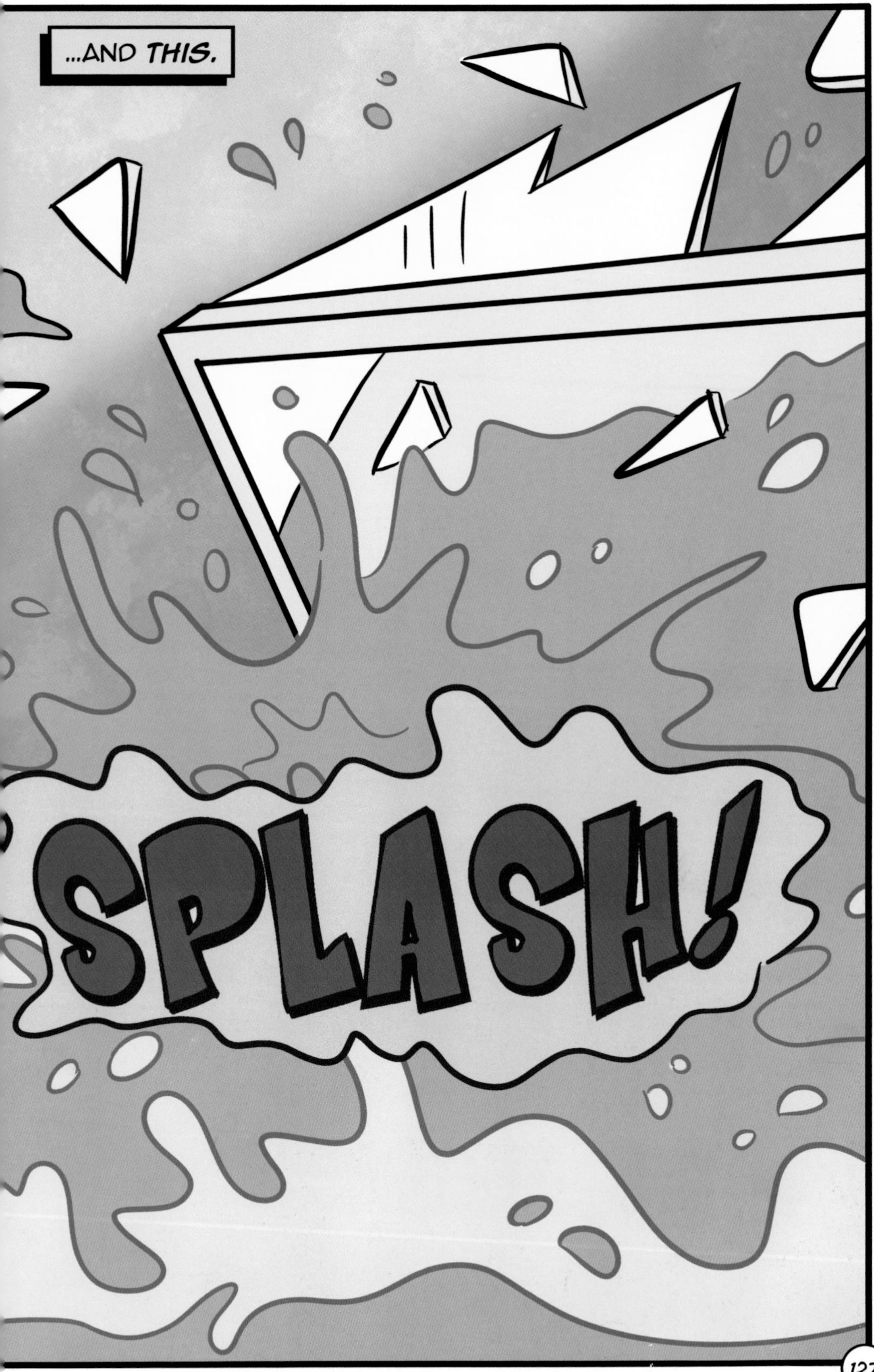
...AND THIS.
SPLASH!

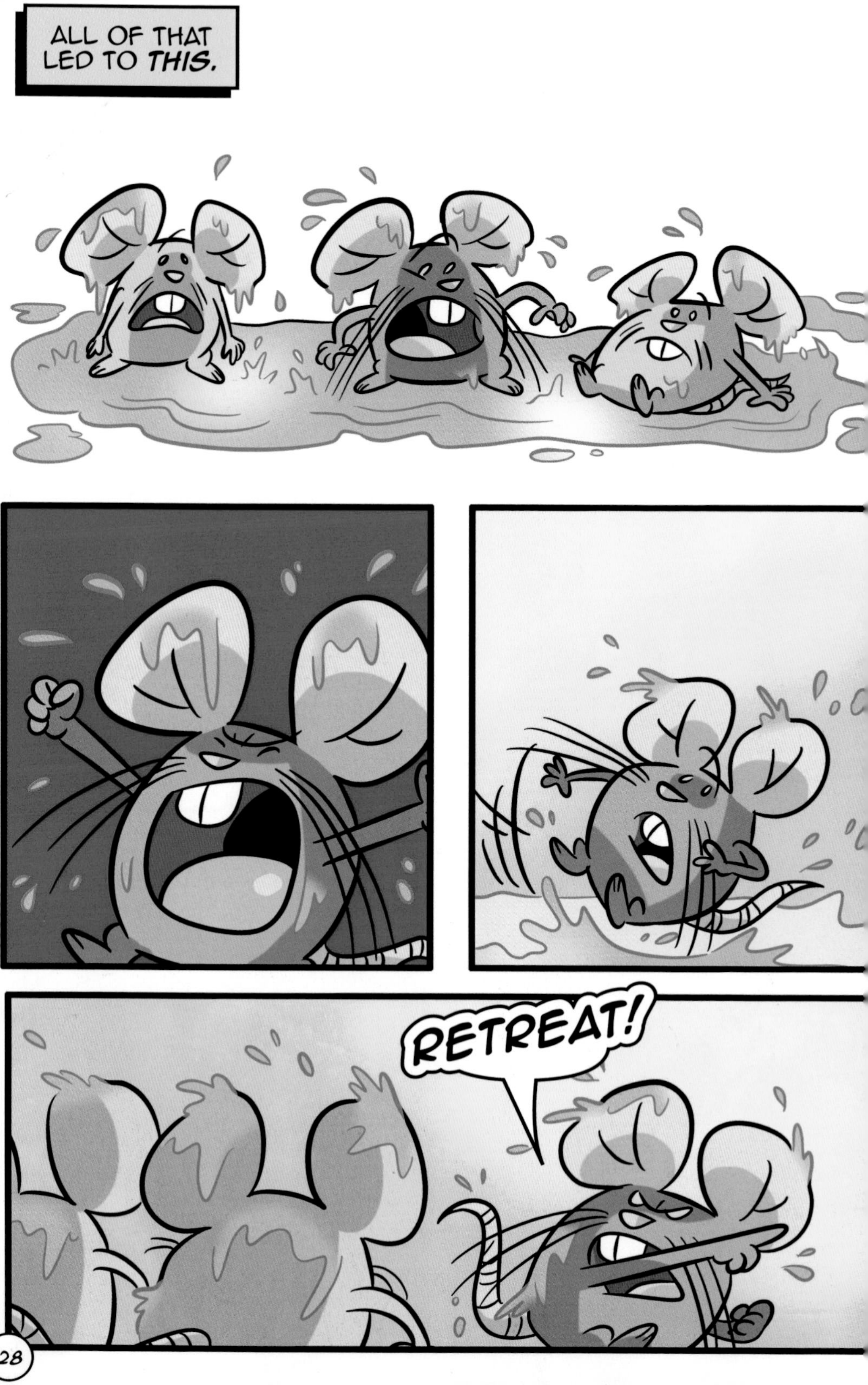
ALL OF THAT LED TO THIS.
RETREAT!

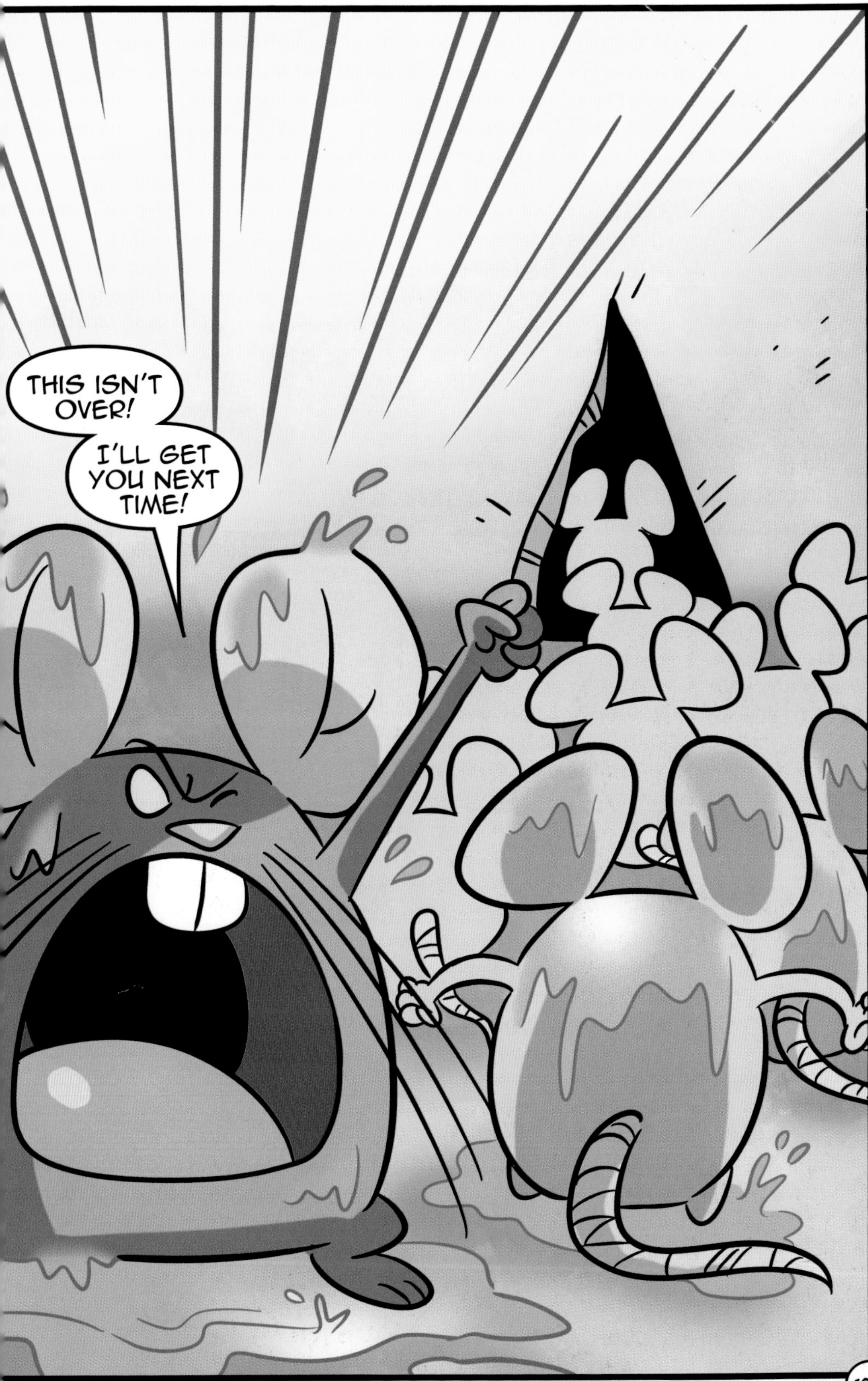
THIS ISN'T OVER!
I'LL GET YOU NEXT TIME!

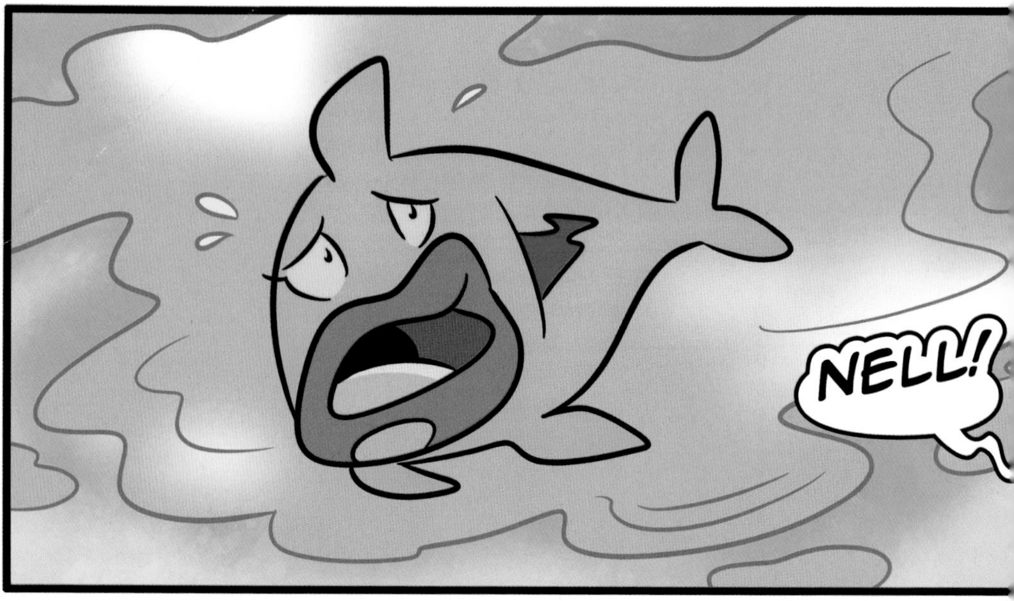
NELL!

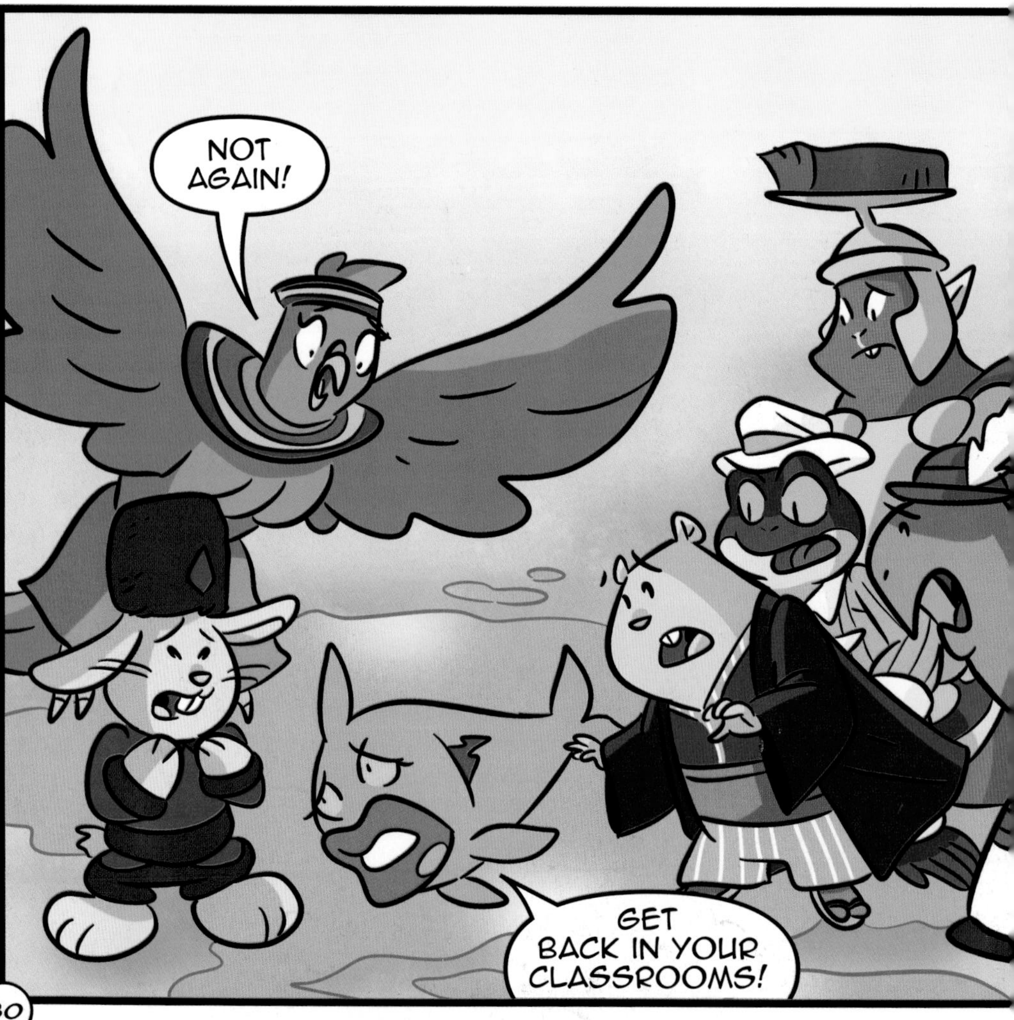
NOT AGAIN!
GET BACK IN YOUR CLASSROOMS!

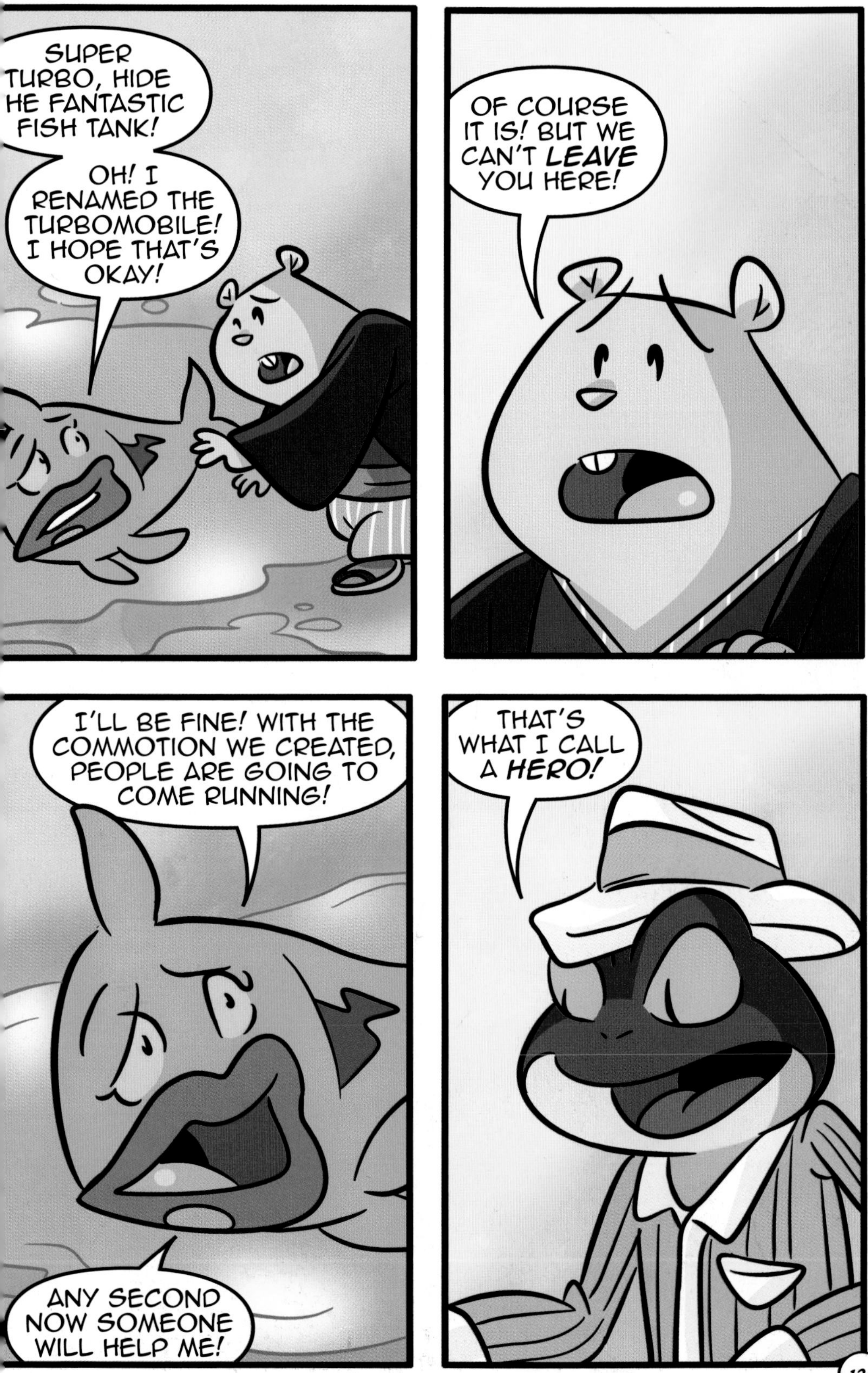
SUPER TURBO, HIDE HE FANTASTIC FISH TANK!
OH! I RENAMED THE TURBOMOBILE! I HOPE THAT'S OKAY!
OF COURSE IT IS! BUT WE CAN'T *LEAVE* YOU HERE!
I'LL BE FINE! WITH THE COMMOTION WE CREATED, PEOPLE ARE GOING TO COME RUNNING!
ANY SECOND NOW SOMEONE WILL HELP ME!
THAT'S WHAT I CALL A *HERO!*

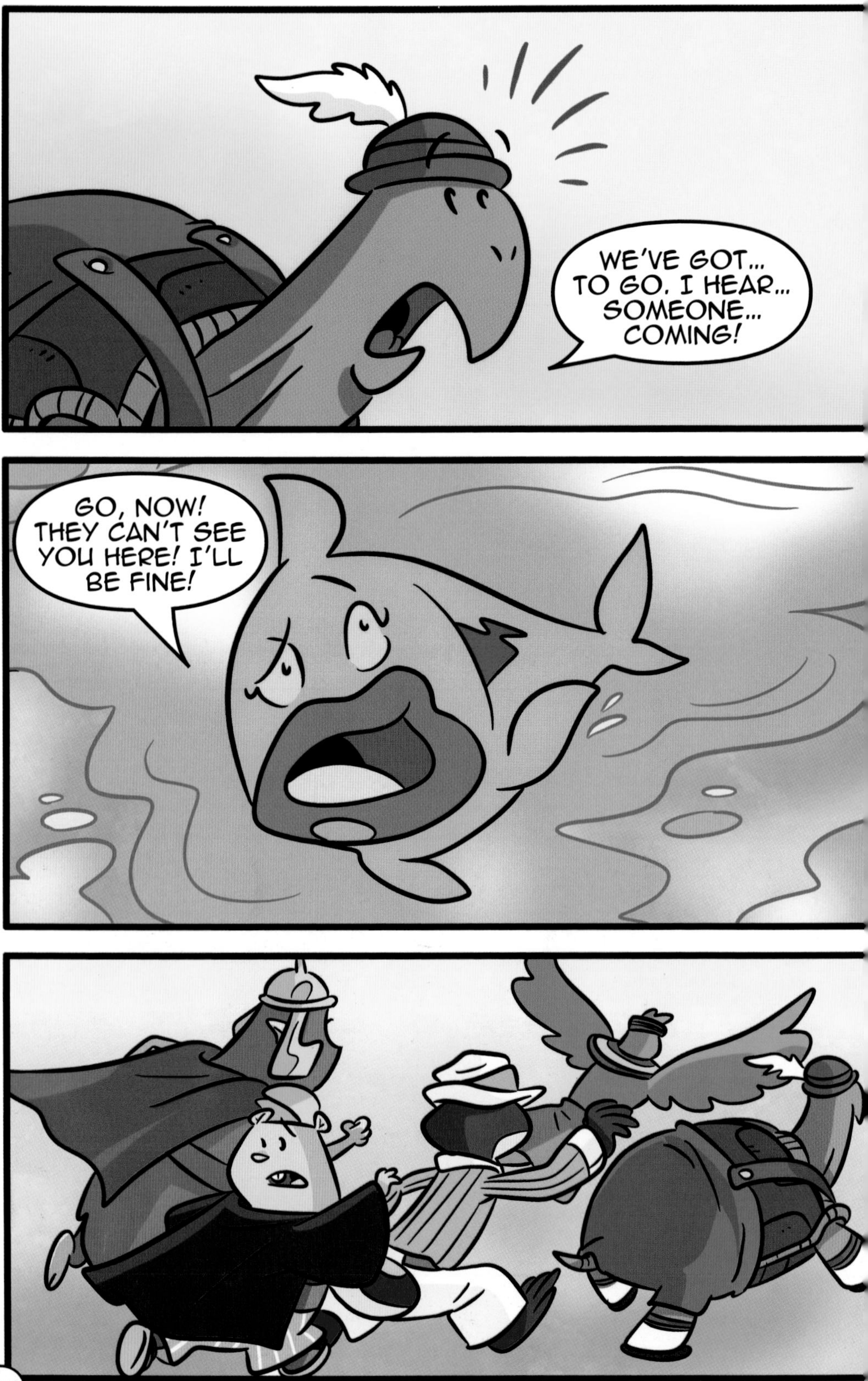
WE'VE GOT... TO GO. I HEAR... SOMEONE... COMING!
GO, NOW! THEY CAN'T SEE YOU HERE! I'LL BE FINE!

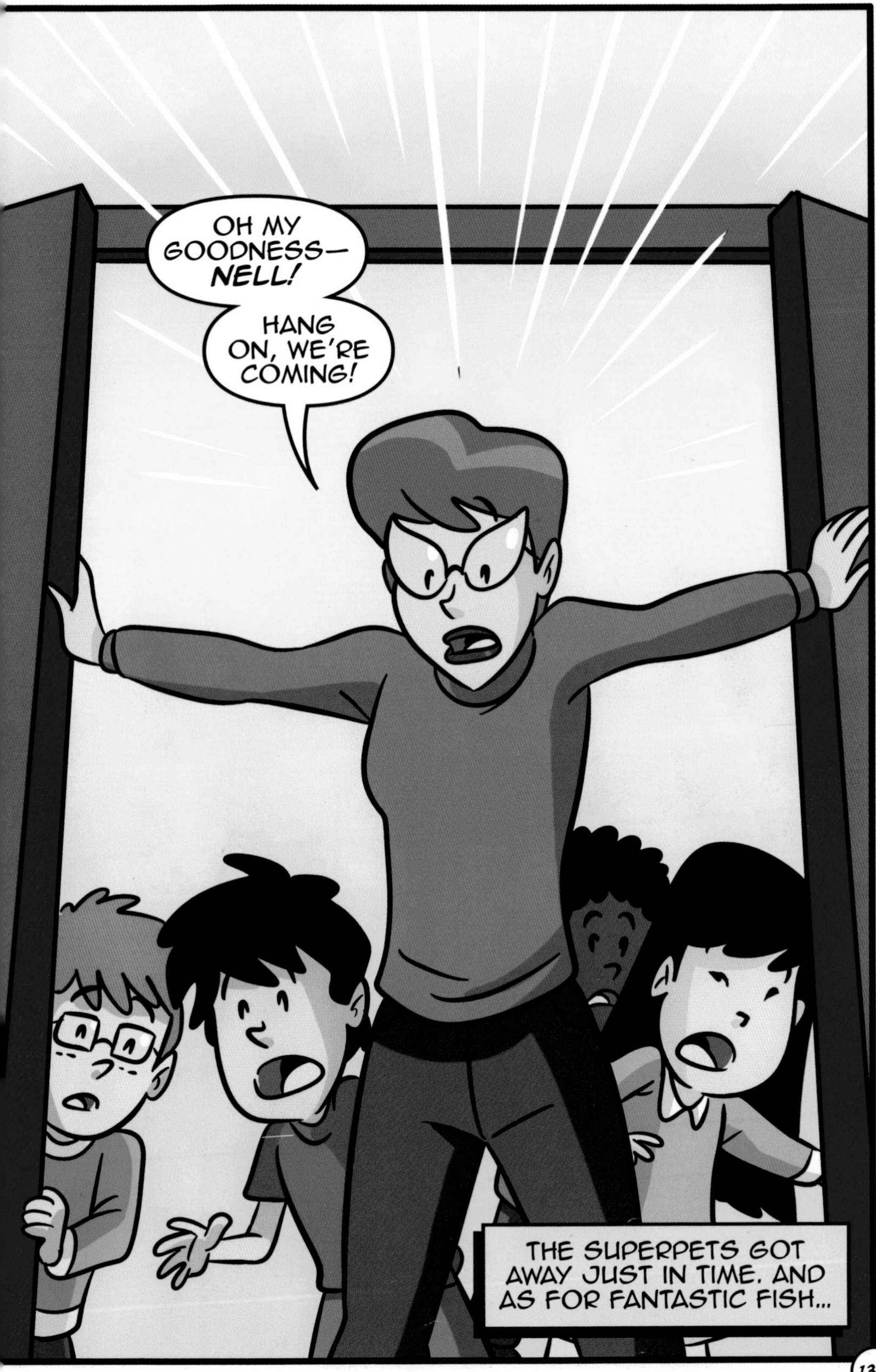
OH MY GOODNESS— NELL!
HANG ON, WE'RE COMING!
THE SUPERPETS GOT AWAY JUST IN TIME. AND AS FOR FANTASTIC FISH...

CHAPTER 10

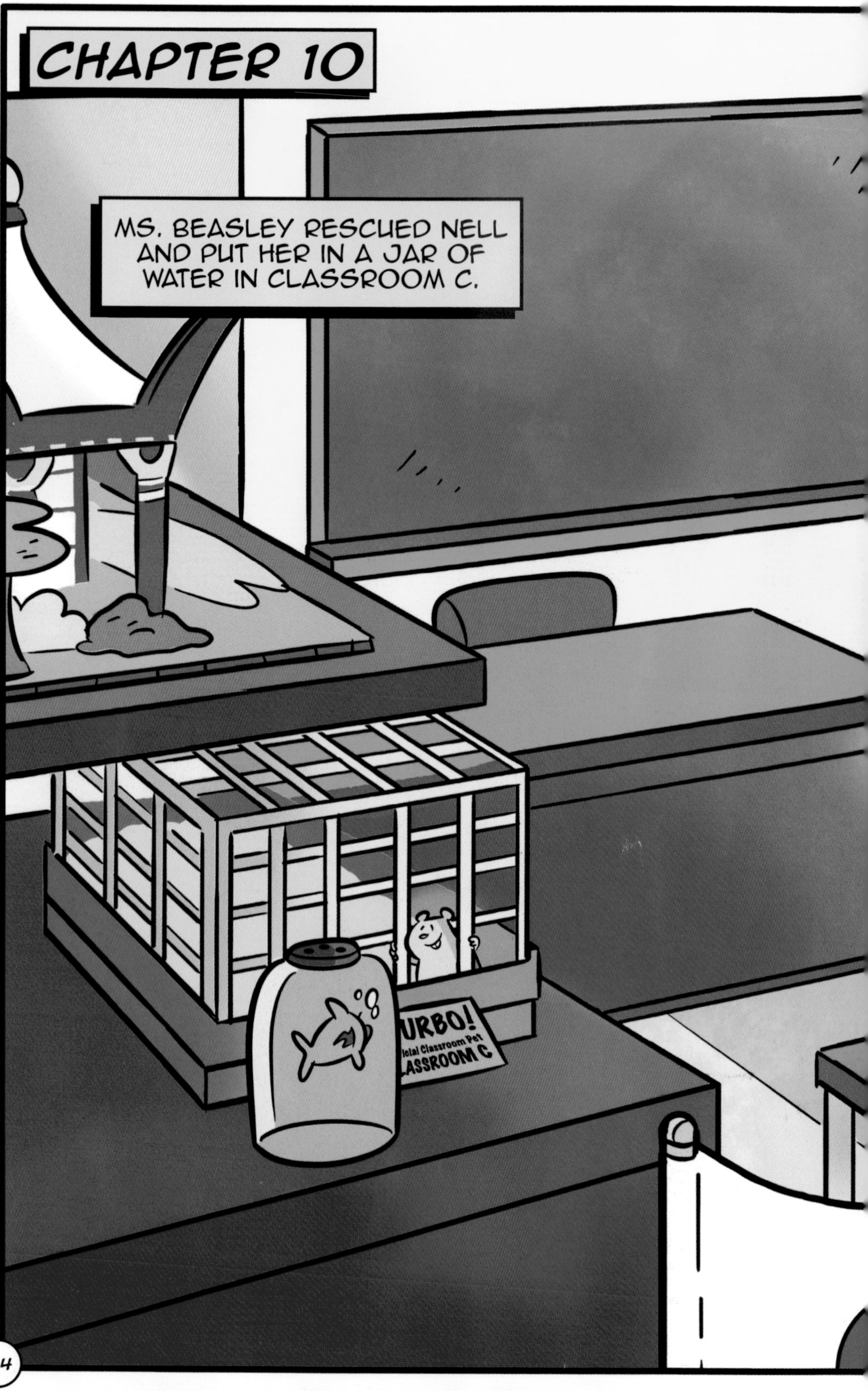
MS. BEASLEY RESCUED NELL AND PUT HER IN A JAR OF WATER IN CLASSROOM C.
URBO!
LASSROOM C

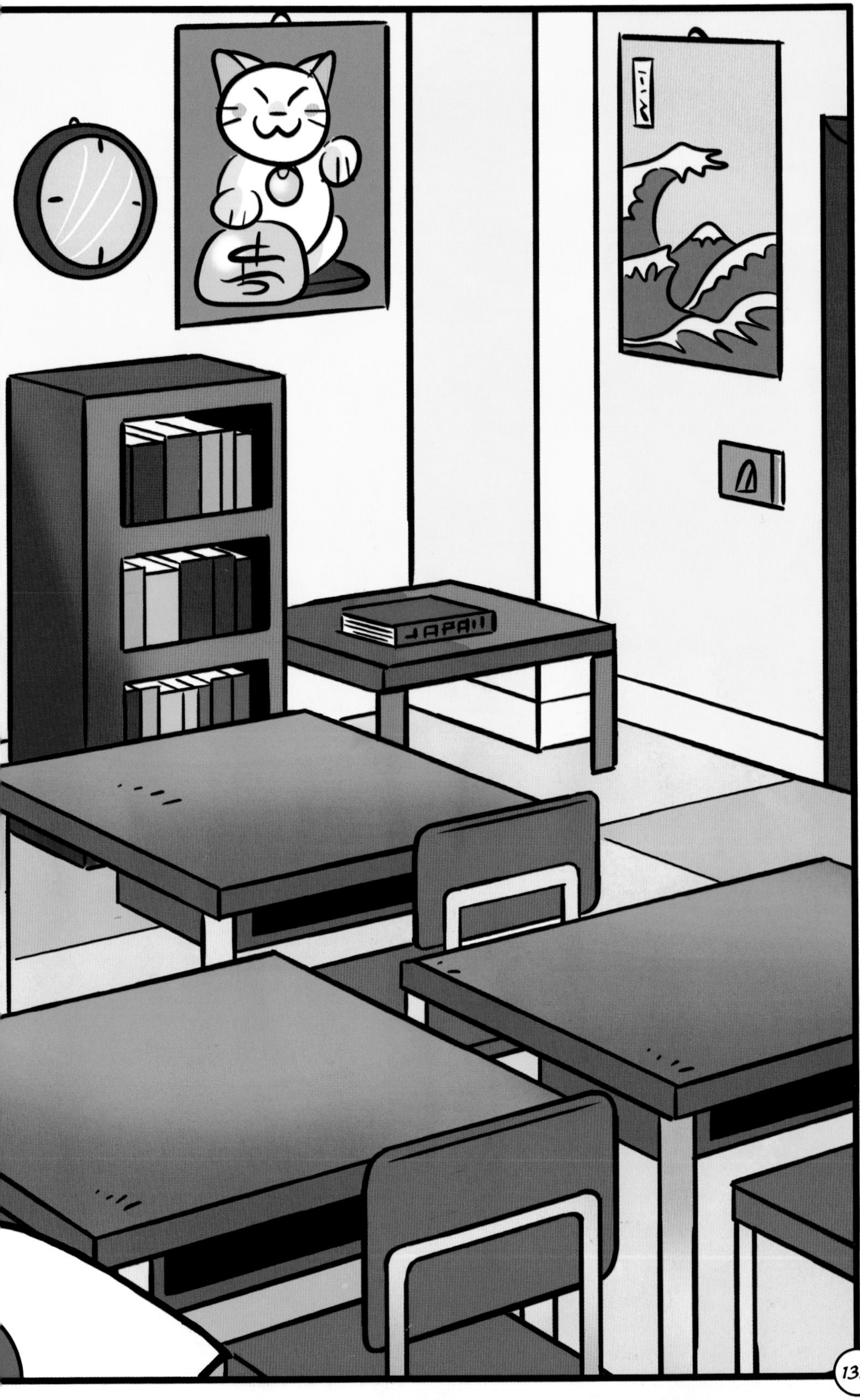
JAPAN

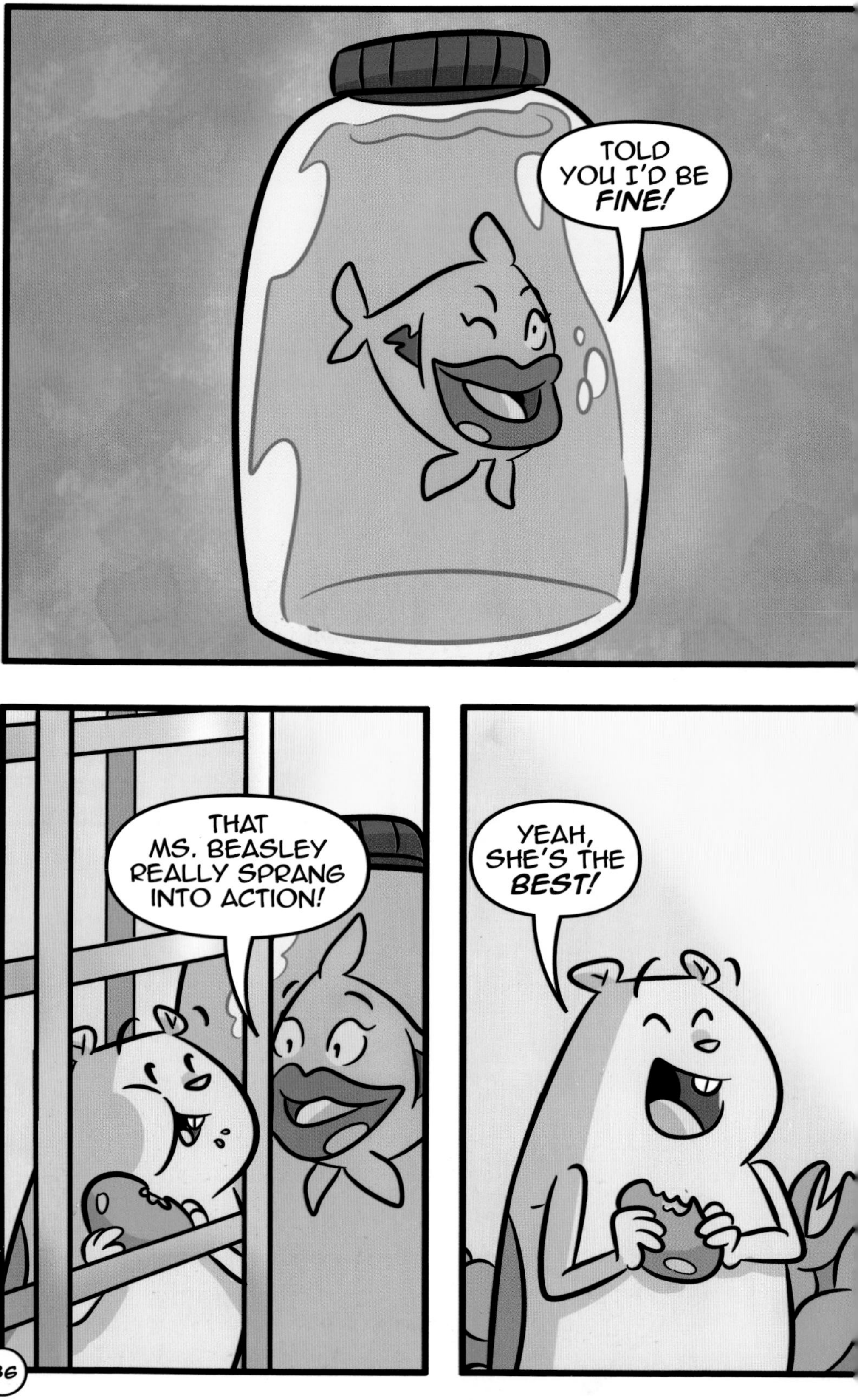
TOLD YOU I'D BE *FINE!*
THAT MS. BEASLEY REALLY SPRANG INTO ACTION!
YEAH, SHE'S THE *BEST!*

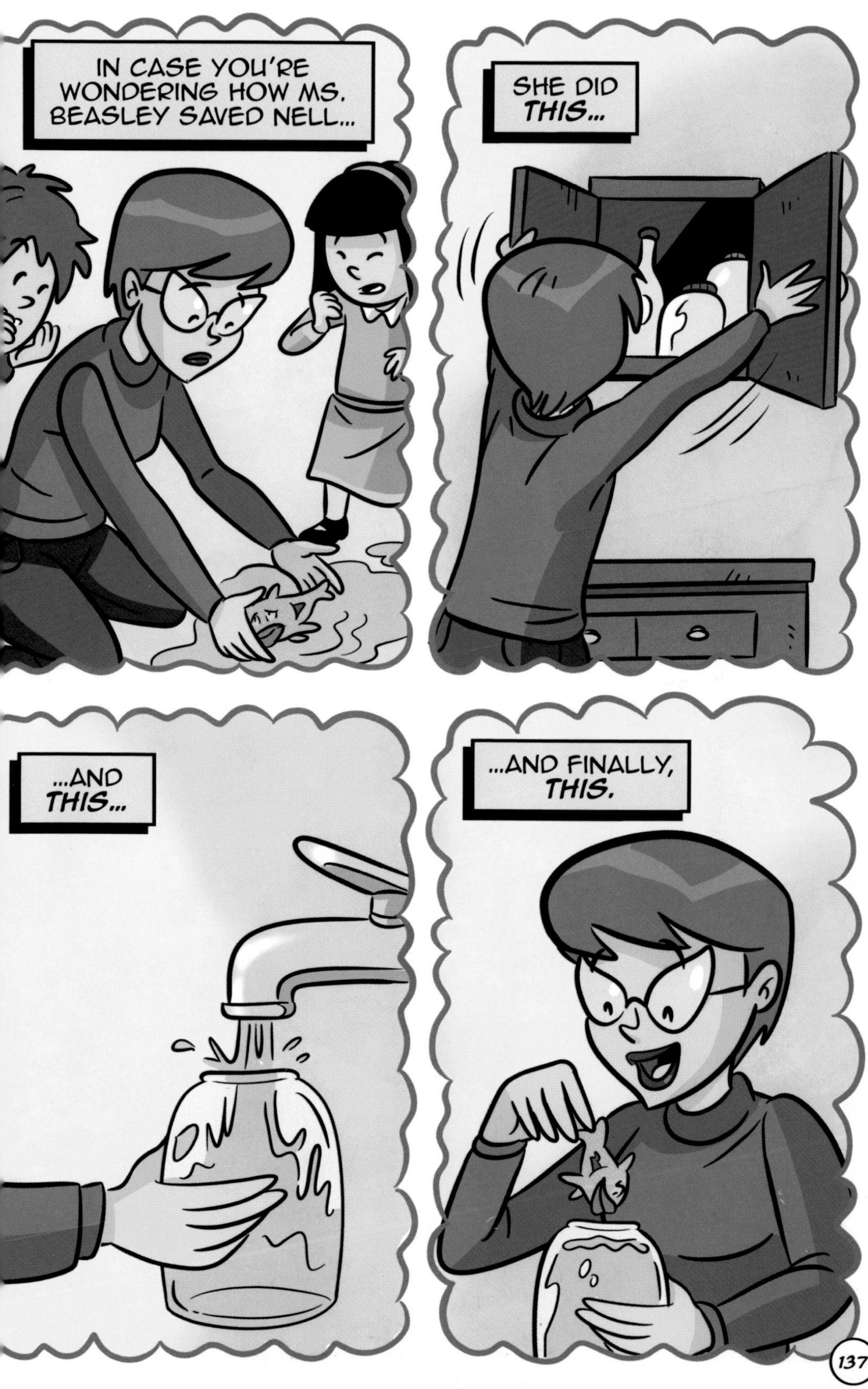
IN CASE YOU'RE WONDERING HOW MS. BEASLEY SAVED NELL...
SHE DID *THIS*...
...AND *THIS*...
...AND FINALLY, *THIS*.

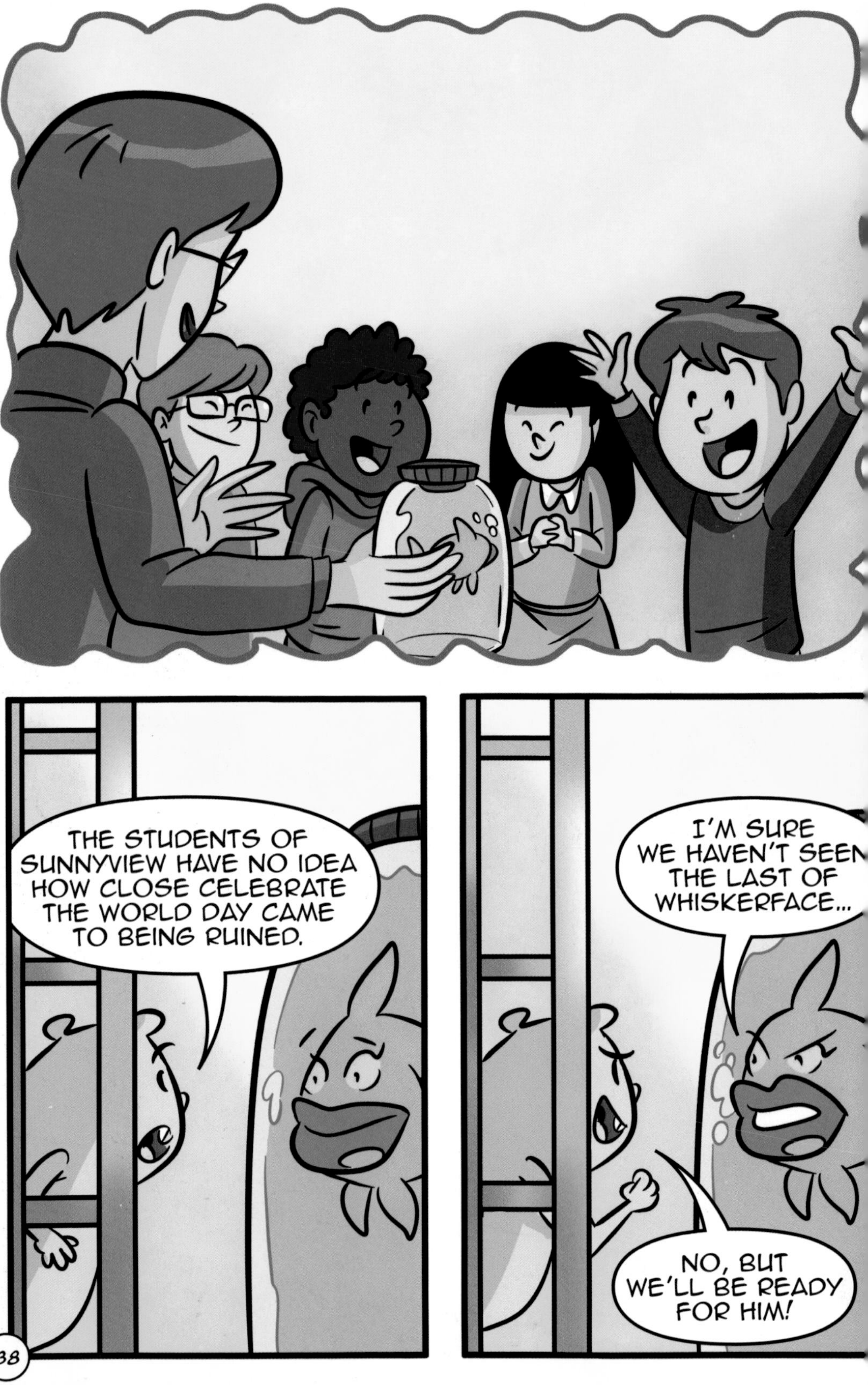
THE STUDENTS OF SUNNYVIEW HAVE NO IDEA HOW CLOSE CELEBRATE THE WORLD DAY CAME TO BEING RUINED.
I'M SURE WE HAVEN'T SEEN THE LAST OF WHISKERFACE...
NO, BUT WE'LL BE READY FOR HIM!

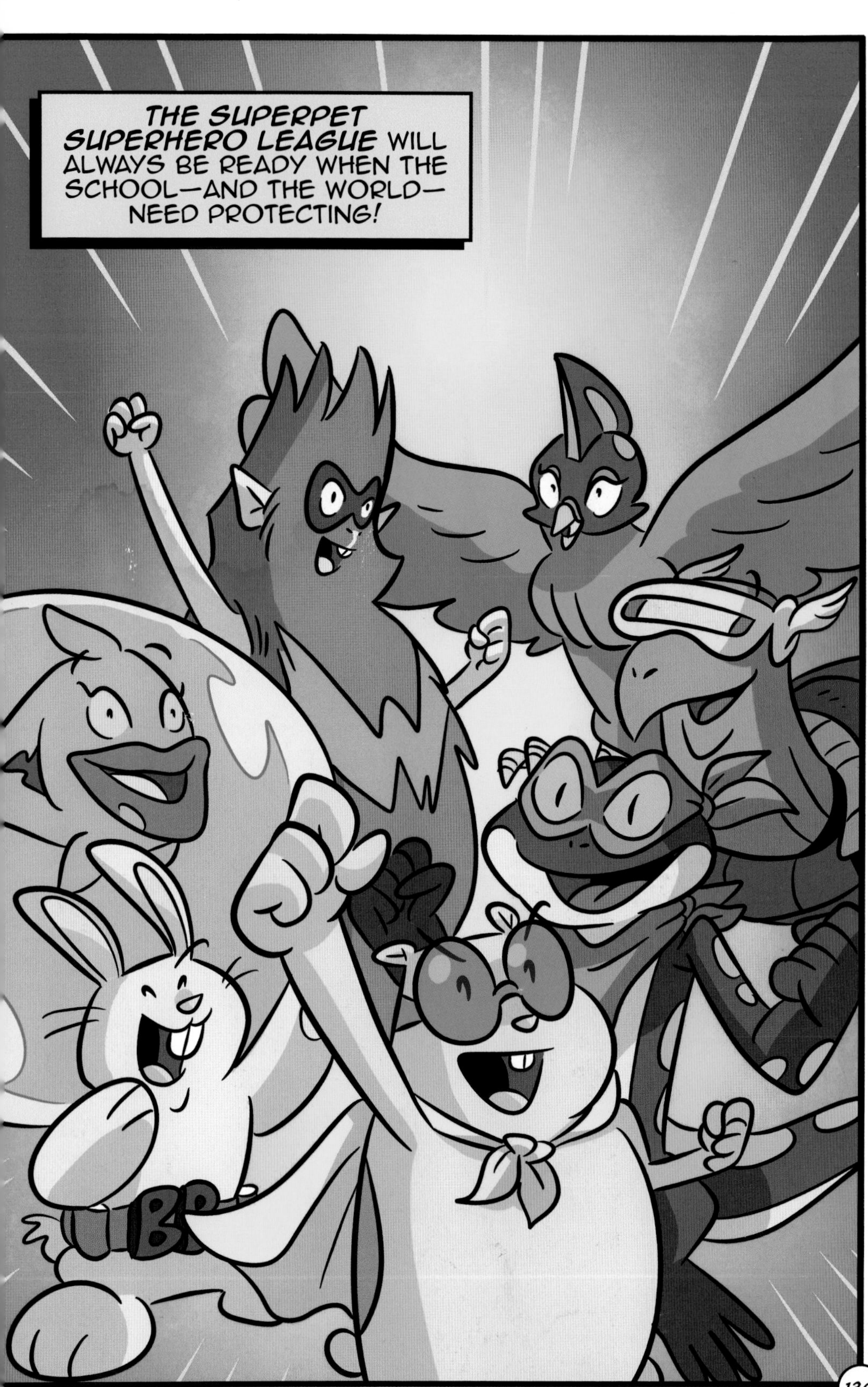
THE SUPERPET SUPERHERO LEAGUE WILL ALWAYS BE READY WHEN THE SCHOOL—AND THE WORLD—NEED PROTECTING!

CAN'T GET ENOUGH OF THE **SUPERPET SUPERHERO LEAGUE?** CHECK OUT THEIR NEXT ADVENTURE...

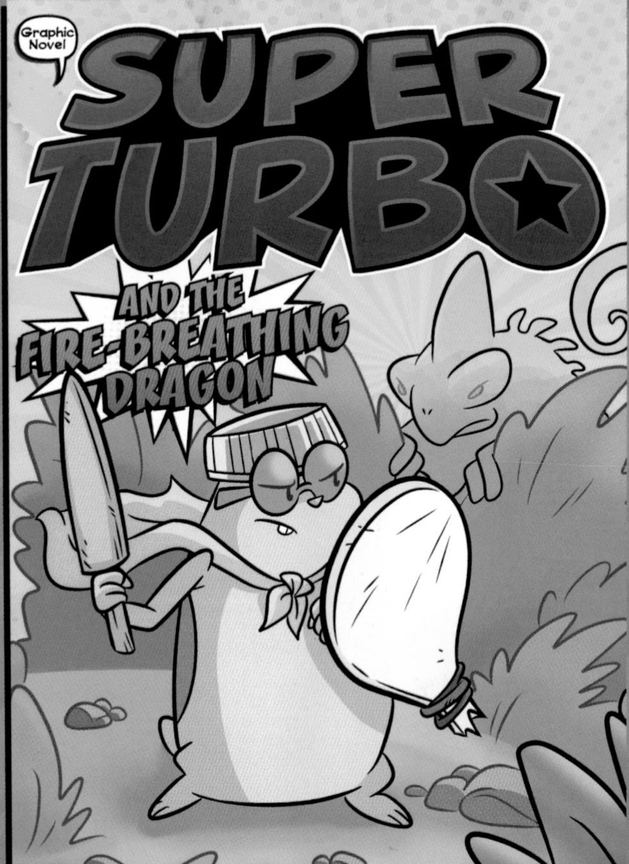
Graphic Novel
SUPER TURBO
AND THE FIRE-BREATHING DRAGON

TURN THE PAGE FOR A SNEAK PEEK...

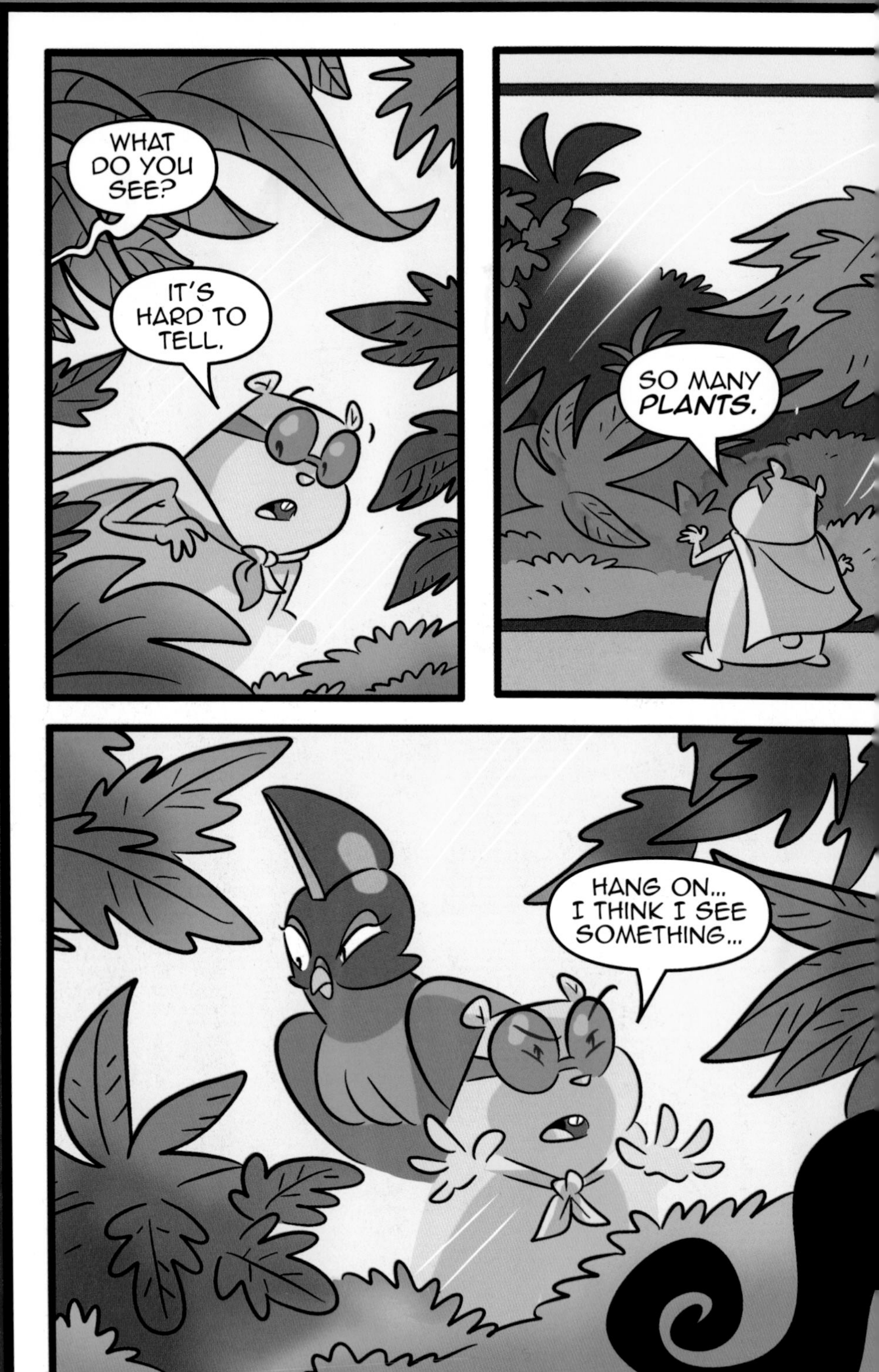
WHAT DO YOU SEE?
IT'S HARD TO TELL.
SO MANY PLANTS.
HANG ON... I THINK I SEE SOMETHING...

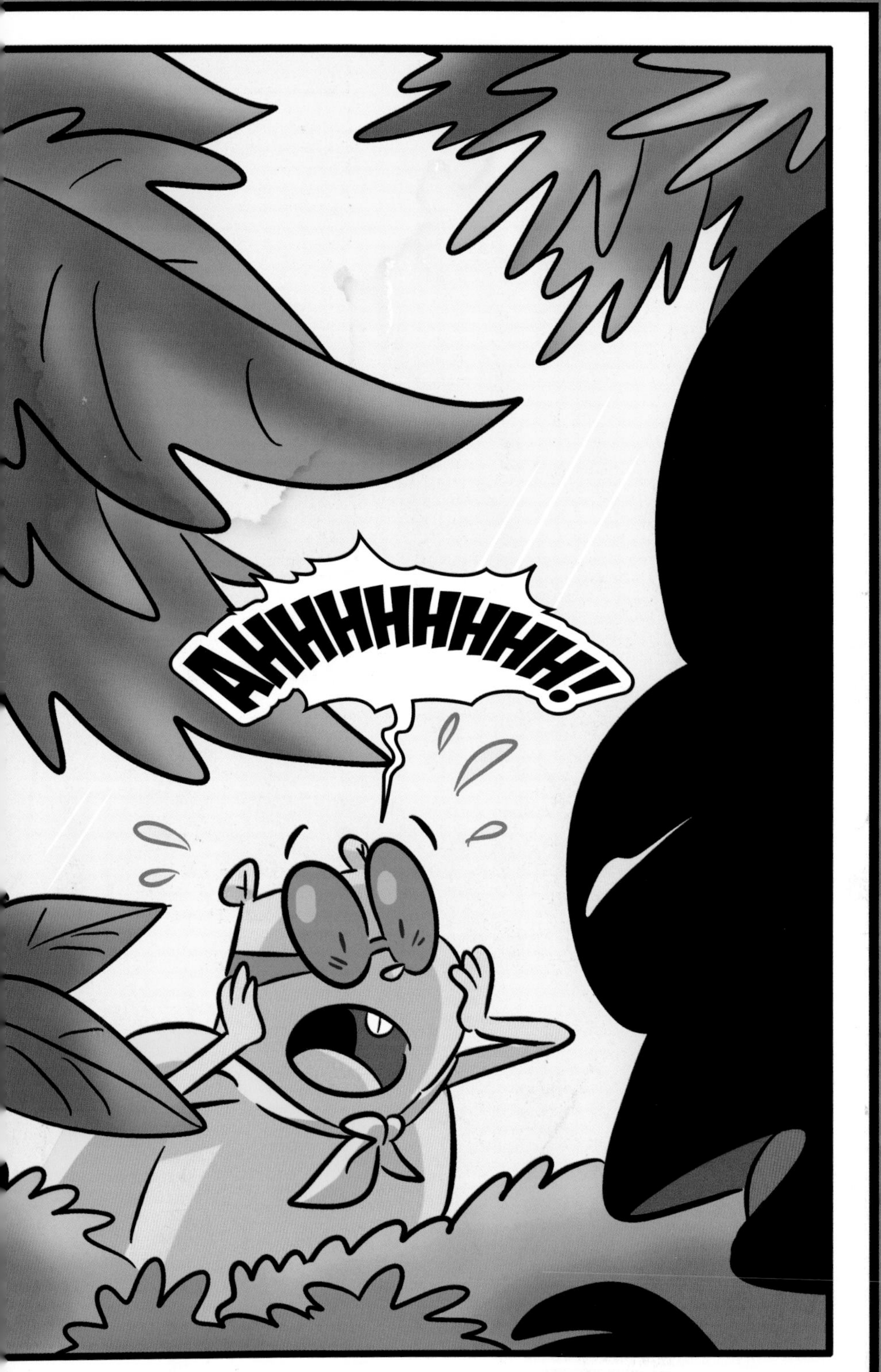
AHHHHHHHH!